LOVABLE
Lawyer

KAREN DEEN

Lovable Lawyer

Copyright © 2020 by Karen Deen
All rights reserved. No part of this book may be reproduced or transmitted in either, electronic, paper hard copy, photocopying, recorded or any other form of reproduction without the written permission of the author. No part of this book either in part or whole may be reproduced into or stored in a retrieval system or distributed without the written permission of the author.
This book is a work of fiction. Characters, names, places and incidents are products of the author's imagination. Any resemblance to actual events, locations or persons living or dead is purely coincidental.
The author acknowledges the trademark status and owners of products referred to in this fiction which have been used without permission. The publication and use of these trademarks is not authorized, associated with or sponsored by the trademark owners.

Published by Karen Deen
Formatted by Kellie Clarke
Edited by Contagious Edits
Cover Design by Opium House Creatives

About the Author

Karen Deen has been a lover of romance novels and happily-ever-after stories for as long as she can remember. Reaching a point in her life where she wanted to explore her own dreams, Karen decided now was the time to finally write some of her own stories. For years, all of her characters have been forming story lines in her head, just waiting for the right time to bust free.

In 2016, Karen put pen to paper for the first time, with Zach and Emily being the first characters fighting to have their story written.

From that first word, she hasn't been able to stop. Publishing Love's Wall (her first novel in the Time to Love Series) in 2017 has ignited her passion to continue writing and bring more of her characters to life.

Karen is married to her loving husband and high school sweetheart. Together, they live the crazy life of parents to three children. She is balancing her life between a career as an accountant by day and writer of romance novels by night. Living in the beautiful coastal town of Kiama, Australia, Karen loves to enjoy time with her family and friends in her beautiful surroundings.

Contact

For all the news on upcoming books, visit Karen at:
www.karendeen.com.au
Karen@karendeen.com.au
Facebook: Karen Deen Author
Instagram: karendeen_author

DEDICATION

To the power of imagination and dreams and the places they take us.

LOVABLE LAWYER

KAREN DEEN

Chapter One

LEX

"Thank you, Counselor, is that all?" The judge looks straight through me like I don't exist. Pompous Prick.

Actually, *asshole* probably suits better.

"Yes, thank you, Your Honor." Taking my seat, I look at my client Michelle, trying to put her at ease. This woman has been through enough. It's the shitty part of the court system. The victim has to sit here, in the same room, mere feet from the person that has totally turned their life upside down.

Sometimes you take on cases where you just want to do more than stand in a courtroom and argue points of law trying to get justice for your client. Like today, where I want to jump the table and grab the smug guy on the stand who has completely destroyed Michelle and her family. Staring at him, I know he has no remorse, what-so-ever. My fist could teach him what it's like to feel the pain that his victims are battling through every single day.

That noise, of the chair legs scraping across the floor, sends shivers across my skin.

Then the clicking of her heels as she strides to her client.

Counselor Jacinta Nordick.

The woman who tortures me most days both in and out of the courtroom. Her back to me, I eye her slender body. The way she dresses portrays an image of power. Her shoulders back, posture straight as an arrow. Her hair always the same for court, pulled tight into a ponytail high on her head. It sways back and forth as she walks.

Her voice then fills the courtroom. It's forceful and her words are always sharp, in a take-no-nonsense way.

"Mr. Digby, tell me what you were doing the night of the car accident," Jacinta says to her client while still standing ramrod straight waiting for his answer.

"I was at my office working hard as I always do. Sometimes I'm there late into the night, trying to keep my business afloat and support my children. Then I realized I was supposed to be at my ex-wife's house to pick up my kids. She gets mad if I'm late. She always starts carrying on, asking me what woman I was with."

"Mr. Digby, just the facts, please," Jacinta snaps.

"Argh sorry, yes. I left my office and hurried to my car. Driving out from the underground parking lot, I saw it was raining. I proceeded to drive cautiously in the weather to my ex-wife's place. I was on route then the Lewisham's car just stopped suddenly in front of me. They didn't give me any time to stop. With the water on the road, my car just skidded, and I couldn't stop in time. It wasn't my fault their car then went into the path of the truck…it was just an accident, they should have swerved around the truck."

Hearing Michelle gasp next to me, I stand abruptly.

"Objection, Your Honor. Mr. Digby is not qualified to make that statement." The judge looks at me and nods.

"Sustained. Proceed, Mr. Digby, and leave out the judgements of what anyone else should have done. I'm more concerned what you did or did not do that night."

My heart's pounding in my chest.

My blood pressure just hit the roof, which is solely from the urge to kill him.

How dare this man judge another driver. The fuckwit was

drunk, under the influence of drugs, and there were no signs of him braking at all. My anger is peaking, but I have to keep it under control.

My father always told me don't get attached to the client. Ignore the emotions. It's just about the truth, and it's your job to argue the facts.

Maybe that works for him, but never for me.

How can you ignore another human in such pain?

The morning continues on with the cross examination and more witnesses. Michelle having to take the stand and battle through the pain of retelling the events that led up to the death of her parents in the car accident where she was the backseat passenger. How she sat in the rain holding her mother's hand as her spirit left her, while her father, lying motionless next to her, had already died on impact, taking the full force of the truck that hit them.

Court recesses for the remainder of the day and we head back to one of the meeting rooms with my assistant and Sam, Michelle's husband. Giving her time to pull herself together before leaving the courthouse. Also, so she doesn't have to face the dickhead that hit her car. Hopefully he'll leave straight away. As I brief her on tomorrow's procedure, her husband wraps her in his arms. When they start to leave for the day, Sam stops at the doorway and goes to shake my hand.

"Thanks, Alexander. We appreciate all you're doing for us." We shake and he guides Michelle out of the room.

Watching them go, I can see how much he loves her and wants to protect her from the hurt. It's eating him up that he is so helpless.

One of the biggest things I struggle with in life is feeling powerless. I need control, and right now I don't have it.

That just makes me a very pissed-off man.

"How do you think she'll cope with another day on the stand tomorrow?" Greta my junior lawyer asks as we pack up our files.

"She's a strong woman and has support. I just hope to god it will be enough to get her through another round of questioning." With my arms full and my coat over my arm, my head is full of all the evidence that was submitted this morning.

Court is like playing chess.

Strategic moves, analyzing your opponent and patience.

Backing them into a corner when they least expect it.

Check mate is so sweet coming off my lips.

Unfortunately, it doesn't always happen, and those days truly suck.

That voice comes from behind me as I'm walking down the corridor. The one that has the hairs on my neck standing up.

"Better bring your A-game tomorrow, Counselor. It's going to take more than a few tears to get the jury on your side. It's me you're up against, not some useless duty lawyer." That smug grin on Jacinta's face as she passes us gets to me every time.

And so the game of cat and mouse begins.

Being against her in a case just adds a whole new level of angst.

"See, that's the thing. The game I need to bring to the table with you on the other side of it is far lower on the alphabet than an A, Counselor. Walk in the park when all the facts are on my side. See you tomorrow." Turning to walk down the hallway to the elevators that will take me to the garage, I hear that laugh of sarcasm as I get farther away.

"Every time you're up against her, I see your shoulders pull back and that little eyebrow twitch starts going. It's sort of funny." Greta smirks as we enter the elevator.

"Not funny, Greta, she drives me wild," I grumble. "Makes me want to go all crazy. So, make sure you keep me on a short leash in there tomorrow. You never know what I'm capable of when she's around."

If only Greta knew what sort of crazy she makes me. No woman has ever drawn this type of reaction out of me before. Make me lose sleep or have her in my head at ridiculous times of the night. I can't seem to shake it, and that's not a good thing.

I always know what is happening in my head and where I'm at. It pisses me off that she is burrowing in somewhere I've always managed to keep solely for me.

Arriving back in my office, I unload my files and run through this morning's proceedings with Greta. I give her the instructions of what we need researched and the information we need for court tomorrow.

"How do you think Jacinta is going to try to argue past the point of him being under the influence?" She looks up at me from her laptop.

"Fuck if I know, that's the annoying part. I'm trying to get into her head and it's always a challenge. One that actually gets my blood going, I must say." Rubbing my neck, I look out the window of my office.

"Well, to me she is just a stuck-up bitch. It's like she has a stick shoved up her ass most days. No one likes her," Greta mumbles as she types away.

"She's not all that she seems on the outside," I say, turning to look at Greta. Running my hand through my hair, my watch alarm starts to buzz on my arm.

"Okay, are you all right with that? I'm heading out to lunch now."

She stands and starts to pack up her laptop and the files she needs. "Lunch, yeah right. I wish I could eat any part of that lunch."

"Greta," I grumble at her.

"What, we go through his every Thursday. Yet you still won't take me to 'lunch' with those hot men. You are so mean."

I just roll my eyes at her.

"Because I know all you would do is drool the whole time and make yourself look pathetic. I'm saving you from losing your self-respect. Plus, they're a little old for you." I walk to open the door for her.

"Pfft mere details, Lex. You should know I would find a counter argument for your issue. I don't want to touch, just watch and drool. But whatever. Have fun." With that she's walking down the corridor to her office. I see her stop to talk to Theresa, my secretary, and they both laugh. Probably laughing at me, I'm sure.

Thank god it's Thursday!

Stripping out of my suit and into my shorts and tank top, I know this is what I need. Basketball with the boys. I try never to miss our weekly Thursday match. Grayson, Mason, and Tate are my best friends and more like family. They're the ones who are always there no matter what. They put up with my sorry ass even when I'm a grumpy, moody bastard, like today.

If I was to describe the four of us, people would wonder why we're friends.

But we just are.

It's that simple.

Since that first day at high school, we fit together like the perfect puzzle pieces. Well, maybe not perfect, but we joined to make the picture whole.

Grayson's the softest of all of us. Gentle in nature which suits his job as an OB/GYN. Yet he loves a good joke and thinks he's the prankster of the group. He's always been the glue that holds us together, made us part of his family. There were times I didn't even realize how much I needed that. His dad and his sister Bella are part of my circle. You know, the people you would move heaven and earth for.

Although they are both doctors, Tate is not like Gray. He's the shithead of the group. Pain in the ass and the one I will most likely be bailing out of jail one day, and probably more than once. You can guarantee it will all revolve around a woman. Being the top neurosurgeon at Mercy Hospital here in Chicago, he plays the field well. It's bound to bring him unstuck sooner rather than later. Despite what Gray thinks, Tate wears the crown for the class idiot.

Mason is quieter like me but is my friend who carries the most baggage in the group. Understandable after spending time as a pilot in the military. His deployment was hard on him, and while we did what we could with the goofy care packages we would send him, nothing can erase the memory of life in a war zone. I doubt it's possible to come out from being in a war and not be carrying something deep inside. Regardless, he is the protector of the group. If it came down to it in a crisis, he would be the one to stop the bullet and save your life.

Pulling into the parking lot, I see none of them have arrived yet. While we would love to be able to meet here every week, it's not always possible. Mason never knows his flight schedule because it can change last minute. His current job of being a private jet pilot for the owner of a multi-billion-dollar company has him flying her all over the country. Plus, Tate and Gray, being doctors, we're never sure when they'll get called for an emergency. So, the days that we can all make it for a game together are precious.

Deep in thought, I sit in the sun on the short fence that surrounds the parkade. Feeling the warmth seeping into my skin, my muscles start to relax for the first time today. Every time I'm in court with Jacinta she sends me into a tense state. Watching her has me turned on and that makes it hard to concentrate. The power she exudes must be what has my heart racing a bit. Yet I'm not entirely convinced it's not just the thrill of the chase and my determination to defeat her. I can't seem to work it out. Either way, she infuriates me, and I wish to hell she didn't.

Pain radiating in my right ear alerts me to Tate arriving. His signature move, a flick on the back of the earlobe when you least expect it. He used to do it all the time in high school when he sat behind me in English. Pissed me off then and still does now.

"How's it hanging, sexy Lexy?" he says, already laughing at himself.

"You are such a dick, you know that, right?" I stand up to start walking towards the court.

"A big dick, you said? Well thanks for the compliment, but don't say it too loud, it's weird when another guy talks about the size of your dick."

"Hard of hearing as per usual. There was no use of the word big in that sentence, my friend. In fact, not sure that could ever be used in relation to your manhood." Smiling for the first time today, I watch Tate scowl at me.

"Always the serious one, aren't you, lawyer boy. You need to loosen up a bit. Let me tell you a secret, sex is the best natural relaxant known to man."

I just roll my eyes at him as the other two guys walk up to us.

"Who's needing sex to relax?" Mason comments with a smirk knowing full well who Tate is referring too.

"Old grumpy here. The one whose nuts are strung so tight they can't breathe." Tate takes the basketball from Mason's hands and starts to dribble it.

"Fuck off, Tate. You have no idea how tightly I'm strung. If you knew Jacinta, then you would understand. That woman has a vice around my dick on the best of days, and I have no fucking idea why. Now shut up and let's play ball. I need to whip someone's ass badly." Looking at Tate about to open his mouth, I hold my finger up to him.

"Not a single word. Not one, do you hear me?"

Grayson laughs hard from behind me.

"Seriously, Lex, maybe you need to take Tate's advice. Get some sex, man. Let go once in a while." Gray looks sympathetically at me.

"I am, but that's the problem. Not sure it isn't making it worse. Now all of you shut up and play. I'm with Mason because at least he hasn't said one stupid comment so far about me or my sex life."

"Give me time, buddy." He thumps my arm. "I'll try to bite my tongue, though. Let's um, how did you say it… *'whip these guys asses,'* shall we?" Mason throws his arm around my shoulder and drags me onto the court, and it's game on.

"You wish, Mason. Nothing can beat the power of two," Gray yells at us from down the court.

"What, two dumbasses? Not sure there is any power in that. But yeah, let's see what you've got. Bring it, baby," I call as Tate starts running at me, dribbling the ball while Gray tries to use fancy footwork to get past Mason. The stupid smirk on Tate's face as he gets closer is enough to get me fired up. I may be the shortest and smallest of the four of us but that doesn't mean I don't know how to stop him. I'm quicker than him, and if my stress does anything to my body it's that it has the adrenaline pumping.

"Come on, pretty boy. Let's see your best attack." Light on my feet, I'm bouncing side to side mirroring him. "You've got nothing." I'm full of mouth today, not afraid to gear him up.

"Oh, you think you've got a chance against the master, little man? Watch and learn, buddy, this is how it's done." He spins to the left to roll around me, but I jump at the same time, anticipating his move, and the ball is vulnerable in his hand about to shoot. I tap it at the right time and it's loose behind him. My feet hit the ground and I'm off with the perfect bounce into my hand. My legs pumping me down the court as he recovers, turning to chase me.

"Shit," I hear Grayson yell as he realizes that the ball is loose.

"Yeah, Lex!" Mason yells as I start my lay-up and dunk the ball in the hoop. I might be smaller than them, but I'm still a tall man.

Tate reaches me as my feet land on the ground.

"Correction, brother, that there, is how it's done," I tease. I jog backwards up the court as he retrieves the ball, and Mason passes me for a high five as we prepare for the next attack.

"Fuck, you are an angry little man today, aren't you? No being nice now. Shit just got real." Tate and Gray have a little word and they are on the attack.

In the fifteen minutes since I've been here, I can already feel my body starting to unwind and my tension about to be laid out on the basketball court for the next thirty minutes.

I love these guys.

Man, it's so hot that the sweat is dripping off all of us as we wind down from the game. I pour water over my head to cool down, knowing I'm going to need a cold shower at the office before I can get this sweaty body back into a suit for the afternoon. I feel like that's all I ever get to wear. Stuffy suits and ties. I hate them so much. It's all I can remember from an early age of being suited up by my mother and paraded around at her social functions as the next future Chief Judge of the district court of the Northern District of Illinois. From the age of four all I can remember is her telling me I was going to become a lawyer, then judge, then on to politics. My father is a lawyer but has never progressed any further than that, so I'm not sure what makes her think I want to.

"Want to tell us what's up your ass today, Lex?" Grayson's voice snaps me out of my thoughts.

I can't even tell them because I'm not entirely sure what has me off rhythm. Of course, there is the normal stress which I'm happy to share, but I know deep down there is more to it and it's just frustrating the shit out of me trying to work it out. I'm a man of facts and solutions. I hate the unknown. My life has always been black and white, with nothing in the middle.

"Just a shit morning in court. This case is tough, man. How can you drive a car drunk and high on drugs? Kill two people and show no remorse and then blame the deceased, saying he should have swerved to miss the truck. For fuck's sake, I just want to grab the jerk and beat the shit out him."

"Wow, that's not the right attitude, Counselor." Tate smirks at me.

"What a dick. Surely the blood tests will prove that. Isn't that just a fact that should make the case cut and dry?" Mason asks, before chugging more water down.

"Except the idiots who handled the first blood samples messed it up, and by the time the second samples were taken, then of course there were only traces in his system. He and his team know that I will struggle to prove how bad he was. Jacinta will make sure he uses it to her advantage. I just wish I knew what she has up her sleeve." Running my hand through my wet hair, I can't stop myself from thinking about her again. I feel the muscles in my shoulders tense up.

"What is it about that woman that you find appealing? She's a dragon, in my opinion," Tate blurts out without any care.

"Tate!" I growl at him. No matter my feelings towards her, he doesn't get to say that.

"What? It's true. You just can't see it. Fuck if I know why, maybe you're blinded by the witch spell she casts over you," he continues, totally oblivious to the death stare I'm giving him. Time for me to leave before I say something I don't really mean.

"I'm out. Need to get back to the office, sort out shit for court tomorrow." Standing, my legs feel a little stiff after a tough game.

"Thanks for letting me whip your ass today, Tate. I must say it felt great. Look forward to next week, I'll make sure my whip is warmed up and ready." Mason and Gray both spray water out of their mouth and are laughing and coughing at the same time.

"Fuck off, Lex. You got lucky. Won't happen again," Tate grumbles. If there's one thing Tate hates, it's being beaten. Competitive is his middle name.

"Blah, blah, all I hear is white noise," I yell over my shoulder as I walk to my car.

Anyone hearing us would think we hate each other. It's totally the opposite, I couldn't live without these guys. It's just how Tate and I are. I'm black and white and he is all shades of gray in the middle. Pushing the boundary of every shade there is, which of course drives me crazy.

The afternoon dragged out as Greta and I pawed over all the case notes. Analyzing what had come out in court today and trying to be prepared for what tomorrow might bring. By the time I leave the office for the day, I know we need to find a golden ticket. Something to nail this bastard. I just don't what that is yet. I need the check mate move.

Finally, I'm home and sitting on my balcony sipping a smooth scotch.

Just breathing.

Taking in the stillness of the night. I can hear the noise of the city, but it's a relaxing noise. I feel calm because the chaos is out there. Where all the lights glisten, the horns sound, and the music blares. The voices are a mixture of laughing, talking, and the occasional scream. Yet it's still peaceful because it's not here.

My personal bubble is quiet and calm.

Everything is in its place and just the quiet music playing in the background. The smell of my dinner in the oven keeping warm, which Ari my housekeeper left for me. One of the privileges of being a trust-fund baby. More money than I can ever spend and a lifestyle that I have never known any different. A life of someone always taking care of me, life has been easy. Whatever I want is at my fingertips, and if it's not, then it can be within a blink of the eye.

It wasn't until I met the guys in high school that I saw what other families were like. They all had money but nothing like the old-money wealth of my parents. One that just accumulates and grows as it is handed down through the generations. No one person will ever be able to spend that amount of wealth in a lifetime.

My phone buzzes on the table from a message. I want to ignore it, but it then starts ringing.

Seeing her name light up, I'm torn. I don't have the energy for her mouth tonight, but I could certainly do with the endorphin release.

Before I make a decision, it stops ringing. But another message is already buzzing through.

Jacinta: I know you're home. Tell your henchman on the door to let me up.

Living in the penthouse, I have an exclusive elevator, and the doorman knows who is allowed up without permission and that is only a very select group. Which does not include the impatient woman standing in the foyer. I'm sure she will be tapping her foot and have a stare that could strip the paint off the walls.

"Hey, Austin. It's fine to let Miss Nordick up." I call the poor doorman to put him out of his misery.

"Thank you, Lex. She doesn't like the word no, does she."

I can't help but start laughing. He hit the nail on the head. "Not even in her vocabulary, man. Sorry for the tongue lashing I'm sure you got."

"Not a problem, happens every time she arrives. Never going to change. On her way up." He chuckles as he hangs up.

His words are still ringing in my ear while I walk into the foyer of my apartment.

'*Never going to change*'.

The doors open and the words are spilling out of her mouth. "Why do we have to go through this every time? Just tell him I'm your girlfriend and I'm allowed to come straight up. Better still, give me a damn key."

Like that is ever going to happen. No chance in hell.

I'm not in the mood for her smart mouth tonight.

While it might turn me on in the courtroom, it's not doing it for me right now.

"You know you aren't my girlfriend, Jacinta, so stop the crap. We fuck, that's what we do. That's all we'll ever do"

She stops walking and spins to look at me.

"Bedroom, now!" I tell her forcefully.

"Pardon? You don't get to…" Her face has the look of fire on it.

"Bedroom now! We both know why you're here. To be fucked, not to talk. So, move before I change my mind." My voice becomes more demanding.

She stalks towards me, her heels clicking on the polished concrete.

"You want to play boss tonight, Alexander? Fine. But we both know who holds the power in the relationship." I hate when she calls me that. Walking away and up the stairs to my bedroom, her ass is swaying in the tight skirt she's still wearing from court today.

Fuck, she has the tightest little ass cheeks. I'm going to enjoy pulling them apart tonight and sinking deep inside her. Hard and fast.

"Don't make me wait, Lex. You know what happens if I get impatient. I start without you." Her voice gets fainter as she heads down the hallway to the bedroom.

My heart is fired up with pure adrenaline again.

Why does she have this pull over me?

The man I am with her is not the man I am in my world.

She makes me someone I don't particularly like.

Yet it's part of me, that I can't deny.

It's like I can't break free, and I can't work out if I even want to.

Striding up the stairs, I need to show her I'm more than playing boss. I'm going to fuck her until she screams my name in pleasure.

I walk into the room she believes is mine. I could never sleep at night if I had the thought of her swimming around me in my actual bedroom. Jacinta is already stripped down to her underwear. A pale purple matching lace set. It always surprises me when she peels off her power suits to find that she's hiding a glimmer of her feminine side. I asked her about it once and won't bother going there again. The answer just sounded like the lawyer in her giving me the premeditated answer she has given every man before me, that she likes the good quality.

I'm not in the mood for games tonight.

"No talking. On the bed on your hands and knees. You want to wave that ass at me all day then you can feel me there now."

She's about to open her mouth, but I glare at her. She closes her lips again, but the smirk pisses me off.

Dropping my sweatpants to the floor, my dick is hard and standing up ready. Already naked, I reef my shirt over my head. Grabbing a condom from the side drawer, I suit up. This I must admit is the only suit I do enjoy wearing.

"This is what you want, isn't it, Counselor. To be fucked hard in that snug pussy. While I finger you like crazy in your tight little puckered rose." She moans as I run my hand over her smooth butt cheek. This is just how I like it; her facing away from me, taking all the power away from her. She won't admit it but it's what she wants too. That's why she's here. To let go and get out of her head for a little while.

Slowly swiping my finger through her dripping pussy, her back arches, her ass lifts higher in the air, and her head looks to the ceiling with her mouth open. Just perfect. At my mercy.

Continuing my finger all the way to her perfectly bleached puckered hole, I smooth her own wetness around while I tease her. Leaning forward, my other hand finds her clitoris and starts to rub back and forth, which brings out her heavy panting. Feeling her getting wetter, I push my thumb slowly deep inside her ass. She moans out loud this time which tells me she's getting close. Pushing two fingers into her wet sex, I'm not gentle. She doesn't like softness. This is what she longs for. Her body rides my fingers in the same rhythm as my thumb sliding in and out of her ass. My third finger slips easily into her as I pull my thumb free. Leaving her wanting a little more.

Lining up my cock with the opening to her sex, I push my thumb straight into her ass as I pull my fingers free from her pussy and sink deep inside her and feel her grip me hard.

Jacinta screams like a wild animal who is in pain, but then starts begging for more.

"Harder, Lex… more…oh…ohh…" I keep pounding her hard like she asks. Feeling my balls tightening and knowing I'm about to blow my load deep inside her.

Just as she is about to come, I pull my thumb from her and smack her hard on the ass as I come hard. Her screaming gets louder as her orgasm rips through her and her body finally lets go. Watching her quivering at the power release reminds me of what she is to me.

Just a good hard fuck and nothing else.

I'm sure there should be more to sex, yet it's just not here between us.

The only comfort I feel in knowing that is that she's told me she doesn't feel a thing for me either.

Chapter Two

LEX

"Good morning, Greta. Thank you for meeting me early. I just had a thought during the night I think we need to investigate." I look up from my desk where I've been working since six am.

I couldn't sleep last night after Jacinta left. After helping her to dress, we both had a beer and talked briefly. Well, she talked and I listened. Never about work. That is the rule. We can't work against each other if we even start to discuss any case. Getting into the each other's head is a bad move for both of us. You then start overthinking in the courtroom which can be the worst thing for your client.

Jacinta mainly talked about my mother and the upcoming charity events we are both supposed to be attending together. Oh, did I forget to mention that my mother thinks that Jacinta is the woman I will be marrying? The power couple of the Chicago legal fraternity. As far as Mother is concerned, Jacinta is the woman who will help me to secure the chief judge role. She is an asset for me in the high-society circles we both socialize in.

Since when do you choose your future wife based on whether

she is an asset to you or not? That's just so demeaning to any woman—or man, for that matter. The years of arranged marriage are almost behind us, or so the public believes. But in the secret lives behind the social circles of money, it's still happening.

No matter what Mother thinks, I can guarantee I will never be marrying Jacinta.

"What did that brain of yours that never sleeps think of?" She places her bag on my chair, pulling out her laptop onto the table. Her other hand places down the tray of coffees.

"Oh, woman, you are worth more money." Reaching over to take mine, I see that it has "insomniac" written on the top of it.

"You better remember that at salary review time, boss, otherwise you never know what special ingredients will start being added to your morning coffee." Laughing, she pulls her chair closer to get started. "Now spill your brilliance—or it better be brilliant to have me here at seven am." Greta looks at me, waiting.

I'm lucky to have her as an assistant. She is super intelligent and has the drive to become an amazing lawyer once she gets the experience behind her. I've had a few assistants in my time, but I think without a doubt, Greta is the best I've worked with. We spend so much time together and sometimes late into the night, and I've never had to worry about her dedication to the cases. We have become great friends, and I hope I can keep pushing her along to get her to where she deserves to be in this firm. I would never interfere with her promotions, but I'll be making sure the people in the know see her ability.

"Right. So last night I was sitting having a scotch after a friend left my apartment. It was my second for the night, plus a beer."

"That's not like you, Lex, three drinks on a school night." She smiles a cheeky grin at me.

"Haha, smarty pants. Anyway, when I started on the third scotch—yes, it had been a long night—I thought to myself, 'Lucky there are no cameras here watching me, to see me getting drunk on my own.' That's when it hit me."

"What, that you should video your own solo drunken parties?"

"No. Very funny. Now just listen and keep up." I glare at her.

"Okay, sorry, no room for comedy this morning. Continue," Greta says, drinking her coffee.

"We may not have a blood sample that is going to prove how much Mr. Digby had to drink that night or what drugs were in his system, but…" I hold my chin and rub my thumb on my beard while I process my thoughts, "…what if there are security cameras in his office that show him drinking or taking drugs in the few hours before he left to drive to his ex-wife's house."

"Shit, we didn't think of cameras in his office. We were so focused on his blood samples, and his driving route once he left the office. I'm on it." Greta's fingers are madly typing away.

"Exactly, and if there are cameras, why hasn't Jacinta used the footage? It's not like her to miss a piece of evidence to prove her point. It leads me to think there's something she doesn't want me to see. I can't believe I didn't think of it. I'm not thinking clearly." I'm pissed off with myself for missing this.

Greta tells her phone to call Blaine, the investigative security expert we use.

I'm almost finished the summary I've been working on of what things I want looked for in his office, so I can send it to Blaine after we speak.

"Morning, sexy lady. Where did you disappear to so early this morning? I was going to finish where we left off last night." Her face goes bright red. I can't help but start to laugh.

"Morning, Blaine. Something you need to share about my assistant lawyer?" I ask him as she just closes her eyes, shaking her head and still typing away.

"Yeah, Lex, tell my wife she needs to wake me up before she sneaks out to see the other man in her life that early in the morning." Blaine chuckles to himself, knowing full well that Greta will be ready to kill him.

"Jealous much? That's what happens when you're second fiddle, man." I try to keep a straight face and not laugh at her.

"Can you two both stop your bullshit and get on with work. We don't have time to continue with you guys trying to one-up each other. Blaine, we have a job and it's urgent. I'm getting the search warrant as we speak. Lex will get the detective handling the case on to executing it. But we need it this morning." Both Blaine and I know the tone of her voice means we are no longer joking, and everyone switches to work mode.

"Sure thing, G, fill me in."

Greta starts talking while I'm sending through the brief to Blaine. We quickly tell him what we're looking for and the time frame we need the security tapes scanned.

He's already running checks on the building and gathering intel as we speak, so he's ready to go as soon as we have the warrant to get in there legally. I can't afford anything to blow this case. This bastard needs to pay for what he has done.

Blaine and Greta met on the job and hit it off straight away. I told her at the time if I didn't get invited to the wedding then I would fire them both. Must admit it makes it handy when you have your own investigator on standby. No matter what he's working on, he won't say no to his wife. They make a great team both professionally and in life. They make me think about the sort of life that hopefully awaits me somewhere down the track. Where I am right now with relationships is not even close to the happiness they share.

"Okay, so we're all good to go, Blaine. As soon as we get the paperwork I'll be in touch. David is standing at the judge's chambers waiting to get it signed off." I finish scanning over the message from David saying that the judge has arrived at the courthouse.

"Perfect. Talk soon." With that he's gone off the line, and Greta doesn't even flinch that he didn't say goodbye to her. Work is work and the rest is for out of the office, otherwise it can just get messy when it blurs the lines.

"Right, now let's get ready for court and pray that Blaine works his magic and we have something to present to court this afternoon." I take another sip of my coffee and look out to the day breaking outside. Let's hope by nightfall we have the evidence that will have this case signed, sealed, and delivered, and Michelle will have the justice she deserves.

"You should thank that friend of yours, Lex. She gave you some clarity with her little visit." Greta laughs as she continues working at the corner of my desk.

"More than you realize, Greta. Though I'm not sure she'll be happy with either bits of clarity she left me with last night. Both epiphanies of how my life needs to change are likely to end both situations badly for her." My eyes are still focused on the clear blue sky.

"That's a little deep for this time of the morning, boss. Care to share?" Greta stops typing. I know I could tell her anything and it would never leave her lips if I asked her to keep a secret. It's not fair to burden her with my troubled mind, though. When I'm ready, the boys will get that messed-up conversation. After a few drinks, I'm sure.

"Thanks, but nobody needs my complicated thoughts this early in the day. We have more important things to worry about." Getting up and walking past her, I squeeze her shoulder to let her know I appreciate her friendship.

"Maybe so, but just know I'm here anytime you need." Her fingers start typing again so I know she's letting it go. Obviously, the guys aren't the only ones to notice I'm not myself at the moment.

I can't have my mind all cluttered with my own shit. I need to focus on work. People rely on me being at my peak in the courtroom.

Leaning on the window for a moment, I roll my shoulders around a few times and rotate my head once to just loosen my muscles.

"Talk to me, Greta, give me the points for my first argument today."

Her work voice is back, and we click into the mode I need.

Black and white, cold hard facts.

"So, Mr. Digby, you were injured in the accident and taken to the hospital that night, where mandatory drug and alcohol testing took place, is that correct?"

"Yes," he answers, looking smugly at me.

"However, those blood tests were lost, so they can't confirm your levels the night of the accident, is that correct?"

"Yes." Again, he looks at me like he holds all the power here. Well, I've got news for you, sunshine.

"Your blood, sample C, that was taken the morning after the accident. It shows in the report tendered to the court, traces of alcohol and cocaine in your body. Can you confirm that this is correct?" I stand very still in front of him. A copy of the report in my hand.

He nods his head, looking down.

"You need to speak for the court, Mr. Digby," I instruct him. "Care to explain why this is the case? When did you consume these drugs?"

He looks sheepishly at the court like he's unsure how to respond. "I was in shock and needed something to calm my nerves after the accident. I couldn't sleep so I had a drink and a little something extra to help relax," he talks, now looking down.

"I need you to be more specific, Mr. Digby. What exactly was the little something extra you had to help relax?" Yeah, come on, asshole, keep squirming.

"Um, a little cocaine that a friend gave me. They said it would help," he mumbles.

"So, you admit you took an illegal substance, Mr. Digby?"

"Yes, but it was the first time. I've never done it before. It was a mistake I made when I was in shock. It was a tiny amount." Oh yes, play the victim, that will just make you look more of a fool when I'm finished with you.

"Objection, Your Honor. What Mr. Digby did after the accident is irrelevant in this case," Jacinta voices from behind me.

"Sustained, Counselor. Get to the point, Mr. Jefferson." Oh, I am, don't you worry.

"Yes, Your Honor." I turn back to the accused. "Mr. Digby, at any time during the day or night before the accident occurred did you consume alcohol or any illegal substances?"

"No." He tries to be quite adamant in his answer.

"So, if the blood sample was not ruined it would have shown that there was nothing in your system?" Keep digging that hole, jerk, tell me you were clean.

"Objection, the question is irrelevant as we don't have the results of the samples," Jacinta calls from behind me.

"Overruled. However there better be a point to this question, Counselor. Please answer the question, Mr. Digby." The judge looks at him, awaiting his response.

"Sure, the samples would have been clean. I promise. I didn't have anything."

I walk back to my desk where Greta is sitting with the documents I need, and Blaine sits behind her with his smug look on his face.

It hadn't taken long for him to find what we wanted. As soon as he gained the footage from the building security company, he had the report and footage to us at the court by eleven am. Just before morning recess, so I've had time to view it and review the report. Now time to deliver the little bombshell to the court.

Giving Jacinta my best self-assured look, I turn back to the court and walk towards the bench.

"Your Honor, I would like to submit exhibit K to the court. Contained is security footage and reports on the footage from the building where Mr. Digby's business is located. The footage is time and date stamped from the four hours before he left the building and drove towards his ex-wife's house when the accident occurred." Placing the file on her desk I turn and walk back to the center of the room, facing Mr. Digby while the television screen on the wall turns on.

"As you can see on the video, the accused is meeting the unknown man at the back door and handing over cash for that package of a white powdery substance." I pause as the video rolls on. "And now in the kitchen with the same bag and snorting it through a straw. Picking up what can be seen as a half-empty whiskey bottle. Please notice all the time stamps on the video as we progress." The video now cuts to later in the night. "Now we have the empty bottle of whiskey and a half-full glass of an amber liquid.

Mr. Digby now struggling with his keys in the door and later dropping them several times while approaching the car. Time stamp showing us all eight forty-two pm."

The video stops, and I listen to all the whispers from the people in the court. Digby's face drops into his hands, and defeat is evident in his slumped shoulders. Time for my final move. I take a few steps to the side so I can see Jacinta as well as Mr. Digby.

"Now, Mr. Digby, I'll ask you again. Had you consumed any alcohol or illegal drugs before leaving your office the night of the accident and driving your vehicle?"

The look on Jacinta's face doesn't change but her tell sign of leaning back against her chair instead of sitting up tall, shows her frustration of not knowing I had any of this.

"Yes," he whispers, looking into his lap.

And there it is – checkmate! Got you, asshole.

"No further questions, Your Honor." I walk back and take a seat next to Greta and Michelle. I place my hand over Michelle's and give it a squeeze.

"You may stand down, Mr. Digby. Court will take a ten-minute recess to allow for the accused to consult with his legal team while I review this evidence and then we will convene back here at two fifteen pm." Banging her gavel onto the desk, the judge stands and leaves the courtroom.

"What's happening now?" Michelle whispers to me in between silent sobs.

"His legal team will talk to him about changing his plea to guilty, and then we will come back, and the judge will bring down her verdict of guilty. Another date will be set for the sentencing." She turns to look at her husband behind her who reaches out to hold her hand. Sharing his strength, the only way he can in the courtroom with a barrier between them.

I look across and see Jacinta talking with her client and looking quite forceful and probably on the inside mad as hell for being blindsided by me. She was obviously counting on the fact that up until now I hadn't sourced the footage.

Before long, the bailiff announces the judge back into the

court, and within five minutes the guilty verdict is handed down and we all walk out of the courtroom. Guiding everyone into one of the meeting rooms so we can talk on our own, I only make it two steps in before Michelle jumps into my arms, crying and hugging me.

"Thank you, Alexander. Thank you so much. I feel like my parents' lives have been given value. You cared and you fought for my father's name to be cleared of any wrongdoing. It won't bring them back, but at least they can rest easy knowing that there has been justice." Her husband pulling her back and into his arms is a relief, and also, I can see he isn't overly comfortable with her hugging another man. I totally get that.

"You are welcome. I'm just glad we managed to get it worked out quickly for you and you weren't dragged through a long court case. You need to thank Blaine here who came up with the goods as quickly as he did. I'm lucky to have such a great team to work with." I can see Greta smiling with pride for herself and having her husband acknowledged too.

We spend the next little while all talking and just coming down of the euphoria of a successful result. I don't say anything, but in my heart, I also have the weight of knowing my actions have just put the wheels in motion for another person to end up in prison. I'm okay with the process of sending people who break the law and do the wrong thing to jail. I just struggle with it being me putting people there. Which is a ridiculous thing to feel as a lawyer, but it's just who I am. I've never shared that with anyone, and I know if my mother had even an inkling, she would lecture that out of me over and over again. Mother is telling everyone I will become a judge; how could I possibly have a hidden moral weakness? It would never be good enough in her eyes. She'd tell me to ignore such nonsense and just do my job which is putting the bad people in jail. I hate to tell her, but it's not always the bad people that are the ones sent to jail. Money and power talk in this system. Justice can be bought, and that infuriates me.

Tonight calls for a celebration, though. After Michelle and her husband leave, I turn to Greta and Blaine.

"Dinner and drinks on me, we've earned it," I say, picking up my bag and files.

"Anytime the boss is footing the bill, who am I to say no?" Greta laughs as she also picks up all her files.

"Well, I'll be there because I need to watch the shifty guy that just asked my wife on a date. Plus, it'll be even funnier having him pay for my dinner while he tries to hit on her in front of me." Blaine slaps me on the back of the shoulder.

"See, that's where you are wrong. I'm trying to teach you how to treat her right, so you stop being the second fiddle in this situation." Greta just rolls her eyes at both of us and walks out. She knows it's all in good fun, and she just ignores us both.

Another day over, and after dinner I'm again sitting on my balcony watching the city wind down at the end of a week. Friday night is where you finally take a deep breath and let it out slowly. Ridding yourself of all the crap from the week with it. I'm not even bothering with a drink tonight. After a few red wines with dinner, I just feel like sitting and relaxing. Today was intense, and my mind is still hanging on the uneasy feelings that keep crawling under my skin.

I think I need a vacation. Somewhere far away from here. Sunshine, a beach, beautiful ladies, and not one lawyer in sight. Actually, maybe we need a boys' trip. We haven't had one in a long time. This adulting takes away all the fun. Either way, I think I need a break from reality for a while. It's been too long since I didn't have to worry about being anywhere on time or fulfilling my duties as the only child of Mr. and Mrs. Dustin Jefferson II. I want a day where I get out of bed and think, *What am I going to do today? Oh, actually maybe nothing.* Yeah, like that's ever going to happen. Even on my weekends there's work stuck in my head. It's hard to switch it off.

My phone starts buzzing on the table. I ignore it.

I know it's her.

I just can't tonight.

It rings next. As it goes unanswered, several messages come

through, then another call. Since I'm not replying, then my intercom phone from the front desk is ringing. She's really not taking no for an answer tonight. I'm sorry, Austin. You will just have to deal with her crap tonight, because I don't have the energy to.

I leave it an hour and open her messages but don't read them. I just type what I need to say.

Lex: We need to talk. Meet me at the grower's market tomorrow morning. Pick a time.

Jacinta: 10am sharp and don't be late. You pissed me off tonight.

Lex: 10am. See you then.

I don't even enter into her baiting me, so she can start her rant. As I stand and lock up on my way inside, turning everything off as I walk upstairs to my room, I know what I need.

Throwing my phone onto my bed, stripping my clothes off, I step into my en suite and my huge shower that is big enough for four people easily. The hot water starts to pound down on my shoulders, and I stand under the stream with my head dropped forward. I wash the day away and try to clear the fog that is stuck there. The problem is I don't really know what the fog is from, just that it's there and it's making me feel like shit.

Dragging my weary body from the shower, drying off, I crawl into my large king-size bed. I can't help but laugh to myself. The huge and very expensive bed has only ever had me sleep in it. I've never shared it with a woman. I've always used one of the other rooms. I like my space to be perfect and untouched by chaos. I could roll over three times and still not fall out the other side.

I'm lying here thinking stupid facts. It's definitely time to close my eyes and get some sleep. Before I become even crazier than I feel already. I need sleep to deal with seeing Jacinta at the market in the morning. I've got a feeling it won't end well.

The sound of the market is getting louder as I walk up the sidewalk. Getting close to the entrance to the park. Watching all the people coming and going with their bags of fresh produce. As the crowd parts, I see Bella, Grayson's sister, just in front of me walking towards the road with her head down.

Shit.

She's not looking at the car coming towards her. Panicking, I lunge out and grab her. Pulling her backwards, we fall on to the footpath with a thud. She scrambles quickly to her feet.

"Lex, oh god, thank you." She looks shocked as to what just happened.

"Shit, Bella, what are you trying to do? Get yourself killed or something? You didn't even look." My words rush out sternly. Fuck, just what I need to start the day, having to call Gray and explain his sister just got run over in front of my eyes.

"Sorry, I was preoccupied. I don't know how I missed that. Thank you for saving me."

I roll my eyes at her. "Like I haven't been doing it most of your life. Just like I'm constantly saving the other boys. One day I'll just stop being there to catch you. Then all of you will be fucked." I grab her and hug tightly. This girl is like a little sister to me. I've known her since she was five and not long before she and Gray lost their mother to cancer. She is just as special to me as the guys are.

"Oh, stop complaining. What would you do with your life if you weren't being our hero half the time?" Slapping me on the chest, she looks up at me with those same eyes of the little girl that we all fell in love with.

She's right, though. I'll never admit it, but I love hovering over them all, making sure they're safe. It's what I'm good at. Being in the background and keeping everything in order. Picking up after them.

"Maybe then I'd have time for a life of my own," I say to her, knowing I'm full of shit, but it sounds good right now.

Chatting and heading into the market, she starts talking about a crazy lady Martha and her husband George. Before I know it, I'm being dragged through the market to meet them and listen to some crazy words. George calls me her boyfriend and then Martha corrects him, saying that I'm one of the friends, a protector, and not the boyfriend. The hairs on the back of my neck are standing up. What boyfriend? I don't know anything about a boyfriend, which means Gray doesn't either. Oh shit, today is already full of surprises.

"Since when do you have a boyfriend? Care to share, Bella?" I stare straight into her eyes and watch her squirming trying to change the subject and brush me off, saying that the crazy lady doesn't know what she's talking about. Hmm, nice try, Bella, but I'll give you a few minutes. As soon as we are alone you will be spilling the details.

Being a smart woman, an almost fully qualified doctor, she knows how to deflect well by turning the questions to me. I think she forgets who she's up against, though. I'm the master of reading people and getting information out of them when they don't want to share.

"Let's go back to the question at hand. What brings you to the market this morning?" Bella asks me as she nibbles on some blueberries she just purchased.

"You have to promise, what happens at the market stays as the market, Bella. None of this reporting to your brother with bits of crappy gossip about me. Otherwise I'll let slip the old lady's crazy—or not-so-crazy—statement about the boyfriend. Do we have a deal?" She thinks I'm joking, but I'm actually not ready to share this with Gray yet.

"Deal. Now spill it, Alexander," she says as we sit on a park bench.

"Wow, my full name, Miss Arabella. This must be a serious chat." My full name only gets used by my mother or at work. Bella is full of sass this morning. She knows I hate my friends using it.

"It'll be serious in a moment if you don't start talking." She points her finger at me like I'm a schoolboy.

"See, this is why I stay away from women. You're all killing me at the moment." And I know the day isn't going to get any better.

"Now that's a good start. It's about a woman. Not that I thought you were gay, but that clarifies it for me."

"Far from it, you weirdo. You've seen me many times with women. I like certain parts of the female anatomy way too much to be gay. Just saying. Mind you, it concerns me we're even having this conversation, but I'm not going there, otherwise this is going to take too long."

As she continues to try to interrogate me, I find I'm enjoying the banter back and forth. Until I hear the voice that seems to overpower every other voice around us and make them fade into the background.

"Alexander, there you are finally. Thought I said ten am sharp if you wanted to talk. Typical of you to be late." Jacinta glares at me.

Fuck, I didn't want her to see me with Bella. You know the saying, *'and never the two shall the meet.'* Jacinta is not someone who belongs in the same world as my special people. These worlds are never supposed to cross over.

I jump up to try to stop her in her tracks, but I'm too late.

"Who are you?" Jacinta says, looking down at Bella with her righteous attitude.

Oh god, Bella isn't going to take that. She's a little firecracker when she wants to be.

"Doctor Arabella Garrett, sister to Lex, and you are, besides rude?"

"Bella," I growl at her.

Even though Jacinta deserves that, my upbringing still won't let people disrespect her.

The two of them start verbal sparring, and then Jacinta straight out tells her we're fuck buddies.

I need to get out of here before this gets worse.

I can just hear the phone calls I'll be getting from the guys later today when Bella spills all this to them.

Apologizing to Jacinta, I pull Bella away and tell Jacinta I will call her later. I need to go into damage control. Bella and I end up in a heated discussion, and I know it comes from a good place, but she's overstepping the sister role she loves to have with all us boys. After calming her down and making her promise to keep this run-in to herself if I keep her boyfriend secret, we part, and she heads off to see the crazy lady again.

I take off in the direction Jacinta left in, hoping I can catch her before she leaves. I see her in the distance buying some flowers. I get there just in time to shove some money in the hands of the vendor and tell him I'll pay. Jacinta just stares at me. Taking her flowers and walking away from me.

"Wait," I call after her.

Stopping, she doesn't turn but waits for me to catch up to her. I walk in front of her then reach for her arm.

"Can we just sit for a moment? We need to talk." She doesn't say a word but follows my lead to the seat. I asked her here so this could be done in a public place. That way I can stay strong to do what I need to do. I don't want a debate with her screaming at me.

"Well?" she says sternly.

"Jacinta, I know we've been using this mutual agreement to satisfy a need we both have at times. No strings attached and no feelings. But it's not working for me anymore."

Her eyes open boldly. "You've developed feelings?" Her voice is a little softer with a hint of a smile.

"God no. I just can't do this anymore. It's not healthy for either of us. I want to find someone for a meaningful relationship. You deserve that too. Let's just keep the respectful friendship. I'm sure you agree. It's time to move on."

That's when I get the biggest shock.

Fuck, how did I miss this?

The momentary look of longing in her eyes. Which quickly flicks to sadness and despair at my words.

Jacinta has developed feelings for me that she has hidden behind the power struggle. This was never supposed to happen. Her words to me were that she just needed the sexual release and that we could enjoy it while it lasted. When we'd had enough, we would walk away.

They were her words.

Fuck, fuck, fuck.

She blinks a couple of times and that vulnerable look is gone and the blank expression returns.

Standing, she puts her hand out and takes mine to shake it.

"Thank you for your time, Alexander. Good luck in your future. Please pass on this change in arrangement to your mother."

As she stalks off across the park in her normal power walk, I'm left sitting there totally floored.

That is not how I expected this to go down at all.

I need a stiff drink and it's only just after ten am.

Can today get any worse?

Well of course it can.

Now I get to visit my mother. This change in her master plan is not going to sit well with her. She feels it's her right as my mother to control my life.

Well, today she's about to find out that's not the case.

And people think Jacinta is a dragon and is as cold as ice with emotions.

Elouise Jefferson has been known to bring the toughest men to their knees within five minutes of meeting them.

Yep, a drink sounds like a good option.

Chapter Three

MIA

Kicking a toy block across the room, my mind is saying every swear word I can think of.

With the kids in the room I can't say them out loud, but I can scream them in my head.

"Mommy, why does he yell at you all the time?" Jack looks at me.

I promised myself I would never let him see me cry again after that night we broke free.

"Because he is an angry man sometimes. Don't you listen to him. Just keep singing in your room like I taught you when he comes, okay?"

He still looks concerned about me. "I don't like him, he's mean. I'm going to yell at him and tell him next time."

"No, you won't. I'm just going to go to the bathroom for a minute. You just keep watching Kayla in the playpen for me." I hold it together until I close the door, my back then sliding down the wall. I fall to the ground and curl my arms around my legs, crying silently.

I can't believe it's happening again. Two months have passed and yet, for everything I went through that night, I'm right back there again.

Different place but same situation. With a man controlling me and threatening our safety.

I want to scream and cry out loud.

But just like before, I have to cry silent tears and not show any signs of my weakness.

What the fuck even is my life!

Laying my head back against the bathroom wall, my mind takes me right back to that night. The one where I ran to what I thought would be a better life.

What a huge lie that's turning out to be.

My memory always starts the same way, with an immense feeling of fear.

"Jack, baby, you need to be really quiet for me. Like a creeping lion. Remember how Mommy showed you. No noise." His big eyes look up at me with complete trust. Nodding his head, he tells me he understands. My heart is pounding so loud I can hear it in my ears.

My poor little boy is only four years old and he should not be living a life like this. With Kayla my eight-month-old daughter strapped to my front in her carrier, luckily sound asleep, and a backpack on my back with the necessities kids need. I can't afford to make a noise. Picking Jack up, I now have him on my hip and am creeping through the apartment. How has my life even gotten to this point?

I know I'm a good person, yet the universe keeps just dealing me shitty situations.

One after another.

From the day I was born, nobody wanted me.

My own mother left me on the front step of a house which just meant I ended up in foster care. I struggled through life just staying quiet and out of trouble. My foster family didn't have much, but they fed and clothed me and shared what love they had. It always confused me why they fostered children when they struggled financially. But they did what they thought was a good deed, and I'm grateful they gave me a home.

The day I turned eighteen, I knew I was on my own, though. Time to leave and fend for myself. My foster mom cried when I left and wished me well. Told me to keep in touch even though we both knew deep down I wouldn't. Like the kids before me. The moment I left, another child was arriving to replace me. They were good people, and for all the kids they gave a home to, they deserve something good to come their way.

Looking at my kids who are my world, wrapped tightly in my arms, I can't imagine giving them up.

Instead my protective instinct became so strong from the day I found out I was pregnant with Jack. No one is ever going to hurt my children. As long as I'm alive, I'll fight to keep them safe.

My hand on the front door handle, I ever so slowly pull it towards us and am hopefully closing the door on an ugly past. Through the gap that's getting smaller by the second, I have the last vision of my husband. He is passed out on the couch. Drunk and snoring loud enough for the whole unit block to hear him. One of the blessings I had was that he very rarely made it to our bed at night because he was too drunk and passed out. Sleeping it off. Then I would make sure I was up before he woke. I avoided him at all costs, but there were times I just had to do as he demanded, otherwise the consequences were worse.

I'm shaking as the door gap finally closes and I pull my hand off the knob. Taking my finger to signal to Jack that we are still being quiet, he just smiles at me. His innocence kills me. He never questions my love or the trust he places in me. Something I will always treasure. Maybe I've never been wanted by anyone else, but these two little angels in my arms give me the reason to keep living. One day I will explain to them how much their love held me together and gave me the strength to take this step tonight.

I rush down the stairs as fast as my legs will take us, in the limited light that there is and trying not to fall. Stopping on the second floor, I lightly tap on the door just next to the stairwell. It quickly opens and Rita hands me the little bag I had left with her earlier with some food for the kids, just to get me through the next day. She has tears in her eyes and grabs us in a quick hug and then quietly closes the door again. She knows she can't let her husband hear her either, as he's friends with Edward. I don't want her to get in any trouble for helping me. Taking the last few steps before the front door, I can't believe I'm really doing this.

The bottom door bangs a little in the wind anyway, so hearing it opening in the middle of the night and make a noise would not be unusual. Not that anyone around here gives a shit about anything other than themselves. Not once has anyone stepped in to help me.

Finally placing Jack down on the ground, I take a breath of the cool night air. It doesn't smell pleasant, but it never does at any time. Where we live is a dump, and I make a promise to myself right now that somehow, I will make sure my kids grow up in a safe home and somewhere that smells far better than this shithole.

Crouching down, I kiss Jack on the cheek.

"Great job, little man. Now let's go on our adventure on the big bus. We have to stay quiet and not talk to anyone. Okay?" I whisper to him.

"Yes, Mommy," he whispers back.

"Now we need to hurry to make the bus."

Taking his hand, we start running down the road a little. I want to get away from here as quickly as possible. I don't want to get on the bus at our usual bus stop where Edward might ask around about us. So, I'm running towards the back of the diner I work at. My boss Anna is there waiting for me. She has been looking out for me for years and has been keeping some of my wages safe for me, ready for this moment. I knew the day I found out I was pregnant again from one of those nights where I just did as I was told, that I had to get out. To Edward I was just money for him. The kids were an inconvenience, and I knew before long would become the next target for his frustration. He gambled and drank away all our money, so he needed me to work to support his habit. He didn't care if we ate or not, as long as he had cash to feed his addiction.

Seeing Anna at the back door locking up the dinner, I feel like I can take a little breath.

She bends down and Jack runs towards her and into her arms. She has been like a grandmother to him and Kayla. Feeding them and letting them stay in the back room while I'm at work. I never trusted Edward with them or to leave them with anyone else.

If he hurt me when his temper flared, then what might he do to them? I wasn't ever going to give him the chance to find out.

But if I didn't work, then I couldn't feed or clothe them. I've been so blessed with this job.

"Great job, Jack my boy. Did you run here with Mommy?" She stands with him in her arms.

"Can I talk?" He looks to me, and I try not to laugh at my gorgeous boy.

"Yes, my brave boy, just quietly," I say as I catch my breath and put the bag in the back of Anna's car, next to the bigger bag she has been keeping for me. Slowly I've been bringing clothes and things I needed to take with me to work each day and filling up the bag. She's been here waiting to drive me a couple of suburbs away to get on the bus.

"Good, because Mommy, I really need to pee. All that running made my pee want to come out." He screws up his face.

Anna and I look at each other and giggle quietly.

"I know what you mean, Jack. Being a mom, when I run it makes my pee want to come out too." Anna just keeps laughing at me quietly, knowing exactly what I mean. Right now, Kayla decides she wants to start to wake a little and fuss.

Damn!

"Jack, we don't have time to go inside. Come with me." Anna puts him down and we walk over to near the dumpster.

"But Mommy, you said we always had to pee in the toilet because it's yucky to pee outside like Daddy does." He looks up at me a little worried.

"I know, baby, but tonight we are just this once going to break that rule. Otherwise we are going to miss our adventure bus. So, can you do it, just this once for me?" Knowing the lure of the bus will have him listening, I strip his pants down and tell him to aim for the wall. What is it with boys and wanting to make patterns? This kid has never peed outside yet here he is making lines on the wall in the dim streetlight. Can't wait until he is a teenager!

"Done," he says proudly as he pulls up his pants. "Mommy, that was fun, can we do that again another day? It wasn't yucky." I don't have the strength to argue or explain now so I use my favorite word that just pushes this discussion to another day.

"Maybe."

Anna already has the car going and the door open for us to climb in the back seat. I lay down on the seat and pull Jack down with me and wrap my arms around him and Kayla who is still trapped to my chest, thankfully now settled again. What we are doing is highly illegal, but we don't want anyone to see us in the car. Desperate times call for desperate measures. Anna slowly starts to drive away, knowing she has precious cargo in the back.

"Sing to me, Jacky boy," Anna says. "I'm not going to see you for a long time while you're on your adventure, so I want to remember your beautiful voice."

Lovable Lawyer

I can see her eyes in the rearview mirror with tears leaking from them. She has loved these two like her own and been the only person I truly trusted in my life.

Jack looks up at the stars out the back window of the car. Singing Twinkle Twinkle Little Star over and over again. This song will forever be my song of hope, as I also wish upon the stars above to keep us safe and find a life worth living.

Standing at the bus door, I don't have long to say my goodbye.

Anna starts to really cry now, and we both hug tightly which starts Kayla crying.

"Know that you are loved, precious girl. No matter what. I will always be here. I don't trust this brother of yours, but then he can't be any worse than Edward. Just be careful." She looks me straight in the eyes and finishes with possibly the last words I will ever hear from her. "You are beautiful inside and out and have more strength than you realize. Don't ever forget that. You are going to do amazing things in this life, I just know it. One day you will find a nice man, and don't let your fear of the past hold you back."

My tears are really flowing now. I can hardly speak.

"Thank you. For everything. I will never forget you." Hugging her again quickly, I pull back and take Jack's hand. "I don't know how, but somehow I will let you know we are okay. Just look for a twinkling star."

I then push Jack to step up into the bus, and I follow him with Kayla and our bags. The bus doors closing behind us. Taking a seat, Jack is already kneeling on the seat and waving at Anna outside. I can't believe we made it. Feeling the bus start to move, I blow Anna a kiss, watching her wipe her tears and trying to smile and look happy for Jack. She slowly disappears into the night as we pull out onto the road and start our adventure trip to Chicago.

I don't know if I'm making the right decision, but I'm following my gut. Surely Bent, the brother I never knew I had, will look after me and help me find my feet. He promised he would take care of us and give us a place to live until I can afford something of my own. He even said he found a job for me and would explain more when we got there. He is doing so much for us, and really, my life couldn't get any worse, so trusting him poses no greater risk, surely?

It's still crazy to believe, after all these years, I have a brother.

Bent started coming into the diner and talking to me a few times over the past couple of months. Then one day he asked me if he could talk to me. I was hesitant because men make me nervous. But I figured everyone was around us so

I should be safe. He then dropped the bombshell that he was my brother and that he had tracked me down through the foster system and then my marriage license details. He knew everything about my mother and how she left me on a step. My date of birth and the house address where I was abandoned. He knew too much for me not to believe him although we look nothing alike. He even told me to go home and get over the shock and he would come back tomorrow. He was on a vacation from his job as a chauffeur and came to find me.

The next day he came back again and said he wanted to take me away from here. To help me and the kids have a better life. If I could get to Chicago he would look after me and we would be safe. After thinking about it, I decided his appearance might the universe's way of getting me out of danger. What did I have to lose? Life couldn't get any worse than it already was. Plus, he was family, one I didn't know I had. He wouldn't come looking for me if he didn't want me in his life. Would he?

After the bus drives for a little while, the excitement of the night catches up with Jack, thank goodness, and he falls asleep on the seat next to me with his head in my lap. Kayla has settled down again and is fast asleep on my chest in her pouch.

Again, I stare out the window and wish on a star.

Not for me but for my kids.

I wish for a better life for them.

Kayla's crying brings me out of my daydreaming that's more like a memory of a reoccurring nightmare. The first few days in Chicago gave me a false glimmer of hope, but all too quickly I'm right back where I came from. I may live in a classy building and nice apartment, but the rest is the same old crap. Now I have two dangerous men in my life, I fear. One I'm hiding from and the other that is threatening to tell him where I am. How did I fall into this trap again?

I drag myself up from the floor and wipe my face to try to look normal for the kids before I open the door. Kayla's still crying and working herself up to that higher pitch she gets when she's being ignored. I look for Jack as I walk to the playpen and pick her up. The crying stops instantly.

"Jack, where are you, buddy?" Walking towards his room, I notice the front door of the apartment open. My stomach drops.

"Jack?" I yell louder, running into his room and then mine.

Fuck, he's gone. Racing into the hallway, I see the elevator numbers counting down as it reaches the ground floor.

I run and thump the button repeatedly, trying to get the car back to my floor so I can get down there.

What if he leaves?

What if Bent takes him?

Or anyone, for that matter?

"No, no, no. Come on, elevator," I yell. Please, baby, just wait for Mommy, I'm coming for you.

The doors open, and I'm in and slapping the door closing button and the ground floor over and over again.

I can't lose Jack.

It's my job to protect him.

So far, I've done a shit job, but please give me another chance, Universe.

Please keep him safe.

The doors open, and I gasp as I see him in her arms.

Rushing forward, I grab him from her.

You can't have him, bitch.

He's mine.

You got the charmed life. You have it all, but you aren't getting the one thing in my life that is worth more than all your money.

Squeezing him so tightly, my heart slows a little. *He's safe. You have him, he's safe.* I keep repeating it in my head.

I hear her soft voice. "Jack, is this your mom, Mia?"

He starts to nod as I jerk a little.

Shit, does she know I'm her sister? Has she known all along? Bent will kill me if he finds out that I've blown the cover. He didn't tell me about her until we arrived in Chicago, but from what I know, I don't want her near me or my kids.

"How do you know my name?" I snap without even thinking.

"It's okay, Jack and I were just chatting until you came. I didn't want him to wander off and get lost. He told me. My name's Paige, by the way." *I know who you are*, I think in my head. *Bent told me how awful you are*, yet there is something weird being so close to her. A funny feeling, I'm not sure what it is. I quickly dismiss it because I know I need to get away from here.

"What have I told you about talking to strangers, Jack? You can't tell them our names. We have to go." I stand up tall, taking his hand.

"Wait, please, let me help you. I think you're in trouble and need some help." She looks at me weirdly. "If you're in danger, we can help to keep you safe. My boyfriend is military, we can help you." I don't want to hear all this. It's lies, all lies. No one helps me. They just promise me the world and deliver hell instead. I bang the elevator button trying to get it to open back up.

"Please, Mia, is someone hurting you?" She's almost begging me to listen.

The doors open, and I quickly drag Jack in with me. My heart now racing as I try to get away from her and whoever that man coming behind her is. She has no idea what she's saying. She is helping to destroy my life again. Trying to block her words out, I say the only thing that makes sense to me.

"You can't save me from you," I mumble as the doors close again.

I know I need to run again.

Just this time, I can't.

I used every bit of money I had last time and now I'm stuck.

I know I promised not to cry in front of Jack again, but I can't stop the tears from falling.

I've never felt so trapped in my life, and I have no idea how to get out.

"Mommy, I'm sorry I made you mad like Bent. The lady was being nice to me, cause I was scared."

I can't say a word. I just need to get back to the apartment and shut the door on the world. Hold my kids and pray that I can figure something out soon.

Jack stays silent the rest of the ride thinking he's in trouble, so he's not about to speak.

Once we're in the apartment again, with the door closed and locked, I just flop onto the couch and think about what the hell just happened.

Everything Bent has told me about Paige has made her out to be some awful woman. Yet she was so gentle with Jack and trying everything to give me some help. She seemed to know that something is not right in my life. How the hell would she know that?

"Jack, come here, little man. Come sit with Mommy." He slowly crawls up and into my lap.

His bottom lip quivering.

"Sorry, Mommy," he whispers, looking down into his lap.

"Oh Jack, it's okay. But why did you leave and go down in the elevator?"

"I got mad that Bent made you cry again. I wanted to yell at him and tell him he is a meanie and leave my mommy alone."

My precious boy. Why is my four-year-old the only man who has ever stood up and fought for me.

"Jack. Mommy needs to look after you. I'm the big person. So, don't worry about me. Please don't leave this apartment again without telling me. Do you understand? It's very dangerous."

"But I'm big now. I'm four." As he holds up three fingers to me.

"Yes, and that is much bigger than when you were three. But Mommy is thirty-eight, which is a lot bigger than that. So, let me be the one to tell Bent he is a meanie and you can just look after Kayla for me, which is a very important job for a big brother. Is that a deal?" He starts nodding with a big smile on his face.

"I'll be the bestest big brother ever." I hope so, Jack. Because my brother has turned out to be a selfish asshole. To be honest, you might be the only chance she's got.

Squeezing him tight, I pray that they never know the hurt that a family can bring. Growing up, all I wanted was to have a family. Someone who belonged to me. To love and be loved back. That you shared something with, that no other human on this earth has. The same DNA. The thing that is supposed to give you such a strong bond, it can't be broken no matter what.

How naive I was.

It's almost a twisted fairytale. The happy ending you imagined is just a horror story after all.

Just because we share common genes does not make us the same. I could never treat another person like Bent has treated me. And from the stories he's told me about Paige and how she turned her back on our mother when she needed her, then I'm damn sure I don't want any sort of relationship with her either.

But as the thoughts of Paige go through my head, there is some little part of me that just keeps rethinking the stories I've heard. I can't put my finger on it but there's something niggling at me.

I push it to the side.

My past track record shows that I'm a hopeless judge of character.

Every boyfriend I ever had turned out to be a scumbag.

My husband.

Now my brother and perhaps my sister.

Maybe I'm just too trusting or gullible. Anna told me to be careful of Bent, she hadn't trusted him. I know I could call her, and she would get me back home, but I'm too embarrassed. Plus, I can't let Edward know where the kids are.

He threatened if I took his meal tickets away, he would kill them. He would hunt me down and kill them. He knows that if I fear for their safety that he holds the power over me. I knew then, that I was going to run and never look back.

What man would ever speak about his children like that. I don't know what I ever saw in him. Another of my bad judge of character moments. That and some very good acting skills on his part until he had me in his bed. He said all the right words and did all the right things to convince me he was different.

Oh, he was different alright. Pity I didn't find that out until after I was pregnant with Jack and he had convinced me we needed to get married straight away. No son of his was going to grow up a bastard child.

I just didn't realize he was the bastard.

That revelation came later when the 'honeymoon period' wore off. A crying baby, a wife who was useless because I wasn't interested in sex and couldn't go out and work to get more money for him. Apparently, every other woman he knew spat out a baby and was at work the next week. There was something wrong with me, which he was happy to tell everyone he knew.

When I went back to work with Anna, she would give me longer shifts so I could sleep in the middle in the back room and feed Jack. She tried to tell me then, to leave Edward. But he was the only family I'd ever had, and I thought in his own weird way he loved me. Otherwise why would he marry me and have a baby together. I kept making excuses that he was stressed about money or tired from working so hard because he would come home so late at night. He must be working overtime to make sure we had enough money.

It wasn't until I overheard him and his friend talking about the much-younger woman he went home with the night before and fucked until her father came home and kicked him out. They both laughed that she was a much better fuck than me because at least she let him bang her ass too.

I slunk back into the apartment and made sure he didn't hear me.

That was the first night I thought about leaving.

It took me four more years to find the courage that I didn't know I had.

Now I need to dig deep and find that strength that Anna told me she sees in me.

I didn't think I'd need it so soon, but I can't see another option.

Looking down at my kids now playing on the floor together, I know it's my only option.

Time to wish upon a star again.

Maybe this time I need to find a twinkling one.

Not one that is shooting in the wrong direction.

There has to be a star out there with my name on it.

I have to keep believing.

There is no other choice.

Chapter Four

LEX

Visiting my mother is always like visiting the First Lady. You can't just arrive unannounced. She needs notice, and way more than five minutes. I look at my friends' families and don't think they appreciate the normalcy of their lives with their parents. Growing up in this life was all I knew, and everyone around me was the same.

Be seen not heard.

Speak only when spoken to.

Perform like a monkey on cue, and god forbid don't embarrass your family by making a mistake.

Win at all costs and be the best.

Never show public displays of emotions. No matter if you are a child and have just fallen and hurt yourself. I can still hear those awful words.

Men don't cry, Alexander.

Looking back now, I realize how fucked up that sort of life is, and if I'm ever lucky enough to have children, they will never live like that.

They will have ice cream for breakfast.

Play in the mud and then run it through the house.

Laugh and giggle while I chase them through the yard.

Say the silliest things at the most inappropriate time.

Make disgusted sounds while they watch me kissing their mother like she is the only air I can breathe.

Pulling up in the white pebble circle drive in front of my parents' home, I drop my head back on the seat. I don't know where all those thoughts came from. I've never really thought about a family in my life. The way my mother has my life mapped out, it didn't really fit in. All I knew was that if I was going to follow that path, there would never be room for love, let alone children. I would not put them through being a token trophy family. I lived that life, and I won't do it to anyone else.

Yet recently watching each of my friends discover there is that possibility of something more, I find myself confused as to what I really want. For thirty-five years of my life I have been told what my life will be. It was easier to just agree. I learned from a very young age watching my father, that to do as mother wanted made life a happier place. But today will be the start of me standing my ground and finally saying no.

Sitting in my car I sound brave, but I know my upbringing will weigh me down as soon as I walk in through those front doors.

Looking towards the front stairs, remembering hearing the crunching of the pebbles under my feet, I'm taken back in time to the little boy who just wanted to be shown love. I don't doubt my mother loves me, she's just never shown it. I'm not even sure she knows how to.

"Alexander Jefferson the third, stop those tears this instant. Look at the mess your blood has made on the white pebbles. Get inside and get cleaned up while I sort out your mess. Charles, have the groundskeeper replace those pebbles now. I can't have people seeing blood and thinking we are dirty people." Mother's voice is so loud when she yells.

Trying so hard to stop my tears, I look up at her. It really stings. The blood is still dripping down my leg from where I scraped my knee trying to climb the tree in the yard. Why doesn't she make it better? Reaching the back door to the house because I dare not enter the front door, Nanny Sue is there waiting with her arms open. Hugging me, she wipes my tears with her apron.

"It's okay, Alexander. You are very brave. I know that hurts. Let me get a special bandage that will make it all better." Sitting me down on one of the kitchen chairs, she cleans me up and puts band-aids on the scratches. "Now run upstairs and get changed before your mother sees that you have ripped your pants. I will have some cookies and milk waiting for you when you come back down."

Walking upstairs, I hear my mother and father arguing.

"You are too hard on him, Elouise," Father's voice comes from his office.

"Nonsense, Dustin. It's your fault he is such a baby. If you were a stronger man, then he would look up to you more. Have a better role model. Instead you are a wimp, and I have to do everything in this marriage. It's about time you stand up and start to show him what his role in society is. It's not like you are going to become anything more than a lawyer. I had big plans for us, and now it will all fall on Alexander to make something of this family name. Your mother promised me more than this life. We had plans for you."

I stop on the stairs, listening for my father in the cold silence that fills the house.

"Are you going to say anything, Dustin?" Her impatient voice fills the halls.

"What's the point, Elouise? You make it perfectly clear every time we have this discussion what a failure I am to you. I'm the man you married for the status and money. You got both of those, so stop complaining." Hearing his shoes stomping through his office, I run up to my room before they see me.

I don't understand what they're saying. I just hate when they fight. They don't do it when all the people come here for the parties. Just when it's only us—oh, and all the staff. Hearing her shoes on the marble floors downstairs, I close my door and quickly get changed. I don't want to make her any angrier at me. Keep quiet and do as she asks. That's what my father always says.

My car door opening next to me jerks me out of my memory.

"Thank you, Charles." I look up to find my parents' butler. Slightly more aged now than I remember as a kid, with grey hair, but still the same smile for me.

I step out and shake his hand, although my mother frowns if she sees me do it. To her, he is the hired help. To me he's a childhood friend who then became my keeper of late-night secrets as a teenager.

"Master Alexander. How are you today?" He smiles, closing my door after we release hands.

"Well, it's been an interesting morning so far, let me just say that. How is Mother today?" Rolling my eyes at him, he just laughs.

"The same as usual. She is expecting you and is waiting in the sunroom." We start walking together.

"And Father, where is he?"

"As usual in his study, hiding—oops, I mean working." We both have a laugh as he opens the front door for me.

"Nothing changes in this place," I mumble under my breath, walking past him and towards my father's study.

He might be my father, but I still knock before entering. This is his sanctuary, and he deserves the respect of being invited in.

"Enter," his deep voice calls.

"Hi, Dad." I only get to call him that when we're on our own. Apparently only the common people use that word.

"Son, how are you? I didn't hear you arrive." Standing, he comes to me and shakes my hand with a slap on my shoulder. And that's about as close to a hug as we get.

"Good, thanks. Busy, but you know what that's like. The cases never stop landing on my desk." I take a seat on his brown leather chesterfield. My mother has control over the decorating of every room in this house, except this one. This couch has been here for as long as I can remember. His room is like my father in a way. Nothing much changes, it's safe, comfortable, traditional, and a true gentleman's office. Nothing flashy, but classy and old world to show the wealth of history in his family. Some of the artwork and photographs of my grandparents and great-grandparents that lived in this house are something he's proud of. Heritage means a lot to both my parents. It's just my mother is more in your face about it than my father.

"Absolutely. I feel like I'm working seven days a week now and still never seem to clear my case load." He shakes his head a little. I know he works on the weekends for the distraction, but I would never call him out on it. "So, to what do we owe the pleasure of this visit?" he asks. Which reminds me that I don't visit them at home that often anymore. I see them at the events I'm summoned to attend and that ticks off my son duties.

"I need to talk to Mother, and I'm sorry to say she will be in a bad mood when I leave."

He just grins at me. "Normal day then. Why, what have you done?" He leans back in his office chair, waiting for my answer.

"I'm about to piss her off when I tell her that I'm not seeing Jacinta anymore. Not that we ever had a relationship to begin with, but in Mother's eyes there were wheels in motion for a society power marriage."

Dad just starts laughing. Not just a little bit, but a deep belly laugh. "Oh, I can't wait to see this. Let's go and see her. This will be my entertainment for the day." He stands and walks towards the door, turning towards me.

It's like he's looking at me for the first time. Trying to understand what lies behind my outside layer. I don't think he has ever studied me like he is in this moment.

"No matter what she says. I'm proud of you, son. Don't settle for what's easy. Find the love that's hard, the one worth fighting for."

Then he keeps walking and leaves me standing there totally dumbstruck. Never have we had a conversation like that. Today I feel like I'm in the twilight zone.

I'm pathetic. At the age of thirty-five and I feel like I'm still a child about to tell my mother I've broken her favorite plate by dropping it on the kitchen floor. Yep, it was like the world ended that day.

"Hello, Mother." She looks up from the book she's reading in the sunroom. It's at that moment I see how much she has aged. I'm used to seeing her all dressed up at functions, and while she is still completely styled, because she would never not be, she looks old. My parents were both in their thirties by the time I was born. When it took seven years for her to get pregnant, you would think I would be someone she would have been totally infatuated with. It doesn't make sense how distant my mother is with her affection or lack thereof. Instead, I was just the next steppingstone in her social climb. Looking at her sitting in front of me now at the age of sixty-eight, I see how exhausting that sort of life must have been and the toll it takes on your body. Holding that perfect image up all the time.

"Alexander, I wasn't expecting you to call to say you were going to visit. A change for you to come to the house." She stands for me to kiss her on the cheek.

"Yes, I'm well, thank you." I smirk sarcastically to myself, as she sits and looks at me.

"Yes, yes, I can see that. Although those jeans look like they need to be retired for a new pair. I do wish you would just let me arrange your styling." She picks up her iced tea from the table next to her chair.

"I'm sure at my age I can dress myself, Mother, thank you for the offer, though. I'll have you know these jeans are all the fashion currently and cost me more than I care to mention." I take a seat opposite her, with my father also sitting on my side of the coffee table. I'm sure it's to see her face when I deliver my news.

"Well, I would hope you would only be buying the finest and most expensive clothing, Alexander. You have never had any cheap piece of clothing in your life. A Jefferson always dresses to impress."

Man, I can feel my blood pressure already rising. She is such a rich snob. I want to give her some smart-ass comment about the last time I shopped at Target and grabbed the most comfortable pair of sweatpants I own, yet it's just not worth it.

"Anyway, I'm sure Jacinta will be taking over your styling shortly. It's time you move this forward with her. You know it takes time to organize venues and things. It's not like it will be a small event…"

Before she gets wound up, I cut her off. "What are you talking about? You know Jacinta is not my girlfriend, Mother. Why would she be picking my clothes and what would we need a venue for?" This is not how I planned for this to go, but we may as well rip the band-aid off now.

"Don't be ridiculous, Alexander. You have been seeing her for over six months. She and I, along with her mother, have had discussions on where she would like the wedding to take place and the reception. We have worked out some tentative dates."

"Woah, what? Hold up a minute. You and Jacinta have been

planning a wedding? A wedding between me and her, two people who most days want to kill each other in a courtroom and meet later that night to fuck out that frustration." I can't believe I've been so stupid.

"Alexander!" both my parents yell at me. I don't think I've ever even said shit in front of them, and now I've just dropped the F bomb. I'm up and pacing.

"I have told you so many times that we were just friends. I'm not doing this. You don't get to marry me off. No, I'm not ending up miserable like you two." I can't even look at either of them.

"Sit down now. You will not speak to me like that," my mother demands.

"You know what, Mother? No, I won't sit down. I'm sick of this. I came here to give you the courtesy of telling you that Jacinta and I will no longer be attending together the few charity events you have us booked into. Not that my private life is any of your business, but we are done seeing each other. For some reason, I actually want more from a relationship. Not that I even know what that is because lord knows I didn't grow up seeing it. So, from now on, do not even contemplate getting involved in my personal life."

"Well, I never. I have never heard such rude and disrespectful words out of your mouth in all my life. How dare you speak to your parents like this. This is not you, Alexander, what has gotten into you?"

Still my father hasn't said a word. Man up, Dad, and stand up for yourself or maybe for once your son.

"See, that is where you are wrong, *Mother*." I accentuate the ridiculous word. "This is the most honest and real I have felt in a very long time. You're right about one thing, though. This is not your Alexander." I wave my hands up and down. "This is me, Lex. The man I am. The man I've always had buried inside, and it's time for him to finally show the world who he really is. So, you can choose to accept that or bury your head in your pompous world and continue to see your puppet son Alexander. I will never embarrass you, Mother, but I sure as shit will not be on the end of your strings anymore. I'm sorry this happened this way, but I'm done with all this crap. I need some space." Picking up my phone off the table, I see my dad smiling like he is proud of me, but to be honest, I'm just as hurt by his behavior as my mother's.

As I storm out of the house, I hear her yelling my name.

"Alexander Jefferson the third, you get back in here right this minute. I will not stand for this! Dustin, do something!" She's now yelling at my father as I hear her storming through the house.

Charles is waiting with my door open on the car.

"Proud of you, Lex," he says as I approach him. The hired help hear everything.

"Thanks, Charles, it means more than you know."

"I know. We all care about you and are damn proud of you." Shaking his hand, I know I won't be seeing him for a while.

I start to put my foot into the car as I hear her voice scream from the front step, "You know you need to marry to get total control of your trust fund money." She's standing ramrod straight with her hands on her hips, and as per usual my father is standing behind her.

Something inside me snaps.

"Fuck the money. I choose happiness."

I'm done.

Her mouth drops open, and I don't wait to hear any response. Not that I think she has anything. For once I have rendered her speechless.

Speeding out of the driveway, I make sure I slam my foot on the Audi's gas pedal, flooring it and spraying her precious white pebbles everywhere.

I don't think I've been more worked up in my life before. I can't even see straight so that I'm a danger on the road.

As I get down the street a little farther, I pull to the side to try to calm myself.

What the hell just happened?

I went there knowing my mother would be pissed at me, but I had no idea that a lifetime of emotion would start surfacing.

Slumping forward and resting my forehead on the steering wheel, I can't help the tears from falling. I don't know why, but they just continue to fall. The last time I cried was when Grayson's mother died. Real men don't show emotion.

A thousand thoughts are churning in my head, and they keep circling back to the point, the one reason for the tears. But I won't acknowledge it because then I have to accept it.

It's all part of that grey area I've always avoided in my life.

Emotion is not black or white.

I don't do grey!

Slowly I pull myself together and head back to my apartment. I don't even want to see the boys. They all know something is going on with me, they keep asking.

But I can't process my own thoughts, so I certainly won't be able to explain to them.

I turn off my phone and change into my workout gear.

Lacing up my runners, I head out.

Not knowing where I'm going, I'm just running.

Running until I can't run anymore.

Then maybe this fog will clear.

Either way, life has changed today, and I need to find the strength to follow my own destiny now.

Whatever that may be.

It's amazing what a few days of distance from something can make. It now seems so much less of a drama than it was at the time. Well, that's what I'm telling myself. My mother hasn't called, and I know that's because she will be waiting for me to apologize to her.

She will be waiting a long time for that call.

The simple—or not simple—act of working and being in court this week has been a good distraction. Thank god I haven't seen Jacinta at the courthouse which has been an added bonus. My mother's outburst just reinforced the lightbulb moment I had at the market. Jacinta had developed feelings for me and thought that there was more to our arrangement than there was. For that, I feel like a total ass. I wish she had said something when things changed

Lovable Lawyer

for her. I could have saved a whole world of hurt for everyone. Instead she let my mother manipulate her and thought that way she would end up together anyway, without making herself vulnerable to me. That woman is such a hard-ass, with something soft on the inside. I just wish she would show more people that side of her.

My day has started well with a message from Mason. Dinner at his girlfriend/boss's place. Finally, after hearing him pine over his boss for six months, he got his shit together and made his move. I'm looking forward to getting to know her better. From the few times we've met she seems like she is exactly what he needs. Someone who won't take his shit but is also strong enough to help him through things when he needs it.

I'm sitting in the courthouse meeting room running over some notes with Greta when my phone lights up with Mason's name.

"Mason, what's happening?" I say, hearing he's in the car.

"Hey, Lex, glad you can make it tonight. Just wanted to talk to you about something, though, quickly if I can."

I will never turn a friend away when they ask for help. No matter how busy I am. Especially Mason. He never asks for anything.

"Sure, man. What's up?"

He fills me in about a woman in Paige's building who they feel might be in some danger of domestic violence. Which then leads into explaining the other drama Paige has in her life at the moment. Someone is trying to sabotage her business and embezzle money.

Holy shit, I thought my life was complicated.

Between Paige's drama and this lady he called Mia, who sounds like she needs someone to reach out and help, it sounds like they need a distraction. Hence dinner with the family—well, the only family I'm interested in.

"So, if you can give us any information that will help us to help her, it would be appreciated. Of course, that's if we can get Mia to listen." Mason sounds like Mia is already pulling on his heartstrings. Plus, from what he has told me, she has two young children, and if the three of them are in danger we need to get them out of there, so they're safe.

"I'll email you a list of some organizations that can help her, and I'm happy to assist her with anything legal if needed."

Greta taps me on the shoulder to tell me we need to get into court. Mason and I sign off and I make a note to send him all the information I have as soon as I get out of court. Then we can run through it tonight. I've missed the guys the last few days. I distanced myself while I sorted out my head, but with them all now having a significant other, I'm getting fewer text messages and calls the last few weeks anyway. Can't blame them for that, though. I'm looking forward to seeing them tonight. Maybe I'll get a chance to talk to them about how I'm feeling.

Arriving to a man hug from Mason and a warm kiss on the cheek from Paige, I'm already relaxing.

It's not hard to tell Paige has money. Her penthouse apartment is similar to mine. Big enough to be a house, but instead, sitting on the top of one of the exclusive apartment blocks in Chicago. I'm the first to arrive since I'm always the one to be punctual. I hate being late, and Tate loves to poke me with the late stick no matter where we're going. I'm sure he stands outside the bar half the time just so he can walk in late to piss me off. I don't do chaos, and he thinks that's hilarious because his life revolves around chaos.

I couldn't live the life of a doctor. Both he and Grayson always need to be ready to drop everything and switch themselves to doctor mode within seconds. Now that we have Bella joining their ranks, she'll be another one who disappears in the middle of dinner. I can't even imagine what Tate and Bella's life will be like. Recently they have finally given into what we all could see, that they're made for each other. Now living together, it will be crazy having two doctors in the one house. Way too much chaos for me.

"Here's your beer, man." Mason hands me the bottle and then clinks his to mine.

"Cheers." I can feel myself settling for the first time in a week.

"Thanks for the email today. Paige wanted to rush straight down there, but I distracted her with other things." His smirk lets me know exactly what he's talking about.

I hold my hand up and laugh at him. "Don't be Tate. You know I don't want the details."

"Man, you can guarantee one thing. You will never hear one word from me about my private life with Paige. I don't need to brag, buddy. I mean, look at her."

"Actually, I value my life, Mason. I pity the poor guy you catch checking her out, now that she has you as a boyfriend."

"You got it in one, Lex."

We both take another swig of our beers.

"So, tell me about this Mia woman. Have you seen the husband?" Sticking my hand in my jeans pocket, I get a flash in my head reminding me of my mother's comment about the state of my jeans. Wow, wouldn't she love these ones with a few tears in them, and ones that I brought already ripped? What a travesty.

"No, Paige has just met her twice at the elevator. But the second time I arrived in time to see her after her little boy ran off on her, and Paige found him on his own in the elevator. He's a cute little guy, but he explained to Paige that Daddy is a cranky man but doesn't live with them. And whoever this current guy is, Jack calls him mean and that he makes Mia cry and calls her a bitch. I just want to find this dude and show him what mean is. I have my buddy Ashton watching her and her apartment. Until we can work out what's going on, the least I can do is try to keep her and the kids safe."

This whole thing sounds fucked up. No one deserves to live in fear. I see it way too often in the courts where it's too late to save the victim.

"Thank god your girlfriend has a sixth sense. She may be the person to save this woman and her children's lives. Doesn't sound like she's a very good judge of character."

Before we get to finish the conversation, the rest of the noisy crew all arrive, and then there are three conversations going at once and you need more than a beer to make any logic out of any of it.

This is what I love.

Exactly what I need to remind me of what normal is.

I look around the table, Mason and Paige fussing about getting everyone food and drinks. Tate and Bella trying not to show too much public display of affection in front of Gray because he's still getting used to his sister dating his best friend. Although Grayson is too busy being all loved up watching Tilly, his girlfriend, and her friend and business partner, Fleur, tell a story about a function they organized today.

As much as I say I hate chaos, this is the perfect kind of crazy. Happiness, laughter, and love that you can't get just anywhere.

The normal banter starts, and I'm the first to join in. I mean, it's time to punish Mason in front of his girl. That's what friends do, right? We might all be in our thirties now, but we're all still sixteen-year-old testosterone-filled males who can't wait to stir the crap out of each other. Now it's even better with the girls involved. Bella knows a lot of our secrets from growing up but has been a little outnumbered, until now. She has found her support network too. The way they gang up together against us is brilliant.

All the fun things are coming out now. Tate pulls out his phone to play the infamous recording of Mason's drunken karaoke the first night he arrived home from his last mission. We went out to celebrate and parts of that night are blank for all of us. We were so happy to have him home safe, and I think he was too busy trying to bury demons he had left behind. Which resulted in some really bad singing and severe headaches the next morning.

"Come on, Paige, you have to agree how bad it is," I yell across the table over top of all the laughing.

"All I see is a sexy soldier on the stage whose got some moves." We all start groaning.

"Yeah, that's my girl." Mason grabs her in for a kiss. Then offers to get drunk with Paige one night and give us a karaoke duo.

Paige just laughs at him. "I thought you liked your friends. Why would you want to punish them like that?" She fits in perfectly.

"That's what friends do," I tell her. "They punish each other. That's part of the fun. I mean, we're punished every day just having Mason as part of the group." I wink at Paige as Fleur pipes up.

"You're all crazy, that's all I know." No truer words have ever been spoken.

Fleur then sets the girls off into talk of a girls' night out, and before we know it, everyone is talking at once again.

Just the usual, really.

Mason takes a phone call in the middle of all the laughter, and he and Paige disappear from the room.

"Are we ever going to find out what the FF boys stands for?" Tate keeps asking, and all the girls lock down tight with sealed lips.

"I think it stands for Fabulous Fellas," Gray replies to Tate.

"Fellas… what are you, an eighty-year-old man? Who even uses the word fellas?" Tate starts laughing.

Mason comes storming into the room heading straight for the elevator, and Paige runs after him screaming at him, "Mason, please, no, just stop. Don't go. I can't lose you."

The room is silent except for the sounds of my, Tate, and Gray's chairs on the floor as we jump up to help with whatever the fuck is happening.

My guess is it's Mia, and there is no way in hell he is going alone.

Chapter Five

MIA

The night is finally settling to a little moment of peace. The kids have been bathed and fed. Not that dinner was very exciting. Macaroni and cheese for Jack, baby food for Kayla with a bottle, and just a slice of toast for me. I can hardly stomach anything at the moment. Plus, I don't have any money, and Bent who promised he had a job for me, lied. The job he had was to live in the apartment and spy on Paige, reporting back to him anything I see or hear about her. He gives me a little money for food, and that's it. Of course that traps me here, right where he wants me.

I'm not sure what the hell I'm supposed to find out. She lives in the penthouse and I live on the eighth floor of a twenty-floor building. I don't have access to her. I've only seen her twice, and to be honest, I'm scared to be near her. I don't really understand what is going on with Bent. I'm doubting more of what he tells me every day. I know I'm in danger, and I don't want to be involved in any trouble with her.

Everything he's told me, about her stealing all our mother's money and then not helping her when she was dying, just doesn't sit right with the person I've seen glimpses of. I'm so confused. Somehow, I just need to get out of this situation.

"Time for bed, Jack. Let's pick up some toys and move the playpen into your bedroom for your sister." Standing up like a good boy, he picks up his few toys he has. There aren't many. His favorite red truck, a couple of cars, an airplane, and of course his t-rex. They were all we could fit in the bag to bring with us, but I wanted him to feel some sort of normalcy. Kayla is too little to understand, thank goodness. Hopefully Jack is too little to remember the bad times of his father, and if I can get out of here soon, he will totally forget this as well.

Kayla is lying on her back on the floor just watching her brother move around her. She is totally mesmerized by him, which I think is the most adorable thing. He's so gentle with her. Always making sure she's okay, and if she cries, he is straight over to comfort her as best he can. The sad part of their childhood so far is they haven't really had a chance to make friends and play with other children. I couldn't afford childcare, not that I would want to leave them with a stranger anyway. So, when they came to work with me, occasionally they would see another little one in the diner, and Jack would get so excited.

"Done, Mommy." He stands proudly next to his toys lined up along the wall.

"Good job. Now, can you watch your sister and I'll move her bed?" I asked Bent if he could buy a permanent crib for her to which he just laughed and said, *'Ask your sister, she's the rich bitch.'*

"Clap hands," his sweet voice says behind me as I'm struggling with getting her bed through the door. "Good girl, clap hands for Jack." Even though she's getting tired, I can hear Kayla clapping hands and giggling at him. The sound melts my heart. That's what it should be like between siblings.

I lean against the doorframe of the bedroom, just taking a few moments to feel the love that is in their little bubble. Taking my phone out, I snap a few pictures for later. I don't own a printed picture of my kids, but my phone is full of them. I guard my phone like it's one of my children. It's the only material thing I own but is worth more to me than anything money can buy. Those photos are irreplaceable.

Laying Kayla down into the crib, I hear the front door open.

Fuck.

I hate that he can just walk in whenever he wants, and I have no choice.

Before I even have time to leave the kids' room, he's in here with us.

"Bent, what are you doing here?" I try to remain calm while guiding Jack up into his bed.

"None of your business, bitch." He grunts, carrying a bag over his shoulder.

"Paige said you're a meanie, when she helped me," Jack blurts out, and I die on the inside. I see the rage on Bent's face.

"What the fuck did you do!" He screams at me and drops his bag on the bed.

I try to get myself between him and the kids. I know he's about to lose his temper, and I will take whatever I need to, so he doesn't hurt them.

"Nothing, it's nothing. He's confused. Paige helped him when he got lost in the elevator. That's all. Calm down…" I'm talking quickly, words pouring out of my mouth trying to stop him from getting crankier.

"Stupid kid's as dumb as you. You need to shut your mouth, boy!" He starts moving towards Jack, and my heart races.

"What do you want, Bent?" I interrupt, trying to distract him.

"It's time to teach our sister another lesson. Move, you little shit." He pulls his laptop from his bag and sits on Jack's bed, pushing me to the side while I grab Jack and pull him farther up the bed away from Bent. His fingers are madly typing away.

"What are you doing, Bent? Take it out of here. The kids need to sleep." He looks so focused and it's as if he isn't hearing me. "Bent?"

"Shut the fuck up. You can watch me take what should be mine." My head is spinning, trying to work out what he means. He's doing something bad, I can just feel it.

"Jack, come with me." I take his hand. But Bent grabs his other one.

The banging on the front door stops us both from moving or making a noise.

"Ignore it," Bent whispers.

The banging starts again.

"Get rid of whoever it is," he growls at me

"I'm not leaving the kids," I say, standing defiantly.

"This piece of metal under my jacket says you are. Shut your mouth and no one gets hurt."

I must look like a deer in headlights and can't seem to move, knowing he has a weapon.

"Now." He glares at me.

"Stay still and don't talk, Jack," I whisper. I back away slowly, with a stabbing pain in my heart.

As I close the door to the room, I thank god Bent seems to be focusing more on his computer than on Jack. My little boy has a look of fear in his eyes as I leave him with Bent.

Just breathe, keep calm. Get rid of them, and the kids are safe.

Stay calm, and they stay safe.

"Who is it?" I ask without much strength in my voice.

I hear a man's voice, but I don't recognize it, "Maintenance, checking the smoke alarms, as per the email we sent."

My hand is on the doorknob, and I'm trying to think what to say. I'm trembling and can't find any words. My brain is scrambling thinking of my kids with that maniac.

"Won't take long, ma'am. We'll be in and out in five minutes. Otherwise the fire department has to come in and do a thorough inspection." Shit, I know that can't happen, Bent will lose his shit if I let more people in here.

You can do this. Five minutes, then they're gone.

Slowly I open the door, and with as much strength as I have in my voice at the moment, I say, "My husband's not home. I'm not allowed to let people in when he's not here."

The man in front of me is tall and doesn't look like he should be messed with. Shoulders that take up the whole doorway and the sort of face that tells you he's not messing around. Yet as I look at his eyes, I sense a hint of kindness there. I'm not sure why, but I don't fear him. I fear the man in my apartment far more than this man looking at me now.

"That's okay, ma'am, it will take five minutes, and we will be out the door again. If you would feel more comfortable, you can wait outside with your kids while I'm inside. Here's my ID card." He holds something up.

Feeling like I don't have much choice, I move to the side slightly for him to enter.

"Okay, but I'm leaving the door open, and only five minutes. Don't touch anything."

I'm almost begging him to come and do what he needs and just get out.

Walking past me, he gives me a little smile which I ignore. I can't let my guard down. As I watch him walk towards the living room, I startle as another person comes in behind him. Crap.

"Who are you?" My scattered brain tells me he's familiar, I just don't know why. I'm having trouble thinking straight right now.

"His assistant. Looks like you have children here. Where are they, asleep?" he asks in a soft calm voice.

"Umm, yes umm, sleeping in there. You can't go into that room." I step between him and the door.

He just stands in front of me while the first man is looking at the smoke detector in the ceiling.

"Ouch, that hurt," Jack's voice cries out, and my heart stops.

Everything happens so fast. The man in front of me shoves me towards the first guy, and his arms grab me while the other bursts through the door to the kids.

I'm struggling and screaming, trying to get free. His soft voice whispers quickly in my ear.

"My name's Ashton, he's Mason. We are here to save you and the kids. I need you to stop now. Trust me." Something about the words *'save you and the kids'* takes all the fight from me for a moment. Just a second, and then he steps me in front of the door so I can see what's going on. He asked me to trust him which I can't do, but I need his help and I can't deny that.

Sitting on the bed is Bent, typing madly on his laptop while trying to hold onto Jack.

"You can stop now, Bent, and let the boy go, it's all over," Mason calmly says to him.

"What, do you think I'm as stupid as that? These kids are my insurance policy. If I hand them over, then I'm screwed." Bent doesn't even look up from the computer.

"No matter what, you are not leaving this room without handcuffs or in a body bag. You choose," Mason says, and I shudder. No, I don't want my kids involved in this. Once again, they are being used as pawns in some sick man's game.

I barely notice when Ashton lets me go and steps past me into the room. He thrusts Kayla into my arms.

"Go, Mia, now," he says quite forcefully.

"No, not without Jack. I can't leave my baby. Not like she did." He is never going to feel like I do every day, that he wasn't enough. I'm not leaving here without both of them. I'm not like my mother.

It's all becoming too much, I'm petrified, and the tears are running down my face.

"Mia, we've got him. Go," Ashton says.

"She's dumb, my sister, she never listens," Bent says, gasping and trying to breathe at his words. "She wasn't supposed to talk to anyone, but of course she opened her big mouth. Talking to her and letting her find out their names."

"If she's your sister, why are you treating her like this? Why are you scaring her and hurting your nephew?" Mason is keeping Bent focused on him.

"She's just my half-sister. She's not worthy of any attention. That's why Mom got rid of her."

My legs wobble, and I want to sink to the floor. The weight on my chest is making it hard to breathe, but somewhere deep inside, I drag what strength I find and start to fight. I need to fight for my kids.

"You're a liar. She was protecting me," I start yelling at him. How could he say that about me, he's my brother!

"You're such a stupid bitch, just like that other stupid sister of ours, your dad didn't want you. You were girls. The weaker sex," he yells loudly at me.

"Fucking asshole, why would you say that?" Mason yells at him, and Bent looks at him with vengeance. My eyes are still glued to Jack, and he doesn't stop looking at me with fear.

"So, Mom got rid of them. She finally got it right and left their dad and got remarried, then had a baby. Me, the perfect male. Just what my dad wanted. He was so proud of me. He didn't need or want any more children."

Oh my god. I can't help but look away from Jack and at the man who is supposed to care about me and be my brother. But instead Bent hates us both. He's just been using me to try and get close to Paige. What have I wound up in the middle of? Bastard, he doesn't want me at all.

I'm so focused with anger on Bent that I feel Ashton's hands on mine, and I see out of the corner of my eye he has Jack and is taking Kayla from me. I look at him, and I've never trusted any man with my kids, but right in this moment I know it's the right thing to do. If he is with Mason who I now recognize as Paige's boyfriend, I have to believe what she tried to say to me. That they wanted to help me. He will keep them safe. I feel that in my gut. He tries to signal me to go too, but I need to finish this. I need to make a stand in my life. I make the toughest decision of my life to let him take my children so I can finally stand up for myself and my life. Everything happens so quickly as they exit the room, and I'm left feeling filled with hate for the man who hurt me in ways he will never understand.

I start towards Bent because I just want to hit him and hurt him for what he is saying about me and Paige. She might not know about me, but I will defend her because deep down I have a feeling she would do the same for me. Mason's arm juts out to the side to stop me from going any farther. Then I hear her voice behind me.

"Bent… are you my brother?" Paige is standing in the room and appears calm as she hears for the first time what I have known for a while. She has a brother and sister she didn't know ever existed.

"Paige and Mia, out now," Mason demands.

"What's wrong, lover boy, don't want your meal ticket getting hurt? Well, it's too late. She took what should have been mine, so I took it from her." Bent looks like he's crazy, his eyes starting to get wider, and I've seen that look before. In my husband right before he would let loose. But Paige isn't seeing it. She's probably never been in a life with a violent man. She just keeps going.

"Bent, please, I need to know, are we all related?" I want to yell at her to stop, that she will push him past the point that we all want. Then I remember he said he has what I can only assume is a gun under his jacket. I need to do something, but I don't know what. I'm useless, just like Edward always told me.

"Don't you listen? Christ, you run a big company with all that money, and you're just as dumb as her. We all have the same mom, but your dad was a dick and didn't want a girl. He used to beat our mother. So, she got rid of you before he had a chance to hurt you. The perfect mother protecting her kids." Bent is yelling loudly now.

Paige and I both gasp at his words. He never told me that part before. My mother lived a life like mine. Holy shit, this is a mess.

"So why are you stealing from one sister and holding the other one here and hurting her?" Mason yells at him to get his attention back on him.

"Fuck off. I'm just taking back what is mine that she stole from me. My father died years ago. Everything was left to Mom. But instead of leaving it all to me when she died, no, she wanted to leave her precious girls something."

Paige's eyes meet mine as we both gasp loudly. I can't help the tears again. My mother is dead, and I never got to meet her. Until this moment I didn't think I wanted to, but with everything I'm hearing, my heart just cracked for a woman I will never know, but who was brave enough to let me go, to keep me safe.

"Girls I didn't even know existed, until I found the scrapbook on the ever-successful Paige Ellen in her will. With a letter explaining about two baby girls she had and what happened to them. But here's the kicker. Until I found you both, nothing from the will would be distributed. But imagine the jackpot I found with one of my sisters and her wealth. So, for years I was living with no money until I managed to get the job driving little miss precious here wherever she wanted. To be at her beck and call. Listen to her order me around like trash. But all the time I was working out how to get to her and her riches."

Mason moves a few steps closer to him and stands with his arms by his side, fists clenched.

"I'm going to take you down for this. You don't realize what you've done and who you're up against. These women are strong. You might think you've played them, but it looks to me like that's over now and they have you back into the corner with nowhere to go."

"Bent, why? Why didn't you just come to me? I would have given you the money, to both of you. As much as you needed. I'd have taken care of you. All I wanted all my life was a family. To know where I came from. You don't understand what that feels like." Paige's voice starts to break. Her words touch something inside me, like no other person could understand but her.

"I do." My broken voice follows Paige's. "I didn't get the happy family, Bent. Or the money and good life. No one wanted me. I ended up in foster care. I got a family who didn't really want me but felt sorry for me. They tried but had other mouths to feed. Lying awake at night, all I ever dreamed of was a family of my own. Look where that got me. Married to an asshole and then blackmailed by a brother I didn't even know, who was going to give me up to the abusive man I was hiding from. Once you found me, Bent, you could have saved me and the kids, but instead you continued our hell. I'll never forgive you for that."

I'm broken and all the strength has left my body. I quietly sob and try to just breathe. The room starts to become too small and I can feel a panic attack coming on.

Paige steps forward and wraps me in her arms. I don't know how to deal with the emotion, it's too over whelming.

"Ashton, now. It's time." I can hear Mason's voice, but it sounds in the distance.

A hand on my arm and the pain of it squeezing me snaps me back from where I was spiraling to.

Ashton is dragging us from the apartment and thrusts us out the door into the arms of other men, I have no idea who they are. Paige is screaming she doesn't want to leave Mason in there. I can't concentrate on her as I see Jack and Kayla in the arms of one of the men. Breaking free from Paige, I rush at the man to grab Kayla and pull Jack with me. I drag him down the hallway a little farther and just stand holding them tight. They are safe. That's all I can think. He didn't hurt them.

I have to get out of here. Away from them all.

I need to run.

Standing up from where I was crouching with Jack, I turn to run only to come face to face with the man who had been hanging on to Kayla.

He holds his hands up to stop me but doesn't touch me.

"Woah, stop. We're here to help you. He will never hurt you again." His voice is quiet and calm. I just stand looking at him.

"No one ever helps me. Please let me go. Please, sir."

"Well, let me be the first. My name is Lex, and I promise I will never let anyone hurt you again. With everything in my powers, no man will touch you like that again."

There is still screaming and yelling coming from behind me. Kayla is starting to cry, and Jack clings to my leg, with his arms wrapped so tightly.

"We need to go. Let me help you to Paige's apartment while we wait for the police. Please, Mia."

The way he says my name is so soft and gentle. He holds his hand out, and I don't know why but I take it, and he leads me into the elevator. Smiling at me with such gentleness that I can't deal with it. Not now, I just can't. I cower into the back corner of the elevator, trying to shrink and hide.

He then stands holding the doors as the other two men, who are still wrestling with hysterical Paige, start pushing her towards us.

Jack, seeing Paige upset, starts crying as well. Both kids are distressed, and I'm numb, my body just can't deal with much more.

The elevator starts the ride up to the penthouse. I'm standing in the back corner like a caged animal. Trying to soothe Kayla, and I can hear Jack singing softly in a whispering voice, Twinkle Twinkle Little Star. He is doing like I've always taught him. When he's scared, sing away the bad noises.

The doors open and everyone walks forward to a group of women, and Paige falls into their arms sobbing. The men keep walking to give me space. Again, Lex stands outside the doors and offers me his hand for reassurance. Hesitantly stepping out, I don't know what to do. My eyes scan the room, and I have never seen anything like this. My apartment downstairs is like a five-star hotel to me and nicer than anywhere I have ever lived. This is like a royal castle. One thing Bent didn't lie about is how much money Paige must have. Jack is still clinging to my leg and not willing to move.

You need to be brave, Mia, that's the only way forward.

"Paige," I finally call hesitantly to her.

Slowly she turns to look at me. For the first time it feels like I'm looking into the eyes of someone who really sees me. Eyes that are shaped similarly to me and full of tears and emotion like mine. One of the girls offers Jack food, and I feel him release me, and another takes Kayla, looking at me with compassion as she walks to the kitchen, rocking and patting her. I don't want to let them go, but I feel like I'm in a trance.

"Mia, I'm so sorry. I didn't know. Did he hurt you? Are the kids okay? Oh, my sister Mia, whatever he told you, I had no idea." Paige's voice is so concerned, but I can't cope hearing someone care about if I'm okay. No one cares about me. They just don't.

We both fall into each other's arms. Her body heaving with mine from the emotion that breaks free. Feeling like everything I have been holding in for so long is landing on her shoulders in my tears.

I need to tell her. I can't get it out, but I need to tell her I didn't mean it. I didn't know, Bent lied to me, and I was so desperate that I believed him.

"I'm...so...so...sorry," is all I can manage. It's all my fault she's hurt.

"Mia, no, you didn't do anything. It was all Bent." Paige stands up straighter, and I see a strong woman in front of me.

"I believed him, but I should have asked you." I wish I was like her.

"No, no, no. We can talk about this later. But don't take any blame for anything. You're here with me. You and the kids are safe, and nobody will ever hurt you again." She places her hands on my shoulders so she has my full attention.

She doesn't understand. It's always my fault. "You can't say that. My life is always like that." Before I can say another word, Lex is beside us.

"Not anymore. Now that you have Paige, it means you have family. We're all here to protect you. That's what we do." His voice is so soothing. Like a warm blanket wrapping around you. I just keep looking at him. Who is this stranger who is being so kind to me? The two men are both now behind him like a tribe. My eyes flick from them to the kitchen to see Jack laughing and eating and Kayla now sleeping soundly while being rocked. I feel the tension in my body settle but only slightly. I'm still so scared and unsure what is going on.

"Mia, these are my friends...actually, sorry, they're *framily*... friends who are family. They will protect us all. You're safe here, I can promise you that. Once Mason gets here, he'll make sure of it."

I don't know what to say. Everything is so strange, and I've heard words like this before only to be slapped in the face with the opposite.

Paige then starts to yell at one of the others that Mason hasn't come back yet. They all start talking at once and the noise is too much for me. I step away a little, just needing to hold my kids. I look towards where they are in the kitchen. I know these people are being nice, but I need my kids back. I just need to center myself.

"I'll get them for you." Lex speaks softly next to me.

How did he know what I was thinking? I just smile at him as I find it hard to talk to him. There's something about him that makes me feel defenseless, and that's dangerous.

"Bella," he calls, and the woman with Kayla looks up and must understand his signal. She walks straight over and places her in my arms. I pull her in close and lean down and kiss her forehead and smell her. My baby is safe and calm.

"She's adorable," I hear her say as she steps away. "Do you want Jack?" she asks gently. I see him laughing and having fun and decide he's okay. If this helps him forget what the hell he just witnessed, then I should let him go.

"No, it's okay, thank you." She just nods and walks away.

Lex doesn't move. Instead, he stays beside me as the doors to the elevator open and Mason and Ashton walk in. Both men have such a strong presence in a room, but not once have I felt afraid near them.

"They're good men. They would never hurt you. They would have laid down their lives before he got to hurt you or the kids," Lex says, looking across at his friends. Paige is now in Mason's arms and everyone is cheering as he kisses her like he almost lost her. Never in my life have I seen such love between two people. My sister lives a blessed life; more important than her money, she has love.

The cheering starts to unsettle Kayla again, and all the girls start scolding the boys. I don't know how to handle this many people in one room. It's overwhelming.

Lex turns to me. "We need to get you Kayla's bed and anything else that you'll need tonight for the kids. I'll speak to the policeman and get what we need. Actually, I don't know anything about kids. Tell me what you need, and I'll bring it up."

Why is he being so nice to me?

"I don't have much, Lex. To be honest, everything I own fits in a bag. I had to be able to carry it." I don't know why I'm being so honest with him.

"Well, that changes right now, Mia." He looks angry but not at me.

"Um, I need the playpen the diapers, and maybe a few toys for

Jack so he feels safe. Everything else can wait. I don't want to put you out. I'll manage with just that, I always have."

His hand touches mine lightly. I don't understand why it doesn't freak me out, but my body doesn't react negatively at all.

"No one should just have to manage. I will make sure you have everything you need." He stops short on what he was saying as Paige comes towards us.

"Please come and sit with me. You must be exhausted, and I'm sure Kayla's getting heavy." She places her hand on my elbow and leads me to one of the couches. It wasn't until she mentioned it, that I feel the exhaustion in my bones. The adrenaline is starting to wear off and sitting down sounds like heaven.

"Paige, I was just saying to Mia, I'm going to go downstairs and see if the police will give me the baby's playpen. If not, I'll go to the nearest Target and grab one and some diapers. The rest we can figure out tomorrow." Lex speaks in a quiet calming tone. Paige is looking at him a little confused, which I don't quite understand.

"That's awesome, thanks, Lex. I can't even think clearly, and to be honest, I know nothing about kids." Paige kisses him on the cheek as she sits down next to me. "I guess I'm about to learn. You do know I want you to stay here with me, Mia, for as long as it takes to sort this mess out and get you somewhere to live on your own."

My head is spinning. I can't stay here. I don't know how to live like this. Plus, what if Edward finds me? Maybe Bent did tell him where I am.

It's just the two of us now with Lex slipping away.

I have to be honest with her, tell her everything, no matter how ashamed I feel about my life.

"Thank you, but I don't have any money or any way of getting any. I can't have anything in my name. I ran away, Paige, from my husband. He threatened if I ever left and took his meal tickets with him that he would hunt me down. I can't stay here for long, just tonight. I don't want you in danger. Plus, I don't know if Bent told him where I am. He threatened to so often that I'm scared he did." I can feel the fear in my body rising again as I try to tell her.

"Mia, look around you. Every person in this room is now on

your team. No one will let him hurt you or the kids again. Lex is a lawyer, and he already knows your story and said he'll help you. If there's one thing I'm certain of, it's that Mason will sort your husband out, I promise you that." Paige has hold of my hand and squeezes it tightly.

"Damn straight I will," Mason says, joining us. "Mia, you're safe with us. He will never get near you, and by the time I'm finished with him, he'll wish he never met you, or your family. That's more than a promise, it's a fact." Mason sits on the armrest of the couch next to Paige.

The way he speaks makes me want to believe him, to trust someone for the first time in a long time. I'm still waiting for the bad news which will follow, because it always does. Nothing good happens to me without something bad coming straight behind it.

"I'm so sorry you've had a hard life, Mia. I feel guilty for all I've had, but I can assure you from now on, life will be full of love, happiness, and comfort for you and the kids." Her hand reaches for me. Oh god, I hope so, I pray this is not all a dream.

"And family?" The words slip out of my mouth before I realize.

"Forever. You are my family forever." We both sit leaning into each other with our heads on each other's shoulders. Quiet tears run down our faces.

I can hear her and Mason talking, but I can't deal with everything she just said. I have a family, I have a sister, and she wants me. Please god, don't be cruel enough to take this away. Pulling back from her shoulder again, I try to pull myself together.

"I'm going to leave you two to talk," Mason says, standing. "There's so much you need to work out. I'll send all this rowdy bunch home, so you can get some quiet time. Plus, I think Jack needs some quiet time otherwise getting him to sleep is going to be interesting." Mason leaves us alone.

"They do exist," I whisper.

"Who?" Paige looks at me confused.

"Real men, kind ones," I say as my eyes follow Mason across the room.

"They sure do. The ones in this room are some of the best. I've only just found Mason, and I'm very grateful. One day, you'll find your real man. He's out there tonight waiting for you."

I doubt that, but it would be nice to believe it's possible.

But I'm just not sure I have any of that sort of fairytale belief left in me.

Chapter Six

LEX

"Playpen, diapers, clothes, toys. What else, think, man." I make a list on my phone while I'm heading down in the elevator.

"Fuck the old stuff. They deserve new things. Nothing touched by that asshole." I'm talking to myself which tells me that I'm nervous. I don't do it very often, but right now I can tell my head is trying to process what the hell just happened.

The moment I saw her coming out that door with fear and terror radiating from her body and written all over face. I just wanted to protect her and her kids. I have never had a reaction like I did in that instant. I've been around vulnerable people all my life through the court system, yet nothing like this has ever happened.

I watched as her body language told me she was about to run again, and I knew I needed to stop her.

Mia was in shock and panicking. She had just had some intense things revealed, and she wasn't coping. The hunched shoulders, the eyes that told me she was on overload and trying to think a rational thought was as hard as breathing for her. I needed to help. My instincts just took over. Approaching her slowly and keeping my voice calm and soft, I knew that was the only way not to frighten her any further. From what I'm piecing together very quickly, every man in her life has hurt her. She was petrified of all of us standing there, with Paige screaming and Mason and Ashton still in there. I know she won't trust me, but I need her to place a little faith in me, to get her to safety. She had no idea on how her life is about to change.

Laying my head back against the back wall of the elevator, I think it all through. I don't even know how I managed to get her upstairs to Paige's apartment. I was surprised she took my hand when I offered it.

Her hands are so tiny and soft. Not in a way where they've been pampered and had expensive creams rubbed into them all day. No, instead in a naturally soft way like she was born with them like that.

Tender, yeah, that's the word.

"What the fuck is wrong with you?" I ask myself, walking into the foyer and out to my car. All the police cars are parked in front of the building with the lights flashing. Mason and Ashton told us it was chaos at the scene with Paige's uncle arriving just after we left along with all the police.

They're just hands, you idiot. You've seen plenty of women's hands. Held them, had then wrapped around your dick, and even tied a few of them up. Why are you obsessing about Mia's hands?

Climbing into the Audi, I get the lightbulb moment that it's not her hands that have me spinning. It's the feeling I had when I touched her. I can't work it out, but something was different. Very different.

Then watching her in those minutes after we got her to safety, I could read every thought she was having. Years of watching people in court have made my reading of body language spot on. She looked so lost, scared, and had no idea what was happening around her. Then her escalating panic had her soul reaching for her children which is understandable. As soon as she held her daughter, her shoulders relaxed slightly.

Paige was dealing with so much that she'd forgotten about Mia. I have a feeling her whole life Mia's been used to standing in the back corner, which is where she retreated to now. What's that chick flick line? Something about not putting someone in a corner. Well, I'm saying it right now. Mia is not being pushed to the back anymore.

Pulling up to the Target, I run through the list on my phone. I know I'm missing things. I'll start with what I have, and I'm sure there will be other things I see.

I'm standing in the aisle with all the baby things and it all may as well be written in another language. There are about ten different playpens. Fuck, I don't even know what the hell they really do, except the baby sleeps in them. Okay, for once I'm being my mother. The most expensive one has to be the best, so I throw that one in the cart.

Diapers next. Hmmm this is a problem. Do I just need them for Kayla or Jack too? Surely, he's toilet-trained. Man, this is complicated. Right, there are boys' and girls' ones, so look at the pink boxes. Shit, different sizes, how the fuck do I know? Well, she's not a newborn, or is she? Mason said she was nine months old. Read the box, idiot. Great, some of them overlap ages. Fuck it, I'm getting some of each, and I grab a boy's box of the pants that are like diapers for Jack just in case. I mean, it's not like he hasn't had the fright of his life tonight. Who would blame him for wetting the bed?

Clothes, I'm sure Mia can borrow some off Paige because I'm not sure she'll want something I pick, but I better get some for both the kids. If Jack does wet the bed, he needs something to change into. Okay, kids' clothes. Pushing the cart towards the clothes, my mind is racing. I have no idea what size clothes to get. How can I be a grown man, who I would like to think is intelligent, not have any idea what to get two little children? What world have I been hiding in? Yeah, a snobby, rich socialite world where nothing is real.

I'm in the boys' section getting frustrated when I hear a voice behind me.

"I've been waiting for you," an old lady's voice mumbles to me.

"Sorry, what did you say?" I turn to see the crazy old lady from the market, Martha.

"Nothing. Now you look lost, young man. Do you need help?" I don't know what she said to me initially, but she's right, I need help and it's all taking too long.

"I need clothes for kids, and I don't know what size. How do I work it out?"

She starts laughing out loud at me. "What a ride this is going to be for you. Now tell me the ages and I'll show you." Why does she always talk in riddles?

"Jack is four and Kayla is nine months old. I need sleeping clothes and something for the daytime. Not budget stuff. Something nice."

Smiling, she starts walking along the racks and just starts throwing things in my cart. This is good. She seems to know what I need. She might be crazy, but she's helpful.

"Oh yes, this is a must." She holds up a little pink one-piece suit that is covered in glittery stars. "She will love this one."

I look at it, and I mean, she's nine months old so not sure how much Kayla will even care as long as it keeps her warm.

"Yep, okay. What next?" I need to hurry along.

"Food, have you got any?" Shit, that's what I was missing on the list.

"Nope, need that too. What do babies eat?"

Slapping me on the arm, Martha laughs as she then links her arm in mine. "Baby food, of course, silly. You really have no idea, do you." We start walking.

"Not a damn clue, Martha, not a damn clue."

After grabbing some jars and spoons, a couple of bowls, some bottles, then the formula, the cart is getting full.

"I need some toys for them. They need to have a reason to smile," I tell her.

"Oh, that reason started tonight. But yes, toys, that's a good idea. Come on, let's play Santa Claus."

I don't think I've ever stood in the toy aisle of a store before. There are some super cool things here.

"Not too much, rich boy. You will overwhelm them. Little steps." Martha picks up some books and slips them into the cart.

"Yes, you're right." What do boys like, a truck, a car… or look, a plane. Mason will like that. Yep, let's get them all. A ball, every kid needs a ball. Dolls, yes, Kayla needs a doll and some soft fluffy teddies. Seeing one that is just perfect, I reach for it. Soft, pale brown, with a pink heart stitched on its chest where your heart should be. I put them on top of the cart that is almost full. Just before I turn away, I grab a teddy for Jack. One that is bigger than Kayla's and is a dark brown color, dressed in a black shirt with a yellow star on it. He might need someone to cuddle up to tonight.

"Bedding, you will need some for the playpen." Martha continues steering me to that aisle. Thank god she's here, otherwise I'd be screwed.

"I think you've just bought the whole store, son." I still think she's crazy, but I have a fondness for Martha now. We both stand together, laughing at how much I have in the cart.

"Thanks, Martha, I don't know where you came from, but I really appreciate the help." Holding out my hand to shake hers, I'm shocked when she leans in and kisses me on the cheek.

"You are a good man, Lex. I've seen it in the stars." Her face lights up with a smile, and before I can say anything, someone bumps into me from behind. Turning to see what they're doing, I quickly apologize for blocking the aisle. By the time I turn back, Martha's gone. Just like she appeared from nowhere, she has now disappeared just as quickly.

There is something weird with that old lady. I need to talk to Bella about her when it's just the two of us. No way I'm having that conversation around the boys.

Now, how to get all this in the car and up to the penthouse. I have a feeling I went a little overboard, but who cares. What's money for if you can't spend it on people who need your help?

Only just enough room in the elevator for me as well as the bags, I press the penthouse button after Mason messaged me the code. I was glad to see most of the police cars gone when I arrived back, which means Bent is now in custody, and I have messaged my detective friend to keep me updated with what happens tonight and when the bail hearing is set for. Paige's uncle arrived at the apartment before Mason and Ashton came back up to us. So, he was the one with everything the police needed. I didn't know, but he had already been working with them on the case for a few days. He will be helping represent her in the court proceedings, and I'm sure Paige's lawyer will be all over it for her and the business side of it, but I will be handling Mia's case. I'm not letting anyone else near her.

The doors open to a welcoming committee, everyone standing in front of me just staring.

Paige's eyes almost pop out of her head.

"Lex, what the hell have you done?" she asks with a smile.

"I just grabbed a few things that Mia and the kids will need. I figured new things would be better, you know, fresh start." I feel like everyone is just looking at me and no one is saying anything. Which is not like the guys. I was expecting a whole lot of crap, especially from Tate.

They make me feel nervous.

Paige reaches in and starts grabbing bags to help me. I'm trying to pick up as many bags as I can so everyone else can use the elevator to leave. Mason starts taking things from my hands and we finally empty the space, so everyone starts piling in. Still no words from any of them, which freaks me out more.

Mia's timid voice gets my attention.

"Lex, I can't pay for this." Her face is one of sheer panic, and she's gone a little pale.

"What? No, I don't expect anything. This is a gift for you and the kids. You needed them tonight and I got them. It's that simple." Black and white, you needed it, I can provide it.

She looks down towards the ground, but I see her eyes peeking up just enough to see me.

"You're very kind, I don't know how I can repay you for all this."

"Just seeing you smile once tonight will be payment enough. Now let's get this set up so you can get these little ones to sleep, and you and Paige can finally talk. I'm guessing it'll go long into the night," I say, trying to make her feel more comfortable. I just want to get this all settled, and it won't look so in-your-face with all the bags.

Mason gives me a chin lift to let me know I did good.

"Let's go, Lex, I'll show you the guest room where we can set them up. They can sleep in there with Mia. I doubt she wants her kids too far away at the moment."

"Thank you, for everything, all of you. It means more than you know," Mia says in her soft voice. Tears brimming in her eyes.

"This is just the beginning, Mia. Welcome to the family," Paige says and wraps an arm around her shoulder and steers her towards the room she will be staying in downstairs.

The main priority is to get the playpen set up so Mia can get Kayla settled in for the night. Mason and I pull it out of the box and start to put it up. He's a pilot and I'm a lawyer. Surely it shouldn't be this frigging hard.

"Where's the instructions, Mason?" I ask, getting frustrated.

"Real men don't need instructions. Come on, man, I can fly a plane, surely we can put this up without a piece of paper." He steps in to try to take over.

"Alright then, Mr. Pilot. Show me how it's done." I roll my eyes at him.

Paige and Mia are behind us changing Kayla's diaper and putting those pull-up diaper things on Jack. Lucky I grabbed those. It's alright, little buddy, I've got your back.

I can hear Paige having a little giggle watching us.

"What are you laughing at?" Mason glares at her, and I can see he is just as frustrated as I was.

Mia is still dealing with Kayla, but Jack is all done.

"Jack, honey, can you help Mason and Lex please?" Mia asks.

"Sure, Mommy. It's easy, you just push this button and this button and then pull this bit and push that bit. See?" He turns proudly to us with the playpen all assembled before our eyes.

Mia lets out a little giggle at the shocked looks on our faces. We just got shown up by a four-year-old. But I'll take that any day, to hear that laugh again. It's that first moment of a tiny amount of free spirit coming from Mia since I met her. It's only small but so beautiful.

"Well, Jack, you are a superstar. High five, buddy." Mason puts out his hand for him. Jack slaps it nice and hard with a big smile. I grab the bedding, and Paige starts putting it in the playpen and then arranging the bed for Jack to get into.

I start going through the bags when Paige calls my name.

"Lex, leave them, we can sort the rest in the morning." I just ignore her until I find what I'm after. There they are.

"I just needed these. I thought, you know…maybe the kids… um, you know, might need them tonight." Why do I feel stupid all of a sudden? They probably have their own and these will just be thrown to the side and not help.

"Lex," Mia says quietly standing with Kayla in her arms, all ready for bed. "They're beautiful. You're very sweet." Sweet, that's not a word that has ever been used with my name before.

"It's nothing, just thought it might help."

"Is that for me?" Jack asks so softly, I can feel his hesitation to ask.

I walk over to him where he has climbed up onto the bed and is looking so tiny on such a big bed.

"He sure is. He even has a star on him, because I think you're a big star because of how brave you were tonight. What do you think you'll call him?"

"I've never had a teddy bear before, do I really get to keep him?"

My steel heart almost breaks in two. "He's your bear forever. So, think up a really cool name for your new friend. I know. How about you call him Lex, I'm pretty cool." Before I can say anything else, he jumps up, standing on the bed, and throws his arms around my neck.

"Thank you, Lex. I will love him forever and ever. He will be my best friend." I slowly put my arms around him because I don't want to overstep the boundaries with his mother.

He's gone out of my arms and the hug is over as quickly as he jumped into them.

"I'm going to call him Ted. You know, because that's his name, Teddy Bear." He looks to us all for validation that the name is okay.

"Perfect," I tell him and ruffle his hair. Something I remember Charles doing to me when I was younger and running around in the yard getting up to mischief, when I should have been inside sitting quietly. It was always done with a smile, and it made me feel happy.

Looking over at Mia, I see she has tears again. Shit, I've made a mistake.

"Sorry, Mia, did I do the wrong thing?"

"No, Lex. It couldn't be more perfect if you tried." She swipes the tears from her cheeks.

"I have this one for Kayla with the little heart, so she knows she's loved too." Handing it to Mia, I know I need to get out of here. There's too much going on so that I have no idea what to say or do. The more I open my mouth, the more I'm saying things that she doesn't need to hear from a stranger.

"Umm I'll go and make some coffee or drinks or something." Turning and leaving, I hear Mason talking then following me out.

Walking beside me he puts his arm around my shoulders. "Thank you, man, you went above and beyond tonight. Paige and Mia won't forget it."

I just nod as we keep walking. Once we reach the living room he stops and lets me go.

"But you need to tell me what the hell was that in there. I don't even know that Lex, and I've known you a very long time."

Shrugging my shoulders at him I just blurt it out, which is totally out of character for me. I'm normally so calculated with everything I say. "To be honest, I don't know, Mas. That Lex is new to me too. Tonight, something just switched the moment she ran from that room. I wanted to wrap her in my arms and protect her with my life. I don't even know her and never laid eyes on her before, yet she is pulling feelings out of me I don't even understand. It must be the craziness of the whole night." I walk away from him towards the window to collect my thoughts. I can feel him now standing next to me.

"You're right to an extent. Tonight, has probably been like no other night you've experienced before, and the same for Mia. The adrenaline rush does funny things to you. I can tell you from years of experience. But I'm going to say this. The sparks that are flying between you two are lighting up the room. Now, that might just be like you said, the craziness of everything, but if it's not, you need to be careful and give her time to breathe. That woman in there has been to hell and back and then was heading straight to hell again. The last thing she needs is another man in her life that will want to dominate her. She needs to learn to trust first. We're expecting so much of her with so many new people around her, that she should just accept we're good people. Trusting a friend will be a challenge, but trusting a man will be a huge mountain for her to climb."

"Fuck off, Mason. I know I could never be the man for her. She needs soft and gentle, someone to treat her like a princess. Not an arrogant prick like me who's a grumpy asshole most days, or so you all keep telling me." I can't tell him that my emotions are already scrambled from the week I've just had, because we haven't had that conversation yet. I'm sure tomorrow she'll just be another client that needs my help.

"You can think what you like, Lex, but that man who bought half of Target and just stood in that bedroom, is no arrogant prick. I think he might be the best part of you that you haven't discovered yet. Take it from me. The right woman brings out the absolute best in you. It's like you've been saving it all for them."

I don't say a word because I can't.

Black and white.

I have no idea about the grey or any other color in between.

"All I'm saying, man, is take it slow. She's going to need time to heal. Then if you still feel that insane pull that I know you have tonight, make your move. Until then, just enjoy the blue balls, man, because your life is about to become hell." He slaps me on the shoulder and starts to walk away.

"Bastard," I mumble under my breath which just makes him laugh harder.

I'm sitting on the couch just watching a rerun of an NFL game when the girls finally come from out of the hallway.

"Sorry for keeping you. They took a little while to settle." Mia looks embarrassed that they were more than a few minutes.

"Don't be silly. They've been through a lot today." Mason and I both stand as they get closer.

Mason takes Paige in his arms and kisses her on the forehead.

"Drink, Tiger?" he asks. "Mia?"

"Make it a strong one please, baby," Paige replies and turns to Mia who looks unsure. "You can have whatever you want, including just water, Mia. No pressure."

"Sorry, I just don't drink, there was enough of that in my house and it never ended well."

Paige picks up on her pain straight away.

"Tea, let's have tea instead. Mason, can you get it ready?" He nods and then relief shows in Mia's face. I follow after him with both our beers and leave them in the kitchen.

"Tea for you too, man?" Mason grins.

"Fuck off and bring back four teas and make it snappy, maid." I'm not sure I could have handled this with Tate or Grayson. They would have had me so wound up by now, that I probably would have stormed out. Mason gets me. On a level they don't. That's why we all work. We each give something different to the others. At times I need the comic relief, but right now I just need the silence and straight-down-the-line attitude.

We all have baggage in life, and Mason is the first to see mine finally creeping out.

As I take a seat on the couch across from Mia and Paige, I can see that they both look mentally fatigued and physically exhausted but neither wants to give in and leave the other.

"I'm just in total shock," Paige says. "I woke up this morning not having a family. Tonight, I'm sitting with my sister and I have a brother too. I just don't even know how to take this all in. I almost feel like I'm going to wake up and find it's all been a dream. I know what you thought you knew about me is different, but you've still had time to get used to the idea of a sister, Mia. Holy shit, I have a sister." She leans over and hugs her for the umpteenth time. "My head is spinning and that doesn't happen very often." Paige is still trying to work it all out and her eyes haven't left Mia.

"So, I'm thirty-nine, how old are you?" Paige asks Mia.

"Thirty-eight." She pauses. "Oh god, can you imagine what our mother went through giving you up and then getting pregnant so soon with me and then having to do it again? I just can't even deal with what she must have felt through that whole ordeal. My heart is hurting for her. All these years I hated her, and now I just want to be able to tell her I'm sorry for what she went through. I couldn't have done it. I just couldn't." Paige reaches out and grabs her hand.

"I don't have children, but I can't imagine what it felt like for her. You are a brave woman, Mia. To manage to keep your kids safe through all of this."

"I don't feel brave, I feel stupid. Twice I let danger near my kids. Never again."

"Don't put yourself down," I say way more assertively than I should. I try to pull the emotion back a bit. "Nothing in any of this makes you stupid. The world is full of terrible men who prey on innocent women. They use your vulnerability to their advantage. But you have managed to keep your babies and yourself safe. Now you'll never have to worry again. Like Paige said, you are the bravest woman I have met. In my line of work, I see the awful side of society all the time. Mia, you have used so much strength that you can't even see, to get yourself out of a situation that was bad. That took a lot of guts to run away with two little children. I take my hat off to you. One day you will look back at today and see what a turning point it was in your life. Time to clear out all the bad and move on to the good times of your new life."

Mason smirks at me as he places the tray of tea down on the table.

"Thank you, Lex. It's just going to take a very long time to process all this. I know you keep saying I'm safe now, but I'll be honest, I'm still sitting here petrified that something is going to happen. Something bad. Nothing good ever happens to me, so you're going to have to give me a chance to get through all this. I'm waiting for the other shoe to drop." This is the most I've heard Mia speak since we found her. I know she doesn't realize it, but her gut instinct is to trust us, otherwise she wouldn't have just told us how scared she is.

"We understand that, Mia," Mason says with his understanding look. "We don't expect anything from you, and we all know it's going to take you a while to trust any of us. Just know, that won't stop us from caring and keeping you safe. Ashton, who you met tonight, is an Army friend of mine who now runs a security firm. I've already spoken to him, and he will be your bodyguard until we get these dirtbags dealt with."

"I don't need a bodyguard." Mia sits up straight, almost spilling hot tea over herself.

"Yeah, honey, you do," Paige says. "Just until we can sort out your husband and Bent so neither of them can ever hurt you again. You won't even know he's there." Paige is rubbing her arm now to help Mia calm down.

"I just can't even work out this world you live in. Big houses, bodyguards, money, it's all just so foreign to me," Mia says, looking into the teacup in her hands.

"It won't take long and it'll feel normal. What is mine is yours. You will never have to worry about money again. I have more than I can spend in five lifetimes. But we can talk about that later. Just know that you will never have to worry."

"Paige, no, I'll find a job," she says, shaking her head.

"It's late, so how about we talk about that tomorrow," I interrupt. "We have more pressing things to sort out first. The police interviews tomorrow and getting the legal processes started, like a restraining order against your husband. I will be your lawyer for everything, Mia. I'm here to help you as we go through the legal mess." I want to make sure that she understands I'm the one she will be leaning on.

"I don't think I can take any more tonight. Sorry. I just need to go to bed before the kids wake up early like usual."

"Of course, it's really late," Mason agrees. "We all need sleep. Lex, do you want to just crash here tonight?" he asks.

Until everyone started saying how tired they were, I hadn't even realized how exhausted I am too.

"Yeah, actually I might, if that's okay with you, Paige. I didn't think I was tired, but it's crept up on me."

"Don't be silly, of course you can. I'll make up one of the beds upstairs." Paige stands and looks like she could fall asleep standing up.

"No, I'll sleep here. I just need a blanket. That way Mia can feel safe that no one will come near her room because they have to get past me."

"Lex, no…" Paige starts to argue, but Mason puts his finger on her lips to silence her.

"Baby, let him be. If that's what he wants to do, then it works for me. Saves me having to patrol down here tonight, plus having him near our bedroom, you know it would get awkward." Mason winks at me.

"Mason, don't be rude." She drops her head onto his shoulder. "Fine, Lex, I'm too tired to argue. I'll send a blanket back down with Mason." She and Mia hug and start to walk towards the hallway.

Mia stops and turns to look at me.

"Thank you, Lex, you don't know how much I need this tonight. You are my star." With that she's walking away, and I'm left standing there wondering what the hell I'm feeling.

"Good luck, man. You're going to need it. That arrow she just shot went straight through your pathetic heart. Welcome to the club of men who get dragged around by our hearts. But I wouldn't have it any other way."

I might be tired but lying here staring out at the sky through the wall of windows, I keep going over what she said.

You are my star.

I don't know what that means, but I'm committed to the time it'll take to find out.

I have a feeling this apartment is going to become my favorite place to visit.

You might be starting a new life tomorrow, Mia, but you won't be the only one.

Chapter Seven

MIA

My eyelids feel so heavy, but I can't sleep. I'm too wired and confused.

Today I feel like I've been through a month in a day.

So many emotions have been circulating my body since I got out of bed this morning. Not once was it one emotion at a time. A multitude of things are racing through my mind. Even now I'm still trying to separate all the feelings.

Lying here listening to my kids' breathing as they sleep, I feel relieved we're safe for another night. Yet I'm still so scared and perplexed. Who are these people and why are they being nice to me? No one is ever kind to me without wanting something in return, yet Paige is my family. If I had found her a few months ago before I met Bent, maybe I wouldn't have this feeling of dread in the pit of my stomach. I want to trust her and believe her, but where I've come from has me full of mistrust. My gut tells me she's genuine, and I don't have any doubt that she means everything she says. But my gut has let me down before. Trust is always going to be a huge stumbling block for me with anyone, even a sister I never knew I had.

Rolling to my side I'm facing Jack, who's curled up with his bear in this huge bed. I don't think I've ever slept on anything so soft, and the sheets feel so luxurious. So out of my league. I'm praying hard that Jack doesn't wet the bed tonight, even though he has pull ups on. They've been known to leak, and god knows he had way too much to drink before bedtime. It'll be so embarrassing to tell Paige I've wrecked her fancy bed.

Softly running my hand over his head, I just feel better having him so close to me. With the blinds still open so it wasn't completely dark for the kids, I can see his face from the moonlight. He's smiling, and I don't think I could pry Ted out of his arms if I tried. I've managed to give him some toys over the years by saving some of my tips from the diner. He's had a birthday present and something from Santa every year, but I could only ever afford one toy. Anna always seemed to have a little something for him as well and some apparent secondhand toys from a friend which looked too new to me. I don't think she wanted to embarrass me. It was totally the opposite. No matter what, I will always put my children's happiness first, so if she was able to spoil them a little too, I was so grateful.

Jack's moving his face a little. I try to work out what he's doing, and then I realize he's rubbing his cheek against Ted's head. It's so soft and smooth. Not like anything he would have played with before. I'm both sad and happy at that thought. Total mixed emotions at the revelation.

Feeling restless still, I roll onto my back and stare at the ceiling again. My mind keeps drifting back to this man Lex. The one who's asleep on the couch outside my room. His sole purpose he said was to make me feel safe, after he spent probably the equivalent of a year's salary for me on things for the kids. I know he thought he was doing the right thing, but our old things were fine. I'm grateful to him, but I also feel so awkward. I don't know him, yet he's showering me with gifts.

What does that even mean?

Is he expecting anything in return?

No one in my world would do something like this without expecting some sort of repayment. My rational brain is telling me not to be so stupid, but it's hard at times to stop the crazy thoughts from circling. My mouth goes a little dry and my breathing gets a little quick. It's slowly taking over my body. The sweat building up and my hands feeling all clammy. It's now that I find my reality sinking in. I'm totally lost. I've run from a world where I had nothing and lived in fear every single day. A place that was scary and not somewhere I wanted my kids to grow up. But instead of running to find a place a little better that turned out to be hell, now I've fallen into a fantasy land. It can't be real. They'll work it out soon that I don't belong with them. I'm just a mere waitress in a diner. A mom to two small children. The woman who is hopeless at everything and will never succeed at life. Maybe I'm more like my mom than I realized. A magnet for horrible men. The dirtbags, scum of the earth. It makes me think about what kind of man Bent's father was. For Bent to turn out so badly. Did my mom fall for the same type of guy all over again, just like my father? Is my father still alive? Not that I would ever want to meet him or even know who he is. I gave up wanting to know anything about my parents when I lay on my bed in my foster home, longing for them to come and find me. I wouldn't have even cared if we lived a poor life. To me it would have been rich in other ways. To live a life as part of a family full of love.

Is that why I don't know how to handle all of this today?

I don't know how to be loved by anyone, just for being me. I've known Paige for about seven hours, and she wants to give me the world. Yet I don't know how to take that. My brain is trying to work out how to push her away, so I don't get hurt or hurt her back. I thought I cried out all my tears earlier yet they're running down my face. Wetting the super expensive pillow under my head. I just want someone to hug me and take the fear away. Just for a moment I want to feel no fear or panic. Not have to drag strength from the bottom of my soul.

Jack murmurs a little in his sleep and then resettles. I think about what I tell him to do when he's scared and doesn't need to hear the bad things around him.

He should sing so he can just forget what is going on around him and not be worried.

Not wanting to wake him or Kayla, I lie hugging my pillow as my teddy bear. The tears running faster down my face and quietly singing to myself. Twinkle Twinkle Little Star. Feeling like that little girl again who was scared all the time and just wanted to fit somewhere. I would look up to the sky and wish upon a star, that one day someone would love me. Thirty years later and I'm still looking up into the same sky and wishing the same thing.

For someone to love me.

Not because I'm their mom.

Not because I'm the cash cow for their drinking, gambling habit, and the occasional fuck if they were lucky.

Not because they need to use me to get to Paige.

Not because they found out I'm their sister, so they feel obligated.

To love me because I'm me. Just little old broken me.

The girl that nobody wants.

Not even my mom.

So why would anyone else?

The one person who is supposed to love you no matter what, but she was the first to walk away. I'm trying to tell myself for a good reason. But here, in the dark at three am, that doesn't sink in.

All that makes sense in my head is that I'm the girl who nobody loves.

I need to close my eyes and sleep.

Let the dreams take me away from here.

Before the morning light is peeking in again, and Jack and Kayla are awake, and I need to be super mom again. Who knows what tomorrow will bring? I'm almost afraid to wonder.

For some reason I think the answer to that question is a whole lot of trouble.

His little voice brings me out of my sleep coma. It feels like I only just closed my eyes. His words are followed with the sweet little giggle of my girl. I do not want him to see I'm awake, so I look through my only partially open eyes. Jack is standing over the top of her playpen and waving Ted above Kayla's head. She is just lying on her back and smiling at him, her arms and legs moving in glee at her big brother.

"Look at our new friend, La. His name is Ted." He's whispering to her, and she starts giggling at him again. I try not to laugh at his name for her. When she was born, he struggled with her name, so he shortened it to La and it stuck with him. He uses both now, her full name when he wants to appear like a big boy and La when they're playing.

"I like the nice man Lex. He isn't mean like the others. He's nice to Mommy and brought us teddies." He waves Ted above her head and then taps it down on her tummy, and Kayla giggles again. She is such a calm baby considering what she's been through. From the time I found out I was pregnant with her, I've always been stressed and anxious. It should have rubbed off on her, but instead she's the opposite. It's like when I hold her, she calms me.

"You will like him too, La. I saw he got you a dolly. It's in the bag. But don't tell Mommy I sneaked a look."

I thought I was completely empty of tears, but more have sprung from my eyes. This time happy tears, though. I haven't seen Jack so relaxed in a long time. He was always jumpy when Bent was around. He could sense he's a bad man. Jack knew the moods of his own father and when it was time to hide away from the yelling and sing his songs. He also knew when to just obey and do as he said so he didn't get in trouble. So, to hear him feel so comfortable with Lex, a man he doesn't even know, is a shock to me.

Wiping my face so he doesn't see me, I need to get up and use the bathroom and get the kids fed before they start making too much noise and wake the others. Sliding the covers back, Jack spots me and goes to talk—or should I say yell—to me.

I put my finger on my mouth to signal quiet. "Morning, my good boy, Mommy just needs to go to the toilet. Can you keep Kayla quiet for a little bit longer and keep whispering?"

He nods his head at me, and I quickly run into the en suite. I leave the door open so I can see and hear the kids. They're used to seeing me on the toilet. No place is sacred once you become a mother, so it's easier to leave the door open than have Jack bash it until I answer him. My head is still spinning that the guest room has its own bathroom. I'm still wearing my clothes from yesterday, and I look like a wreck. The person I see in the mirror is a mess. I can't go out in the kitchen looking like this.

After washing up, I start opening a few cupboards quietly and thank goodness find a new toothbrush and some toothpaste. I'm sure Paige won't mind if I use them. Cleaning up my face and pulling my brown hair up into a messy knot bun on my head, I go back to the kids who are still playing and giggling.

"I'm hungry." Jack looks up at me with his big brown eyes.

I'm lucky he waited this long really. As a baby, he was the child that from the time he opened his eyes he was screaming to be fed. Kayla is the complete opposite. Will happily lay in the crib until I can get to her. Thank goodness Jack grew out of the screaming for food stage, although he always seems to be hungry.

"Okay, baby. Let me see what I can find for you. But you need to be very quiet, so we don't wake up Lex on the way to the kitchen. Now let me see what's in these bags first. Hopefully there are some bottles for Kayla so she can have her milk while you eat."

"There are, Mommy, and clothes and toys and food. Lots of food and diapers. A dolly and a plane and lots of things…" Stopping mid-sentence, he realizes he has just given himself away for looking.

"Jack, have you been looking in the bags?" I try to look serious, but I can't do it for long because it would have been like Christmas for a four-year-old with all these mystery bags.

"I just looked, but I didn't take them out. Sorry." As he drops his head, I walk to him and lift it back up to look at me.

"It's okay, bud. I know it's exciting to have all these surprises. We have to remember to say thank you to Lex when he wakes up. We are very lucky that he got all of this for us." Understanding that he isn't in trouble, his feet start marching on the spot.

"Can I take out the plane please, Mommy? Paige said Mason flies a plane." His eyes are nearly popping out of his head.

"Okay, but nothing else. First I need you to show me the bags with the food in them and then we need to change diapers for Kayla and take your pull-up pants off."

The whirlwind that is my son starts buzzing around me, pulling out what I need and then running for the bathroom to go to the toilet and take off his diaper.

"Remember you need to be very quiet," I whisper to Jack as we creep down the hallway towards the living room, so we can get to the kitchen.

"Like when we play creeping lions?" he whispers.

"Yes, baby, but this is a new fun game that's better than that one called tiptoeing tigers." I pray that Kayla doesn't take that moment to start crying or squealing.

Looking at Jack, he's smiling thinking we're playing a game. All I can think of is the last time I had to get him to be so quiet to get away from my apartment. This morning is a whole different situation.

We almost made it through the living room when I hear his gravelly voice from the couch that I was trying not to look at.

"Morning." Lex's voice sends shivers down my spine instantly. I almost drop Kayla with fright at him speaking.

"Lex!" Jack yells and runs straight for him and jumps up on top of him before Lex even has time to move. "Thank you for my plane. It's cool. Can I keep it like Ted?"

The panicked look on Lex's face makes me let out a little giggle.

"Jack, get off Lex, I'm so sorry. He's pretty excited this morning."

"It's okay," he sleepily says. "Hey, buddy. Of course, you can." He sits up with Jack on his lap, still looking a little lost.

I'm certainly not lost – instead I'm frozen in my spot.

Lex stands up with Jack in his arms, and I can't breathe.

He's shirtless and standing in just his jeans.

He looks like a model straight off one of those magazines that I see in the supermarket.

Holy shit.

His abs are so solid like a washboard, and his arms are so strong and firm-looking. I feel tingles in places I've never felt tingles before. Dropping my eyes a little, there's a small hint of sandy blond hair like the color of the hair on his head and his beard. It's just above the top of his jeans that are currently sitting just below his waist, with the button popped open. The muscles on his stomach with that perfect V shaping downwards. It's like he's too perfect. No one looks like that in real life.

"Morning, Mia." Lex speaks in that same low morning voice which makes me snap out of my lusting and leering at his body.

"Umm yes. Morning. Umm yeah, sorry… for umm, ah yeah, about Jack." Oh my god, shut up, woman, you sound like a lunatic.

"He's fine, aren't you, bud. This is the best wake-up call I've ever had, let me assure you."

His eyes find mine which are stuck looking at him.

Last night he caught my attention, but there was so much happening I didn't really see him. Not like I am in this moment.

His hair is all messed up on the top of his head from sleeping, but long enough I could run my fingers through it. Not blond, not red, not brown, but a mixture that pulls me towards wanting to touch his beard that's covering his strong jawline. I've never kissed a man with a beard before.

Shit, I shouldn't be thinking about kissing this man either.

I'm done with men. They hurt too much, and I can't let myself be that vulnerable again. But it doesn't mean I can't appreciate the hot specimen standing in front of me with my son in his arms. Man, my ovaries are screaming at me. That man would make a perfect baby daddy. For fuck's sake. I need my body to calm the hell down. We are not going there again. Two kids are more than enough for a woman to cope with on her own.

"Please, Mommy, can we?" Shit, what did he say? I break from my trance and hope I don't have drool running down my chin from ogling. I see Lex with a sexy smirk. He knows exactly what I'm looking at and thinking about it. Of course, he would think it was funny. I'm sure he makes women speechless on a daily basis.

"Sorry, what?" I ask, trying to get myself back in the conversation.

"Make you breakfast. Me and Lex. He said I could help him, while you feed Kayla." Jack looks way too excited for me to deny him even though I want to. I don't need anyone to look after us. I've been doing it all my life, and no man is going to sweep in on his horse and try to rescue the poor lady who he feels sorry for.

"Okay, but no hot stuff. Lex looks after that." I make sure Jack is listening. He has a habit of getting so excited that the listening ears shut down. "Maybe Lex should put his shirt on too, so he doesn't burn himself." Oh my god, I did not just say that to a grown man. I feel my cheeks pink up as I head towards the kitchen to try to get away from him. Putting the bag on the kitchen counter, I look down at Kayla who is just taking in everything around her.

"I'm such an idiot, ladybug. You're just lucky you're not old enough to understand how embarrassing your mother is," I whisper to her, and she just smiles up at me with those big eyes that suck me in every time.

"I would say beautiful, not embarrassing." Lex walks past me with Jack in tow. Not turning to look at me, he opens the fridge to look for food.

Great, he has perfect hearing too!

Stay strong, legs, don't let me down now. You can't melt into a puddle when you have the baby in your arms. I must have misheard him. No one has ever told me that, and I doubt Lex would think that either. I can't take it any longer, and I take out the bottle, formula, and jar of food with the spoon. I need to get this taken care of and get as far away from Lex as I can right now. Within reason. There is no way I'm leaving Jack with a stranger unless I can see him from a distance.

"I hope everything you need is there. I can always run out and get anything I missed." From the voice that had me tingling all over to one that is full of uncertainty. Lex has turned back from the fridge and is watching me intently.

This man baffles me. All the confidence of a moment ago is gone and he's looking for reassurance.

"Lex, you didn't forget a thing. I'm so grateful, you will never understand how much. I don't know how to repay you," I whisper.

"Oh good. I was worried. I can take you to the store today to get anything else you need."

"No," I yell louder than I should have. "Sorry, I mean no, thank you. You've done enough." His head drops a little. Which makes me feel bad. "We are fine thanks, Lex." His head rises back up and looks at me with a serious look.

"You haven't seen anything yet. My help has only just begun." With that he starts talking to Jack, and I hear the words bacon and eggs and toast with juice. Jack starts jumping up and down on the spot with excitement. He has only had bacon a couple of times at the diner when Anna would sneak him a little piece which she got the cook to make extra just for him. She would try to feed me too, but I would always refuse. She already did so much for us, and I would rather she give it to the kids than me. I was so used to surviving on very little that it was no different for me.

Snap out of it, woman. Kayla may be a patient child, but if I don't feed her shortly then she'll let me know that she has reached the end of that patience.

Grabbing the plastic bowl, I spoon out the food and heat it a little in the microwave. Sitting her on my lap at the table, she's like a baby bird. As the spoon heads towards her, her mouth drops wide open and shakes back and forward trying to latch onto it. Watching Lex and Jack from here, I can see them talking and laughing. Well to be honest, Jack is doing most of the talking and Lex is listening while he works. He has Jack standing on a chair next to him at the counter mixing eggs and milk, getting ready to cook.

I'm still having trouble getting past looking at his body. He might have put his shirt on but it's a button-up one and it's still hanging open, which is worse because every time he moves, I just get sneak peeks. That's just mean. He knows what he's doing to me and obviously is enjoying the torture.

Kayla starts fussing, and that's when I look down to see that I have nothing left in the bowl and I've been trying to feed her an empty spoon. No wonder she's complaining.

Right, formula and bottle. Get moving. I can feel her starting to squirm in my arms as she sees me shaking the bottle getting ready to warm it.

"Nearly there, ladybug, just hang tight." Her complaining is getting a little louder, and I start to panic a little. I don't want her breaking into a full-blown tantrum in front of everyone.

"She must really want that bottle. I've hardly heard her fuss up until now," Lex says to me. Grabbing the bottle from the microwave and testing it on my wrist, laying her in my arms, I put it to her lips, and she latches on immediately. Kayla has a love for milk. It's her go-to when she gets upset. It calms her. The room goes silent instantly.

"Wow, just like that the noise is gone. It's magical." He looks a little fascinated.

"Milk fixes everything apparently. Well, in her world anyway." Her eyes start to get that mild drunk glazed look.

"I remember that when I was little. Milk and cookies were the best thing when you were sad. They fixed everything." Lex is staring at her lying in my arms, just going off into her own little trance.

"Can we have cookies too with the eggs?" Jack pipes up to ask.

"Yes," Lex says as I say, "No."

"Oops sorry, buddy. Mom said no. So, not today." My heart just opened a sliver listening to Lex actually back me in my decision, like my opinion matters.

"Sorry, Mia, I shouldn't have said that without checking. It was wrong of me." He picks up Jack and carries him around to my side of the counter and sits him in one of the bar stools there.

"Okay, Jack, I'm going to use hot things now, so I need you to stay on this side. I don't want to ever hurt you. Do you understand, little bud? You're such a good helper, but now I need you to watch me and make sure I do it right. Is that okay?"

His words hit hard in my chest… '*I don't want to ever hurt you.*' I could only pray for a man like that.

Watching Jack, he would never complain, and he is just as fascinated with Lex as I am. So, he just shakes his head and makes himself comfortable. Lex looks at me for a moment like he's thinking hard and then he blinks and shakes his head a little.

Going back to the frying pan, he throws the bacon in. The sizzling is loud, and while that's cooking, he pours the scrambled eggs into a second pan, then leans over and pops down the toaster.

This man knows his way around a kitchen. I've never really had anyone to watch but have taught myself the basics. We didn't eat very fancy growing up, and when I was older, I didn't have the money anyway, so I stick to the basics. I stayed out of the kitchen at the diner and just concentrated at being a waitress for that reason.

I'm used to not eating much breakfast, but my stomach is growling at the amazing smell coming out of the kitchen. I'm hungry, and this will probably be the best meal I've had in a very long time. I sit Kayla up on my lap and rub her back to bring up any gas. Jack jumps down from his seat and climbs up next to me on a chair.

"Are you ready, Mommy, for our Lex breakfast?"

I know what Jack means, but for a split second my mind went there. Oh yeah, I could have a Lex breakfast. Like I said, a split second, and that moment is lost as soon as the voices behind me start speaking.

"Nice to see you making yourself at home in my kitchen. There better be plenty for us too, chef," Mason's voice booms across the room, and Paige tries to shush him so he doesn't scare the kids.

"You wish, man. I have cooked breakfast for Mia and Jack. There is enough for Paige, but you can cook your own. That's what you get for being lazy and sleeping in." Lex is plating the food and laughs to himself at his own joke. "Plus, since when is it your kitchen? Pretty sure this place belongs to Paige and she just lets your ugly mug visit sometimes."

"Well, she obviously likes the look of this ugly mug because I'm moving in, so technically yes, you are in my kitchen now." Both Mason and Lex start laughing at each other.

"Paige, you'll be sorry. Don't say I didn't warn you." Lex just laughs as he keeps cooking.

"Smells good, buddy, and it's okay, there's enough, I'll just eat yours." Mason slaps him on the shoulder. They seem close, the two of them.

I feel Paige next to me, her hand on my shoulder as she leans down and kisses me on the cheek and then Kayla.

"Morning, my favorite girls." Then she leans over to kiss Jack on the forehead and give him a hug. "Plus, my big boy Jack. How is all my family this morning?" Jack starts chatting away replying. Paige then turns to me after he's finished talking.

"Ready for a big day, the first day of your new life?" she asks.

How can I tell her no? That I'm shit scared and have no idea what the hell that means. But instead I do what I always do and tell her what she wants to hear.

"Sure," I reply.

Looking down at Kayla in my lap and kissing her on the head, I ground myself for a moment before I look back up with my shield up and activated.

"You can have some of my food, Mason, I don't eat much."

I offer a change of subject so I don't have to tell them that I just lost my appetite worrying about what today will really hold for me.

As much as I hated it, maybe I was better off back in my apartment with Edward. I knew what to expect there.

Here I am so out of my league that everything scares the shit out of me!

Chapter Eight

LEX

I don't know how long I've been lying here looking at the stars outside. My mind can't seem to turn off. Why am I having this reaction to a complete stranger? Someone I know very little about except that she is the most naturally beautiful woman I've seen. She isn't hiding behind all the makeup and clothes of my stuffy socialite world. To be honest, she doesn't need it.

Watching her with her children and being the protective momma bear of her cubs is not something I'm used to. Daisy who is Hannah's daughter is the closest I've ever been to little kids. Yet there's something so innocent about them. The way Jack knew he could trust us all, and there was no hesitation from him. That surprised me when I know he has come through a situation with two different men that he's scared of. What makes him trust us?

Why does he trust me?

Kayla in her mother's arms had me feeling things that I've never even contemplated. What would it be like to have a baby of my own? Someone I could love unconditionally and never leave to wonder if they're loved or not. Mia may have had a tough life in more ways than one, but she loves those two kids more than the air she breathes. You can see it all over her face when she looks at them.

Feeling restless and needing to pee, I know I should get up and go to the bathroom, it might help me to sleep. Throwing the blanket back then sitting up, I try to get my bearings in the dark. I move slowly down the hallway so not to make a noise. Moving past Mia's room, I find the bathroom at the end of the hallway. Afterwards, as I'm walking back past her room, I hear a little noise. I know instantly what I heard. Mia is crying herself to sleep. Standing outside her room, I want to open the door and take her in my arms to soothe her. Tell her she doesn't need to be scared anymore. I won't let anyone, or anything, hurt her again like she is hurting right now. Unfortunately, I know that's not even close to an option for her. She is so far from being okay that only time and support will get her past her pain. It doesn't stop me from wanting to do it, though.

Slowly I place my hand on the door and lean my forehead forward to touch the wood. Her angelic voice is now singing so quietly. I can't make out all the words, but it sounds like she's struggling between tears to say them. I feel her pain in every sound. My heart is waking from its cold place, and she is calling it like a siren. There's something so different about Mia that I can't work out why she's making me stop and take notice. I know it's not her wounded soul, although that pains me all over, but it's not what is calling to me. There is a special quality in this woman that I want to explore further. It's crazy that I've only known her for a few hours, yet I can't stop thinking about her.

Standing with my hand still on the door, the noises get a little quieter, and then I finally hear silence. I hope sleep has finally found her and will give her some peace for a few hours from the weight she carries on her shoulders.

'Hang in there, angel, I've got you. Even in the hard days to come, I'll be here. You are not alone anymore.'

Lying back down on the couch, I know what I need to do. Just like Mason said. I need to just be there as a friend and help her heal. Get to know her, let her get to know me. To find out not all men are assholes. When the time is right and if these weird feelings haven't left me, then I'll know she's the one.

One thing I know with certainty, though, is that I need to be the man she needs first. The lawyer who will make sure the men who have gone before me, pay for the hurt and pain they have caused. No one gets away with hurting one of my own, that I promise with every bone in my body. She is one of my own.

Mia, Jack, and Kayla are now in my circle. The one that holds all the people I will never turn my back on. The ones I will fight for no matter who the enemy is.

Closing my eyes, I try to turn off the pictures that I keep seeing. The fear in her eyes the moment I saw her, to the change for that small moment of laughing in the bedroom. I never want to see that kind of fear again, so I concentrate on the smile and the sound of her laugh as sleep finally claims me.

Hearing faint noises from down the hallway, I know they must be awake but are trying to keep quiet. I can hear a little baby giggle every few minutes from Kayla which sounds so cute. Lying with my arms clasped under my head, I hear the door open slowly. Holding in my laugh as I hear Mia whispering to Jack to be quiet, so they don't wake me up. Lying so still, I watch her step out from the opening and look down at Jack to hold his attention. Kayla on her hips is looking straight at me with her big eyes and smiling at me. Her chubby little cheeks and grin are sucking me in. Now I know why people always talk about pinching baby's chubby cheeks. They're like a magnet.

Just like I remember from last night, Mia is a vision. Tiptoeing across the floor barefoot, in jeans and her white t-shirt from yesterday. With Kayla pulling the shirt to the side scrunched in her little baby fist. Showing more skin that I'm sure Mia is aware of. Just enough to start my body taking a lot more notice than I should be. They almost make it across the room to get past the couches when Jack looks up and sees me. The excitement in his eyes has me smiling.

"Morning," I say, letting Mia know I'm awake before she freaks out that Jack wakes me with whatever he's about to scream out.

I startle her, if I can judge by the way her body reacts to my voice. Watching her reactions to me is becoming interesting.

"Lex!" Jack yells, and before I have time to move much, he jumps at me to catch him. Luckily, I get my arms out from under my head quick enough to stop his knees from landing right in my crotch. This kid is quick, I'll give him that. Especially this early in the morning. "Thank you for my plane. It's cool. Can I keep it like Ted?"

This kid is like he has woken up ready to tackle the day at full speed. All this excitement before coffee is a little hard to take. Then I hear that giggle that hardens my cock again. Shit, I need to move this kid away from my body. So I can adjust myself. She doesn't need to see what she's doing to me and think I'm just another dirty man.

"Jack, get off Lex, I'm so sorry. He's pretty excited this morning."

"It's okay," I say, looking to Jack. "Hey, buddy. Of course, you can." Sitting up with Jack on my lap, I try to find my feet on the ground in the blanket that's still wrapped around my legs.

Standing up with him in my arms just feels so natural. He's talking flat-out while I just stand there watching Mia. Her eyes are leaving heat on my body as she looks me up and down. There is no way I'm not affecting her the same way her body is doing things to me. The pink on her cheeks tells me she likes what she sees. I'm trying not to react, but I can't help but feel a little cocky. It's been a long while since someone has reacted to me like this. Especially where there is far more going on than just getting naked to fuck.

All of a sudden, I feel two little hands on my cheeks turning my face to him so I'm paying more attention.

"Are you hungry too, Lex? Because Mommy is going to find me some food." This kid seriously is the funniest thing.

"Why don't you and I make breakfast for Mommy while she feeds your sister. I'm sure Kayla is hungry too." Jack and I stop talking to look at Mia, waiting for her answer. She looks like she's in another world until Jack speaks to her. Shocking her into realizing she hasn't heard a single word we said. I can't help but smirk. Oh yeah, she feels it too. There is no doubt I'm not on my own here. I grab my shirt and put it on after Mia's comment worrying I might burn myself. Yeah right, I'm sure it was more than that.

Softly, softly, Lex, I tell myself as we start walking. Give her space. Don't rush this.

Getting into the kitchen, I find plenty of eggs and some bacon in the fridge. Jack's eyes light up at the word bacon. Decision made. I don't get to cook very often, having a housekeeper, but that doesn't mean I don't enjoy it. When I was away at college living in my first apartment, I didn't want to be that kid that stood out as the rich kid with privilege. So, I refused to have anyone help me and I looked after myself. Cooking, cleaning, washing. My mother thought it was ridiculous, but I told her it was a rite of passage, and when I went into politics it would help me bond with the everyday American voter. She bought the crap I was spinning her, for which I was thankful. It had nothing to do with that. I just wanted some space to find out what life was without her hovering and ordering me around. No one reporting back to her every move I was making. Plus, college days are for discovering life, having adventures, making friends, meeting girls, and having sex…lots of it.

I set Jack up on a chair next to me like I remember Nanny Sue doing with me when we baked. Usually when Mother was out at some garden party or charity event. Licking the spoon and bowl after making chocolate cake is a childhood memory I haven't thought about in a very long time. Mia's not far away from us, sitting at the table feeding Kayla. Shit, I should have bought a highchair. I'll go back today and get that and anything else she's thought of that I missed. Not that I could have fit anything else in the elevator last night, but I should have also gotten a stroller for her too. I'm sure Kayla gets heavy carrying her all the time.

Just as I'm getting close to having everything cooked, I hear Mason's deep voice behind me. I kind of forgot about him and Paige. Which I know is ridiculous since we are in Paige's home. But I just got so wrapped up in feeding Jack and Mia, I wasn't even thinking about cooking for them. Oh well, bad luck, Mason can figure that out.

Mia tries to tell Mason he can eat her share as she doesn't eat much.

Not a chance.

Her being put behind someone else stops today.

If Mason is that desperate, he can eat mine and I'll cook more. I'm feeding her whether she likes it or not. She is so tiny. I just have this awful feeling that it comes from not having enough to eat at times. That pulls on every heartstring I didn't know I owned. Between Paige mothering her and now me, Mia is never going to be without anything going forward, especially not food.

Finally coming to a compromise with Paige pulling out some muffins and fruit, there is plenty to go around. We all sit down at the table and listen to Jack talking and telling us so many stories. Mia tells him at times he needs to stop so we can all talk which lasts about a minute, if that, and he is off on another story. He's fascinated by Mason being a pilot and of course wants to ride in his big plane. Which Paige reminds him is her plane just to annoy Mason. Finally, I see Mia relaxing a little at the constant chatter and seeing how happy Jack is. Paige is now holding Kayla so Mia can eat, and although she's picking little bits of what's on her plate, I make sure she eats something.

Paige offers to take Kayla and Jack to the bedroom to get some of the toys so she can set them up in the living room. I take this opportunity to broach the hard topic of what today holds for Mia.

"How did you sleep last night, Mia? I can't imagine it was easy." Knowing full well she had a rough start to the night crying herself to sleep.

"It was okay. I didn't get much sleep, yesterday was a lot to digest." I can see the worry lines coming back to her face.

"Yeah, I can imagine," Mason says, as he's sipping his second coffee of the morning. I must admit I'm thinking a whole lot clearer now that I'm on to my second boost of caffeine.

"We need to talk about what will happen today." I watch her face lose the small smile that had been there for part of the morning.

Her head just nods, not wanting to really acknowledge what is about to happen.

"I just want to explain what will happen this morning, so you aren't worried at all. Most importantly, I want you to know I will be with you every single step of the way. I won't leave you for one moment. Are you okay with that?" I don't want to force anything on her, but I need her to know I am here to help.

"Yes, I appreciate that. I have to admit I'm a bit lost and a whole lot scared of what's going to happen now. What happens when they let Bent go? He'll come after me and Paige. He hates us. And my kids, I have to keep them safe and I'm not sure I can do that here." Once Mia starts talking, all her fears are pouring out; she doesn't understand this is just what I wanted her to do. I can't help her if I don't know what's in her head. "What if he did tell my husband Edward where we are? He told me he would kill me and the kids if I left. I don't know where to go or what to do. I don't have any money, I used everything I had to run last time. I'm just so confused and scared." She's trying so hard not to cry, but the tears are bordering on spilling down her cheeks again.

I can't stand seeing her so scared. I lean across the table and take her hands, giving them a tight squeeze. "Mia, look at me and listen." It's a little more forceful than I needed to be, but I needed to snap her out of the panic she's slipping into.

Her head suddenly looks up at me the moment I touch her and speak. Her eyes are wide but not with fear, which I'm thankful for. I'm hoping it's from the electricity running through her arms like is running through mine from a simple touch.

"You and the kids will be protected for as long as you need to be. If that is for the rest of your life, so be it. Mason has Ashton in place for that, plus you have Mason who's a badass, and when he's not with you then I will be. No one, and I mean no one, is going to get near you and hurt you. That's a promise." I keep her concentration on my words.

"Damn straight. Not on my watch," Mason growls, letting me know how pissed he is at hearing her scared. I hear you, brother. I'm ready to hunt down her husband and kill him myself.

"I know that's hard to understand and take on board, but the more you spend time with us the more you will see, we are here to help and protect you. We weren't joking last night when we told you, you are part of the framily. You may be family to Paige, but with that you also inherit the framily of all of us. You may regret that later once you get to know us, and how annoying and loud we are, but we protect our own. So get used to that. We aren't going anywhere. So, if you run, we will follow you, not to hurt you but to keep you safe. I know it sounds like the safest way out is to run again. But I need you to understand the safest thing you can do for your kids, is to stay and fight to finish this once and for all. Help us to put Bent behind bars and then let Mason and I deal with Edward. I can assure you I will have him so scared to come near you and the kids that you will never see him again. Plus, you just say the word and I will have the divorce papers drawn up tomorrow and filed with the courts. Getting you full custody of the kids and restraining orders, that he can never come anywhere near any of you, unless he wants to spend time behind bars too. I know this is a lot to take in, but I do this shit every day. Let me help you get your life back." I feel like I'm giving the speech of my life. I need her to let me in to help. I'm almost begging her.

"Lex, I'm scared," she whispers, and my heart bleeds for her.

"I know, but let me carry that fear for you. Let us all take a piece of it and share the load." She starts to slowly nod her head up and down a little.

I see Mason go to put his arm around her shoulder, but then thinks better of it. Instead he stands next to her to gain her attention

"Let us take the whole load, Mia. We've got you." Then he walks to the kitchen to grab a tissue for her. Reluctantly I let her hands go so she can wipe away the tears in her eyes.

"Now, let's talk about how this morning is going to go and then we can take a step at a time. How does that sound?" I watch for her body language as she pulls herself together again. Her shoulders have relaxed a little, but she's trying to bring the strength to the forefront again to push away any weakness she's showing. One day I hope that she no longer feels she needs to always be strong. That it's okay to be vulnerable in a safe place.

"Okay, I'm listening." Her voice picks up a bit and she sits taller in her chair. "Let's do this."

"Attagirl," Mason says, and the three of us start running over what will happen. I explain that I messaged my detective friend last night and have organized the police to come to the apartment to take both Mia's and Paige's statement along with Mason. Paige's father's friend who had been helping, went to the police station last night and presented the full case to them about Bent and the embezzlement. That was enough for them to hold him last night, and today we press charges for anything else we can in the way he blackmailed Mia and virtually held her and kids hostage. By now Paige has joined us and the kids are just playing on the floor with all the toys I grabbed last night.

Mia asks questions and wants to understand everything about the process. She is far smarter than she gives herself credit for. I wonder if given the same opportunities as Paige was if there would have been two smart women running the company. Hopefully one day when she has claimed back her life, she feels she can pursue something for herself that stimulates her intellect that she has been ignoring while just trying to survive.

Paige slips her hand into Mia's. "I know this morning is going to be hard, Mia, but I was hoping after it's all done, I can take you and the kids to meet my father. I know he's going to be just as shocked as I was, but he will love to meet you all. I understand if you aren't up to it." Paige looks like a little girl full of hope.

Mia is slow to respond as she takes in what Paige just asked her.

"I think I would like that. I still can't get my head around that you're my sister, so I may as well keep putting my head in a spin and get it all out there. Are you sure he won't mind? We're a lot to take in as a package. I mean, Jack is not a quiet little boy."

Mason bursts out laughing.

"Oh, wait until you meet Jonathan, he's not a quiet old man either. They'll get along just fine." Paige swats his arm and then looks back to Mia with such a big smile on her face.

"Shush, you. Daddy kind of had a reason to yell at you. He did get a shock meeting you the first time. I mean, you were in the middle of telling his daughter all the dirty things you were about to do to her. Pretty sure that would have been grounds for murder in any court of law."

I can't help but laugh and look at Mason who looks proud of himself. "Oh, I need to hear this story, man. Did you piss off the father-in-law straight up?"

Mason just rolls his eyes at me. "Let's just say if he had a gun, I'm sure you would have been attending my funeral. And to be honest, if I was in his shoes and Paige was my daughter, I might have done the same." Mason stands and starts clearing the dishes off the table. "But the little ears around here don't need to hear those details, plus I don't kiss and tell, man. I'm not Tate." He disappears towards the kitchen.

Fair point. Tate does like to overshare at times. Thank god he's now with Bella and we don't have to hear those stories anymore. I mean, I would be worried more about the wrath of Bella than I would of Grayson killing him.

We send the girls to play with the kids and give Mia the chance to shower and change into some of Paige's borrowed clothes. Mason and I clean up from breakfast. My mind is already processing everything I know I need to do. Put in place the legal actions I can, to keep them all safe. I'll email Greta later, lay out everything I need her to work on first thing Monday morning. This takes priority over everything we have on our workload. I need the documents drafted and then filed in the courts as soon as possible.

Ashton arrives around the same time as the police, and we go through the slow process of statements and full recounts of yesterday's events. I'm sitting with Mia because the others don't need me. Although Paige has had a hard time, it's nothing compared to Mia. Plus, Paige has Mason to lean on when she needs someone. Ashton on the other hand is cool and calm, just as I would expect. I'm glad Mason has him on board. Looking at him, I know his appearance would be enough to make most men back away, but I guarantee that Edward is some gutless guy who gets his thrills from standing over women. Yet as soon as a real man stands up to him, he'll cower away like the rodent he is.

"We'll be in touch once we investigate and process all of this. You've all been very helpful. Let us know if there's anything else you think of or become concerned about." Detective Benson shakes my hand as they step into the elevator.

"Thank you. We appreciate you coming here. I'll call you Monday if I don't hear from you before then." I let go of his hand and the doors close as the elevator starts its trip down to the foyer.

Walking back to where everyone is sitting, I take my seat back next to Mia.

"I'm really proud of you. That was not easy to do, but you handled yourself well and were clear in everything you told him. That makes it easier for them to nail this bastard."

Patting her hands again, I realize I keep doing that. It's like she has this pull that makes me want to connect with her physically every so often. I seriously need to get control of this. Mia is going to think I'm way too touchy for someone who doesn't know her.

"Thanks, Lex. I couldn't have done that without you. I was so nervous, but you made me feel like I was doing okay." Her voice is quiet, letting me know that it took a lot out of her.

It's never easy to talk about something that is so personal. Telling other people about things that have happened to you, things that aren't considered normal in their eyes. Looking back, you now see some of the things you did weren't smart and should have raised warnings at the time. Hindsight is something we all wish we had at one stage of our lives. I've told so many clients that I don't judge them. What happened at the time is no reflection on how you see the same situation once you get distance from it.

"You did great, and the first step is always the hardest. Now forget about all that for the rest of the weekend and leave it up to me to do some groundwork with Edward." Before I get to say another word, Jack comes over and climbs up into my lap.

"I'm hungry, Lex, can we have the cookies now?" he says so sweetly and looking so innocent.

"Jack," Mia gasps.

But the rest of us all start laughing at him. Having little mouths to feed constantly will take some getting used to.

Paige takes him off to the kitchen to see what she can find for him while we settle with Ashton what the schedule is for the next few days.

"Thanks, Ashton. We'll be in touch once Paige sorts out her work schedule for next week. I've got this for the next few days until I'm needed back at work." Mason and Ashton talk a little more in quiet voices near the elevator, and I'm guessing it's details they don't want the girls to know. After years together in the Army, these two are close, you can tell. I can imagine when you're relying on someone to keep you alive, there's no stronger bond than that.

"Are you coming with us to meet my dad, Lex?" Paige asks as Jack crawls back into my lap with his crackers and cheese. Not exactly cookies, but he looks just as happy. It seems my lap has become his new favorite spot to sit. I don't know how Mia feels about it, but she hasn't said anything, so I let him get himself comfortable.

It just dawned on me that I'm still in my clothes from yesterday and could do with a shower. Plus, that is a family moment that I don't need to be part of.

As much as I don't want to leave Mia, I need to back off and give them time to start to get to know each other. I've already intruded enough.

"No, thanks for the offer. You guys need to do that as a family. Plus I have some work to get done and perhaps a shower might be a good idea." I look at Mia as I say it, trying to see her reaction. She doesn't give much away and just stands to attend to Kayla who is starting to fuss.

"You're welcome to come, but I understand you need to get home." Paige looks at me with appreciation for being here through it all.

"Man, can you just hang here for a little longer while I run to the store and grab some car seats for the kids? I don't want the girls on their own." Mason stands, grabbing his keys and wallet from the counter.

Damn, I should have added car seats to the list too.

"I can go if you want?" That way I can get the stroller and highchair too.

"No, it's fine. Let me buy the only part of the store you didn't buy last night," Mason says as he kisses Paige and disappears into the elevator.

Turning back to see Mia rocking Kayla to sleep in her arms, I can tell she's struggling again with us buying more things. I didn't really think of it from her shoes. If I were her, I would hate it too. Having to rely on other people is not my thing at all.

I'm starting to learn it's not Mia's either.

She's been on her own all her life and overnight we've just taken over.

I need to talk to the others about this later.

She needs to feel in control, otherwise we aren't any better than every other person who has gone before us, trying to dominate her life.

She needs space, and we need to give her that.

Otherwise we risk losing her.

Chapter Nine

MIA

I think back to everything that has happened since I got out of bed this morning, I didn't think it was possible, but today has been just as draining as yesterday.

I hadn't slept more than a couple of hours and my mind was scrambled. One of the many things that was weighing on me since last night was Paige wanting me to meet her father. I knew it was important to her, but to be honest, I was scared shitless. All the possible scenarios were going through my head. What will he think of me? He probably thinks I'm just after her money. He won't want to have anything to do with me and my kids. He'll likely tell her to just kick me out and get on with running her business. Not to bring trouble to her life. All these crazy things that I couldn't shake had me absolutely petrified. I tried to hold it all inside, but I have a feeling there was at least one person who could tell how worried I was. But I just had to keep it together and get on with the day.

Breakfast with everyone, meeting with the police, and then meeting Jonathan and Beth, it was enough to make today feel like a week all rolled into one. My nerves were peaking as I walked into

Paige's family home. Never in my life have I seen such a beautiful and extravagant home. Yet it was homely, and as soon as I met them, they made me feel so welcome. Jonathan straight away told me he wants to be my father for the years he has left, and will love me like his own daughter. All my fears came flooding out as he hugged me. I cried on his shoulder. I didn't know how much I needed his acceptance until I had it, and it came straight away without one ounce of hesitation in his voice. He and Beth just doted on the kids, and I have a feeling we will be seeing a lot more of them, with Beth already offering to babysit. Although I'm not anywhere near that stage of leaving my kids with people I don't really know. Maybe in time I can work up to that.

The kids fell asleep in the car on the way home, and Paige had Mason stop at the mall so we could get some clothes for me for a few days until we can get some things figured out. I tried to tell her I would just go to my apartment and get my clothes, but she refused. She said she would send Mason down there if there were any keepsakes we need, but the rest can go to charity. Her favorite words today are new life, fresh start. There are a few things that are in my backpack that are important to me, so I made a list for Mason for later. I still feel uncomfortable with the handouts, so I didn't get much. Just a couple of pairs of jeans, shorts, and tops. Plus underwear, which I just picked the cheapest I could find. Paige told me I could have whatever I wanted, but that didn't seem right. I'm sure my boring white bra and panty sets are nothing like the expensive lace and satin that she would wear.

When we got back to Paige's apartment, we unpacked everything that Lex had bought and put it away in the cupboards. The room is now more organized, and we know what I have. Dinner was simple tonight with just cheese on toast for the kids and me. Paige wanted to order in for us, but I just couldn't take it tonight. I'm not used to so much food and the richness of it. Plus, the emotions have my stomach feeling all churned up. Mason can see I'm struggling, and he's good at pulling Paige back from pushing too hard. I know she means well, but she's overpowering at times. I understand why she has the position she has in the business. She is a very strong woman. Something I wish I was, but I'm not even close.

Bathing the kids and letting them play for a little while was the first bit of quiet time they had all day. But it didn't take long and they were starting to fall asleep playing so I knew it would be an early bedtime. Sitting on the end of my bed, now that both the kids are asleep, I just need a moment on my own. I feel like I've been smothered since everything happened. I'm so grateful for them all, but there were times today I didn't think I could breathe. It's overwhelming in a good and bad way. I just don't know how to navigate it all.

Paige just wants to give me the world. I can't believe I thought all those awful things about her. She is totally the opposite to everything Bent told me. I want to say no to her generosity, but I can't and that is hard to accept. I have no home or money for food, so I need to rely on her. As soon as I can pull myself together and we have this stuff with Bent done with, then I need to find a job. So I can look after my family and stop feeling like a leech, taking money from Paige. I know she can afford it. I mean, look where she lives, and her father's house is a mansion. But that is beside the point. I want to—no, actually I *need* to stand on my own two feet.

I won't be able to afford a very nice place to live, but I will find something to suit us that is still close to Paige. As long as it's clean and safe, then I'll be fine. I don't want to be that annoying family member that takes what they can get and keep expecting the handouts. But after spending a day with her, I do desperately want her to be a part of my life. There is an undeniable bond between us. One that I have longed for all my life and finally have found. I'm not giving that up for anything. I also want my children to grow up in a family environment. I know already, deep down in my heart, that if something were to happen to me, Paige would take care of them and love them like I do. She has shown that from the very beginning, and they both respond to her like they've known her all their lives. I can see she loves the connection just as much as I do. We grew up differently, but one thing we had in common our whole lives is the craving for a family. Now we've discovered each other, there is no turning back.

I look down at Kayla in her playpen, the star mobile that was in one of the bags now hanging above her. She is snuggled in the cutest sleepwear, pink and covered in sparkling stars, and my mind again goes to him.

Lex.

Who is this man and where did he come from?

I'm more confused about him than I am about everything else put together.

Why does he make my body react and tingle as soon as he's near me, but at the same time, he calms my soul? I thought once he left today I would finally feel better and not have to battle the weird feelings. But instead, more strange sensations filled my mind.

I missed him this afternoon.

His smile, calm voice, and just his presence. Now that it's time for me to go to bed, I didn't realize how much he made me feel safe. Both him just being near me and sleeping outside my door. It's totally crazy because I don't even know him, yet I wish he was back on that couch tonight watching over me.

I hear a soft tap on the door, and Paige pokes her head into the room.

"You okay in here?" she whispers so not to wake the kids up. They're exhausted. Standing up, I walk to the door to answer her quietly.

"Yes, I think I'm just going to shower and then jump into bed too. I'm so tired."

"Me too. That sounds like a good plan. I think I'll do the same. If you need anything during the night just come and find me or call out and we will be straight down." It's like she's not ready to let me out of her sight either.

"I'll be fine." I hesitate on how to say what I need to say. "Thank you for everything today, Paige. You've opened your home and family to me. I'm very grateful. More than you will ever know."

She reaches out and pulls me into a tight hug. "You are my family. I will always be here no matter what. I'm the grateful one to have found you. We will never be apart again. I promise. Now get some sleep and let's have a lazy day tomorrow." With that she steps back out of the hug.

"Sounds great. Goodnight," I say, starting to close the door. I hear her say goodnight as she walks back up the hallway.

We've already developed a bond, and it's close, but there are still times of awkwardness. It will just take time to get past that.

There is something about a hot shower when you feel totally exhausted. It's like it washes some of the worries away. The things that you shouldn't be wasting energy on. Then it helps to soothe the big things. The things that won't wash away completely, but they just don't seem so heavy while you're standing under the water.

Maybe after a day to catch my breath tomorrow, I'll have the energy to battle through the next challenge. I just don't know which thing to pick, which will be the next problem to tackle. My life is crazy. No one would believe me if I tried to tell them.

Curling into the big comfy bed tonight feels different than last night. Tonight, I feel so tired I don't have the energy to think. I need to just breathe out and start to accept some of the changes happening. They may not be exactly what I want, but to be honest, we are safe, in a home where we are wanted and have food to stop us from starving. That's more than I've ever had. For that I'm extremely grateful.

The rest will fall into place.

At least I hope it will.

Closing my eyes, I try to blank out my thoughts, but it's impossible. Lex keeps appearing in my reflections of the last two days. His soft smile, that deep laugh that makes me laugh with him on the inside. I hear his voice in my head. The words he said to me on repeat over and over again, *'Let me help you get your life back.'* I know I am nothing more than Paige's sister, and he's helping me because he feels sorry for me. I'm not like any of the women he would have in his life. Wealthy, beautiful, and powerful women is what I imagine his world is full of. The only poor, single mothers he's met would be in the courtroom, who he turns the other way from as he defends his rich client from something that they've been accused of. Who am I kidding, he probably has a girlfriend, and that's where he was today. I'm thinking stupid thoughts again that I shouldn't be. He could never be part of my world. More to the point, I could never fit into his.

But part of me wants to imagine he sees me. Just for once I let myself go off to sleep dreaming that I would be good enough for Lex. I know it's a crazy thought, but a girl can dream.

And this girl knows in reality dreams never come true, so it's okay to live in my dream tonight.

No one will ever know.

One of the most frustrating things with kids is their sleep patterns. The mornings you would give anything for just ten more minutes of sleep are the days they are up as the sun peeks over the horizon.

Not today, though. I'm the one lying here wide awake and the kids are still snoring. Yesterday really wore them out. I try so hard to go back to sleep, but it's just not going to happen.

Sneaking out of bed to use the bathroom, I decide I'll leave the kids sleeping with the door open slightly so I can hear them when they wake. Trying to be as quiet as a mouse, I make a coffee and curl up on the couch facing out the floor-to-ceiling windows. Just taking the view in. The sky is clear, and the sunrise is showing me the start of the sky for today, being blue for as far as I can see. There's something so peaceful about the early morning light. Like nothing bad has touched it yet and the day is still so pure. Taking in a deep breath, I just sit and take in the peacefulness.

Until I arrived in Chicago, I had never been in a building this high off the ground. It's a strange sensation to be up above everyone. It's like being a princess in the castle. Paige is the princess that lives here, and I'm just visiting. She has her Prince Charming. Just watching her and Mason together, I see what real love is. He adores her and treats her like a precious glass object that may break if not protected. Yet he still manages to give her space to be herself. I don't think she's the kind of woman who can be caged. But it's also easy to see Paige needs Mason to ground her. He is her rock when she needs the strength. I think her life is all about control, but when she comes into her castle, she just lets go, and Mason takes the load for her. It seems an interesting dynamic but works, and there's nothing but love between them which makes then inseparable. One day I hope I find that sort of love.

Although I'm mad that I couldn't sleep, the time I've had sitting here this morning in the silence is just what I needed. A moment of peace in the middle of the chaos.

I hear quiet footsteps coming down the stairs and look up to see Mason wearing that just-awake look. Hair still messy, eyes open but not wide awake. Smiling at me, he waits until he's beside me to talk quietly.

"Morning, Mia, you're up early. Are you okay?" His early morning voice is just like Lex, low and coarse.

"Morning. Yes, thank you. Just couldn't sleep, so I'm enjoying the sunrise with a coffee." He places his hand on the couch next to me, which should make me shudder from a man being this close, but it doesn't. The respect he shows me is what I imagine a big brother's kindness would be. This is going to take some getting used to.

"Sounds perfect. Mind if I join you?" he asks softly.

"Not at all." Surprisingly, this morning I'm not saying yes just because I think I should. I actually wouldn't mind the company.

"I'll just grab a coffee. Want another one yet?" I shake my head no as I'm sipping mine.

We both sit there for a little bit, not speaking, just enjoying the changing morning picture in front of us. Then Mason looks seriously into my eyes.

"How are you doing, Mia? And not the answer you would tell Paige. Tell me how you are really doing." He may be the toughest-looking of his group of friends and the one that I'm sure carries the most demons, but to me he is such a gentle giant. The way he charged in to protect my kids and was prepared to kill Bent to keep them safe, it still makes me shiver. I think he understands me more than Paige. He has seen life that is hard and not like this luxury.

I feel totally comfortable talking to him.

"If you were Paige, I would say I'm fine and change the subject." He grins at me, knowing that's what he was expecting.

"But I'm not Paige, so you want to tell me the truth." He smirks at me.

"Will you tell her?" I don't want to upset her.

"If I think she needs to know, yes. I don't keep secrets from her. But if this is just you needing a shoulder, to talk things over and help clear your head a little, then that's just a conversation between friends. I don't tell her every conversation I have in a day."

I can't help but giggle a little. Just like I said. This is my version of a big brother.

"The truth...hmmm, I'm not sure I even really know what the truth is. I have a husband I'm scared of who may or may not know where I am. A brother I never knew I had who blackmailed me to hurt Paige, and I followed him which then put my kids in danger. I found a sister that I didn't know I had, was told she was a monster, but she turns out to be the most beautiful woman I've met. So… to say I'm confused is probably the only word I can use to describe how I am."

Taking another sip of my coffee, I just stare out the window. "On top of all of that, I don't even know how to cope with all of this." I wave my arm around the room. "You have no idea where I've come from, Mason. My world was so different. I'm scared if I let my guard down and then someone comes along and pulls the rug out from under me again, it might be the final straw. Do I want to live in this world and see my kids never know the poverty and hurt I've suffered? Absolutely. But I can't live here and sponge off Paige for the rest of my life. I need to take care of my family, that's my job, and I don't want them getting used to this and then when I can't give them the same, they resent me. Those two are all I have in this world. They are all I live for." Trying to sort my thoughts, I just sit silently for a few moments.

"That's a lot of worries for such a small set of shoulders to carry. But I have a feeling there's more you need to get out." He sits patiently.

"Ughh, you are worse than my friend Anna from the diner. She knew when I was hiding something and wouldn't give up until she got it out of me." I shift my legs to stop the pins and needles starting in my feet.

"Can't wait to meet her one day then." Mason chuckles quietly. "So, spill it. The more that's out, the lighter everything feels. Take it from me. I have plenty of experience with holding things in."

"Lex," I say straight out. I wish I could take it back, but it's too late and I've said it now.

Again, he chuckles.

"Mhmm, go on. Now we're getting somewhere."

I swat his arm. "It's not funny."

"Oh, from where I'm sitting it's hilarious." Smugly he places his cup on the table.

"You're so annoying. How does Paige put up with you?" Placing my empty cup next to his, I relax back into my seat.

"I'm so annoying that I don't give her a choice, but that's a story for another time. I'm sure she'd be happy to tell you how persistent I can be. Now what about Lex?"

Why did I even open my mouth? This was supposed to just stay in my head, for nobody but me.

"I don't know. He just appears from nowhere, wanting to be my knight in shining armor, turns up with everything he thought I needed. Sleeps on the couch so I feel safe, makes me feel that perhaps there are nice men in this world when I had given up on that a long time ago. I know I'm just someone he feels sorry for, I get it. But I don't know what the hell to think about the way I feel around him, the way he calms me. And to top it off, why does he have to be so goddamn hot." Oh god, I slap my hand over my mouth. I can't believe I said that out loud, and to Mason who is Lex's best friend.

"Oh god, Mason, please don't…shit, I'm such an idiot. Just please don't repeat any of that and pretend I didn't say anything." Dropping my head into my hands, I can feel the heat on my cheeks at the embarrassment of just blurting all that out.

"See? I told you it's funny from where I'm sitting. Mia, look at me." I can hear him but I'm not about to look up.

"Mia." I know he won't give up until I do. Slowly I lift my head and feel my cheeks going red again.

"Firstly, your secret is safe with me. Remember, friends just talking. Secondly, you are not an idiot and I can guarantee that Lex is not doing all this because he feels sorry for you. It's far from that. I'll tell you a little secret now too. I have known Lex since we started high school, so a long time. In all the years I've known him, I have never seen him act the way he does around you. He's almost tripping over himself to do things for you, and that has nothing to do with where you've come from or what has happened to you. Do you get my drift?"

I hear what he's saying, but it's not easy to hear.

"Yes, but none of it makes sense," I mumble.

"It usually doesn't. I'll tell you what I told him. That your life is complicated, and while you work on taking back control of it, everything else will take a back seat. You need friends in your corner, and he is a loyal one who will be there for you no matter what. Let him be that friend. Then when life is more stable, if those feelings you're having, the ones you don't understand and are so unexpected for you at the moment. If they're still there, then explore them further."

Trying to take in everything that he's saying, my head is whirling again with the thought that Lex is as confused as I am about this.

"How could you tell what was in my head?"

"Mia, when you and Lex are in the same room, there are enough sparks flying between you that you could light a bonfire. I know it seems strange that at the worst time in your life, something like this can be happening. But the universe chooses when and who. We are merely along for the ride. So just enjoy it and wherever it may take you both. Whether it be friends or something more." He pauses for a moment. "Now let's backtrack over some of the other points you said before you started blushing like a schoolgirl."

"Oh god, I am never going to live that down, am I?" We both laugh together.

"Not a chance. Welcome to the framily, Mia. Being made fun of is how you know you belong with us. Now I'm getting another coffee and then we are going to continue this chat. How do you take yours?" Mason gets up and heads to the kitchen, leaving me to digest what he just said.

"Umm, white with one sugar, please," I mumble.

Shit.

How the hell am I going to be able to look Lex in the eyes again if he's thinking the same things I am? Surely Mason didn't mean it like that. I mean, there is no way I'm sharing everything I've had going on, when I'm thinking about Lex. The fantasies I had last night about how he looks under those jeans. If his chest is anything to go by, then I might just pass out. Damn, woman, get a hold of yourself. It's been a while since I've been touched, and that's been a good thing. My cravings for sex have never been strong, but what was there has died a long time ago. But I know whatever Lex is hiding would be like nothing I've ever had before, and I'm pretty sure I'd have no idea what to do with it either.

Mason placing my coffee in my hands snaps me out of my fantasy, and we continue to talk about my fears and how trauma can affect a person. Sharing some of his stories of the PTSD he suffers. When he talked about friends in my corner, I know he's going to be one of the most important of them all. He gets me and understands my fears and especially my confusion over where to go from here in my life. Listening to him talk about Paige and how she feels about having me here, I understand a little more that this is not just about me. She needs me close while she deals with everything that has happened to her too.

"So why were you awake at five thirty am, Mason? I mean, if I had a choice, I would have still been asleep, but my body had other ideas."

"Early mornings are normal for me. When I fly, I'm up checking the weather and flight schedules. I'm used to not sleeping much. A habit from my Army days I haven't managed to shake yet. Although since I've been with Paige, she does give me a reason not to get out of bed too early." His smirk tells me exactly what he means.

"Um, I might have just met her, but that's my sister and I do not need to be thinking about that image, thanks." We both can't help it and the laughter is loud. Which of course means the next thing we hear are little quick footsteps running down the hallway.

"Mommy?" Jack calls with a little panic in his voice.

"I'm here, baby. It's okay." He runs to me and crawls up into my lap and snuggles in for a cuddle. There's something so special about those early-morning hugs from your kids. They're still warm from the bed, quiet, and only just waking up. Probably the only time that Jack is this quiet in the whole day.

"Morning, bud. Did you sleep well?" Mason asks as Jack just nods up and down.

We all sit quietly for a few minutes, and then like a switch, Jack is awake, and the day begins. Mason takes him upstairs to jump on Paige to wake her up, while I get Kayla up and ready for the day.

We're just all sitting down to breakfast that Mason and Jack have cooked for us when the elevator opens, and boxes start sliding out of it across the floor before I can even see a person. Mason doesn't look shocked or worried, so I'm guessing he knows what's going on. Paige stands and starts walking across a bit tentatively.

"Hello?" Her voice is a little wobbly.

"Morning, Paige. Can you grab this one for me?" Just like that, I look at Mason and give him the dagger look to say you could have warned me. To which I get a sly smile, a wink, and he places the extra plate on the table for breakfast. Bastard knew he was coming and knew I would panic if had warning. In such a short time, I've got a feeling he knows me better than I thought.

"Lex, what have you done now?" Paige says as the last of the boxes slides out of the elevator, and he stands up straight looking very proud of himself. Hearing Lex's name, Jack takes off running across the room.

"Lex!" he yells as he launches himself at Lex, and thank god he was ready and catches him.

"How's my star man this morning?" That's all it takes for Jack to start talking flat-out, telling him about everything from yesterday after he left. I stand with Kayla in my arms and walk towards them.

"Hi, Lex," I manage to say without stuttering.

The way he looks at me, I can see that everything that Mason said is true. There is so much more than friendship behind those eyes.

I'm just not sure that I can ever manage to be anything more than this.

"How are my two favorite girls this morning?" He steps forward and taps Kayla on the nose with his finger which has her giggling and her hands flapping up and down.

What is it about Lex that my kids gravitate to?

Maybe it's not just me that senses the good in him.

I have a feeling he's casting a spell on all of us.

"What, I'm not your favorite girl anymore?" Paige pretends to be offended with her hands on her hips, and we all laugh.

"Well, obviously," Lex replies as he puts Jack down. "Now, are you going to help me get the highchair out, Jack, so Mom can eat her breakfast in peace and not have to hang on to Kayla the whole time?" Jack is already bouncing at the thought of more presents.

"No, Lex, not more. You have to stop. I can't repay you for this." Paige just takes Kayla from me and heads back to the table. Lex takes a step closer so he's by my side.

"Mia, for me this is nothing. Please, it's the only way I know how to help without smothering you," he says in nothing more than a whisper.

"Lex, if this isn't smothering then I'd hate to see what is." I let out a little giggle.

"I'm almost scared to think that too." He laughs a little and looks at me with a bit more confidence now.

"Thank you. One day I'll be able to show you how grateful I am."

"I can't wait," he says as he turns and starts pulling open the box with Jack.

With his fitted black jeans and bent over in front of me, I need to walk away before the drool starts running down my chin.

I thought his arms and chest were hot.

That ass needs a warning sign.

There is something to be said for a man in a perfect-fitting pair of jeans.

Not that I'm saying a word, but the view from the front-row seats is just perfect.

I may not become anything more than friends with Lex, but that won't stop me from admiring the masterpiece in front of me.

Chapter Ten

LEX

I know I should've waited a day before I showed up again, but I couldn't. I mean, Mia needs the highchair and stroller to take the pressure off her. Well, that's what I tell myself as we sit here eating breakfast together.

Kayla looks pretty pleased with herself and is playing in the mess she made with her food on the tray of the highchair. I had no idea that kids make such a mess when they eat. Thinking of my mother, I can't imagine her coping with this kind of thing when I was a baby. Trying to remember back, I actually can't picture her ever feeding me when I was younger. Most of my meals were at the table in the kitchen with Nanny Sue. The only time I ate with my parents was when there were guests there. Probably so she could parade me like the puppet I was.

I watch Mia as she takes it all in her stride and doesn't seem stressed at the mess one little bit. I love that the kids can just be normal, and there's no pressure to be perfect. The conversation flows freely, and we all sit for a while, no one in a rush to move.

"Just letting you both know that I have talked to Mason, and I'm working from home this week. No flying for meetings. Mason will have to work, though, as there are a few trips my vice president can attend for me. Then he has a special trip at the end of the week to take one of the kids he mentors, Leroy, for a job interview. I promised we would get him there, but Mason can take the plane without me." She talks about her travel like it's an everyday occurrence.

I sit there watching Mia looking stunned. Just like that. She has a plane and it just flies across the country for some teenager's job interview.

"It's okay. That's her normal life. You'll get used to it," I say to her quietly as Paige answers a question Jack asked about the plane.

"Oh god, I just can't even comprehend this," Mia mumbles under her breath.

"Don't let it worry you. One step at a time. I've got you," I say and then join back into the conversation to try to keep things a little normal. Watching Mia, it's like reading her mind, and I know exactly when she starts freaking out. Just when she thinks she's getting a bit of a handle on everything, then something else makes her feel so out of reach of this type of life.

"So, Ashton will be around this week when Mason isn't here," Paige goes on. "He's going to come tomorrow morning, and we can all talk before Mason leaves for the day. But let's worry about that then. What about if we take the kids for a walk to the park today?" Mia still looks stunned at everything she has just said. I'm sure Paige is so used to running a business, that without meaning to, she is micromanaging Mia too. I don't know how she feels about it, but like most things at the moment, I think she's just going along with everything. I plan on talking to Paige later about it.

"Breathe," I whisper from beside her. I hear her take in a deep breath and let it out slowly.

"Can we, Mommy? I want to go to the park!" Jack jumps up and down.

"Sure, little man. Let's clean up first." He jumps up high in excitement.

"We can do that," Paige says.

"No," Mia says, and it sounds a little snappy. "I mean, no, we can do it. Jack has to learn to help too. Right, Jack? You know how to pick up your toys while I wash the dishes. Don't you?" Her voice is a little coarse, and I know she's feeling closed-in again.

"Yes, I'm the best helper." He runs over to the few toys that are on the floor where he was playing earlier.

I stand up quickly, so no one has time to question it. "I'll help Mia if you two want to help Jack and unpack the stroller from the box, and I'll take Kayla and clean her up."

"Okay, sounds good." Mason looks at me and gives me a chin lift. I think he can see Mia's struggling too.

Stacking the plates, I start carrying the dishes to the kitchen where Mia is trying to tidy. I don't speak, I just let her do it her way. Placing the plates on the counter, I just continue to bring things to her. Watching her work, I wonder if she doesn't need to take up boxing for a sport. There's a lot of pent-up anger in there. I don't think it's directed at Paige, but she's lighting the fuse without even realizing it. On my last trip into the kitchen, I see Mia slowing a little and her shoulders not so tense.

Coming up beside her at the sink, I just stand there until she looks at me. I don't step into her space until she acknowledges me there.

"You know she doesn't mean it. Actually, she is completely oblivious to her controlling nature. It's just who she is. Everything she's doing and saying comes from a good place."

Mia just lets out a big sigh and leans with her hands on the edge of the sink. "She makes a perfect bossy older sister." She looks at me and rolls her eyes.

"That she does." I agree totally but don't want to make it worse.

"I've being doing this on my own for a long time. I don't need her to take over. I know that makes me sound ungrateful."

"Not at all. I understand what you're saying, Mia. It'll take time to get to know each other. But don't feel you have to agree with everything Paige says. You get a say too. Don't be afraid to have a voice here. Remember what I said. You're reclaiming your life, and I will back you no matter what. Now, let's finish up here and get out in the fresh air and some sunshine. See if we can wear Jack out a bit for you. I never knew kids his age had so much energy. You mothers deserve a medal. Seriously!" I need to pull Mia out of her head and thinking about something else. I knew the thought of the kids would help.

"You haven't seen him at his best, or should I say worst yet. You think that's hyper, wait until he's full of sugar, that's what I call extreme parenting. I'll call you over to help on those days." She starts to laugh at the face I pull just thinking of Jack any crazier than I've seen so far.

"Um, not sure I'll be the man for the job with my zero experience with kids, but hey, I'll give it a go. I mean, how hard can it be, right? He's four years old. Surely a grown man can manage him." I stand and clench my fists and arm muscles. Bringing them in front of me, making a tough-guy pose like a muscle man.

"Oh, you just keep telling yourself that. Aren't you the man who relied on said four-year-old to help put up the crib?"

I love listening to her giggle. "I'm never going to live that down, am I?"

"Not a chance," she replies as we both head over to where the others are again being shown up by Jack. Man, we all need to get our act together on the fine art of opening and closing baby items. They should run a class on this crap, so we don't look so stupid.

After several attempts from the useless adults in the room, Mia figured out the stroller and we finally headed out for the morning. She makes this parenting look so effortless when it really would freak the hell out of me, every single second of the day.

The rest of the morning flew past, and I knew I needed to give them all space again. As much as I wanted to be there, it'll crowd Mia if I spend every minute of the day with them.

It's Sunday night and I'm sitting on my balcony just going over the day and how we finally got Paige to understand how Mia is feeling, while Mia was off playing with the kids. Well maybe, let's see how she handles the next few days.

I don't feel like a drink tonight, so I'm just sitting with an iced tea in my hand when my phone chimes. Expecting it to be one of the boys, I'm shocked when I see it's from my father.

Father: *Alexander. You need to contact your mother and apologize. She is upset at your outburst!*

"Are you fucking kidding me!" I yell to no one in particular. How dare he send me a message like that. Looking at the message I see the prior message was sent to me on my birthday. My once-a-year text message. Normally he would call me or send me an email.

I can't believe he thought this was an acceptable way to talk to me after what happened. The respect I have for my father is getting smaller every day. I have never had any interaction with friends with children to understand the relationship between a parent and a child. Grayson and Bella's dad, Milton, has been the closest role model I've had to compare my own parents' behavior, against what's normal. I always knew they were so far on the other end of the spectrum to Milton, but the last few days watching Mia with her kids. It makes so much sense now.

I'm a man who has grown up and never once told someone I love them.

How fucked up is that?

Not even my own parents have heard those words from me.

Who lives a life like that?

Part of my heart started beating a little more today just watching Jack being pushed on the swing by his mother. The higher he went the louder he laughed, which had Mia giggling with him. Their happiness connected them together. Then later when he was running and Mason was chasing him, he fell on the grass and scared himself. Mia picked him up, brushed off the grass and leaves. Kissed him on the forehead, wiped away the tears, and gave him a hug. That's all I ever longed for.

Some sort of affection from my parents.

Now that I have finally stood up and told them to back off, my father chooses after thirty-five years to try to be the man I craved my whole life to look up to.

Fuck that!

I want to reply and tell him to fuck off, but I can't. Respect has been ingrained in me from before I can ever remember. Even to respect people who don't deserve it.

Pity my parents knew how to preach it to me, but not how to practice it.

Now I'm up pacing the balcony. All the relaxed feelings I had have left my body, and I'm ready to release my pent-up anger. It's circulating through my limbs and raising my blood pressure. I can hear the blood thundering through my body. I know it's a mixture of anger and sadness that I don't know how to control. I don't normally get this worked up unless it's in the courtroom.

Stopping dead in the middle of my pacing, the thought hits me like a lead weight. I'm such an awful man.

Fuck, poor Jacinta.

I used her.

I fucked my anger and frustration out with her. She never said no when I messaged her, just like I could never seem to turn her down when she called on me for the same reason.

If this happened last week, my fingers wouldn't have hesitated to phone her. I can't even call it a booty call, because I don't think it even had that amount of emotion. It's closer to hate sex. Not hating her but hating whatever had pissed me off. It became the addiction of choice for both of us. How did I get to the point of hard, fast, pounding sex with a beautiful woman, and there was absolutely no emotion involved? Not even the slightest ounce. The boys know me more than anyone in my life, yet they don't know this part of me. I'm ashamed to even admit it to myself.

Pacing again, I take some comfort that I wasn't the only one in this fuck fest. Jacinta used me as much as I used her. If the truth be known, she was using me far more than I realized. I became the pawn for the two power-hungry women. Making sure they got what they wanted to make the play in their societal climb.

I feel sick thinking about it.

My anger is subsiding slightly to one of disgust.

Disgust at my actions, but more so at the way they treated me, and sadly I let them.

Deep down I knew what they were doing, I just didn't want to admit it to myself. That and I needed to find the strength to make a conscious choice to take control of my own life direction. Part of the reason was I never wanted to admit a weakness. All my life, I wanted to make sure I never became like my father and yet that was exactly where I was headed.

Not now! Not ever!

So much has changed in the last week. It's like someone has told the universe they need to shake things up around me.

My anger might have subsided slightly, but my cock is still solid as a rock and he's telling me it's time for that release.

Nope, not happening. You can suffer, buddy. Time to find a new way of getting rid of our frustration.

Where I didn't feel like a drink earlier, now I'm busy slamming down a scotch and thinking about a refill. Hearing my phone chime and thinking it's my father again, I'm about to throw it off the balcony completely before I see it's Paige. I grab it in a panic, thinking that something is wrong with Mia or the kids.

Opening the message, a warm sense of calmness and an odd feeling of happiness I'm not used to washes through me.

Paige: Hi. I thought you might like to see some of these from today xx

What is it with girls and xx on every message? I mean, it's not like she wants to kiss me.

Scrolling down the message, pictures of Mia and the kids at the park with me today pop up. I don't feel like I have a right to these photos, but I already know I will treasure them. There are several as I scroll down. Each one making me smile harder. Until I get to the last one.

A vision of an angel.

The sunlight shining through her light brown hair, flowing in the light breeze. She is totally unaware of the photo being taken. The moment captures her perfectly laughing at something as she's looking off to the side. The stress on her face that we normally see is completely missing and her smile lights up her face, and my world.

Everything from earlier in the night is not worth the energy spent on it.

This beautiful woman is where I need to be. Standing right beside her.

Finding the way to make that smile never leave her face.

If only Mia could see how bright her future is. Once we clear the darkness she will never look back.

Standing for god knows how long just staring at her, I save this image to my phone. I never want to lose that first glimmer of a better life ahead. For both of us.

Lex: Thanks, Paige. Perfect shots of great memories being made.

I want to say so much more, but I can't. For the time being I need to stay in the background. Be the friend to Mia that I hope she will lean on. Be the lawyer she needs to get through all this mess. Then hopefully when we come out the other side, I'll be something more.

Stripping off my clothes and crawling into my bed for the night, I can still feel that frustration in my cock, but I chuckle to myself, turning off the lamp. I know this time it's not for the same reason as when I felt the intense anger earlier and the need to fuck it out of me.

This pain is just as bad but in a far better situation. For the first time ever I'm drifting off to sleep thinking about a woman who will always mean more to me than a quick fuck. She only deserves to be treasured like a sweet angel.

I rub my hand over my cock trying to get Mason's voice out of my head. *'Enjoy the blue balls, man'* with the stupid glint in his eye.

I'm not going to be that guy that lies here and jerks off to a woman he hardly knows while looking at a picture of her. That's just got weirdo written all over it. Yet the more I rub over my cock, the more I want to...badly.

Suck it up and show restraint, I tell myself, rolling over to my side and leaving my phone on the bedside table. It's not my fault that Mia is still on the screen and staring at me while I tell myself to close my eyes and sleep. A pure coincidence, of course. Like the hand that keeps reaching out to touch the screen, so it doesn't close to dark.

Eventually after more taps on the screen than I can admit, I feel sleep claiming me and my eyes closing, the room going dark and the vision of my angel burnt in my memory and now walking in my dreams.

"I promise I will never hurt you, beautiful. I have waited a lifetime for you, nothing is going to ruin this. I just want you to touch me and tell me it's okay to touch you. We can take our time."

Her pupils are dilated, and I know she feels it too. "Yes," she whispers.

I lie to the side of Mia so I can't crowd her. As much I want to lay her out and kiss every inch of her body. I know I would start in the arch of her foot and then slowly drag my tongue up the inside of her leg. I feel her quivering under my hand that is holding her legs apart, ready for me.

I just need a taste, just one. I know it will be like heaven.

Not being able to stay away, I shift in between her thighs and I'm now acting out my fantasy.

"Lex," her sweet voice trembles as I get closer to her sex with my mouth.

"Mmm," I murmur from her leg, just to the right of her pussy.

I don't want her to feel embarrassed that it's too much. "Say the word and we stop, baby," I whisper.

"No. I need this, and I need it from you. Show me how it feels to be touched by a real man without fear."

Feeling ten feet tall, I swipe my tongue up the center of her pussy.

Her body rises off the bed as I work her over and continue the orgasm building. She needs to know we only go as far as she wants.

Her hands on the back of my head, I can feel her nails starting to dig into my scalp. She's quiet, and I need to know she trusts me.

I lift my eyes to watch her.

Her head back, eyes closed, cheeks flushed and mouth open as she's close to letting go.

I can feel my cock straining against the bed under me.

I raise up onto my knees, not taking my mouth off her for one moment. Small moans are coming from Mia the closer to the edge she gets.

Dropping my hand to my cock, I run my thumb across the head to take the pre-cum down over my skin. The more she rides my mouth the harder I stroke myself.

Fuck, she needs to come because I can't hold on much longer.

Taking her clit in my teeth and giving it a little bite and then sucking it strongly, she explodes screaming my name.

The most beautiful thing that I've ever heard, my name yelled in ecstasy.

I'm so close and just want relief. I wish it was her mouth or hands on me, but I can't stop. I need to let go and stop that stupid alarm that's taking away the sounds of her moans.

I want to keep hearing her voice, it's my siren.

Oh fuck, my balls tightening is the relief I need.

Feeling the come jerking from my cock and all over…

"Fuck," I groan as I feel the come shooting all over my stomach.

Shit, I've been jerking off in my sleep.

What the fuck!

I've never done that before, like ever. Not even as a teenager. Holy shit.

Laying my head back on the pillow, I stare at the ceiling while my breathing slows down. I reach out with my hand to hit my phone and shut that alarm up.

Trying to go back to my dream, I know I want to finish what I started. But feeling yucky with this all over me, I climb out of bed and turn on the shower. Stepping in and standing under the hot streams of water, I feel so disgusted in myself. How could I treat Mia like that? Such disrespect. I've known her a few days and I'm using dreams of her naked to get myself off.

It was all that anger last night that I didn't deal with.

That's what it must be!

Nothing to do with the beautiful picture I fell asleep with tattooed on my brain. Or the fact that every moment I spend with her she's making me feel emotions I have never dealt with before.

My world is never like this. I don't do this fuzzy, fluffy shit. Hence why I haven't had a serious relationship in my life. Besides, no one was ever good enough in my mother's opinion, although to be honest, no one ever caught my eye anyway.

Not like Mia.

From the moment I saw her she had me.

There is just something about her. I can't shake it. At first, I thought it was that she needs me. But I'm not stupid enough to ignore that there's more.

What that more is, I have no fucking idea.

All I know is that felt like the best sex I'd had, and it wasn't even real. I'm struggling to imagine what the real thing would be like.

Standing in the shower for a few minutes and guilt hanging over my head, I know I have to keep my horny cock under control. Mia is a long way from being ready for any sort of relationship. She does not need me making her feel uncomfortable around me.

Friends!

I need to be the friend she can rely on.

Isn't that what good relationships are built on? A great friendship?

Well, ours is about to be the greatest friendship of all time.

One I could write a book on!

"Here is your Monday morning pick-me-up. Now tell me what the hell all the emails I received yesterday are about. You are a criminal lawyer. Why are we lodging restraining orders, divorce papers, and custody orders?" Greta smirks as she places my coffee on my desk.

"Before that crazy head of yours creates a backstory like one of those drama series you keep binge watching, Mia is Paige's sister. Paige is Mason's girlfriend." She sits looking at me like there's more gossip. "I am helping a friend, that's it. Now, can we get on with this before they get here? We have a busy day and I need this taken care of and out of the way." I take that sip of caffeine that my body is craving.

"Okay, then why do you sound all wound up about it?" Greta leans down and grabs her laptop from her bag.

"Sit back and listen and then you might understand. This woman has been to hell and back. I'm putting a stop to that starting today. Start taking notes."

Greta senses my seriousness right away and we spend the next hour getting everything in place. Then we move on to the other work that we already had on the schedule for this morning and smash through it to free up some of the time that I need. Delegating a to-do list to Greta, I work on some case notes for a court case later in the week. Trying to distract myself.

The phone on my desk startles me a little as it starts ringing.

"Yes, Theresa."

"Your appointment Mia Kennedy is here, along with Mason and a few others. Do you want to use the conference room?" I can hear the confusion in her voice.

We are using her maiden name when we list her for any legal matters. That was her choice. She doesn't want to be known as Mia Walker anymore.

"Thank you, I'll be using both, my office for the meeting and the conference room for the kids. On my way." I know Mia is not ready to be too far from the kids yet. Hence why they're here.

Standing and buttoning my suit jacket, I take a deep breath.

Now walk out there and act like a true professional to your new client and don't show her any indication that you were jerking off to her this morning. Not once but twice. That one in the shower was to make sure I was completely done.

Well, that's what I'm telling myself anyway.

Walking down the corridor I can hear a little voice trying to whisper, just not very successfully. Turning the corner into reception I feel my nerves rattle at seeing Mia sitting there fussing with Kayla in the stroller.

Her eyes widen as Jack jumps from Mason's lap.

"Lex!" he yells as he runs to me and jumps at me like he has every time I've seen him.

"Jack," Mia quietly tries to scold him.

"It's okay," I mouth to her.

"Hey, buddy. Have you been a good boy this morning?"

"Yep. You smell funny and you look funny. Why do you have one of these on? They look dumb." He grabs hold of my tie, and I can't help but laugh. Mia is looking down into her hands, completely embarrassed.

"I'll let you in on a big-boy secret. They are dumb, but some people think they're important. Now let's get you settled with a donut from the breakroom so I can talk to Mommy. Is that okay?" Like he's going to turn down a donut. It's not something we usually have, but I made sure Greta had a couple ready for Jack's arrival.

"There better be a donut for me too?" Mason says as he walks forward and shakes my hand. Jack just giggles at Mason being silly.

"Right, let's get this show on the road. Follow me."

Walking to the conference room, Jack has not stopped talking. There is so much to see for a little boy. Everything is new and exciting.

Getting them settled in, I turn to Mia. "You ready to come with me?"

"I'm coming too. Mason will watch the kids." Paige stands.

"Umm, I …"

Reading between the lines, I step in. "I think it's better if you stay here with Mason. Mia would feel more comfortable. I mean, I'm not sure I'd trust him with my pet dog," I say, trying to break the moment.

"You don't own a dog," Mason replies.

"Wow, you're smarter than I thought."

Paige is torn and I can see she wants to be in both places.

"We'll be back soon. Message me if you need us." I don't give either Paige or Mia time to think about it.

Holding my hand out to signal for Mia to step through the door, she looks up at me with a scared look.

This is a huge step. Come on, Mia, take this first move towards the future.

"I've got you," I whisper softly.

Lovable Lawyer

Her eyes hold my gaze, she takes a deep breath, and then steps through the door.

My heart swells a bit.

The first sign of a little trust.

Now let's keep building on that.

Chapter Eleven

MIA

I stand looking through the doorway and then back at Lex.
I don't think he understands how big a thing this is for me to leave my kids here.

Alone.

Without me.

I know they aren't really alone, but I'm not going to be here with them.

His eyes are telling me to trust him, and more importantly, to trust Paige and Mason. I'm so torn in my decision. But I know if I don't do this then I will be running for the rest of my life, and I'm sick of it. I want to give my kids a stable place to live. One with no fear and a house they can make memories to tell their own kids about one day.

A home.

I take one last look back at the kids, who are too busy being entertained by Mason. I do what I need to do for them and for me. I walk out of the room and towards Lex's office.

I take a seat in the black leather chair that Lex guides me to. It's not at the desk but a couch that sits along the wall. Looking towards the view out the window. What is it about rich people? They always have these big windows with the breathtaking view. All I see is a place for lots of dirty handprints and hours of relentless cleaning for me. I doubt Lex has ever had any children in this office.

"Can I get you a coffee or water?" Lex stands next to his desk, waiting for my answer.

"Umm a coffee would be great, thank you. I have a feeling I'm going to need it."

He just smiles while picking up his phone. "Theresa, can you bring in two coffees and some water, please?" He stops to listen for a moment. "No, I don't care who it is. I'm not taking any calls. And can you also let Greta know that Mia is here whenever she's ready with the papers? No rush. Thank you."

I watch him work, noticing that he has a presence about him. It's not arrogance or trying to impress me. He just exudes confidence in his domain.

"How are you feeling, Mia?" Lex takes a seat beside me but leaves a gap between us like he usually does.

"I'm okay," I reply, not wanting to give too much away.

"Right, so that's the answer you will give anyone who politely asks you. Now let's hear the answer you tell me." His smile is so welcoming and soft. He just makes me want to smile and that never happens for me.

"How do you do that?" I can't help but ask.

"Do what?" Like he has no idea.

"Just talk and your words always make me feel calmer. I don't get it. I don't even know you." I can't help myself, words are just coming out of my mouth which I'm sure make me sound like a crazy woman.

"I'm glad to hear that." His confident smile gets a little bigger. "You might not know me, but I would like us to be friends and get to know each other better. I enjoy your company, but I think you already know that." I'm not sure how to answer that. "I want to be your go-to man for anything you need. I mean anything. Whether it's to do with legal things or absolutely anything in your personal life."

"But why? I don't understand why you're being so nice to me. What do you want in return?" My insecurities are pouring out of me. I'm anxious about the kids and being away from them. I don't want to be this woman, yet here I am saying all the things that should be staying in my head.

"Mia. Never will I expect anything from you in return for friendship or any legal work I do for you. Do you understand me?" His smile is gone and he's looking at me so seriously.

I'm kicking myself for saying anything. I've upset him and that wasn't my intention. I just have never had a man do anything nice for me and not be after something.

"I'm sorry, I didn't…" I'm stumbling over my words

"Don't. Mia, don't you apologize to me. You have nothing to apologize for. I just want you to feel comfortable with me. That's what friendship is. Being able to be ourselves and not having to worry about being someone else that other people expect us to be." Lex runs his hand over his beard, looking like he's frustrated.

"You're looking at me like you're still confused?" he says.

"My whole life is confusing. But yeah, I am? I'm not used to having friends I can trust, especially men. I've learned to stay away from them and stick to myself. But you're different and I don't know why. My head is still trying to work it all out." Leaning back into the couch, I let my head fall backwards to lay on it. Looking at his office ceiling is easier than at him.

"That's totally understandable, Mia. That's why I'm here offering friendship. We need to build up your trust in me and the others. I know it won't happen overnight, but I'm hoping it will happen." He pauses then his voice becomes softer and gentler. "Do you feel it? That something extra between us?" Hearing the uncertainty in his words, I can't ignore him, it wouldn't be fair.

I slowly lift my head and sit up straighter.

Taking a deep breath, I can feel my palms sweating. He's just waiting for me to talk. I want the words to come out but I'm struggling with my answer.

"It's okay if you don't…"

"No, it's not that. I don't know what it is, I can't tell you how I feel. All I know is when you're near me, I feel safe and my heart slows down. My chest doesn't feel so tight. I've never felt that before. In the two days you've known me, you have seen more of my soul by looking past my armor, than any person in my life. I don't know how you do it, but you seem to know my inner thoughts and fix things before I can even voice them. Paige is my DNA, yet you read me better than she does which makes no sense." Stopping, I try to find the right words. "So, if that is what *'something extra'* feels like, then yeah, I'm feeling overwhelmed by it." I can feel my cheeks blushing and want to take back everything I just said. I can't seem to keep my words tucked inside where they're safe when Lex is around me. He manages to get me speaking about emotions I'm not ready to share.

"That's all I need to know. I never want you overwhelmed, that's why I'm offering my friendship. That's all you're ready for. One day maybe you'll be ready for something more, but if not, then we'll be great friends and that's a gift for both of us. Does that sound like a plan, something you can feel comfortable with?"

A moment ago, more words than I wanted left my mouth, yet right now I can't find one to answer him. Nodding my head, he just smiles that handsome smile. One I fantasize is just for me.

The knock on the door breaks the moment, thank god. I'm not sure I could have said what I needed to. Lex calls enter and the door opens to his secretary carrying a tray with our coffees, some water, and a plate with a selection of pastries and fruit. Enough on the plate to feed ten people, but I have a feeling that is Lex's way with everything. He doesn't seem to know what's a normal limit with anything. I'm starting to see he is a man of excess, but in a good way. Well, I hope anyway.

"Thank you, Theresa." Lex stands, taking the tray from her and sitting it down on the table in front of us.

"You're welcome, Lex. Greta said she'll be another fifteen or so minutes. Also, Ms. Nordick asked me to let you know she was not happy you refused to take her call." Theresa rolling her eyes at him lets me know there's more to that story.

"Well, she'll get over it, won't she. Thanks, like I said I'm not to be disturbed by anyone, please. Can you also check on Mason and Paige every so often to see if they need anything or help with the kids, please? You have little ones. Those two in there are probably being controlled by the smartest person in the boardroom and that'll the four-year-old, Jack."

I can't help myself, I start laughing along with both of them. Because I know it's true. Jack will be running rings around his auntie.

Shit…his auntie. My kids having an auntie is hard to get used to.

"No problems, Lex. Don't worry, Ms. Kennedy, I have a three- and five-year-old. I can handle this. I know what they're like and I'll rescue them if needed." I like Theresa. She seems down to earth and Lex obviously trusts her.

"Mia, please call me Mia, and thank you. I appreciate that. But if they get to be too much please come and get me. I don't want them upsetting people or anyone getting cranky with them." I'm still feeling nervous they aren't with me. I'm struggling not to worry that someone will start yelling at them or scare them.

"Mia, have you seen Mason?" Teresa says with a laugh. "No one is going to say a word to those kids while their personal bodyguard is with them. That man could make any of the men in this office melt into a puddle just by giving them the look, I'm sure." Theresa giggles as Lex clears his throat. "Oh, of course, except Lex. He's not a wimp like the rest of them," she clarifies.

"Thank you, now you can go and take your smart comments with you." Waving his hand at Theresa, Lex dismisses her as she shuts the door, giggling to herself.

"Ignore the wimp comment, but she's right. No one will even look sideways at the kids while Mason is with them. So, relax." He hands me my coffee after making it just how I like it.

"How do you know how I take my coffee?" I ask, taking the first sip.

"I pay attention, Mia. Not much gets past me. Now let's get all this yucky crap out of the way so I don't keep you from the kids for very long. Although I could sit and talk to you all day, I know that's not possible for either of us. I'm in court this afternoon and you have lots to figure out today too, I'm sure."

"In case I forget to say it later. Thank you. For everything. Just thank you." I can feel tears building, but this is not the place. Lex sees it too.

"You don't need to thank me. I'm happy to help, but before we move on, I just want to clear one thing up because I know you're thinking it. I'm not doing this because I feel sorry for you, or because I think it's the right thing to do out of some moral value. I'm helping you because I want to. Simple as that. Not because Paige or Mason asked me, not because you need me. Because I want to. I like you, Mia. From the moment you came running into my arms out that door. Something in my universe shifted. Something good. So never doubt why I'm here. It's for you." He pauses as the tears I was trying to hide are now running down my face.

"I'm here for *you*, beautiful." His voice is strong and determined to make me understand.

No one has ever been here for me.

"Please don't cry, it kills me seeing your tears." I feel his hand take mine and squeeze it. It's almost like he's squeezing my heart. Why does his hand on mine feel so right when every other man makes me cringe away with the slightest touch?

Reaching into his jacket pocket, he hands me a crisp white handkerchief.

"Let's wipe your tears away. We are here to make things better, not make you cry. Otherwise I'll have Mason in here ready to beat the crap out of me, and I'm pretty sure I wouldn't want to upset Paige either. She is one tough lady." Once again, he has me giggling in between the tears that are starting to subside.

It's a good feeling.

"You could be right." Taking a deep breath, I wipe my eyes. I'm ready. "Okay. Let's do it. I've got this." Trying to prep myself for what is about to happen.

"Absolutely you've got this. Now I need to run through several things, so let's start with Bent and what happened with him. Let's start at the beginning."

Pulling his notepad off the coffee table, Lex starts to take his notes as I retell my story. He knows most of it from the last few days. What I told the police, what Mason and Ashton shared on how it went down. Then there are the talks I've had with them all, about how I met Bent and came to be in Chicago. I try to remember every little detail of the conversations, what he did when we met up, and everything that happened each time he visited the apartment. I'm already feeling drained and this isn't even the worst conversation we'll have today.

"That's a really good start, Mia. I have a detailed timeline to prepare case notes on. Once I speak to the detectives about the charges and what will be needed, we can go further with this part." Lex scribbles something else down.

"Do you need a break, or need to see the kids?" he asks just as there's a knock at the door.

Lex doesn't rush me and waits for my answer before attending to whoever is after him.

"No, I'm okay. I'd rather keep going if that's okay. If I go to the kids and leave again, it might upset them. Can we call Mason, though, and just check on them?" I try to find my phone in my little handbag Paige gave me to use.

"Here, use mine." Lex passes me his phone and it's already dialing.

"No, I haven't lost them yet and there's no broken bones." Mason's voice comes down the phone, and in the background I can hear Jack laughing with Paige.

"Well, I'm really glad about that," I answer, shocking him I'm sure.

"Shit, sorry, Mia, I thought it was Lex. I'm just joking. I promise they're fine. Please don't worry." His panicking voice just makes me smile.

"It's okay, Mason, I believe you. Just keep it that way, please. I don't want to have to shoot you when we only just met," I fire back at him.

"Oh, you've got sass and I like it. Keep it coming, Mia. I'm all for a good joke. But how about I be the only one carrying a gun in this friendship. Deal?" He laughs at me.

"Deal. Okay, we'll keep going."

"Take your time. We're fine here."

"Thanks, Mason." Hanging up the phone, I look up to see Lex standing at his desk going through his papers with a stunning lady. They're standing very close and obviously comfortable in each other's space.

He looks up realizing I'm not talking anymore.

"Everything alright?" His face is one of concern.

"Yes, they are happy and still playing."

"Perfect. Now, Mia, this is Greta, my assistant junior lawyer. She will be helping us with all your cases, and if for some reason I can't take your call at any time, then talk to Greta and she will help you or get a hold of me if it's urgent." They both walk towards me.

"Lovely to meet you, Mia. Lex has been filling me in on everything, so I'm here whenever you need me. I'll give you my mobile number with all the paperwork."

I stand and put my hand out to shake hers. I'm already feeling a little nervous about this paperwork she's talking about. I didn't attend school for long, and although I did well in class, I haven't had to deal with anything legal. In fact, I haven't had to do anything more than writing orders at the diner in years.

"Umm okay, thank you." My voice is a little shaky no matter how strong I'm trying to be.

"Mia, don't worry about anything we give you," Lex says, trying to reassure me. "They're just copies for your records. We will go through every little thing with you. You will completely understand everything we're doing before we have you sign anything. I wouldn't have it any other way. Ask as many questions as you like."

"I appreciate that." His words always seem to be just what I need to hear.

"Thank you, Greta, for all of this. I'll call you back in when we're ready to sign so you can witness the signatures. Unless you would prefer Greta to stay for the next part?" He looks to me and I know what he means. He is giving me the option to have a woman in the room with me if I need it.

"No, I'm okay, and I'm sure Greta has more important things to do."

"No, she doesn't. Nothing is more important than you right now." He glares at me, not happy with what I said. "But if you're fine with just me then let's get started again. Thanks, Greta." Lex dismisses her, and as she's leaving the room, she smiles at me.

"Lovely to meet you, Mia, I have a feeling I'll be seeing a lot more of you." Her smile is then directed at Lex as she closes the door.

"Sassy little thing." He smirks and brings the folders back to where we've been sitting.

"I want you to know at any time if you feel uncomfortable talking about your husband with me and would prefer we stop, you just need to say so. I can leave and Greta can take over. I won't be offended at all."

I don't know how I'm going to feel, and it depends on how much he wants to know. I send a prayer that I can get through this without breaking down. The only person I've ever really talked to about this is Anna and she doesn't know all of the details. She's a smart woman and could piece it together, I'm sure.

"I'd prefer it to be just you." All of a sudden, panic washes through my body. "Oh, god you won't tell Paige and Mason this, will you? What I tell you?" My voice is wobbly with the anxiety I'm feeling. My nails dig into the skin on my hands where they're balled into fists.

"Not a word, Mia. Everything you say to me in here is completely confidential. We will discuss what you want in the court documents as well. Everything about this is your choice. You control the whole procedure. I'm here to guide you and fight for you, but I will never hurt you in the process. My job is to protect you, not make you feel more exposed." Every time he speaks his voice settles me.

"Okay good, because I don't want her to know what happened. She'll get funny about it, I can just tell."

"You mean she'll feel bad because she had the charmed life and you didn't. You can't prevent how she will handle this, Mia. Just like Paige can't tell you how to cope or what to do with your life now. She will want to, and that's okay. But you get to choose. Choice has been taken away from you for far too long. That's why we're here. To give you back control of your life, your choice to do what you want, when you want, where you want. You need to try to let that sink in. Life is for living now."

I just nod my head as I let what he's saying settle in. Lex doesn't say anything further until he can see I'm ready. He is so patient with me.

"Will you help me tell her that?" I whisper. "I'm not strong enough."

His hands are once again are on top of mine, just this time he is slowly pulling them from the tight fists they've been balled in.

"Of course I will. I told you I'm here to help however you need me. From where I'm sitting, I think you underestimate your own strength, though. Just being here, plus your kids in another room. That is a huge deal. You need to be proud of every step you take forward. Not everyone makes it here. Let me assure you. This is huge. Just like taking the kids and running was so brave. You are so strong, and hopefully we can all help you to see that one day. Now let's relax a little and start with how you met Edward and a bit of a backstory on him for me."

My mind is racing. Where do I even start?

"In the beginning I met him at a job I was working at a pizza place. He used to come in at night on his way home. I should have seen it then. He would visit a bar every night and get pizza after. I was too stupid to see it. I just thought he was being sweet and coming to see me each night. Anyway, he kept chatting me up and trying to convince me we should go out sometime. I gave in eventually, and he took me out to a movie and then a bar afterwards. We had fun and he was nice to me. I'd had a few drinks and then he started to let his hands roam. I was okay with that. I'd known him for a while and things seemed to be going well. I didn't have any intention of sleeping with him that night, though. But he kept saying I owed him after being such a prick tease for months. In the end I agreed because I felt bad." I pause to look at Lex, wondering what he's thinking. He's just sitting there taking notes and I decide I need to keep going and not watch him. Otherwise I'll never get through this.

I talk for while, telling him what I could remember of the time before I found out I was pregnant with Jack. I had changed jobs and was working with Anna by that stage and Edward was changing a little. I had spoken to Anna about breaking up with him, but then I found out I was pregnant.

I thought it would be hard to talk, but once I started it's all pouring out.

"So, he got one of his friends who was a celebrant to marry us because he wanted the baby to have his name when it was born. Especially once we found we were having a little boy. There was no white dress or flowers. Just at the friend's place and then to the bar for dinner with a few of his bar buddies." I run my hands through my hair with frustration at myself.

"I was so caught up on my child having parents and not being an orphan like I was I ignored so many warning signs."

"Mia, I don't judge you or your choices." If only I could believe Lex means that.

"The first week after Jack was born, Edward was like the man I met in the beginning. He looked at me like he loved me. He took care of me and changed a few diapers. But then it all stopped. Three weeks after Jack was born, I overheard Edward and his friend talking about him cheating on me with some young woman. I was upset but not as much as I should have been. I realize that now. Deep down I knew he didn't really love me like I think love should be. It hurt me, though, because it reinforced what I always knew. Nobody wanted me and I wasn't really worth loving." So wrapped up in my own head, I can't believe I said that out loud. The sound of Lex letting out a low growl makes me look up. His face is strained, and he's mad, like really mad. He's scaring me a little.

"I can tell you right now, one day I'll prove that wrong." His voice is deep and forceful like he wants me to believe every word.

"Your husband and any man before him are fools. They never took the time to see what they had. I wish I could show you." As he runs his hand over his beard, I'm starting to recognize that is his frustrated tell sign.

"It's okay, Lex, I know what my life is. I accepted that a long time ago."

"Well, you better start rethinking that because it's changing. That I can guarantee."

I can't handle the emotions that are surfacing when he keeps saying things like that to me. I'm not strong enough or ready for anything like what he's promising. I need to move on and just keep pushing forward so I can get to my kids. They are my world. They are all I need.

"Anyway, things got worse. He stayed out longer at night and came home drunk all the time. The words got nastier and the shoving got harder. Especially when I told him no sex or that I wasn't ready to go back to work. To him both of those things were unacceptable answers." I don't want to tell him everything. I just can't say the words or relive the memories. I stand and walk to the window to put some distance between us. Looking over the skyline.

"Do I need to tell you details? I'm not sure I can." I speak to the window and don't look back at him.

"No, Mia, you don't have to do anything you don't want to. But can I ask you some questions and you just answer with a yes or no? Or if it's too much just don't say anything. Is that okay?" His calm voice is back and that settles me a little.

Quietly I reply, "Yes," scared what the questions are going to be.

"Did Edward ever hit you, Mia?" And there it is, the dark side of my life.

"Yes, a few times."

"Did he ever force you to have sex with him?"

"Yes."

"Did he ever hurt the children?"

"No, I protected them." The tears are running down my face now.

"Are you scared for your safety and that of your children?"

"So much." My body is shaking as the tears are tumbling down. I can't take any more of this. My arms wrap around myself. I'm pulling them tighter and tighter, trying to stop. Hearing Lex behind me, I can't seem to move. I know he's close and I should back away, but I'm frozen with fear.

"Mia," he whispers. "As a friend I would normally hug you now, but I won't touch you without your permission. I just want to hold you and share that pain and take away that fear you're feeling. Tell me what I can do for you, what do you need?"

I'm so confused what the hell is going on with him. But just like before, he draws out my truths.

Turning, facing him, and letting him see the mess I really am, I let my walls down.

"To feel safe and wanted." The dam wall breaks, and the big sobs start as I step forward and put my head on his chest, my hands just grabbing on to his coat and hanging on like my life depends on it. I don't know why I'm even touching him because it is so far from where my life is at.

"Can I?" he whispers above me.

"Please…" is all I can get out between sobs.

I've never wanted to be hugged as much as I do in this moment. I feel so weak that I'm clinging to him for strength as his arms slowly come around me and softly wrap me up. He feels like a blanket folding around me and the warmth that comes with it.

"Let it out, Mia. I've got you."

I've got no choice, my body is in control and the emotions have been released. There is no stopping it now. Having to admit to Lex the life I ran from is admitting to myself it happened too.

I'm not sure how long I've been standing here crying but finally the tears run dry. The whole time he didn't let me go or say anything. He just let me take what I needed from him – his strength.

Relaxing a little, my senses kick in and I'm aware of the sound of his heart beating in his chest. The hard chest my forehead is lying on. It's strong and steady. The constant rhythm is peaceful.

I should let go of him and step back, but I just need a few more moments before I see the pity in his eyes. Feel the embarrassment at what has just happened. I wish I had the courage to put my arms around him and cuddle him properly, but I just can't. That's too much. I'm already overwhelmed with him holding me.

Overwhelmed, but for once in a good way.

How can his touch feel so right?

At the worst time in my life, he walks in and makes me feel.

Something I gave up a long time ago.

If you don't feel, you can't hurt.

So why do I want to feel with him?

It's just foolish. Like every other time, it'll be a big mistake.

We come from different worlds, and I'm fooling myself if I even believe I deserve to be in his. He can't see it, but eventually he will.

Then comes the pain.

Just a few more minutes.

Before I let him go and step away.

For his sake as much as mine.

Chapter Twelve

LEX

I've never wanted to kill anyone.
 I mean, you say it sometimes, but never really mean it.
 Today I want to kill Edward Walker.
 Hate is a strong emotion, and it is the most powerful word I'm feeling the more I hear Mia talk.
 I don't want to put her through this, but I need to have the answers to these questions for her case, otherwise I wouldn't ask.
 With each question, her arms are gripping her body harder. Her shoulders are tightening and moving up and down as she can't hold back her emotions. I move to her even though my head is telling me to stay away. I can't stop myself. She needs me, even if she doesn't realize it.
 Not invading her space, I need her to give me permission. I promised her. Everything now is her choice.
 "Mia," I whisper so as not to startle her. "As a friend I would normally hug you now, but I won't touch you without your permission. I just want to hold you and share that pain and take away that

fear you're feeling. Tell me what I can do for you, what do you need?"

Fuck, there is a pain in my chest like I've never felt before.

It's her pain.

Lodged right in my heart.

Let me take it, beautiful. I'll carry the burden.

Come to me, let me be your strength.

Turning and falling into me, her answer absolutely kills me.

I need her to say the words.

I won't be that guy.

"Can I?"

"Please…" It's all I need as I wrap her in my arms. You cry, beautiful. I'm never letting you go. It will take time for you to heal, but I can't walk away from you. I can be patient. I've waited thirty-five years to feel this. However long you need, I'll wait for you to feel the same. In the meantime, I'll keep you sheltered and make sure every day of your life you know how much you are wanted.

I promise her in my silent words.

I'm yours, and when you are ready, I hope you choose to be mine.

Standing there, I let her take as much as she needs from me. But after a while I know I need to step away. Fuck, I don't want to, but I've done far more than I should have. My head is screaming at me to back away and give her space. There are so many reasons that I shouldn't be touching her.

She's fragile, and a stranger touching her is not what she needs.

To have a client wrapped in your arms is totally unprofessional. If any of the boys saw this, they would be telling me what a hypocrite I am about workplace conduct that I've been hounding them about for years.

I promised her I would be her friend until she wanted anything more, yet here I am comforting her like she is so much more than my friend.

I need to pull back. Mia is vulnerable, and I can't risk scaring her away.

"Mia, I'm going to let you go now. Give you a few minutes to breathe."

"No. I can't do this. I'm a mess, look at me." I feel her hands gripping my jacket that little bit tighter.

"I am looking at you, and I like what I see."

"What, a weak, pathetic woman crying all over your suit?" she mumbles into my chest.

"No, I see a strong woman who just needed a moment, and that's okay. One to let it out in a safe place. Plus, you washing my suit just saved me a dry-cleaning bill."

I hear her groan at my bad joke. "You mean I just created a need to get it washed. Nice joke, though."

"You have no idea. My jokes are awesome. Just ask the boys. They get better than that. I'm just warming up."

"You won't beat Jack's." She giggles a little.

"That's a challenge if I ever heard one. I can't have this four-year-old beat me at everything. I'm going to get a complex."

"You give better hugs."

"I'll take that trophy any day of the week." Taking my hand and putting it under her chin, I pull back a small amount while I lift her face to look at me. She's shaking her head trying to say no, but I continue to lift her to look me in the eyes. "Mia, look at me. You've done the hardest part. You told me the truth and admitted what I suspected. It gets easier from here. I promise. Now really look at me. See, I'm not looking at you any differently than when you walked in here, am I?" I keep my voice soft yet determined so she knows that I mean what I say.

"No." She tries to look away again.

"That's because you are the same woman who walked in here ready to move on with her life. I won't lie to you. There's going to be hard days, today is one of them. But each time you get through one of those days it makes you a little stronger to tackle the next tough one. Now, before anyone comes in here and sees you, let's wipe those tear stains, eat a chocolate cookie because they always make you feel better, and have another strong coffee. How does that sound?" Stepping completely away from her now, she stands up a little straighter and blows out a big sigh. I reach for the handkerchief on the couch and hand it to her again. I leave her to wipe her face while I pour another coffee, place a cookie on a plate, and take a seat on the couch. Letting her take her time and come back to me when she's ready.

Sipping my coffee, wishing it was a scotch, I try not to look at her, but her mere presence draws me to her. Forcing myself to look down at my notes, I see I wasn't even writing when she was talking towards the end. Instead there are some very deep grooves in my notepad where I was going backwards and forwards in a line. An angry-looking line. Luckily, I have a good memory and can make notes once she leaves later. Seeing movement out of the corner of my eye, I see her make her way back to me. I stay silent and just continue to sip my coffee as she takes hers and takes a long sip. Still looking a little flustered but a little better, she reaches for the cookie and takes a bite.

"Yep, you're right. Everything feels better with cookies. Can we just keep this secret from Jack? Otherwise he will never eat another vegetable again." And she is coming back to me.

"My lips are sealed. That kid already has me wrapped around his finger. I don't need to give him any more ammunition to get me in trouble." Just letting her settle in with her coffee, I give her a minute before I speak again.

"We don't need to talk about the past anymore today, Mia, but I do need to talk to you about what I propose we do for you. I want to get a restraining order in place for Edward, so he isn't able to come near you or the children. Greta has drawn up the papers we need to file with the courts to keep you safe. I want to make sure this is what you want me to do. Remember, just because I'm telling you that you should do it, the choice remains yours." Her inner strength is coming through strongly now.

"Yes. I definitely want to do that. At the moment, that is my biggest fear. But will it really stop him?"

"Yes, it gives us the power to get the police involved if we need to, and he will end up in jail if he breaks it. But also remember we have protection in place for you anyway. This is just to make sure he understands in black and white that he can't come near you. Not now, not ever." I can tell she's feeling stronger now.

"Okay, then tell me what I need to do."

Opening the file Greta left for me, I start to run through everything she needs to know and let her ask as many questions as she wants. By the time we get through it, I need to ask the next question.

"I would also like to file on your behalf an application for a divorce and full custody of the children. I believe we have sufficient facts to convince a judge that due to the concern for the children's safety, they should agree to this. Unfortunately, it will take time as it's not an instant thing like the restraining order. But if we can get it filed now, then the timeframe will at least be ticking down and be over before you know it." Mia is reading the papers while I continue to talk. "From what you told me, I don't think he will contest the divorce or custody. He's a bully who thinks he has all the power. But the day you left, you took the power from him. I'm sure he'll see how much support you have and back away. Plus, he won't have the money to fight you in the courts. There is no way he can afford the legal team to beat the best lawyer in Chicago."

She looks up from her papers with the first hint of a smile today. "Who would that be?" she asks so innocently.

"Oh, the hurt is real." I pretend to grab my heart. Then I hear that small laugh I love so much.

"Bragging about yourself, Lex?" She smiles at me, baiting me for a smart reply.

"No need. I know I'm the best. Which means you are the lucky one."

"I already knew that." Her voice is soft again as she goes back to reading.

We spent time going over all the paperwork and then called Greta in to witness Mia sign everything. I expected her to hesitate, but when it came time to put the pen to paper, she was signing without hesitation. Ready to get out of my office as soon as she finished, though. It was almost as though she needed to distance herself from what she had just done.

As much as I don't want to think about it. I'm sure at one stage she loved Edward, enough to have a child with him and marry. It must hurt to finally start the process of severing that bond forever. No matter how much he hurt her, the human brain is strange. Part of her will still love him and hope he'll change.

"I better go and rescue Paige and Mason. I've been longer than I anticipated. I'm sure they'll be regretting offering to babysit, and I've probably turned them off ever having kids of their own."

"I'll walk you to the boardroom to meet up with them, but before we go." She stops at the door to look at me. "I'm so proud of you. Today was tough and you never gave up. You might not let those walls down often, but I'll always be here if you need to do it again. What happens between us, stays between us for as long as you want it to."

"Thank you, Lex. For everything. But mainly for being my friend. I know I just need a friend right now." I smile and take her hand and squeeze it.

Then I open the door for her to walk through. I must be the biggest idiot around. I've convinced the most amazing woman I've ever met to put me in the friend zone. Tate is going to have a field day with this one, I can already hear him laughing hard at me.

Before we even make it into the boardroom, Mia is looking worried.

"It's too quiet. Something has happened." Her feet move quicker down the corridor. Swiftly opening the door, she stops dead as I come up behind her.

The vision in front of us is not at all what she was expecting.

Mason is walking up and down the length of the room rocking a sleeping Kayla, her little hand wrapped around one of his fingers. He looks up and smiles as he sees the stunned look on Mia's face.

Paige and Jack are sitting at the table with a picture of a plane and are coloring it in while they talk quietly together.

I must admit I'm just as shocked as Mia. I wasn't expecting the room to still be in one piece, and I thought Theresa would have had to step in by now. Mia's shoulders lower as the worry leaves her body.

Jack looks up and sees us looking at him, but he puts his finger to his mouth to tell us to be quiet. I almost choke on the irony of the talkative child being the one to tell the adults not to make a noise.

"Kayla is sleeping," he whispers. "I get another donut if she doesn't cry."

Ah, and there it is. The age-old bribery used by every parent at some stage. Food.

"Good work, bud," Mia whispers as she gets closer to him and reaches to take him in a cuddle. His little arms coming up and latching around her neck. I'm doing a very immature dance on the inside knowing she thinks I give better hugs than Jack. Seriously, I'm losing it. What grown man thinks things like that. Well, we won't answer that question, will we.

Mason walks towards me with Kayla.

"Can you take her, man? I've been needing the bathroom for about thirty minutes, but I wasn't about to move her or leave Paige on her own with them without protection."

Before I even have a choice, he places Kayla in my arms. Carefully but also with speed. She stirs a little but nuzzles into my chest just like her mom did. Her little hand takes hold of my jacket and then she's back off to sleep. I've never cuddled a baby before. Fear is radiating through me, but not in the way I imagined. It's a sense of worry that I might hurt her in some way. Where I thought it would be a panic of being near a baby in general. Children are not something I really wanted anything to do with until two days ago. Yet the feeling of this little girl in my arms, so tiny and innocent, is doing something to my cold heart. I can see myself wanting to protect her with my life. Just like her mother, she is planting herself firmly in my heart.

Staring at her sleeping, I'm oblivious to Mia picking up Jack and she and Paige have packed up all the kids' mess. Paige is pushing the stroller towards me and the door.

"We'll wait for Mason in the reception area. Do you want me to take her?" Paige stands to the side of me. Looking down at my sleeping angel in my arms, I'm not ready to give her up yet.

"It's okay, I'll walk out with her. She's happy at the moment." Looking up, my eyes meet Mia's. The sparkle in them makes me wonder what she's thinking. Smiling at me, she walks past me towards the reception with Jack. Following her I hear Mason come up behind us and whisper but not low enough so I can't hear him.

"What a cute little family man our big tough lawyer makes."

"Mason, stop it," Paige quietly tells him. "Leave him alone. He looks too cute with Kayla curled up in his arms. Any man in a suit with a baby is like porn."

I keep walking imagining the look on Mason's face.

"Woah. Don't you ever mention Lex and porn in the same sentence again, Tiger, otherwise there will be trouble. Yes, and what you're thinking is exactly the punishment I'll be dishing out." There is no whisper this time but a very low grumble.

"Bring it on, magic man," she replies.

Christ, this is not a conversation I need to be hearing and neither do Kayla's innocent ears. I walk a little quicker to keep up with Mia and leave the other two behind to talk dirty.

Turning the corner into reception, I hear her voice before I see her.

Fuck.

"I don't care if he has a full calendar. I will wait. He *will* see me as soon as he is finished with this appointment. If you had put my call through earlier then I wouldn't have had to come across town to see him to deliver these documents. I'm sure once you tell him I'm here he will rearrange his schedule." Jacinta stands in her normal power stance trying to intimidate.

"I suggest you either leave the papers with me or take a seat, Ms. Nordick. It could be a long wait, though. He is tied up with a very personal lady friend and has advised he is not to be disturbed by anyone. Which would include you. Just like I told you on the phone when you called an hour ago." Theresa then looks back down at her desk and continues with her work. The politest way she can dismiss her without saying something to provoke her further.

Jacinta looks pissed as she turns from the desk only to see us walking towards her. Without even thinking, I take my free hand and place it on Mia's lower back as she slows walking. I can tell

Jacinta is already intimidating her with her mere presence. I just want her to know I'm here and there is nothing to be afraid of.

"Alexander!" she snaps. I can tell by the look on her face that she's a bit shocked.

The loudness of her voice frightens Kayla which has her letting out a little cry. Without even thinking, I pat her little bottom gently and feel her relaxing back into my arm. Looking back up, I see Jacinta's mouth open, speechless for the first time since I've met her.

"Sorry, Lex, I'll take her," Mia whispers to me. Her voice has lost all the bravado it had a few moments ago. I'm not having her feel like she needs to cower to anyone. Sliding my hand from the middle of her back around to her side, I gently pull her closer to me. Her body is stiff as a board, but the moment we touch I feel her relax a little.

"No, I've got you all," I whisper back.

We stop a good distance from Jacinta. Mason and Paige have now come up beside me.

"Jacinta. What are you doing here? I don't remember seeing you on my calendar this morning." My courtroom voice is now kicking in. She wants to come into my domain and throw her weight around, then let's play the game.

"I'm not. However, I have some documents I need to deliver, and we need to talk so I knew you would see me." Her snarky reply pisses me off.

"I'm sorry, I'm extremely busy this morning. I'm just seeing my family out and then I have back-to-back meetings until after lunch where I'm due in court. So, I really don't have time today, I'm sorry. Theresa will be able to find a time tomorrow for you, I'm sure, or you can leave the documents with her like she told you." I keep my directness so she understands I'm not backing down.

"Family. They aren't your family. You're an only child. With no woman in your life except me. He is just one of those annoying schoolboys who you can't seem to get rid of, not family." Her hand waves in Mason's direction. Instantly Mia's body stiffens next to me and she tries to pull away but I'm not letting her.

How dare she speak like that in my office and in front of

anyone, let alone my family. Her green-eyed monster is out in full force, but she is no match for the people surrounding me.

Stepping from beside me, Paige extends her hand out. Jacinta is nothing to her.

"Paige Ellen. Nice to meet you. This is my sister Mia and her children, along with my boyfriend, Mason, one of Lex's brothers. Who I can confirm is far from a schoolboy. He's definitely all man. So, it seems you're mistaken about the family. Because as far as I can see, we are all related. And while we are on the topic of wrong assumptions. Being someone's beck-and-call girl does not make you the woman in anyone's life." I love Paige, but if she thinks that is going to make Jacinta back down then she is mistaken.

"Alexander, are you going to let her speak to me like that? Or are you just going to be pushed around like usual." She's still giving death stares to Mia. "Why are you holding that baby? Surely someone else can be doing that for you. Give it to the mother."

"Enough, Jacinta. Don't speak another word. My family are just leaving and then you have five minutes to explain yourself before I ask you to leave. And for the record, who I choose to spend my time with and give cuddles to is none of your business. In fact, it's never been any of your business. Sit and I'll be back."

Not waiting for her to say another word, I guide Mia and the kids past her, with Mason and Paige following.

Mason mumbles under his breath, "Yep, just like I thought, grade-A bitch," which gets him a slap on the arm for using that word in front of Jack, who is surprisingly quiet which worries me. Like his mom, he's wary of any confrontation. Jacinta will have scared him.

Putting a little distance between us, I look down to Mia beside me. Not letting my arm drop at all.

"I'm so sorry, Mia. You didn't need to be caught up in that. Just ignore her." But it's too late. She's shutting down on me.

"We need to go. You're very busy." With that she puts Jack down on the ground. Taking Kayla out of my arms, she pushes the button for the elevator. Taking Jack's hand in hers, she walks right into the car as soon as the doors open.

"Thank you, Lex," she says, dropping her eyes to the floor as she waits for Mason and Paige to follow her.

Paige leans up and kisses me on the cheek. "Thank you. Good luck with the witch. I'll talk to you later. Don't worry, I'll watch her, she'll be fine." Pushing the stroller, she enters the elevator.

"What a piece of work. She better have been worth it, man, because that there just looks like hard work and a whole world of pain. Good luck with that one. Call me later and we'll talk about tomorrow." I'm too angry with Jacinta to even reply to the comment from Mason.

"Look after them for me. She'll need support today. It was tough." He pats me on the shoulder as if he knows what I mean.

"Sure will. Now go slay the dragon, man." He walks into the elevator and the doors close behind me.

I watch Mia's face as they're closing and all I can see is the walls back up and the armor in place.

Time.

It will take time and trust.

Neither can be rushed.

Walking back towards Jacinta, my blood pressure is rising. She has picked the wrong morning to come here and try to throw her weight around.

I'm more than happy to let off steam with a fight, because that is all I want from her now. I can't even fathom how I ever wanted anything more than that before.

"Theresa, I won't be long, please hold my calls, unless it's my family." I walk past Jacinta and don't even look at her as I snap my words in her direction. "My office, now. You have five minutes!" I don't know what has come over me. I don't normally speak like this to anyone, except in the courtroom, and even then, I'm not as rude as I'm being to her.

I can hear her huffing behind me, and she hasn't even said a word in return. She'll be furious at the way I've spoken to her in front of my staff. Not that she can't take it, it's more about the image of me being rude to her and not bowing down to her. She obviously hasn't gotten the message yet.

There will not be any more putting up with her bullshit attitude.

I stand at the door of my office as she marches past me with her nose stuck in the air, like her shit don't stink.

Closing the door behind her, I don't have to move much before she spins around and starts the speech she's come here to deliver.

"I don't know what I ever saw in you, Alexander. No man of any class would speak to me like that or allow others to. I don't know what is going on with you, but you need to snap out of it. Your mother sent me here to tell you she is still waiting for you to attend the house to deliver your apology."

"Feeling is mutual, Jacinta, let me assure you." I try to keep my voice down so I don't sound like a raving lunatic compared to her. Determined not to give her any power in my office, I walk over and lean on the front of my desk, crossing my legs and placing my hands on either side of me hanging onto the front of the desk.

"As for my mother, that has nothing to do with you, nor do I have anything I need to be apologizing for. If anything, you and she have plenty to apologize to me for." I try to keep my volume low but put everything in my voice to let her know my anger level. "What, did you think I'd just happily play along in your little game? Did you already have your dress and ring picked out? The proposal all mapped out for me to follow like a good little puppy dog. I mean seriously, do you really see me as that weak a man?"

I never imagined having this out with her, but today I'm ready to tear strips off someone, so her timing is perfect.

"Are you serious, Alexander? You have been fucking me most nights for six months, and I wasn't expected to think that it was leading somewhere? What was I to you? Just a stress relief? That's pathetic. Your mother told me you weren't like your father and you have goals to achieve. How wrong she was." Walking closer to me, her voice lowers slightly. "The dress is white and sexy as hell, the ring is huge and a classy single solitaire. Just so you know, your mother helped me pick them out. Stupid me thought we were close to announcing the engagement. Well played, Alexander. You got what you wanted from me, my body…" Her pause sees her face change. "Too bad I gave you my heart with it." With that, she turns from me to walk away. I can't let it end like this.

"Jacinta, wait." She stops but doesn't turn, just stays facing the door. "I had no idea, I'm sorry. But we agreed it wasn't about that. We both said this was not about happily ever after. As fucked up as it is, we used each other for sex. It was a safe place we could go and feel no emotions. I'm sorry that changed for you. You should have told me, because it never was anything more than that for me. My mother has built it up in your head to be something more than it was, and for that part I apologize for her meddling."

Her shoulders rise and fall at her taking in a deep breath.

"You deserve more than what we had, Jacinta. Sex is good, but I have a feeling love is even better. Look for someone who will love you like you are the most precious jewel he sees. A woman he will protect, stand up and fight for, and tell you every day that you are loved and wanted. Find the man that when he looks at you, he sees nothing else but you."

"Like you look at her… Goodbye, Alexander." Her hand on the door handle, she stops for one last moment. "I hope she'll be worth it." With that the door is open and she's gone.

"Sorry…but I know she will be," I say to myself with her already gone.

"Money and power do not buy happiness," I whisper to my empty office. "And love is not for sale."

Chapter Thirteen

MIA

Twinkle twinkle little star...
Keep singing and the nasty lady will go away.
That's what I would be telling Jack, but this time it's me who needs to hear it.

Paige and Mason's voices are in the background, but I can't really hear what they're saying. My heart is racing, and I just want to get as far away from here as possible. I need this elevator to hurry up. Breathing is becoming harder. My body jolts as the elevator reaches the bottom and the doors open.

"Come on, Jack, we need to go." I drag him with me, striding through the foyer. I just need to get outside. I need fresh air.

Bursting through the doors I can feel my lungs slowly starting to fill, but my breaths are still fast, and the panic is starting to come.

A hand grabs my arm and spins me quickly.

Mason holds me in place with his hands on my shoulders.

"Mia, count with me. Calm the panic. Ten, nine, eight, deep breath… seven, six, five, breathe again." Mason's voice has me transfixed as he slowly counts backwards.

Repeating the words, I feel my heart slowing and the panic subsiding slightly.

"Four, three, breathe… two, and one." I look at him standing in front of me full of concern.

"Mason," I whisper.

"I've lived where you are, Mia. Panic attacks are crippling. You're okay, just keep taking slow deep breaths." Still with his hands on my shoulders, he never looks away but talks to Paige.

"Paige, take Jack to look at the fountain and birds." His gaze still keeps me engaged.

Jack's hand slips from mine. I know he's safe but still feel his loss.

"That's it, a few more deep breaths for me, Mia."

Slowly filling my lungs with the fresh air and then letting it out gradually.

"You are safe. I'm here with you. I can see Paige and Jack, they are safe. Kayla is in your arms and she's safe." My vision's clear now, and I see the compassion of this man in front of me.

"Oh god. I'm a mess, I'm sorry." I'm trying not to cry again today.

"No, you're not. Mia, I've been there. I've suffered PTSD for years and only recently really got on top of it. I know the signs and I know what works for me. We need to find what works for you. Have you ever seen a therapist?" He slowly takes his hands off my shoulders and steps back slightly.

"That costs money I don't have." I look around so I can see Jack. Taking in a big breath now, I can see him playing and laughing. "I'll be okay."

"Mia, I know it's hard for you to take this in, but money is not a problem anymore. It's worth thinking about. Because we want you to live your life feeling more than just okay."

Still feeling unhinged from it all, I snap back at Mason when I shouldn't be, but it just comes out. "Money might not be a problem for you, but it is for me. I'll be fine. I don't need help, thanks!" Walking away, I feel the embarrassment of again exposing my issues to someone else. I get to where Jack is splashing his hand around in the water.

"Can we go now, please? I need to get Kayla home to bed." Looking at Paige, she doesn't comment, just nods, standing up next to me.

"If that's what you want?" she asks tentatively.

"Yes please," I mumble back while taking Jack's hand. "Time to go, bud. We can go home and play with your toys while Kayla has a nap."

Jack looks up at me and just does as I ask. He can tell I'm feeling stressed, he's seen the signs before.

"Do I get my donut then?" his sweet little voice starts bringing me back to the moment.

"You sure do, you have been such a good boy today." Starting to walk towards the car, I feel bad for snapping at Mason like that. As we get to the side of the car, Mason opens the door for Jack.

"Sorry, Mason, I shouldn't have spoken to you like that." I look at him timidly.

"Nothing to apologize for. I get it." Mason just straps Jack in and then looks up smiling at me. "I'm glad you feel comfortable enough to say it how it is with me. Keep it coming." He steps back from the door, closing it so we can head around to the other side.

"You might regret that," I mumble to myself, following him around.

"Never," he replies, laughing at me.

"What, do you have super hearing or something?" I start laughing too.

"I'm just super in general. You'll get used to that."

"Oh my god, don't get him started, Mia. His ego is huge, and it does not need any encouragement, I can assure you," Paige calls from the back of her SUV where she's packing in the stroller.

By now we're all laughing which wakes Kayla a little, in the seat I'm strapping her into.

"Shhh, ladybug. Uncle Mason is just trying to be funny," I whisper as I pop her pacifier into her mouth.

Taking my seat next to her, I look up and see Mason's eyes in the rear-view mirror. They have a hint of water in them. It only takes me a moment to realize why when Paige speaks. "I like the sound of that, *Uncle* Mason." Her hand on his leg. Obviously, Mason does too by the smile on his face.

"I'm still getting used to this. Sorry, it just slipped out. I hope it's okay."

"Just perfect," Paige replies and now also has watery eyes too, looking back through the seats at me. "Something I never thought I would hear, but I love it."

I don't want to cry again today, so I just nod at her, turning to look out the window. My emotions are on overload today, and we haven't even made it to lunch yet.

Hearing the car start, I'm thankful for the distraction for a while.

"Are they both asleep?" Paige asks as I'm coming from the hallway after putting the kids down for the night.

"Finally, thank goodness. Kayla crashed, but Jack was full of chatter tonight. I think every day there are so many new things that his mind is on overload. In a good way, though." I sit down on the couch, and Mason sets a cup of tea in front of me. "Thanks."

"I can imagine," Paige says. "It's hard to remember being so little, but it's amazing what you learn in the first few years of your life. Imagine when Kayla is walking and talking too. You'll be wondering what it was like to live with any quiet time in your life. I have a feeling she'll grow up just like Jack, and if she doesn't, he will speak for her." With that we all start laughing.

"That's for sure. That boy has enough words for the both of them," Mason says, smiling at me over his cup.

"I'm sorry, Mason. You know you don't have to keep drinking tea because of me. Thank you for being so considerate."

"I don't need to have a drink every night, but it's good to know that you aren't worried if I do."

Leaning back into the couch with my hands around my cup, I smile across at him.

"I wanted to wait for the kids to be asleep to talk to you and give you these." Paige gets up and grabs a few boxes from the table, then comes and joins me on the couch.

I'm feeling a little nervous about what she has and is about to say.

"Okay," I tentatively answer.

"I know you want to stand on your own, and I respect that, but right now you need a little help to get started. I've gotten you a new phone and a laptop that is set up with an email account for you. I know you're going to say you don't need it, but please hear me out." Paige looks at me with her pleading eyes.

She's right. The words were ready to come out of my mouth.

"The phone is one that is linked to mine, so for security, Mason and Ashton will be able to track your location if needed at any time. Not that they'll be spying on you but just to keep you safe if required. The laptop is also linked into the phone and my work network. No matter what you do on it, the content is secure, and my IT department will keep your data safe." It's like she's talking at high speed to try to get everything out. I think my meltdown this morning has her a little on edge knowing how to treat me without upsetting me.

"Thank you, but I don't have anything worth keeping safe." I'm hesitant to tell her the real reason I don't need it, but I know if I don't, I'll just seem ungrateful.

"Plus, as embarrassing as this is, I don't know how to use it very well. I did some computer work in high school but haven't touched one since. I'm sure they've changed a lot in that time." We come from such different worlds and every day there are so many things to remind me of that.

"Oh, Mia, even more reason for you to take this gift. Let me teach you. I know you want to look for your own job, and I admire that. Upgrading your skills will help with that. Plus, the other reason is there will be a need for Lex to send you documents and updates about different things via email. That way you can access them on your own computer. I hope you don't mind, but I set your email account up as Mia Kennedy. I didn't think you would want it in your married name going forward." I can see her waiting for my reaction. To be honest, I don't even know what that reaction is. I'm grateful, but part of me wishes I didn't need this handout. I take a deep breath and close my eyes for a moment to process my thoughts.

"Thank you, but can I ask one day when I have a job that I can repay you the money for these? You probably think I'm crazy because I know you have the money. It's just, it's important to me to do this on my own. It will take me time, but I made a promise the day I ran from Edward that I would never be reliant on anyone again. My independence is my safety. I never want to feel trapped again. I hope you understand that." Not knowing what is going through my sister's head, I look down at the boxes between us. My mind drifting, trying to think of the last time anyone gave me a gift. Sadly, I can't remember. I don't even have an engagement or wedding ring. We didn't have the money so decided it wasn't necessary.

"You're right, I don't need the money, Mia, but you are more like me than you realize. I'm stubborn to the core and have been standing on my own for so long that I don't know how to accept help. Just ask Mason, he'll agree that I'm a pain in the ass to take help from anyone." Hearing Mason groaning next to us brings us both a little giggle.

"You have no idea how big a pain she is. Even just getting her to eat breakfast is a major deal. Every day I'm seeing more similarities between you two women. It scares me what I'm in for when you both gang up on me." Mason stands to grab our cups from us so we can open the boxes.

"Baby, be scared. You are now outnumbered in this house." Paige reaches out and takes my hand. "Now, I don't like it, but yes, I understand the need to pay me back. So, let's call these an IOU for a later date, how does that sound?" Squeezing my hand, I finally relax and see she is starting to understand what I need to do for me.

"Perfect. Thank you for not taking offence. This is about me and what is important for me to move forward. I'm blessed to be here, but I also want you to know I don't take it for granted."

"I know, Mia. Now let's open these up and have a little play and

Lovable Lawyer

get you set up. We have also given you a new phone number so no one from your old life can find you unless you want to give them your new number. We have programmed all the phone numbers for us, Ashton, Lex, and the rest of the crew. My dad and Beth are in there too."

"What about all my photos on my phone? I can't lose them. This has my whole world on it. The only baby photos I have of the kids." I look at Paige, worried I might lose them.

"No problems. Mason can back all the photos up to several storage devices for you so they're safe, and we can put whatever you want on this new phone and the laptop. But we will also put your old phone in the safe in my office so that they are never lost. I can't wait to see some of them."

Those damn tears are coming again, I can just feel it.

Looking down into my hands, I tap the phone and bring it to life.

That's it, there's no holding back the tears now.

Staring back at me are my two adorable kids, both smiling and Jack cuddling Kayla. Like they don't have a care in the world. My heart is aching with the love I have for these two little humans.

Looking up at Paige through the tears, I can't help it, it's time to tell her.

"I love you. Thank you for everything." I reach out and grab her in a hug. We both hold on so tight to each other.

"I love you too, little sister, and I'm never letting you go." Just nodding through my tears, we stay that way for a few minutes until the phone goes off in my hand.

We both jump apart, and I gaze at the screen where there is a message titled *Crazy Fam*.

Sliding to open it up, I can't help but start laughing the more the phone starts buzzing in my hand.

Crazy Fam group message

Mason: Welcome to the framily Mia. Everyone, this is Mia's new number. Please don't give it out to anyone without her permission. Plus, remember this phone could be in little person's hands at some stage, so play nice.

Tate: So, no dick pics then??

Mason: Seriously, Tate! Did you not read what I said!!

Bella: Tate, I'll cut yours off if you do!! Welcome, Mia, can't wait to catch up again. Paige, we need a girls' night without the Neanderthals in this group.

Lex: If you don't, I will, Bella. Hey, Mia. Told you that you might regret being part of this family.

Grayson: Hey, don't include me with the crazies. I'm the gentleman of the group. Hi, Mia. Hope Lex and Mason are looking after you. If not, let me know and I'll fix them up for you.

Mason: You wish, Doc. Like you can even compete with me.

Lex: Or me!!

Tilly: My god, all the egos are out tonight. Ignore them, Mia. Now what was that I saw about another girls' night?? Count me in.

Fleur: Don't you dare make plans without me. Mia, I'll protect you from this crazy family. They roped me in, but I'm the sane one in the group.

Hannah: And I'm the old woman of the crew with the crazy child. I'm your go-to for mother support. These lunatics have no clue.

Lovable Lawyer

Tate: I call BS here, Fleur, but keep dreaming. And Hannah, I'm an expert at everything, just ask me.

"Are they always like this?" I ask while I can't stop laughing.
"This is tame, you should see them when they're in a room together, it gets even worse. You will love them all. I've never laughed so hard as the first night I met them," Paige answers as she's madly typing into her phone.

Paige: I'll have you know Mia is here asking if she can disown this family already. Girls night, I'm in. Just give us a few days for Mia to settle in.

Mia: Hey, I am not. I'll take this family, warts and all. Thank you all for being so kind to me. It means the world.

Tate: Oh good, so Lex already told you about the warts. That saves us spilling the secret later.

Mia: Yes, he told all about your wart problems, Tate, and the private treatment you've been getting for them. So unfortunate for you.

Lex: Oh yeah!! It's like she's been here all along. Looks like you are fighting a losing battle now, Tate.

Tate: Christ, another sassy female. Just what we need.

Mason: Try living with two of them.

Tilly: Wait, what did I miss? Have you moved in with Paige?

Paige: More like I can't get rid of him, hehe love you baby xx

Mason: You do remember I am sitting across from you on the couch, right? I can see you laughing to yourself.

Paige: Yep. And yes, I can officially confirm Mason and I are living together, well, once we move his things here. And we are just as happy to have Mia and the kids here with us.

Mia: Thank you, but at least I'm a temporary guest. You are now stuck with Mason.

Mason: Again, in the same room, girls. See what I mean people? I'm outnumbered.

Paige: No one feel sorry for him, he loves it. Okay, we are signing off. Lex, Mia will be on email after tonight. See you all soon xx

Lex: Great, thanks. Will send the email now. Talk soon, Mia, and let me know if you need rescuing.

Mia: Thank you, everyone, for making me feel welcome. You make me laugh.

Grayson: Better than making you cry. See you soon.

Tate: There's still time for us to make you cry. Lex is hopeless like that.

Bella: Tate, behave! Bye, Mia, here if you need anything, for either you or the kids xx

Fleur: I'm here to help if you're going insane. Take care xx

Hannah: Let's set up a play date for the kids. Daisy would love it xx

Mia: Thank you.

"Don't reply anymore, otherwise these weirdos will just keep going." Mason stands up. "Anyone want another drink or anything?" he asks, heading towards the kitchen.

"No thanks, I'm okay." I'm still looking down at my phone in wonder of what just happened.

"Are they like this with everyone they meet?"

"No, just family. They've taken you in whether you like it or not. So, I guess you better get used to it. I'm someone like you, I didn't have anyone before Mason. Believe it or not, having money meant friends only saw the money and not me. But these people, they see the person and nothing else. They want to be your friend, and it has nothing to do with me. Just sit back and enjoy it."

Scrolling back through the messages, I can't help but start laughing again.

"See? If they make you laugh, then they're your tribe."

"Maybe you're right. Just weird to have so many new friends at once. I'll get used to it, I guess."

"Before long it'll be like you've known them forever. Now let's look at this computer." Paige pulls a brand-new laptop from the box. My life has become a continual story of new experiences that I need to get my head around. She almost looks more excited than me at what she has in her hands.

"Okay, let's see how bad I am at this. I'll try not to screw it up on the first night." I laugh a little to try to shake off the nerves of feeling inadequate.

"Everything is fixable, Mia. So, don't be afraid to try things. I pay people to fix up my screw-ups on a daily basis." Opening up the laptop, it comes to life with another picture of me and the kids in the park on the screen. I've never felt so loved having someone take the time to do special things for me.

"I love this picture. It looks so beautiful seeing it bigger than just a phone." I place my hand on the screen to feel the love that is looking back at me.

"Three of my favorite people right there. Now let's have a look at how all this works. Do you want some paper and a pen to write some notes? I find it helps me when I'm learning something, to put it in my own words to look at each time until I remember."

"That sounds like a good idea. Let the lesson begin."

For all the fear I had when Paige opened the laptop, I'm surprised how quickly I grasped it. By the time I packed it away for the night, I had mastered emails and searching the internet for things. We also set up a bank account which we argued about how much money Paige transferred into it, but eventually agreed on just a few thousand dollars to start with, and hopefully I will have a job soon and not need any help. I tried to explain I don't need much, but she just laughed and said, "It's not about what you need anymore, it's about what you would like for the kids or yourself. I don't want you to have to ask me for money all the time. That's just awful and I would hate to make you feel embarrassed. This way you have your own independence. "

Tomorrow is another challenge to conquer. Paige has a meeting she needs to attend, and Mason is flying her vice president to another meeting in Washington. Ashton will be with me tomorrow. I know he will protect me and was so gentle that night, but I still feel anxious. Being left with a man I don't know in a place that is all new to me. I'll never get over this vulnerability in this rich world. Back home, I knew how to defend myself against the jerks in my world, but here is so different. That woman at Lex's office this morning made me feel so small with her words and looks. I didn't think it could hurt more than what I've previously put up with, but I was wrong. She brought out a side of Lex I never imagined he had. He was short and angry with her. Standing up and trying to put her in her place. The way he never let me go even when she pushed him showed how much of a man he is. There was no way he was letting her near me or the kids.

I can take people attacking me, but when they go at my kids then I take offence. I know I didn't leave Lex with the kindness he deserved. She had made me want to hide behind my walls and just shrink into the back corner where no one sees me. She reminded me how much I don't belong in this world.

Sitting in the dark on the floor curled up in a blanket next to the window, I want to leave and find a place for just us three to live a simple life. This feeling of needing to run every time something gets hard is not healthy. I know it doesn't help the situation. Look what happened last time, I just ran to something worse. That won't always be the case, but I need to stop the urge to run from my fears. Maybe Mason is right. I should see someone and talk through my history and fears. It might make me stronger to get past it all. Tomorrow when they're out at work, I might search on the internet if I can find someone that won't cost me much. Not having a job, I don't have health care, so I'm probably wasting my time as the cost will be too much. But it's time to do something. I know that now. I can't keep running, and I need to manage the panic attacks so I'm in control to keep the kids safe.

The stars are shining brightly again tonight, watching over me. They are one constant in my life. They have always been there. Some nights brighter than others. Even on nights the clouds have rolled in, I know they're still there, just hiding. Like what I do at times. Either way, they never go away, and I can rely on them to be my constant.

My new phone is on the floor next to me, and the buzz in the silence almost makes me squeal with fright. Luckily, I manage to catch it before the noise comes out of my mouth. The last thing I need now is for the kids to wake up.

His name is shining brightly up at me in the darkness of the room. I'm starting to think he's my star the more he seems to turn up when I need him the most.

Lex: I hope I'm not waking you

I hesitate if I should answer, but I have this feeling deep in my stomach. It's a longing I've had since the elevator doors closed on his saddened face this morning.

Mia: No, I can't sleep. Just looking at the stars.

There is something about Lex that makes me speak so honestly and freely to him. I've never told anyone my deepest thoughts and fears in my life, yet in the few days since we've met, I can't stop sharing them with him.

Lex: Me either. I'm sorry about this morning.

Mia: You didn't do anything wrong, in fact you did so many things right.

Lex: I let Jacinta upset you, and that's the last thing I want to happen.

Mia: Is she your girlfriend?

Oh my god, I can't believe I wrote that and pressed send. Shit, he's writing back. I need to fix it before he replies.

Mia: Sorry, none of my business

Lex: No, far from it. I'm ashamed to even admit that we were friends with benefits for a few months. Actually, that's not even true. We weren't even really friends.

How do I even respond to that? I can't even picture him with her. Although that's always been my problem, I don't read people well. Yet I feel like I know the real Lex. The one he doesn't share with the world. The man who held me while I fell apart today and keeps my secrets safe.

Lex: I know you probably think differently of me now.

Mia: Actually, I don't. I might be a bit confused, but I feel that's not the real you.

Lex: I'm not sure I knew who the real me was until a few days ago.

Mia: Why?

Lex: I've grown up in a world where from the time I was born I've been told who I am and who I'll become.

Mia: I don't understand. You live a life of choice and money. Why can't you be who you want to be?

Lex: It's complicated, choice isn't easy.

Mia: You keep telling me it is. Yet you're telling me it isn't easy for you?

Lex: I grew up in the society circles of Chicago. My mother feels she gets to have an opinion on my life.

Mia: You're right, it's nothing like I knew growing up. It sounds like money can be as restricting on your life as poverty.

Lex: More than you realize.

Why do I have the feeling Lex is not as confident in his personal life as what I saw today in the workplace?

Lex: Anyway, let's talk about you.

Mia: Do we have to?

Lex: No, but I'd like to, because I can't stop thinking about you.

Mia: Me too.

Lex: Really?

Mia: Why are you surprised?

Lex: I'm not what you need in your life right now.

Mia: Doesn't mean I don't want it.

Lex: Fuck, you aren't making this easy.

Mia: I'm sorry. I'm saying more than I should.

Lex: Never hold back. Not with me. Always tell me what's in your soul.

Mia: I don't know what's in there, but you keep drawing it out.

Lex: As you do with me.

Mia: That's hard to believe.

Lex: I don't share my thoughts often, not even with the boys. Yet I want to share it all with you.

Mia: Tell me one thing no one knows about you then.

Lex: I never wanted to be a lawyer.

Mia: Oh Lex. Then why are you?

Lex: Because it's what was expected of me.

Mia: That's so sad. What would you be if you had a choice?

Lex: Sadly, I don't know anymore.

Lex: Your turn. Tell me one thing no one knows about you?

Mia: That I'm scared.

Lex: I know, baby, and I'm sorry about that. But I knew that. Tell me something else

Mia: You don't understand what I mean.

Do I do this or just hold it tight where I should deep inside? My head is saying to keep it locked tight, yet my heart and that gut feeling are saying let it go. If I were in a room with him right now, there is no way I would say this, yet texting makes it so much easier to be brave and tell him the truth.

Lex: Then make me understand.

Mia: I'm scared I'm falling for you.

Pressing send, I'm already screaming in my head I want to take it back. He will run a mile now. Who wants a single mom with two kids and no life? Shit, the dots are appearing on the screen.

Lex: Don't be scared. I've already fallen.

But I'm not for you, Lex.
I never will be.
If you need someone like her then I'm far from it.
Why now?
Where were you five years ago when I wasn't such a mess?
Maybe we might have had a chance.
Now it's just bad timing.
For you and for me.

Chapter Fourteen

MIA

"Mommy, why are you sleeping on the floor?" Jack's little voice is next to my ear.

Sitting up startled, looking around, I realize I'm still in the blanket next to the window where I spent until early hours of this morning texting with Lex.

"Morning, my sweet boy. Did you have a good sleep?" I try to change the subject so I don't have to answer him.

"Yes. I'm hungry." And there it is, the start of another day with children.

As I try to wake up quickly and start to stand, I realize how stiff I feel from lying on the hard floor last night. The blanket drops to the floor and my phone is still clutched tightly in my hands.

"Okay, we better get you some breakfast then, buddy." Jack runs into the bathroom to go to the toilet and take off his pull-up pants. He knows the routine.

Looking down at the screen, I can't remember the last message or saying goodnight.

Swiping the screen, it opens up still in the message thread.

Lex: Mia?

Lex: I'm guessing you fell asleep

Lex: Dream of happiness and love, beautiful. Because that's what you deserve.

How can this guy get any sweeter than he already is? I don't understand how no one sees the real him. I feel sad that he's hidden that away for so long.

As per usual, I don't get much time to myself. The noise of Jack moving around and talking to himself on the toilet has Kayla stirring and looking for me.

"Morning, my beautiful girl." Reaching and picking her up, I pull her into my chest for that first cuddle of the day. She rubs her face against my sleep shirt and then looks around for Jack. She can hear him and her love for him always draws her to wherever he is.

"Your brother is already up and ready to talk our ear off for another day, sweetheart. Let's get you changed too, and we can all get some breakfast."

She grins up at me and all is right with the world again, until I remember that today is another new challenge. Just like Lex told me last night. Ashton is here to protect me, not scare me. I need to accept that not all men are the same as where I've been.

"Okay, little one. We are strong. Time to show the world that. I'm going to show you a life where you don't know fear." Watching her sucking on her fist while I'm changing her makes me smile. The simple things in life are the memories that are so dear.

"Do I have to be quiet, Mommy?" Jack asks as we step out of our bedroom. I can hear noise, so I know the others are already up.

"No, off you go." I laugh to myself because I'm sure it's a shock to Paige and Mason to have a four-year-old so full of energy every morning.

"Uncle Mason!" he yells as he runs to the kitchen, using the new names that have stuck now.

"Jack! Stop and do not touch Mason," I yell in a panic, seeing

Mason standing in the kitchen in his pilot's uniform. Oh my. Now that is a sight. No wonder Paige fell for him. It would be tough work looking at that every day.

Jack has frozen on the spot.

"It's okay, Mia. I'm sure he's clean for the first five minutes of the day." Bending down to Jack's level, Mason gives him a hug, which Jack loves. I've always tried to show my kids as much affection as possible without smothering them. It's something that I longed for as a child growing up. Seeing other kids getting hugs and kisses from their parents. I knew the moment Jack was born that I would hug him tight every day and tell him how much he is loved. And even more so when Kayla was born.

"True. Morning, Mason, don't you look handsome in your uniform." I walk past him into the kitchen to get the kids' food ready with Kayla on my hip.

"Hey, keep your eyes off my man, sis, he's taken." Paige comes up behind me laughing. Jack now spots her and moves from Mason.

"Auntie Paige." Which brings a smile to her face as she picks him up to give him a hug.

"She can't help it if she has good taste," Mason says, back at the counter pouring the coffees for everyone.

"Well, I can't deny that. Men in a uniform do look sexy," she replies.

"Umm not men, just one particular man, thank you very much. Eyes here and nowhere else." Mason's voice gets a manly rasp to it.

"Pfft, you know they are, but I love seeing you get all jealous." Taking Jack and putting him on a chair at the table, she comes over to take Kayla off me for a morning hug, which makes it easier for me.

"Morning, Mia, and morning to my little niece. Looking pretty this morning in your yellow outfit just like a sunflower." Walking over to the highchair and putting Kayla in, she has both the kids giggling at whatever she does. I've never needed any help up until now, but I have to admit it's nice to have it. The morning ritual is a little less crazy. I just have to remember this is only temporary, like a vacation, so I can't get too used to it.

Sitting down at the table, everyone quietens down as they start eating. Even Jack, which won't last long.

Mason is looking at me with interest. "How are you feeling this morning, Mia? You look tired," he finally asks.

"Mommy sleepeded on the floor," Jack proudly blurts out along with food that's in his mouth.

"Jack, don't talk with food in your mouth." What I really want to say is, thanks buddy for throwing me under a bus.

"What?" Paige nearly chokes on her coffee.

"Everything okay?" Mason calmly asks while Paige gets her coughing under control.

"I'm fine. Stop stressing. I was just sitting on the floor watching the stars out the window for a little while, and I must have fallen asleep there. That's all." I try to hand Jack another piece of toast to keep him eating and spoon another mouthful of food into Kayla's mouth.

"That can't have been comfortable. We need to get a chair there for you so that doesn't happen again." I can see Paige already making a mental note to take care of that today.

"No. I don't need a chair. Stop fussing, it's fine." Knowing no matter what I say, she'll do it anyway.

"Mia, are you worried about today? With us leaving you alone?" Mason never holds back. He gets right to the point.

"No." But I want to say yes.

"I don't believe you, but if that's what you're telling me then we'll run with that." He takes his last bite of food on his plate.

"I won't go to my meeting. I'll stay home. I'll cancel it." Paige is already reaching for her phone.

"No! I can do this. Please, just stop with trying to fix it all. I have to do this on my own." Taking the cloth, I wipe Kayla's face, probably a little rougher than normal. Then I hand her the bottle of milk she's been waiting for.

"Sorry," I mumble. I take Jack's plate and mine into to the kitchen to get away from them for a moment and pull myself together.

The chime of the elevator sounds to alert that someone is here.

Hearing Mason's chair moving, I know it will be Ashton. I need to pull back the bitchiness that just escaped.

"Hi, man. Thanks for coming today. I've got to leave shortly for the airport," I hear Mason greeting him.

Deep breath.

Okay, I can do this.

Walking back to where everyone is standing, I feel my body tensing again.

Ashton is a big man. As tall as Mason and well-built. Just like you'd imagine a special forces guy would look. A few tattoos peeking from under his shirt sleeve, bulging muscles, and solid legs. His stance gives away the military background. Tall, straight back, feet slightly apart, and arms by his side. Wearing black cargo pants and a tight black t-shirt, you don't need to guess how hard his abs are with them outlined through the material. This guy looks scary until he opens his mouth.

"Hi, Mia, how are you this morning?" His whole face softens as he sees me, and his eyes light up with kindness. My heart starts to remember the feelings of that first night where for some reason I wasn't scared of him.

"Hello, Ashton." I walk over to clean up Jack's hands and face before I let him loose for the morning.

"I think I'll stay home with you all today." Paige is still fumbling with things on her phone.

"No, Paige, you have a meeting and I have a flight. You heard Mia, she's fine here with Ashton. He will look after them all. If I had to trust anyone with your life, baby, it would be him, so I know I trust him to keep them all safe too. Now stop trying to control things and go get ready for work. I'll be up to say goodbye in a minute." His tone is not one I've heard from him before. One of dominance but not in a harsh way.

It's the first time I've seen Paige just do what Mason says without question.

After she's gone upstairs to their room, I look across to him and mouth the words thank you. I'm not sure how Paige and I would navigate our new relationship if we didn't have Mason here to be the mediator. He knows her, and even though he doesn't know me that well, he understands me on a level no one else does. Except Lex.

"I know you must be nervous about today, Mia," Ashton says. "You don't know me, and from where you've been that is enough to be unsettling. So, here's a few options I thought of. I can spend all day downstairs at the doors to the elevator. No one can get up here without using it. That way you can be on your own and not have to worry about me. Or I can spend a little time up here this morning, talking and getting to know you and the kids, so they aren't scared of me. Then if you want some quiet time, I will go back downstairs and then you just call me if you need me. Once Mason comes home, I'll leave him to it. I'm not offended either way. My job is to keep you safe, and to do that you need to be comfortable around me. So, your call."

Both he and Mason are now looking at me for an answer. To be honest, my head is still spinning at everything he said, and all I can think of are Lex's words reminding me I have choices now. This is what Ashton is doing. Giving me the power of choice.

As I lift Jack down from his seat, he races off to the living room where his toys are neatly stacked, but I know not for long.

"Thank you, Ashton. I appreciate that. There is no need for you to stay downstairs. I agree the kids and I need to get to know you. I don't want them to be scared of anyone anymore." Picking up Kayla from the highchair and putting her up on my shoulder, I give her a few pats on the back to bring up any gas before walking over to where Jack is and sitting her down. Propping her up with a few cushions. She is sitting on her own but only just, so they help her keep her balance.

"I agree, Mia, and now I'm happy leaving knowing you two can play nice together." Mason laughs at his own joke, walking towards the stairs. "Now I need to go and calm the wild woman upstairs who's probably pacing with worry. She's just lucky we have company, so I can't use my usual methods." The smirk on his face says it all.

"Lalalalala my sister, remember? Visions I do not need." I place my hands over my ears to pretend I can't hear him.

Still laughing all the way up the stairs, we see Mason disappear towards the bedroom.

"Can I help you clean up from breakfast?" Ashton offers, picking up a cloth to start wiping things down.

"Oh no, please, you aren't here to be at my beck and call. Just to watch over me. I can do that." I feel embarrassed at having him here at all.

"You're right, but I'm hoping we can become friends, and friends help each other. If we both do it, then the quicker we can sit, have a coffee, and chat." Ashton just ignores me anyway and continues to help.

With everything in the dishwasher, the kitchen and table wiped down, we're making coffee when Paige and Mason come down the stairs, still having a heated discussion. Obviously, Mason was unsuccessful at calming her down.

"You two okay here? I'm off to the airport, and Paige's driver will be downstairs shortly." Mason walks to Ashton and gives him a slap on the shoulder, then continues past us to say goodbye to the kids.

Paige takes my hand and pulls me back into the kitchen on our own. Whispering to me so the boys can't hear us, "Are you okay? I can stay if you want. I don't want you feeling worried and us leaving you all on your own. I mean, Ashton is a nice man, but I know it's harder for you than others to be left alone…"

"Paige, stop talking and breathe." The irony of all this is that with the speed she's talking, it's almost like she is the one about to have the panic attack, not me. The tough, strong businesswoman standing in front of me is far from in control.

"I'm okay and already feel better since Ashton arrived. I have my phone and can call you or Lex if I'm worried. He told me last night he could be here within ten minutes if I need him. He's not in court today."

Paige freezes and her expression changes as I finish talking. A smile starts to creep up her face.

"What?" I ask. She stands back a little and looks me up and down.

"You were talking to Lex last night, huh? Didn't happen to fall asleep on the floor talking to a certain lawyer, did we?"

I walk away with a smile on my face. "Paige, go to work and stop being nosy," I say over my shoulder.

"But that's what big sisters do." She laughs behind me.

This part of being a sister I think I'm going to like. We might be almost forty, but the teasing is fun and something I've never had the chance to do before. There's a lot to make up for.

LEX

Lying in bed messaging with Mia feels the most normal thing I've done in a long time. I know I shouldn't be doing it, but the innocent flirting that's starting to happen between us is giving me hope that down the track there could maybe be a place for us to explore more. Seeing the bubbles bounce, waiting to hear something she hasn't told another soul excites me that she is trusting me quicker than I was hoping.

Mia: I'm scared

Fuck, I hate hearing how scared you are. I wish I could take it all away, but I can't. It's a process we need to go through. Yet this is something I've known from the first moment I looked into your eyes, I want more than this.

Lex: I know, baby. and I'm sorry about that. But I knew that. Tell me something else.

Mia: You don't understand what I mean.

Shit, what have I missed? Is there more she hasn't told me?

Lex: Then make me understand.

Mia: I'm scared I'm falling for you.

My heart skips a beat. I never imagined that was what she was going to say. Oh, beautiful, the moment you took my hand that night and let me be your strength, I fell hook, line, and sinker. I reply the only words I can.

Lex: Don't be scared. I've already fallen.

My head keeps telling me to pull back, but my heart is having trouble listening. Then she says things like this to me and I'm gone. I have all the control in the world in the courtroom, yet with Mia everything just comes out. I can't be anything but honest with her, and today showed me she is the same.

There are no bubbles of reply coming. Maybe I shouldn't have said that. Clutching at my phone, I'm debating with myself. What should I say? Do I smooth it over, or just leave that hanging and change the topic?

Or do I just be honest.

Lex: I'm sure that frightens you, but know it frightens me just as much. There is no rush to this. We have a lifetime to work it out.

Mia: Why do you always have the right words to calm me and make me flutter at the same time?

Lex: There has not been a romantic bone in my body before you. It's you that's doing this to me.

Mia: Stop, otherwise I'll be here in a wet puddle before long.

Ugh. She's killing me. I doubt we're thinking about the same wet puddle right now. I definitely can't reply anything like that. Then she'll run for the hills.

Lex: I hope we are talking happy tears sort of puddle?

Mia: Yep, let's go with that.

"That's it, woman, there is no way I'm sleeping now." I'm talking to her like she's here, or maybe that's wishful thinking.

I make myself comfortable because I don't want to say goodnight yet, but I need to lighten the conversation for both our sakes.

Lex: Let's do twenty questions about each other. What's your favorite color?

Mia: Mine is yellow like sunflowers and the stars. What's yours?

Lex: I would say it used to be black because I'm boring, but I'm starting to rethink that.

Mia: Favorite ice cream?

Lex: Cookies and cream.

Mia: Now I'm the boring one – vanilla for me. Not that I've tasted many flavors.

Lex: Then it's my mission to introduce you to the finer things in life like cookies-and-cream ice cream. You will never be able to eat your boring vanilla again.

Mia: Don't bet on it. I can't imagine the texture of crunchy cookies in creamy ice cream. It doesn't sound appetizing at all.

Lex: Wow, how dare you pick on my flavor. You will take that back eventually, just you wait.

Mia: Haha we'll see.

Lex: Favorite movie?

Mia: All-time hands-down favorite – *Pretty Woman*.

Lex: Of course, a chick flick.

Mia: Hello – I'm a chick!

Lex: Fair point. Why that movie?

Mia: Julia Roberts and Richard Gere are amazing, but the story every girl dreams of. The prince riding in to rescue the girl. So many nights I dreamed of that.

Tucking that comment away for later.

Lex: You aren't allowed to laugh at mine.

Mia: Why, is it something stupid like *The Hangover*? Oh wait, is that what you four boys are like in Vegas?

Lex: God no, although us in Vegas when we were single was not a pretty sight.

Lex: *Lion King*.

Mia: What? I did not see that coming. Why *Lion King*?

Lex: I don't know, when I was a kid it just really resonated with me. Maybe I saw myself as Simba. Wanting to run away from the life I was destined for. Who knows?

Lex: Wow, that got deep quick. By the way, if you tell anyone that I will deny every single word.

Mia: Your little-boy secret is safe with me.

Why did I even tell her that? It makes me look like an idiot. I need to redeem my man card.

Lex: But if you want to know my big-boy favorite movie – *Braveheart*.

Mia: I haven't seen that one.

Lex: Right, it's a date – movie night, *Braveheart*, while eating cookies-and-cream ice cream.

Shit, why did I use the word date.

Lex: Not like real date but as in the saying of 'it's a date.'

Lex: Not that I wouldn't want to take you on a date. But I know you wouldn't want that.

Lex: Plus, a first date would be better than movies and ice cream.

Mia: Lex, stop.

Mia: I know what you meant, and for the record, one day a proper date sounds like fun.

Oh, it will be more than fun, Mia, you can count on that!

Mia: Favorite song?

Lex: Right now, *Make it to me* – Sam Smith

Mia: *She used to be mine* – Sarah Bareilles

Lex: Want to tell me why?

Mia: Nope, you?

Lex: Nope.

I don't know that song, but I need to listen to it. Give me a little more insight into who the real Mia is. Scrolling through my music app to find it, Mia is already sending another message which means she needs to change the topic, so I don't ask questions.

Mia: Favorite season of the year?

Lex: Anything except winter. I hate playing basketball inside. Much prefer the fresh air. Live my life inside so getting outside is what I love.

Mia: For me it's spring. The new blooms, new beginnings. Coming out of the dark and cold.

Her song is now playing, and my heart is breaking. This was her life. It's like someone has written her inner thoughts. No wonder she loves spring. Well, sweetheart, every day from now on will be spring for you. I'll make sure of it.

Mia: Favorite food?

Lex: Easy – Ribs.

Mia: Such a boy.

Mia: Chocolate.

Lex: Such a girl.

I can't help but laugh at the ease we have been chatting now for a while. So glad Paige bought her the new phone. She doesn't have to worry about using it or what it costs. I know it's easier to chat like this for her at the moment than face to face. I'm okay with that.

Mia: Where are you now?

Lex: In bed, you?

Mia: Lying under the window looking up at the stars

Lex: In bed?

Mia: Not quite.

Lex: Are you tired?

Mia: Mmm, getting a little sleepy.

Lex: I'll stop messaging then.

Mia: No, I like it. You're keeping me company.

Lex: Tell me what you see?

Mia: The stars, twinkling brightly in the sky

Lex: What do they mean to you?

Mia: Hope, a place to wish.

Lex: For what?

Mia: A better

The bubbles start and then stop.
Better what? What is she writing?
There's nothing coming. What's happened to her, it's like she started the message and hit send before she finished.

Lex: Mia?

I hope she's okay. Maybe one of the kids woke up, or she fell asleep. That's probably it.

Lex: I'm guessing you fell asleep

Lex: Dream of happiness and love, beautiful. Because that's what you deserve.

It's hard to imagine that I've only known this woman for a few days, yet she has managed to bury herself so far into my heart I know I don't want her to leave. The rational part of my brain is yelling at me to slow down and that it's not normal to fall this fast. I've dated women in the past and never felt the pull I feel towards Mia. Please, Universe, don't play with me like this. If I'm feeling some sort of need to be the rescuer, tell me now because this is going to hurt if it's not what I'm picturing. Surely, I can't feel this strongly about someone and it just be because they need my help. This is what they write songs about, the things I have been hearing from Grayson, Mason, and Tate.

What if it is real for me but for Mia it is the hero complex? She's falling for me because I'm the person helping her to find a new life. Maybe that new life won't involve me.

Thoughts are swirling in my head, but one thing I know for sure, I'm not walking away, and being hurt at the end is a risk I'm willing to take.

"Greta, have we had any reply from the court about a hearing date after Mia's restraining order was filed yesterday?"

"Not yet, but I'll let you know as soon as I do. How did she cope after the run-in with bitchface yesterday?" Greta replies without even looking up from her computer.

"Greta, don't call her that. She might act like it, but I have to believe deep down there is a nice person in there, just afraid to show her face. Maybe one day the right guy will bring her out." I can't believe that I spent all that time with a woman who has no good qualities at all. Surely, I'm not that shallow.

"Hmm, not sure about that, but all I can say is I'm glad you aren't that man."

"You're like the protective little sister, aren't you? I'm a big boy and can handle Jacinta. I doubt we'll be seeing her for a while." Not after yesterday's heated discussion. I can only imagine what our next court encounter is going to be like.

"Whatever. Just making sure you know if she hurts that gorgeous lady again, then I'll be in the line to protect her too. Now want to explain why you cleared your schedule today? Do we have something big we need to work on?" She finally looks up from her keyboard, which I'm sure is to watch me squirm.

"Just wanted to catch up on a few things, and yes, be available if Mia needs me today. So, don't say a word and just keep working. If I have to put up with you and Blaine, then you can humor me on this, alright?" I look back down at my desk, continuing to write some notes so I don't have to watch the smirk I'm sure she has on her face.

"Yes, boss, not a word. Well, not today anyway. No guarantees tomorrow." Her little giggle makes me smile. We never discussed Jacinta openly, but she knew what was going on. You don't work this closely with someone and not know parts of their personal life. She never pries, but she does care, and that part of her has made us good friends and our relationship be more than a work one.

The morning has dragged on, and I know I need to leave Mia to handle this, but I can't wait any longer. I thought I would have heard from her by now.

Listening to the ringing in my ear, I almost hang up, feeling stupid in making the call.

"Hi, Lex." Her voice fills my ear.

"Hey, Mia. Everything going okay today with Ashton?" Way to go, Lex, just rush into the overbearing friend question.

Hearing Jack laughing in the background, I know things must be fine, but I want to hear her say it.

"Yes, it's gone better than I expected. Hang on, I'll just walk away from these two noisy boys." Her voice is light and without stress which is a relief.

"I'm pleased to hear that. So, you are getting along with Ashton then?" I hear a little bit of jealousy creeping into my voice which is ridiculous.

"He's a really nice guy. Jack is having fun with him, and it gives me a break from trying to entertain him all the time. He gave me a choice if he would stay downstairs or spend the time up here with us. I chose with us, which I'm glad I did. I was nervous at first, but he put me at ease right away."

I should be glad, but instead I'm twitchy at him now spending so much time alone with her. What the hell is wrong with me? I'm not some teenage boy who has a crush. Besides the fact that Mia is not my girlfriend or anything more than a new friend, I have no claim over her. I need to get it straight in my head that Ashton is there to keep her safe and nothing more.

"Well, it doesn't sound like you will be needing me at all then. See? I told you that today would be a good day. Is Paige back from her meeting yet?"

"No, she messaged to say it's taking longer than expected, but I assured her to take her time, that we were all okay here. Mason also called when he landed to check on me."

"Looks like you have everyone checking on you. Sorry about calling and adding to that."

"Don't be silly, Lex. I appreciate you calling me, and I'm sorry I fell asleep on you last night. My brain was exhausted from all the learning on the computer and I just crashed mid-sentence."

"What were you going to say in that message, I'm curious."

"It doesn't matter now. So how is your day going?" Once again, she is good at deflection.

"Busy, but that's usual for me. Did you get my email?"

"Yes, it's my first email ever. I sound like a little kid, sorry." I love the excitement at something simple that we take for granted.

"Don't be sorry. That's fantastic. I'm glad I'm your first. We haven't heard anymore today, but I expect it to be soon. They will give us a court date, where you will need to appear to get the emergency order in place." My desk phone starts ringing, and I know I need to go. "Sorry, Mia, I need to go. I'll talk to you later. Remember you can call me anytime, even if it's just to talk."

"Thanks for calling. Go, I know you're busy. Talk soon." With that she's gone.

I have to snap my mind out of my Mia bubble and get back to work.

"Yes, Theresa."

"I have the detective handling the case against Bent Tolso on the line."

Here we go. The next problem to deal with.

"Thanks, put him through.... Hello, Alexander Jefferson speaking."

Bring it on. I'm ready to battle whatever I need to so Mia can have the life she deserves.

Yet the last words I expected to hear from the detective's mouth are, 'So the DNA proves he's not their brother.'

What the fuck.

Chapter Fifteen

MIA

I love my early morning coffees sitting on the couch, watching the sun rise. It doesn't happen every morning, but on the days it does, I feel an inner peace like I haven't felt before at the beginning of a day.

Things are starting to fall into routines, including the annoying things. Since the night I fell asleep on the floor, Paige creeps into my room every night to check on the kids and make sure I'm in my bed. Scares the hell out of me every time. I know she's just doing it because she cares, but I think she forgets I've been doing this on my own for a long time.

The kids have settled in well, and Jack basically runs this house now. He has every adult wrapped around his finger, including Lex, who we have seen every afternoon after work. Some days later than others, but he never misses a visit. At first, he was making excuses to come here, something he needed to tell me or show me. But by the time we got to Thursday, he gave up and just turned up for dinner. We've just started setting an extra place for him.

Hearing a noise behind me, I know it will be Mason coming

down as he has an early flight this morning. I found out yesterday he mentors kids, and one of them needs to go to California today for an interview. Originally Paige had offered to fly Leroy to the interview, giving a fake story about having a work meeting. Instead she has chosen to stay here with us, and Mason will take the plane out without her. One thing I've learned very quickly about my sister is that she has a big heart.

"Morning, Mason," I half-whisper as he gets close, giving him a smile.

"Morning, Mia, enjoying the quiet again?" He continues towards the kitchen to grab his coffee. It has started to become a little ritual of ours, having an early morning coffee together while the rest of the house is still sleeping.

Coming back to take a seat, he has a smirk on his face. "You and Lex seemed to be talking for a while last night after we went up to bed," he says, taking a sip of his coffee.

"How do you know what time he left? Isn't the idea of going to bed that you go to sleep?" I knew as soon as the words left my mouth that I'd be regretting them.

"Mhmm let's go with that. Anyway, back to you. How are things going there?"

"We're friends, Mason, don't even start." I look back out the window.

"I know that, just checking if there's anything I need to know."

"God, you are worse than Paige. What are you, the factfinder so you can report back to the rest of the boys on their little Lex? Well, you can tell them he is a proper gentleman and an excellent lawyer. Very thorough in all areas." I give a little giggle into my coffee.

"I thought Paige gave me enough grief with her smart mouth, but you are just as bad. Damn, it's getting tough living with you two."

"You love it, stop complaining." We both smile, knowing he does.

We sit for a few minutes just enjoying the quiet and the morning glow appearing outside.

"How are you feeling about yesterday's revelations on Bent after Lex's phone call?" Mason looks a little more serious now.

"I was shocked, but a big part of me was relieved. To find out after the DNA test that he isn't our brother made me feel better. I must admit, I struggled to know how he could have done what he did to both of us if we were his family. But what he did to our mother chills me to the bone."

"Paige is struggling with it too. I know you are both trying to show that you're handling this, but we both know that deep down it's so much to process. I don't know about you, but Paige had a little cry last night." He keeps looking out the window so there's no pressure for me to reply if I don't want to.

"Same. Poor Lex, I'm beginning to worry that he thinks all I ever do is cry on his shoulder." I pause for a moment. "I'm just struggling with the finality that no matter whether I want to or not, I'll never get to meet her. Finding out she's dead has rocked me a bit. For years I waited for her, and then as I got older, I hated her for leaving me in that life. Then when Jack was born, I got a new perspective on the challenges of being a parent and often wondered why she did it. Now I'll never know the truth but only what Bent told us. If you can believe that. I mean, this is the same man who befriended an elderly woman who was desperate for company and tried to rob her of her money. Can you believe people even do that, prey on the vulnerable and then get themselves written into their will? Pity he didn't count on our mother never giving up on us and still wanting to give us something. I bet he was furious when he found out he couldn't get his money until we were found. I just want to hurt him so bad for that."

"Stand in line. He's just lucky Ashton was there that night, otherwise I'm not sure he would be sitting in jail right now and still breathing." Mason looks tense. "He hurt you and the kids, Paige, and your mother. It took a lot of restraint not to pummel him."

"I know. I agree. That night was such a shock, and to be honest, most days since have been a challenge, but I know one thing for sure. I want him to pay for what he did to my mom. No one deserves that." I take the last sip of coffee, and not feeling like I want another one, place my mug down. "Lex said last night that the police called and will be sending over copies of the letters my mother left with the will and the things that they found at Bent's apartment that belonged to Mom. We can't get the originals until after the trial, but I just want to see them. Maybe it will give Paige and me some closure, who knows."

"Yeah, I agree." Mason stands and picks up my cup. "Anyway, I better get some breakfast and get to work. I don't want to be late picking Leroy up. I'm sure he hasn't slept a wink last night."

"You're a good man, Mason. I knew it the moment I met you."

He shrugs his shoulders as he's heading into the kitchen. "Don't believe everything you see. If you ask Paige she might disagree," he says, laughing to himself.

"Pfft that woman is head over heels in love with you. And speaking of my sister, can you tell her if she keeps sneaking into my room every night to check on me that I'm packing my bags and moving out. She scared me half to death last night. I know she cares, but seriously, I'm thirty-eight years old. I don't need a mother."

"Oh, you didn't get a mother, but you sure as shit got a pushy controlling older sister, just like I got a sassy, bossy woman in my life. Welcome to my world, Mia."

With that we're both laughing quietly and start to get on with our day.

Just before Mason is about to leave, Paige comes down the stairs looking pale.

"Are you okay, Tiger? You don't look great." He rushes to her side.

"Morning," she replies a little quietly for her. "I don't feel well, actually. I'm going to get something to take the headache away which will hopefully settle the stomach."

"Shit, I should be here to look after you, but I need to go." Mason looks a little panicked.

"No, go. It's important for Leroy. This could be the start of the rest of his life. I'll be fine," Paige mumbles on her way to the kitchen

"Mason, I'm here. I can take care of her. Plus, Ashton will be here any minute." For the first time since I arrived, I feel useful.

"I don't like it, but I don't feel like I have a choice. I'll message Tate and Grayson before I leave to let them know you aren't well." He's already grabbing his phone.

"Mason, stop. Unless I have a brain tumor or lady issues, then I doubt I need them. It's probably just a twenty-four-hour thing or a tension headache. You heard what Mia said. She's here, now go." Grabbing her drugs and a glass of water, she's already shuffling back towards the stairs to her room.

"I'm coming up to tuck you in." Mason storms after her. I can tell he isn't impressed with leaving her but has no choice.

I'm in the kitchen as I hear the elevator signal Ashton's arrival, and at the same time Mason comes back down from seeing to Paige.

"Hey, man, Paige isn't well, so you need to help Mia keep an eye on her for me." Mason looks stressed as he places her phone and laptop on the kitchen counter. "I've taken these from her so she can sleep. I think everything is catching up with her today. You two girls need to be talking to someone."

"I do. To you and Lex," I reply, probably with a little too much attitude.

"Mia, seriously. When I get back, I'm getting in contact with my therapist for a contact of someone you can see. I'm not letting you both end up in the hell I lived in."

"He's right. Take it from both of us who think we're too big and tough that we can handle it all. But the truth is your mental health is complex, and don't think you can package it away in a box. One day the lid slips off and things start climbing out whether you like it or not. It's worth considering." Ashton looks at me while pouring his coffee.

"Great. I've gone from no family, to a controlling sister, and now not one, but two pretend brothers. And who can forget a friend who I have no idea where he even fits into my world. Yet you wonder why my head is spinning." I laugh to myself to break the moment a little.

"Sorry, Mia, but you're stuck with us now," Mason says. "So, suck it up, princess, and get used to it." Mason laughs too and looks to Ashton for support.

"Hey, don't look at me. I'm happily single for a reason. Women are hard work, man," Ashton replies to him.

"I call bullshit on that," Mason laughs. "You have been out of the country fighting the bad guys. Every day back in the country is a day closer to you being hooked by one of these crazy creatures. They stab you in the heart with this damn arrow and there is no escape. I'm warning you, keep running while you can." Mason slaps him on the shoulder.

"Oh my god, you are both full of shit! I'm done." Smiling, I start laying things out for the kids' breakfast before they wake up.

They both walk off together to the elevator, having their morning chat, and then Mason is gone. Another day begins.

"You know Mason will kill me if he knows you're trying to work," I say, taking a green tea into Paige in her home office.

"Then don't tell him. We need to work out how sister secrets work." She giggles a little and then groans holding her head.

"Headache still bad?" I ask, concerned about her.

"Yeah, but not as bad as this morning. I'll get there. I just have to get this document proofed today. It's killing me not having a personal assistant. For all Tyson's faults towards the end, he was good at his job. They better find me a new one soon. Otherwise, I'm stealing someone else's PA and they can have the nightmare. After all, I am the boss."

"The kids are down for a nap and Ashton's watching the television. Can I help you with anything?" Knowing I probably can't, but I wish I could.

"Were you any good at English at school? Because I sucked at it. Numbers were my thing," she mumbles while looking at the screen with a scowl on her face.

"Does getting straight A's every year count?" I might not have had any support or encouragement at school, but I loved being there.

"Really? Get over here." She points to a chair, and I grab it and drag it over next to her at the desk.

"I know I can trust you, but anything you read is confidential." She looks at me.

"Of course, I understand. Now what are you doing?" I look at the screen which has a very detailed document.

"Don't worry about the content so much, I just need to proof the grammar, spelling, and anything that doesn't make sense." I can see the uncertainty in her eyes.

"I might not have many skills, Paige, but this is something I do know. In fact, there are so many things wrong on that page it's hurting my eyes."

"Well, my eyes are just hurting, full stop." Paige rubs her forehead

"Okay well, that sentence there, you've repeated the word 'continue' which we need to change. Let's change this one," I say, pointing to the screen. "Then I need to teach you what a comma is and how to use it, obviously." Looking at the document, I don't understand what it's really for, but I can certainly make it look presentable.

"See? I told you I pay people to fix up my screw-ups. This is one of the things I'm talking about."

"Obviously, now move over and let me see what I can do. But for god's sake, save it somewhere safe first in case I do something to lose it all. You know I'm not great at this computer thing yet." Sliding closer to the keyboard after Paige saves the file, I take another look at her and she looks so drained. "Now go and lie on the couch over there, and I'll ask any questions from here. It'll help your head if you lie down and rest." I feel nervous to have control of something so important, yet it's the most excitement I've felt in a very long time.

"I thought I was supposed to be the bossy sister," she grumbles as she lies down on the couch and drags the blanket up that was lying over the back of it.

"I've been taking notes and thought I'd test it out today. Plus, Mason is going to come home and be ready to kill me for letting you work. So, I'm looking after myself here too. Now rest and I'll ask when I have a question."

I didn't realize how much I would love this. Totally forgetting where I am, my mind is solely focused on reading and editing Paige's work. It doesn't take long for the strong medication she took to kick in, and she's fast asleep on the couch, and it lets me work in silence. Her phone is on the desk beside me and rings constantly. After a few times, I decided to start answering it quietly and taking messages. Then ranking them in order of importance from what they had told me. Deflecting the ones I could to next week, so she doesn't have to worry over the weekend. I can't believe she's sleeping through the whole afternoon and even me talking in the office. The other amazing thing is the kids are still sleeping. Ashton must have worn them out this morning playing with them. It has allowed me to get completely through the document and then go back and make some changes that I feel sound better. Paige can always change them later if she doesn't like them.

Mason has messaged a few times checking in and is now on his way home from the airport. Hopefully Paige is still asleep when he gets here. She looks so cute curled up sleeping in a room where she is usually full of energy and working hard. This is her space. The powerful CEO, but she looks far from it. Right now, she looks vulnerable, and I know how that feels. I don't think I've even thought enough about how she's been coping with everything that has happened. I forgot that I've lived a life of being knocked down and how you become resilient at shaking it off, picking yourself back up, and moving on. This is probably the first time that she has really had anything so hard emotionally to cope with. I should have been more supportive of her instead of it just being all about me. I didn't think I had a selfish bone in my body, but maybe I do. Looking at her for the first time, I see myself, when the world has gotten to be too much and you just need to take that moment to gather enough strength to get through it.

Paige may have had a charmed life, but at the end of the day, she is hurting just as I am about losing a mother we never knew and the finality of never having the answers to questions we've had for years. I need to get better at this sister relationship. It goes two ways. I need to give back just as much as I'm taking.

Hearing in the distance the ding of the elevator, I know that will be Mason arriving home. His voice fills the silence while he's talking to Ashton, and I know it won't be long before he'll be walking into the office to check on us. The soft footsteps coming down the hall make me look up to the doorway, and I put my finger over my lips as he walks in, so he doesn't wake Paige.

Giving me a smile, he walks to her, and in the moment, I can see how much he loves her. Bending down next to her and gently brushing the hair off her forehead. He then leans down and kisses her gently on the cheek, closing his eyes for the few seconds that his lips stay on her cheek. I almost feel like I'm intruding on a private moment. I've seen movies and read stories but never witnessed this sort of love before. Not just love or lust but complete devotion and adoration for another person.

Standing again and coming to me, his voice drops to just above a whisper. "How long has she been knocked out like that?"

"Around two hours. As soon as I made her lie down, she crashed and hasn't even moved the whole time I've been in here. Even with me talking on the phone while I took messages for her. Her body needs the rest. The headache is a bad one. She was holding her head and squinting trying to read the screen. Luckily, I got her to leave it and walk away. I think we're both as stubborn as each other. I think the emotional exhaustion has hit her today and left her with the headache. Do you think maybe we should call a doctor to check her out? I have a feeling she doesn't get sick often."

Mason smiles at me. "I've spoken to Tate who told me to stop being a drama queen, that she'll be fine. He agreed that the last week has caught up with her, but he offered to come over if she gets any worse."

His whisper wasn't low enough because Paige's voice comes from behind him. "Stop fussing, I'm fine. Now come here, my hot pilot, and give me a kiss."

"That's my signal to leave the room. She must be feeling better after the sleep, and I don't want to witness what happens next." Leaving them to it, I walk and open the door to my bedroom to check on the kids. Jack is spread out like a star fish, lying sideways across our bed. Ted is lying on top of him where Jack must have been cuddling him when he fell asleep. His head back and mouth open wide. Kayla is awake, but just like the little treasure she is, is still lying there sucking on her fist and taking in the world around her. I hope she never loses the beautiful soft and calm personality she has.

I pick her up and make the quick exit out to the living room, making sure we don't wake Jack. She starts making noises and babbling to herself.

"Did you manage to rescue the fair maiden without waking up the chatty dragon guarding her castle?" I can't help but laugh at Ashton. He's becoming a great friend the more time I spend with him.

"The dragon has run out of steam and is restoking the fire as we speak. Don't worry, it won't be long and he'll be out here to talk everyone's ears off. Are you getting ready to head off for the day, now that Mason is home?"

"Actually, I'm going to stay for a beer with Mason after he's checked on Paige. That is, if you don't mind?" I love how respectful these men are towards me. Never once have they assumed anything with me. It's starting to sink in that not all men are like I've encountered before. In fact, Edward and Bent are the minority, I'm learning. These guys are the normal ones, polite, respectful, and who care about you as a person and not just what you can give them.

"Of course. You deserve it after putting up with us all week. That's worth a medal."

Before Ashton can answer, Jack comes hurtling down the hallway ready to jump up on the couch and be with us, in case he's missing something.

"See? I told you he'd be back larger than life," I say. Ashton braces for the launch that Jack is about to attempt to land in his lap. "Jack, what've I told you about jumping onto Paige's couch?"

"I'm not, Momma, I'm jumping onto Ashton's lap." I just roll my eyes at him. Great, we have a rule-bender here. Can't wait until he's older.

My phone starts ringing in my pocket. It can only be Lex. No one else calls me.

"Here, give me Kayla to hold while you answer it." I can't believe I don't even blink an eyelid at handing my daughter to a man to watch her while I'm doing something else. What a roller coaster my life has become.

"Thanks, Ashton." Passing my little smiling bundle over, I see him smiling back at her. Jack may have everyone wrapped around his little finger, but Kayla has them all sucked in too.

"Hi, Lex, how's your day going?" I hear my voice go up an octave as I speak to him.

"Hey, Mia, I'm almost done for the day, and just like they say, thank god it's Friday." His voice sounds a little tired.

"Are you okay?"

"Sorry, yeah, don't worry about me. Just tired and it's been a long week at work. How's your day been. I heard Paige has been sick?"

"Yes, she has a bad headache that I would say is bordering on a migraine. I think she's turning the corner, though. Mason just got home so I'm sure she'll feel better now. Those two are a bit cute together."

Lex bursts out laughing. "Oh, can you wait until I'm there and let me watch as you tell Mason he's cute? His ego will take a slap and it'll be hilarious. For future reference, Mia, no guy wants to be cute. We are way too manly for a girly word like cute."

"Well, you know what I'm calling you from now on then, don't you? I love how you all think you're so tough and manly, yet all I see are big-hearted, soft, mushy men. So nice try with the image." Now we're both laughing.

"You really know how to wound my fragile heart, don't you. Here I was going to say cute was a name I'd use for you, but now I'm not so sure."

"I'm sure you didn't call me to listen to me call you soft and mushy."

"You're right, I didn't, but you did give me the laugh I needed this afternoon." I hear him taking a deep breath which worries me. "I got the notice from the court in Bellevue. Your restraining order hearing against Edward has been set for Monday, and like I explained to you originally, you will need to attend."

I can't help the gasp that escapes my mouth. I knew it was coming, but now that it's only a few days away, the reality sets in quickly.

"Mia, just breathe for me, baby. I'll be there the whole time. Not for one moment will I leave you. Plus, we'll have Ashton with us. It will be okay. I promise with my life, you are safe with me." His voice sounds as pained as I feel.

"I'm…umm, going to have to…umm have to see him, aren't I?" I let my body slide to the floor in the bedroom where I walked to for some privacy.

"Yes, unfortunately. But he may not turn up. It's a big possibility and one I hope happens for your sake. I'm sorry I had to tell you this over the phone, but I need to make arrangements for Monday so I need to know for certain that you think you can do this. Will you be able to stand up before the judge and explain what your life was like? I totally understand if you can't. I can go for you, but it will be better if you are there to plead your case."

My heart is racing. "I don't know if I can, I'm sorry, Lex. I'm trying to be brave, but I'm so scared to see him." The tears are welling in my eyes and my voice is a little wobbly.

"That's okay, Mia. This is really tough, but I want you to know how strong you are. I admire everything you've done so far, so don't even start beating yourself up if you don't make it there on Monday."

Trying to tell myself to not panic, I still feel the tightening in my chest.

"Mia, talk to me. Tell me what's in your head. If you keep it in there, we both know you will shut down on me. Deep breath and then start the words, please?" Lex's voice is like the magic balm for my heart.

"What if I freeze on the stand…or they don't believe me? Then he's seen me and knows where I am. We can't stop him then. He will hurt me and the kids…"

"No one will ever hurt you or the kids while I live and breathe. Are you listening? If you hear one thing then hear that. I will die before I let him near you. Do you understand that, Mia?"

I nod my head up and down before I realize he can't see me. "Yes," I murmur.

"So, all you need to do is tell the truth and I will take care of the rest."

"I want to do this, I really do. I'm just scared, Lex."

"I know, beautiful. You've got this and I've got you. We can do it together."

His words sink in a little deeper. I want to do this for him, but more than that, I need to do this for me.

"Okay, I'll try. That's all I can promise, Lex, and nothing more."

"That's all I ask, Mia, and nothing more." His gentle voice makes the tears I've been holding at bay fall free and trickle down my cheek.

"Now I want you to wipe the tears that are running down your cheek and think about tonight. Because when I finish here, I'm turning up with two tubs of cookies-and-cream ice cream, and we are going to put the kids to bed before we start watching *Braveheart*. You will forget all about this by then. Good company, good food, and the best movie. What do you say?"

Trying not to let on how much I want that, I casually reply, "I'll take the ice cream, but ladies go first, so *Pretty Woman* it is then. I need to show you what a real classic movie is." My mind now distracted, already trying to think of things to say, he has achieved his objective and taken my mind off it.

"I'm not sure my ice cream will go with your *Pretty Woman*. I mean, it is a chick flick, after all. Maybe I'll need chocolate ice cream instead. Isn't chocolate the standard go-to for a woman?"

"Oh, careful, you are on shaky ground here. If you say anything about women and periods and needing chocolate to stay calm, you may as well run now." I can't help but giggle.

"Now that's something Tate would be stupid enough to say. But I'm glad to hear you laugh a little."

"Thank you for just being you, Lex. No matter what, you always make me feel good."

"And I always will, Mia. No matter what, I'm not going anywhere in a hurry. So, get used to the bad jokes and terrible assumptions in regards to women and chocolate. I grew up an only child, so no sisters to educate me when I'm putting my foot in my mouth."

"Well, that makes us even, I don't have any brothers so I didn't get the bad brother jokes, gory movies, and all things testosterone. I'm sure you will fix that."

Hearing him grunt on the other end, I realize what I said. "Oops, yep, maybe hold off on the last one just yet." I can feel my cheeks blushing a little.

"As long as it's on the table one day, I'll hang on as long as you like."

This man makes it hard to ignore him.

Every day I fall that little bit further which is problematic for us both.

But today I need him, so I push it to the side and worry about it another day.

Dangerous, I know, but he's what I need.

Chapter Sixteen

MIA

Pulling myself back together, I walk back out to rescue Ashton from the kids and find Paige sitting with him, feeding Kayla a bottle while Jack is on the floor playing. She still looks a little pale but a lot brighter than she was this morning.

"Are you feeling better after your sleep?" I ask, sitting down next to her.

Mason calls out from the kitchen, "Do you want a drink of anything, Mia?"

For the first time in a really long time I feel like I could use a drink, but I won't. I might start and not want to stop. You can't do that when you're a parent.

"No thanks, Mason." Hearing the noise of the cap twisting off a beer, my body shivers, but I know I don't need to worry. It's just a natural instinct, to still be fearful of that noise and the night it would normally bring from Edward.

Paige's voice snaps me out of my memory. "Mia, did you answer my phone while I was sleeping?"

Shit, maybe she's mad. I've done the wrong thing. I should have just left it. "Yes. I'm sorry if you're mad," I reply timidly, my confidence totally gone.

"Mad? Oh my god, no, I'm so happy. You also proofread that document in record time, and it looks amazing. I can't believe you haven't had more time on a computer or been trained. You're picking things up so quickly. I know you're going to freak out at this, but I want to offer you a job. To train you to be my PA."

"What the hell?" I can't help it, the words just slip out.

"Hear me out, and it's not the foggy brain from the headache talking. I see talent in you. You are more intelligent than you give yourself credit for. I can trust you with my life and not have to worry about you knowing my private calendar as well as managing my work life. We have childcare in the building, and you can work from home some of the time too. When we travel you can bring the kids, and Mason can help watch them when we're in the meetings. But more importantly, it can give you the independence you crave and know that it won't be a handout. You need to work for your money, and this is your opportunity." Pausing and looking at me, she must see the utterly stunned look. "Just think about it for a few days, please?"

"Are you serious? I have no idea what I'm doing. I'm a mess, I don't know the first thing about the corporate world."

"I beg to differ. What you just did in the last few hours from instinct, taking initiative like that, tells me you're just the woman I need. I might be your sister, but I'm a businesswoman too. I can't afford to have you as my PA just to make you feel better. This is a genuine offer, and my gut instinct is telling me to snatch you up before someone else sees the hidden talent like I do."

"Paige, I don't know what to say. It's all a bit much right now."

"Just say you'll think about it. That's all I'm asking." She's almost pleading with me.

"Okay, I'll think about it."

"Thank you, Mia, and believe me when I say, this is what I really want. It could work out as the best scenario for both of us."

Slowly looking between her and Mason, I see he just has this stupid grin on his face.

"What, I didn't have anything to do with it. This is all Paige. I know my place, and that is on her plane being her pilot and now being Uncle Mason's daycare. I never interfere with her work. That would bring a fate worse than death." He and Ashton clink their beers together to agree.

"Glad, you know your place. Now I'm going to go and relax in a bath and see if I can shake this headache completely. Behave while I'm gone." Paige is pointing at Mason.

"I've got no idea what you mean." His innocent look isn't fooling anyone.

"Yeah, right," I say as I take Kayla back from Paige and sit her with Jack. "I'm going to start to get the kids' dinner prepared, feed them, and then tackle a bath with the two of them. But I bet theirs won't be as peaceful as yours, Paige."

"I don't know, I could tell you a few stories," Mason mumbles to himself but loud enough we all hear it.

"Mason!" Both Paige and I say at the same time.

"Yeah, yeah." He waves his hand at us to dismiss the crazy women, then he and Ashton start chatting between themselves.

Boiling up some vegetable for them both, I'm thinking about everything that Paige just said. Could I really do the job? I mean, it sounds amazing, and it would give me my independence. I could get a little apartment for me and the kids and we could really start our own lives, not depending on anyone. But I know nothing about being a PA. Paige must be crazy to think I would be any good. It has to be her good heart again just wanting to make me feel important. I'm not good enough to be worthy of a job with her. Her job is high-pressure, and I'm not used to that sort of environment. I mean, what if I let her down? She'll be too kind to tell me.

Shit, as if I haven't got enough on my plate to think about.

I need to talk to Lex. He'll make sense of it all. He always does.

Oh Mia, what are you doing? You know you should never rely on a man again. You've made that mistake before and look where it's gotten you.

I need to concentrate on dinner and then worry about all this mind fuck later when I have time to myself. In other words, I try to push it aside because it's truly too hard and my brain is spinning.

Okay, food, I need to do food. Pumpkin, peel it. Come on, brain.

Lex, I really wish you were here.

LEX

"Hey, boss. I just got the email through on Mia's court date and time." Greta comes into my office, papers in hand.

"Finally, luckily she's here with us and not in danger. There are just not enough judges to get through all the cases. So, when are we up?"

"First thing Monday morning at 9am in Bellevue Court House. At least you have the weekend to get sorted. You know you're going to need to stay there the night before to be there that early. How will Mia cope with that?" She looks to me for my reaction.

"I don't even know how she's going to react to Monday being court day, so telling her that too is going to freak her out, I'm sure. One step at a time, I think. I need to talk to Mason and Ashton first before I broach the subject of her being away from the kids for a night. She'll hate it, but I just don't want to risk taking them with us. Plus, she'll be nervous enough and the kids don't need to see her like that. If she is on her own, she can just use her energy to get through it and not be worried about protecting them." I lean back in my chair, my hands clasped behind my head, thoughts racing.

"Can you book two rooms for Sunday night at the best hotel that's the closest to the courthouse, please? One suite that has two rooms for Mia and me. Then an adjoining room for Ashton. Charge it to my personal credit card, not the work one. In the meantime, I'll call Mia to tell her about Monday. I'll wait to talk to her in person about Sunday night, though."

"On it. I'll send through the booking details when I'm done. Then I'm off for the day. It's date night, and Blaine gets to choose tonight. After the week we've had here, it better include alcohol, a massage, or both."

"Too much information, G, just go have fun whatever he manages to pull off." I laugh to myself.

"Ugh, Lex, you are hopeless. Really, that's where your mind went?" Greta laughs, making her way towards the door.

"Well, if your mind is not going there on date night then Blaine is not doing it right. Now go. You have things to do, places to be, people to see. Leave me to do all your prep work for Monday while you're out with your husband. I see how it is. He takes priority." As I reach out to grab my phone, Greta bursts out laughing.

"He'll be happy to know he's the number one man in my life and not you. He kind of put the ring on it and has the piece of paper that proves that. But he'll be impressed you've finally admitted it. PS don't message me if you need help. I think I might be busy. You can do the junior lawyer grunt work for a change."

As she closes the door behind her, I know damn well if I called or messaged her, she'd answer right away and be here in a flash if I really needed her. I also know I won't have much to do as she likely has the file perfectly organized, and everything I need will already be sitting there for me. Which I'm grateful for this afternoon, because I want to get out of here to go and be with Mia. Especially after this phone call.

"Hi, Lex, how's your day going?" Hearing her voice sounding so perky makes me sad because I know I'm about to ruin her day.

"Hey, Mia, I'm almost done for the day, and just like they say, thank god it's Friday." I try to match her happiness, but I know I'm failing.

"Are you okay?" her sweet voice asks me. I want to reply no, but I need to be the strong one here. Mia is relying on me, and if that doesn't make me feel ten feet tall, I'm not sure what will.

We spend a few minutes talking, and by the end of the phone call I'm desperate to get to her and make sure she's okay. My job is to take her mind off this over the weekend, and Monday will be here before she knows it.

Pulling together the files I need and packing them in my briefcase, I'm off to the shop to buy us two tubs of cookies-and-cream ice cream. Operation distraction starts right now.

"You seriously brought two tubs of ice cream for you and Mia and none for me? Well, it looks like Tate just became top of my list of friends. Actually, what am I thinking? Gray is top, then Tate, Ashton even rates above you. You are scraping the bottom for the no-ice-cream stunt." Mason is trying to act all serious as I put the tubs into the freezer for later.

"Do you want to yell it any louder so Jack hears you and then starts complaining that he can't have any? And by the way, I can accept Gray being on top, and even Ashton above me, but Tate? Seriously? That's just cruel."

Mason is leaning against the counter in the kitchen just laughing at me, but he sobers as he takes me in. "You look like you could do with a beer, man. Are you okay?"

"Probably, but I won't tonight while I'm here with Mia. As for the question am I okay, no, not really, but I need to be. While Mia is in bathing the kids, I need to talk to you about something."

Sensing my seriousness, Mason stands a little taller and is immediately paying attention.

"Hang on. Ashton, come here for a minute," he calls to Ashton who's still sitting on the couch.

"I called Mia earlier. Court is set for Monday morning at nine am. So, we will need to go down the night before and stay there. Just going is a big thing for her, but to leave the kids here is going to be huge. I wanted to talk to you about how we'll handle the protection of them all. I was thinking Ashton comes with me and you stay here with Paige and the kids."

"Fuck, I want to be in two places, but I know we need someone here with Paige, there is no way I'm leaving them vulnerable." I can see Mason is already thinking of other options.

"Lex is right, Mas." Ashton nods for me to keep going.

"I have another problem, and I need both your support on this. Don't try to talk me out of this either." I rub my hand over my beard.

"I'm not going to like the sound of this, am I?" Mason looks directly at me.

"Probably not, but I'm doing it anyway."

"Great, this is going to get messy, I can tell." Ashton leans on the counter next to Mason like the two of them are giving me the stare down.

"I want to go and see Edward and strongly suggest he sign the divorce papers for me to file and to turn up at court and not contest anything on the restraining order. But to do this, I need someone to come with me, but I can't leave Mia on her own in the hotel I've booked for us all. She needs someone with her the whole time, every second we're there. But I need to see this guy and make sure he understands he is never to come near her or the kids ever again." I can feel the stress making my body get stiffer, and my heart is pounding in my chest.

"Whoa, hang on. Do you really think this is a good idea? You could lose your job over this," Mason says sternly.

"I don't give a fuck. That woman in there is burying herself so deep down inside me, every single moment I'm with her and even the moments I'm not. I'll do anything to make this world a better place for her."

"Including getting yourself thrown in jail, dickhead," Ashton says, shaking his head. "I don't think so. Let's talk about this before I spend my weekend protecting Mia and also saving you from getting the shit beat out of you." Ashton is pissing me off now.

"What, no one can be as tough as you, Army boy?"

"I suggest you back off, Lex," Mason says, moving closer to put a hand on my shoulder. "I know you're agitated and ready to kill someone, but remember we are all on the same team here. I know Mia means a lot to you, we can all see that, and I know she feels the same by just the way she looks at you. But you need to calm that hot head, and let's come up with a rational plan. Man, don't get me wrong, I want to go and beat the shit out of him too. But you have to think about how Mia will look at you. She has just come out of a place of violence and you're going to show her that you're no better. How is that going to help her or you?"

Standing there just staring into nothing, I know Mason is right, but tonight I know that they won't change my mind. With or without them, Edward and I are having a chat.

The silence in the room is deafening. Until Ashton finally speaks up.

"Okay, this is how I see it. I'll get one of my men to come down on Sunday. Lex, you and I go pay Edward a visit while he watches Mia. We have a nice chat and then that's it. Get him to sign your papers and we are out of there. You get to say your piece. No bloodshed and everyone stays out of jail. Then we do court Monday morning and get the fuck out of town and never go back. Understood?" If there's one thing I've learned being friends with Mason after he joined the military, it's that when that tone is in their voice, you listen and don't argue.

"I can deal with that." I nod at him, but Mason now interrupts.

"Nope, I need to be there. I'll drive down Sunday at the same time but separately in my car, with your extra guy to watch over Mia in the hotel. We get Grayson and Tate here with the girls to help Paige, and you can post another one of your guys at the base of the elevator. Then after our little chat. I'll come back here for the night, bringing your guy back, and you can take it from there. If you get to say your piece to the scumbag, then so do I. That woman has become like a sister to me. We protect her as a family. Do you agree?" He is giving me a choice, but not really. I've got a feeling he'd turn up anyway, even if I say no.

"We don't say a word to Mia until we get there, otherwise it gives her time to think about it and panic. Well, more than she already will be about going anywhere near him. Are we cool now?"

"As cool as I'm going to be about a plan that still sounds like trouble," Ashton says, but that's been the story of my life for the last twenty years. Why should now be any different. I'm going to head out for tonight. You know how to reach me if you need me." He holds his hand out to mine, I shake it to seal our plan.

"Thanks, man, for all you are doing. At least I can rest easy knowing they're all safe when I can't be here."

Ashton gives me a chin lift while Mason whines like a girl. "What am I, chopped liver? Pretty sure Ashton is not the only one keeping her safe."

"Whatever, stop sounding a like girl." I start to laugh at him because his pout makes him look like when we were back at high school.

"You wonder why you're on the bottom of the list. I'm going to see Ashton out so we can bitch about you being totally whipped already." They both walk away, laughing at me.

"Assholes," I mutter under my breath, luckily quietly as Jack comes running out of the hallway with just his underpants on.

"Jack, you get back in here right now and get your pajamas on before Lex gets here," Mia yells from their room as he's giggling after already jumping into my arms and getting a hug.

"I think you're in trouble, bud." I tickle him as we walk back towards the room, carrying him as he's squirming in my arms laughing.

"Look what I caught running around in the wild." Jack is still laughing and I'm trying not to with him.

Mia, looking totally frustrated trying to get Kayla dressed, stops and looks up at hearing my voice. Her eyes change and have a little sparkle in them as her mouth moves into a smile.

"Hi there. I didn't know you were here." She picks up Kayla off the bed, who is now dressed for bed and looks so cute.

"I haven't been here long. I was just talking to the boys when this little rascal came running by. Here, swap." Putting Jack down and holding my arms out for Kayla, she puts her cute little arms up and leans out of Mia's arms towards me.

"Hello, my gorgeous little girl. Have you been good for Mommy and not running away like your brother?" I pull her in tight for a hug and take in the distinct smell of a clean baby. It's like they brand you so you can't think clearly when they're near. They hypnotize you.

"God help me when she's moving too. I can't contain one of them, let alone two of them." Mia rolls her eyes while getting clothes onto Jack.

"You are going to be a nice quiet one for your Momma, aren't you, Kayla?" Before I get to say another word, Jack is running around me to grab his books.

"Lex, can you read me a story, please, pretty please? I'll let you pick." He is jumping up and down in front of me.

"Hey, how come I never get to pick?" Mia pretends to protest, while holding her arms back out for Kayla.

"Because you are my mommy. Lex is my new friend, so he can choose."

I swallow my emotions so not to let Mia see them. "Okay, here's the deal. We go and read two books while Mom puts Kayla to sleep. But you have to promise that you will go right to sleep once we're finished. Is that a deal?"

Mia laughs and mumbles under breath, "You'll make a good parent if you know the bribe game already."

I wink at her as I take Jack's hand and lead him to the living room. "Now we have to be quiet and settle down so Kayla can sleep, but I know you're good at being super quiet, aren't you?" Jack is busy nodding his head as we take a seat on the couch.

Mason comes walking past, letting me know he's taking food upstairs for Paige and they're having an early night so she can rest with her headache. I know he's doing it for me and Mia as well, but he'll never admit that.

With Jack snuggled into me on my lap, we start the first story and nearly get all the way to the end and I hear his breathing get that little bit heavier and his body going limp. Looking down, I can see him asleep on my chest. This boy amazes me. He goes flat-out all day, but when he crashes, it's quick and he's in a deep sleep before we know it. Putting the books aside and picking him up, I walk slowly to the bedroom since I don't want to wake him. As I walk into the dimly lit room, I see Mia is sitting on the bed looking down at a sleeping Kayla. Hearing me enter, she looks up and smiles at me.

Pulling back the blankets, I place him down softly and then tuck the blankets up around him to keep him warm. I don't know what came over me, but I lean down and kiss him on the forehead. Glancing at Mia, I see she has tears in her eyes, but I can tell they're not sad tears.

Leaving her in the room for that quiet moment and making sure both her kids are okay, I walk out and just stand looking out of the window. The city is switching into Friday-night mode. Everyone is releasing the tension of the week. From the balcony of my apartment, I'm used to hearing the sounds, but from here I can only see the lights and hear the silence. Strangely, I enjoy it just as much.

Her soft feet on the carpet draw me out of the spell the nighttime view has over me.

"Hey," she says as she reaches my side. I look at her standing in front of me. Not just glance, but really look at her. Her soft pale skin, the fine features of her face. Her hair pulled in a loose ponytail at the base of her head, showing off her slender neck. There is something about the simplicity of Mia that really appeals to me. She has so much inner beauty that she has never let out before. Yet since the day I met her, that glow inside her is starting to shine brighter, even when she feels the weight of the world. Still she is simply stunning.

"Lex?" Shit, I haven't replied.

"Hi. Sorry, I just couldn't help it. You look beautiful tonight." The instant blush appearing on her cheeks just makes her more appealing.

"Don't talk crazy. I'm a mess and we both know that." Her head drops to look at the floor. I can't take seeing her with such a lack of self-confidence. I step closer to her.

"Mia, look at me." I wait for her to lift her face, yet it's not coming. I take a risk when I know I shouldn't.

I place my hand on her cheek and lift her face to see me. Her breath hitches and my heart skips a beat at the chance to touch her.

"All I see in you is beauty, please don't ever doubt that." My thumb slowly strokes her face, and I feel her gently lean into my hand. Oh, how I want to lean down and kiss her. Taste those precious lips. Patience has developed a new meaning. It's the definition of describing the pain in my body right now as I try to hold back. Or as Mason called it, the word to describe blue balls syndrome.

Her lips parting just the tiniest amount now have my cock standing to attention.

"I don't see it," she whispers.

"I know, but I'm going to show you. Just you wait. One day you too will see what I do."

Our faces getting closer, I have to pull back. Now is not the time for Mia. Slowly sliding my hand from her face and down her neck to her shoulder, the soft moan that escapes her is not missed. It may not be the right time, but fuck, I wish it was. And the hardest part of all is I know she wishes it was too. The look in her eyes and her body language is telling me all I need to know.

"Sorry, I shouldn't have done that. But you just keep pulling me closer." Finally letting her go and taking a step away from her body, she looks like she is in a bit of a trance.

"Mia, why don't we get something to eat and have that movie night." I try not to laugh as she snaps out of her little dream. I get it, baby, I'm in that fantasy world too.

"Umm, oh yeah, sorry. Have you eaten dinner? I haven't cooked mine yet, I waited for you." Still a little flustered, she heads towards the kitchen with me following.

"Actually, I haven't, so that sounds amazing. Don't go to much trouble, though. I'd be happy with cheese on toast, because I know what's coming for dessert."

Mia's head whips around with a startled look.

"Ice cream, Mia, nothing more. I just meant the ice cream I brought for you." My heart aches for her fear. It will take some time for that to pass.

"Yeah, sorry. I wasn't thinking." She turns back to the fridge where she's getting out some things. "It's nothing exciting, just some chicken and vegetables like I was cooking for the kids, but I won't make you eat all of yours mashed together like Kayla."

Her little joke breaks the moment for both of us and we laugh.

"Thank goodness. And I promise not to get it all over my face like they do either. Can I help you with anything?" I step to the side so I can see her face as she starts working at the stove.

"No, thank you. I prepared it all earlier when I fed the kids. But you could get the plates out and set the table for us, if you like." She even seems timid to ask me that.

"Of course, okay, I'm on it." I give her space to cook without feeling like she's being watched. I remember her saying that she doesn't feel she has any confidence in the kitchen.

After getting everything ready, I start searching the streaming Paige has to find the *Pretty Woman* movie. I can't say I've ever really watched a true chick flick so tonight will be a first.

Watching Mia carry the plates to the table and looking at her uncertainty, I know she's struggling a little tonight.

"That looks great. I'm starving. Here, let me take them from you." Placing them down on the table, I pull her chair out for her to sit down. The look on her face is priceless. "Yes, this is what a gentleman will do for a lady. So, you better get used to this kind of treatment. Although I don't have a great relationship with my parents, one thing they did teach me is manners and the way to respect women."

Nodding her head at me, she slowly lowers into her seat with a small smile on her face. I take the seat next to her on the end of the table, so we're close together, but I'm looking at her.

"Thank you for making me dinner, Mia. I really appreciate it. The only person who's ever made me dinner is someone I've paid to do it or in a restaurant. This is my first home-cooked meal prepared by a beautiful lady." I cut off a piece of chicken and slide it into my mouth, letting out an appreciative moan at the tasty food. "This tastes so good. I think you underestimate your cooking, Mia."

"Pfft, it's just something plain and boring. Nothing like your chefs would cook for you." She shakes her head and starts to eat.

"Ah yes, but their food always lacks one important ingredient."

She looks at me, waiting for my answer. "What?" Her fork is halfway to her mouth with some beans on it.

"Affection."

Smiling at her and continuing to eat, I know I'm stepping way past the line I was going to stay behind with Mia. Yet I can't seem to stop.

The words are said before I can take them back.

The truth is never a lie

Chapter Seventeen

LEX

Getting through the small talk in between mouthfuls, dinner is now done, and after my suggestion, Mia has just gone to check on the kids while I clean up.

Trying to help, I insisted that she cooked, so it's only fair I clean up. Not that there's much mess for two people, but it's Paige's home and it should be respected at all times. Her letting Mia stay here, and putting up with me being here all the time too, shouldn't be taken for granted.

As I place the last dish in the dishwasher and wipe the counter down, Mia walks back into the kitchen.

"Are they okay?" I ask her, wondering what the strange look on her face is for.

"Yes, both sound asleep." I can see she's hesitating over something.

"What is it?"

"Why are you so kind to my kids and worry about them all the time? Why do you care?" All the words come out in a rush.

"Okay, where did all that come from?"

"I just don't understand. You aren't their father, yet you have shown more interest in them in a week than he ever did. Jack hasn't asked for anyone to read to him except me. Kayla doesn't go to men for a cuddle as easily as she goes to you. And none of this seems to even faze you. Why?"

Standing still, I know this is a conversation we need to have but just not in the middle of the kitchen, but you can't always pick the timing. "To me, it's simple. They are adorable kids who I love spending time with. Plus, they're a part of you. I'm not going to hide the fact I like you, and that there are some serious emotions happening between us. With that, I know the three of you are a package deal." I'm not sure she was ready for that sort of answer, but too bad. "If you've learned anything in the last week, I hope it's that blood relations don't always mean family, it's more about the connection on a deeper level sometimes. So, I might not be their father, but that doesn't mean I don't care about them and want to protect them as best I can. Meeting you, Jack, and Kayla is making me feel freer than I've felt in a very long time. I won't lie to you, Mia. Before now I haven't had one thing to do with any kids besides Daisy occasionally. I'm totally winging this and hoping to god that I'm not doing anything to mess it up."

"You are far from making any mistakes. I've never seen Jack gravitate to anyone the way he does to you. I don't think you had a choice in him wanting to spend time with you. As you've seen he's a whirlwind at times."

"That's what I love about him. He has so much character in him."

"You've brought that out in him, Lex. He must feel safe with you because he has talked more and laughed louder since meeting you." Pausing, she looks at me with such feeling behind her eyes. "Maybe I have too."

Fuck. She does this to me so easily. In a few simple words, brings me to my knees.

But every time she lets a little something slip out, the panic starts to follow. Rescuing her from having to acknowledge her feelings and what she just said, I take control for her.

"Those words mean the world to me, Mia. Thank you. Now let's grab the ice cream and head to the couch so we can sit and talk about any other questions you've got. Or don't talk at all and you can punish me with your chick flick." Giving her space, I turn, opening the freezer to retrieve the tubs.

"Lex."

"Yeah," I respond with my head still in the freezer and trying not to laugh at the note stuck on one tub from Mason: *'Hope your balls freeze off.'*

"I like you too." He soft voice rolls over me, and the feeling that comes with it is one I can't wait to explore further.

Before I have time to turn around, she's gone, and I'm left standing in the kitchen with ice cream, thoughts of frozen balls, but a warm feeling in my heart. I'll take that.

I take my time to get spoons, some serviettes, and of course the chocolate I couldn't resist buying just to be a smartass. Walking into the living room, I find her sitting on the bigger couch getting herself comfortable. I could sit on one of the other ones, but I'm not. Sitting down next to her and placing everything on the table, Mia just looks at the chocolate and any awkwardness is gone, while she laughs.

"You're such an idiot." Her giggle lights up her face.

"Okay, show me this movie you love so much. I'm sure it's just riveting," I say, playfully mocking her now to keep the moment light.

"You wait. I'm going to convert you to love my movies. There is nothing like a good HEA."

"What the hell is an HEA?" Man, I'm so not up with this girl talk.

"Seriously, you don't know what HEA means? You know, as in Happily. Ever. After. You are such a boy!"

"Well, I hope so, because otherwise I've got some extra body parts that you may need to explain to me." I pick up the first tub of ice cream, lift the lid, and pass it to her as the movie starts rolling.

"You did not just say that." She rolls her eyes at me.

"Do I need to repeat it?"

"No." She takes her first scoop while I dip my spoon into mine too.

"Prepare to be amazed, this ice cream will ruin you for all other flavors for the rest of your life."

"That's a big claim, mister. I'll rate it after you have watched this. Now you sit back and enjoy the best movie ever."

"I doubt it, but I've been proven wrong before. Not often, but it does happen occasionally."

"Be prepared for today to be the day then."

We both take our first mouthful, and I'm in heaven hearing her moan with enjoyment. Knew she was perfect for me, just like my cookies-and-cream ice cream.

I can't voice it out loud, but this movie isn't too bad. A little outdated being made thirty years ago, but it's still pretty funny in parts. I can see why Mia loves it. It's the ultimate fairytale for her and probably one she's dreamt about many times. As the movie progresses, she's now lying down on the couch curling into the pillows. Her feet curled up next to me. Her toes almost resting on my leg but not quite. I want to take them, put her feet in my lap and massage them, but I know I can't.

The moment the ending happens, I look to her and there are tears rolling down her cheeks.

"Is this what HEAs do to you?" But she shakes her head a little at me. Up and down but then sideways too.

"Mia?"

"I always cry at happy endings." She sniffles.

"But this isn't just happy ending crying, is it?"

Then her head shake is more pronounced, side to side.

"Talk to me, baby. What is it?" I knew this was coming, and to be honest I'm surprised it wasn't earlier in the night.

"I'm so fucking scared." The words I hate hearing her say.

That's it, I'm not waiting any longer.

"Come to me. Let me hold you." Seeing the hesitation in her eyes, in my head I'm almost begging her. *Take the step, trust me to take care of you.*

Slowly she sits up and then shuffles down the couch to me. My heart is racing for the way she's fighting her own demons for me.

Placing my arm around her shoulder and the other under her knees, I lift her onto my lap. I don't have to worry about how she feels about my touch as she snuggles her head into the crook of my neck and her hands wrap around my body.

Nothing has ever felt as good as having her in my arms. There are so many words I want to say, but instead we stay quiet, both just in the moment.

Her tears have stopped, but I'm not letting go of her until she makes me.

The silence is broken by her soft voice. "I'm scared of heading into my past, but I'm just as frightened of the future."

"I understand the past, but why the future?" I need to see her eyes. They are the window to her soul. I lift her face up to see me.

"What if I let my walls down and then you hurt me. I won't make it through it. I know I won't. Everything I feel already is more than I ever felt for my husband. How can that be?"

"Because he never loved you. Not like the way you should be loved. He wasn't the one for you."

"Are you?"

My hand cups her cheek. "Totally," I say immediately without any hesitation. "Mia…" My face lowers closer to hers. "Can I kiss you? It's okay to say no." My voice is no more than a whisper. "I will never hurt you, I promise…" is all I say before she tentatively kisses my lips.

The moment of finally tasting her will be etched in my memory forever. Letting her lead, the kiss is soft and gentle. Everything Mia is to me. I don't want to rush this. Savoring every part of it. I can feel her body starting to respond to the heat of the kiss as she slowly starts to bring the intensity.

My head is screaming at me to keep it slow, but my body is deaf to my inner voice. My hand now sliding into her hair and pulling out the ponytail. I want her hair flowing and falling all over her shoulders. I need to stop and check she's okay. Pulling back, my lips long to stay touching her.

"Lex?" A confused look is rising in her eyes.

"I won't push you. Is this what you want, Mia? Please tell me it's not just me."

"I should say no, but I can't. I want you, and I can't turn off this feeling."

"Then don't." Taking her lips again, now I'm trying to claim her. My mouth asks permission as it swipes across her lips, both my hands on her cheeks trying to show her how much I want her. "Oh Mia, what are you doing to me?" Breaking the kiss again, I rest our foreheads together.

"You're my star, aren't you?"

"Yeah, baby, your hope for a better life. Let me in and I'll be that for you, for the rest of your days."

"I'm still married."

"I'll wait," I say, kissing her cheek. "You need me to take it slow, and I'm not going to fuck this up. I've waited a lifetime for you." Kissing the opposite cheek now and then softly on the lips. Holding her for a few seconds before separating. "Lay with me. Just let me hold you, nothing more. Take away your fear." Her head nods to tell me that's what she wants. I know Mia struggles to talk when her emotions are running crazy.

Lowering my body onto the couch and bringing her with me, I pull us along a bit farther so we're both stretched out. My back to the back of the couch so she feels she has an out at all times. Lying on our sides so Mia won't feel threatened by my body above her. Settling her head on my arm and drawing her to me. We are front to front, and her legs are entwined in mine. I can feel her heart beating against my chest, and I'm sure she can feel mine.

"You are safe, Mia. Just how you feel now, I will always keep you safe." My hand rubs up and down her back. I'm elated she is so calm, but part of me is scared that she's holding everything inside. In such a short time, she has come such a long way, yet I'm worried that what I'm doing could be pushing her over the edge and sending her backwards.

"Please tell me to stop if you need to. I couldn't bear knowing I hurt you."

"You promised you wouldn't." She takes a big breath. "I trust you, Lex, from that first night, I always have."

And just like that, Mia makes me a mushy mess.

MIA

How am I able to lie here with Lex and not feel one second of panic? I should. From where I've come from, this should be freaking me out. Yet I just want to lie here forever and never leave his arms. His strength wrapped around me is something I've longed my whole life for. Someone to just hold me and care. To want me and to let me know through their simple touches that they will protect me. With his powerful hold on my body, my brain is telling me I should fear him. But how can you fear what your heart is longing for? This overwhelming tingling that is running through my body can't be wrong.

Can it?

Am I dreaming?

Too much imagination of the perfect fairytales. Am I just desperate for Lex to be my Prince Charming?

The universe can't be this cruel, to bring me the perfect man and not let me keep him.

Oh god, why can't my brain just shut up. Give me tonight. Just let me take the calm he always brings me, so I can deal with tomorrow and the next few days. I just want to be Mia tonight.

"Mia, stop overthinking this. I can feel you tensing back up." And there is his controlled voice again. Bringing me the peace I so desperately need.

"How do you always know?" I whisper.

"Because you're the other part of me. I already know that. So, when you think it, I feel it."

His lips kiss my forehead again. I think that is my favorite kiss ever. I feel so cherished.

"I feel you everywhere, Mia, but already you have captured my heart. It smiles when you smile and bleeds when you bleed. Nothing you do can change that. I tried so hard to stay away."

I can't help but giggle even in this intense moment. "How did that work for you?"

He looks down at us joined from the chest down. "Not real well, as you can see, but I'm blaming you. No man can resist your beauty for long. I mean, look at you. You are so sexy, baby." I can see in his eyes he actually means it.

I feel sensations in places that haven't been excited like this in a very long time, if ever.

"I've never been told I'm sexy. I don't feel it, and I can't see it."

"Mia, you have to believe me when I tell you. No woman has ever affected me the way you do. Fuck, every time you walk into the room, I'm struggling not to wrap you in my arms and kiss the hell out of you."

"You don't need to be nice to me." I don't know how to cope with his words.

"Nice is the last thing I want to be to you, sweetheart. My body is screaming at me to strip us both bare and make you see how sexy I find you. Making you come so many times, so you're in utter bliss by the time I sink deep inside you, claiming you as mine. I never want to own you, but god, I want you to be mine like I need to breathe. Fuck, I need to shut up before I scare you." Pulling back from me slightly, his hand goes up and he runs it through his short spiky hair.

"You don't scare me. Tell me more, please...I've never had this before." I wish I could turn on my filter sometimes, but Lex holds the key. With him the words just come out. He gets to hear what I really want whether I've worked it out yet or not.

"Every time you open your mouth tonight you kill me, Mia. More, oh I want to do so much more to you. You have no idea the dreams I've been having since you arrived. The way you respond to me when I touch you. I'm not sure you can handle if I tell you my inner desire."

His face shows the increase in the frustration his body is holding back.

"Tell me. I know I won't cope with more than words, but I want to hear it all." My boldness shocks both me and him.

"You are in control here, just remember that." His arm moves back around me and pulls me a little tighter. Already my body feels the tingles of being so close, but feeling his cock so hard and pressing against my stomach, and knowing he won't force me to do anything, actually turns me on more than I realized was possible.

His head now leans down and the softness of his lips kisses ever so gently on my neck. The words vibrating on my body as he whispers, "When you are finally free and ready to be mine, I will worship you like my queen. Our days will be filled with laughter and happiness, but our nights are just for you and me. I can't wait to lay you out on our bed and just admire your naked beauty. I know under these clothes, your soft pale skin will shiver at my touch." The way his hand slides down over my back and smoothly caresses my ass has the heat in me rising.

I can't hold it back, letting a soft moan escape my lips.

"Oh, how I long to hear you moan like that when I'm sliding my fingers through your wet pussy. I'm making you wet now, aren't I, Mia." This deep sex voice is new, but oh my god I want more.

"Yes," I whisper unashamedly.

"Good girl. I never want you to hide from me. Tell me how you feel. Right now, what do you feel?"

"Tempted, so tempted."

"Imagine when I can touch you. When my hands can take your breasts and make you feel the pleasure. My mouth sucking your rock-hard nipple into it and my tongue playing there. Sending that tingly feeling straight to your clitoris, making it start screaming to be touched."

"Oh, Lex..." How can he play my body like this with just his words? It's like I can feel his intimate touching through his voice.

"You want to come now, don't you? Your body is begging to feel the euphoria I can give you. You're burning with desire. While you're lying there naked, now I would swipe my tongue slowly up your sex and taste every drop you're giving me. Watching you raise your body off the bed because you can't take the sensation. Holding your waist then sliding my finger deep inside you, now you're screaming my name. Inside your head, scream my name, Mia. As my thumb pushes down on your clit and my second finger slides in and starts stroking that spot. Yeah, the one that has you riding my hand like you can't stop. Trying to gain that final release you're longing for."

I can't even breathe, his words have me on the edge of a cliff, and I want it. I want it all. Every single thing he's describing. I can't help it now, I'm grinding against his body trying to ease my aching.

"Oh…oh yes, please, Lex, I need it…oh god." I want him to touch me. For the first time ever, I really want a man to fucking touch me like this.

"Right at the moment when you're riding my hand so hard and you can't quite get there, I lean down and take your nipple that is so fucking hard, and I bite it to the point you want to scream but instead all you can do is moan. I'm sending that pleasure through you, and you've reached the pinnacle. Like now. You are so fucking turned on that you're about to explode. It's coming, Mia, feel that orgasm. Let it overtake you. Let go and know it's me taking you over the edge and you are safe to feel it all. Come, Mia, come for me now!"

His voice is all I need, and I'm lost. Closing my eyes and my mouth dropping open, I can't breathe. All I can see is stars and the waves of pleasure rolling through my body. Like I'm out of my body and floating in the sensations.

His voice whispering in my ear brings me out of the floating experience. "That's it, my beautiful girl, come back to me." Feeling his lips on mine, I open my eyes to see him. I can't do anything but kiss him like my life depends on it. The sexual tension between us is so high that he must be ready to explode.

Pulling apart, he settles me back on his arm and takes me in tight to his body again.

His hand rubs my back while my breathing starts returning to normal.

"Lex, do you…"

"Don't even ask that. This is not about me. I will never forget that vision of you letting go and the ecstasy taking over. The most beautiful sight. That's all I need to feel pleasure."

"But..." His finger is on my lips before I can finish my sentence.

"Shhh, just close your eyes and rest with me. Just give me a few minutes."

Knowing his cock is as hard as steel, feeling it still pushing against me, I feel guilty but don't have the energy to argue.

"Lex."

"Mmm." His voice is soft now.

"Thank you for not pushing for more." I feel so dreamy now, still floating.

"The choice is always yours, beautiful. Always..."

Totally at peace, I know I'm drifting off to sleep, but I'll just take a second to lie here. Everything just feels perfect for this moment. I don't want to lose it.

"Mommy, move over. I can't fit."

"Yeah, bud," I mumble.

Shifting back a little makes Lex groan behind me.

Lex!

Shit!

Where am I? What the hell is going on?

I sit up completely startled. Not meaning to, I launch Jack onto the floor from the couch.

"Jack, why are you out of bed?" I open my eyes more and look around. Realizing it's morning and I've slept on the couch all night.

With Lex!

I've been spooning on the couch with Lex.

Dammit, how am I going to explain this to everyone? I'm a married woman and I'm here sleeping with another man.

"Because I woke up. So, I came to say good morning and I'm hungry." Such a simple answer.

"Morning, Jack," Lex's deep voice comes from behind me.

"Hi, Lex. Can we make pancakes?" Jack's excited voice at having Lex here is just too much this early in the morning.

"Right, morning, yes, um breakfast. Go to the toilet and come back." Thank god he happily skips off down the hallway, doing as he's asked.

"Lex, quick, get up." Turning, I find him lying with his hands behind his head with the smuggest grin.

"Mia, breathe. We were just sleeping, nothing more. He's four, he won't understand. Now come here and give me my good morning."

"Stop it." Smacking him on the arm, I try to stand but he grabs me around the waist and pulls me on top of him.

"Don't do this. Don't shut me out again." His lips take mine before I have time to think. Oh god, they're like a weapon that has a tranquilizer in them. With just his touch and my fight leaves me every time.

"That's better. Morning, beautiful." He looks so hot all ruffled in the morning.

"Morning," I say, resting my forehead on his. My hands on his chest where I can feel every hard muscle.

"Morning, love birds, coffee?" Mason's laughing voice comes from behind the couch. I didn't even hear him coming. All I can do is groan. This morning just gets better and better.

"Great."

As I try to get up, Lex just starts laughing. "It's fine, it's not like he didn't know. I'll talk to him."

Nodding a little, I need to move before Jack is back.

"Okay. I need to get Kayla." His arms releasing me, I stand and straighten myself back up.

Before I can even get two feet away, Jack is back running straight for Lex.

He can't know. I don't want to confuse him. Especially if things turn to shit. Which in my life, they usually do.

"Pancakes. Let's go." Jack is already excited and hasn't even noticed or asked why we were asleep on the couch together.

"Hang on there, buddy. I need to help Mom with Kayla first. Uncle Mason is in the kitchen. Go and say good morning to him." Lex is now standing with Jack in his arms. Putting him down, his little feet are already running as soon as they hit the floor.

"Uncle Mason! Lex is making pancakes for breakfast!" I hear him yelling as I try to escape to my bedroom.

My mind is racing along with my heart. What the hell am I doing? I can't let this happen.

Happiness is not something meant for me. I can't let the kids get hurt anymore. I'm barely functioning, but I won't let anything bad touch them again. If I let them get close to Lex, when he leaves, they'll be devastated.

Stop pretending, it's you that will be shattered. You're using the kids as your excuse, but it's your heart that's on the line.

As I stop over top of Kayla in the playpen, she smiles up at me like the world is the same as it was yesterday. But it's not. My whole universe has shifted, and I don't know how to deal with it.

I feel his hand on my shoulder. He doesn't have to say a word. Just his touch is grounding me a little. Seeing his face behind me, Kayla starts to get excited and her hands and feet are flapping faster now. Now my own daughter is a traitor too. He has put the Lex spell over her just like he has her mother.

"Mia, talk to me. You know keeping it inside is no good."

"What are we doing, Lex?"

Turning me to face him, his smile makes me weak. "We are becoming who we should be, starting a life together. I know you're frightened, I see it written all over your face. But your eyes tell me the truth. They can't lie. You want this, you're just scared to take that step. I get it, and I will let you take the lead every step of the way."

"I can't do it. I don't know how. The obstacles are too high."

"No, they aren't. They might be tall, but I will lift you up. We'll climb them together, I promise. I know I keep saying this, and I'll probably repeat it until I'm blue in the face, but I need you to trust me not to hurt you. It's okay you can't do that yet, but the more I remind you, hopefully one day it will sink in and you'll believe it."

He embraces me tightly like he's trying to imprint me with his words. Then pulls back as he hears Jack getting closer. He bends slightly so we're eye level.

"I'll go slow, but I'm not walking away."

Swallowing a big lump in my throat, I reply, "Super slow," my voice quivering.

"Slow as a snail if you need me to."

"Who is slow as a snail?" Jack is now beside us, and I need to distract myself from the intense situation. Bending down picking up Kayla, I snuggle her tight.

"You are, Jack. You are slow like a snail." Lex takes the reins for me.

"Not me, I'm super speedy like a race car. Just watch me." Taking off back out of the room, he's running to show us.

As soon as I turn back to Lex, he looks relieved.

"I've got you, baby. Relax, and for once, let the goodness overtake the darkness. I promise you will only ever know happiness now."

His voice and words are like a spell. Kayla leans out from me with her arms out for Lex to take her.

Maybe he's right.

I need to take a lesson from my kids.

All they see is sunshine and rainbows since Lex turned up in our lives.

I want to just see that too.

To do that, I need to move on past the darkness.

Easier said than done.

Chapter Eighteen

LEX

I know I need to keep Mia out of her head today.

Her emotions are all over the place. The fear of Monday is always there just below the surface, and we still need to talk about that. The confusion about her feelings for me is mixed with the exhilaration she's still feeling from last night. I'm still trying to process it, so I'm sure for her it's ten times harder.

When I drove here from work, I never expected the night we shared. I just wanted to see her and make sure she was alright. The ice cream and movie were exactly what I had imagined. The sort of night I'm hoping we can share more of in the future. But what came after that has left me feeling on cloud nine. Watching her, I'm just praying I didn't push her to a place she never wanted to go. Although we stayed fully clothed, it was one of the most intimate things I've done with a woman. No one has responded to me like Mia does. She brings out a gentleness in me I didn't know I had. For me, sex has always been a little rough, hard and with no emotion. The women I've been with have wanted the same thing.

Mia's different.

She is soft and gentle. Someone to cherish and make feel like she is treasured. Last night I wanted so much more, but I know I've got to take baby steps. Something I'm not usually very good at. If I want something I go after it and nothing stands in my way. This time no one is getting between Mia and me, but I'm not charging in there like a bull. I promised her slow, and that's what she'll get from me. Part of me is hoping like hell her definition of slow and mine are two different things.

"I just need to freshen up. Can you take Kayla out to the living room with Jack for me?" I know what she's really saying is she needs a few minutes.

"Sure. Come on, ladybug. Let's go and see if we can contain your brother long enough to get some breakfast happening. Take as long as you need," I tell Mia.

Walking out of the room, I'm trying not to laugh at myself. What even is my life? Cuddling a baby girl while I'm on my way to cook pancakes with her four-year-old brother. If only my mother could see me now. She was horrified at me that last day I saw her. This would blow her mind. Actually, I wonder how she would feel about being a grandmother. Had it ever crossed her mind, that one day I would marry and have children? Probably not. She would believe that children would interfere with my career path. I'm still so angry at her, but I know at some stage I need to speak to her and my father. I don't want to sever the relationship, but it will be a distant one. The obligatory visits for birthdays and Christmas. The kiss on the cheek at charity events when we run into each other. Pretending to know everything that's going on in their life when I'm asked by people how Dustin and Eloise are. It's sad, but it's just how it will be. I didn't choose this, they laid the path for the relationship a long time ago. Now they have what they created.

A token son.

Meeting Paige at the bottom of the stairs, she steals Kayla from me for her morning cuddle. I swear these kids will never know a life without hugging and feeling love. It's here in abundance for them.

"Morning, Lex, another sleepover, I see." She just keeps walking, giggling away, and doesn't let me answer. I follow her into the kitchen because I may as well get this over and done with. They're both busting to say something.

"I slept on the couch. It was too late to go home."

Mason just rolls his eyes as Jack once again rats me out. "Yeah, he slept with Mommy." Proud as punch he can add to the conversation.

"You what?" Paige nearly chokes on her own words trying to get them out fast enough.

"Yeah, Lex, please explain." Mason is loving this. Asshole.

"Calm down, Paige. We were watching a movie and both fell asleep. That's it. We slept on the couch together. End of story." Well, not quite, but there is no way I'm sharing that moment with anyone.

"Lex, be careful. She's vulnerable." I can see the concern on Paige's face.

"I know, but she is also a big girl who can choose her own destiny. I won't hurt her. You have to know that." I'm a little frustrated that I need to justify myself to her, but on the other hand, I'm happy she's so protective of her.

"I do, but I also know that whether you like it or not, you're a boy, and boys do some really dumb things sometimes."

"Wow, hurting over here," Mason pipes in. "I never do dumb things. The others, well, I totally agree, but not me." Mason is trying to occupy Jack while I get grilled by his girlfriend.

"Keep dreaming, Mason," she says, leaving him and walking off to the living room with Kayla, the conversation finished. Thank goodness.

Leaning back against the counter, I just take a minute too. From the moment our eyes opened this morning, I feel like it's been a blur.

After I take in a deep breath, it dawns on me that if I'm lucky enough to share a life with Mia and the kids, then every morning will be like this.

Time to suck it up and get on with it.

"Hey, Jack, you think Uncle Mason will be better than me at

making pancakes or am I the king of the kitchen?" I call to him, and he's running before Mason even has time to start to answer.

"I will always be better than Lex at everything," Mason tries to convince Jack as he arrives in the kitchen.

"Nuh uh. He is better at making Mommy smile and laugh than you!" Jack is already dragging the stool to the counter where he knows he is allowed to help.

"Yeah, buddy, I'll give him that one. He is pretty good at that."

I'm still standing there speechless as Mason grabs my shoulder, giving it a squeeze.

"Keep up the good work, man. You both deserve this." Mason's words snap me out of it, and I know Jack is waiting for me to say something.

"Thanks, my little champion. Now let's see how good Mason is at flipping pancakes."

With that, the breakfast feast championship begins.

MIA

"Mia, are you in here? I just wanted to see if you're okay." Paige pokes her head into my room. Seeing me sitting on my bed just staring into space, she takes a seat next to me.

"Oh sorry, time got away from me," I mumble.

"Don't be silly. There's no rush. The boys have the kids, and there's a couple of huge egos swirling in my kitchen trying to compete to make the best breakfast." She laughs, and I can imagine the scene out there.

"I better go and sort out the kids then."

"No, they're fine. I promise. Now, you want to tell me what has you hiding in here?"

"He kissed me," I blurt out.

"Okay, and did you like it?" Paige gently prods me to continue.

"It was so amazing, I don't even know how to describe it," I say, dropping my head into my hands.

"So, what's the problem, did you not want him to?"

"No, I wanted it, over and over again. I almost begged him to do more. What the hell is wrong with me? I can't stand men touching me, but Lex, I want him to touch me in all the ways I never thought I would let another man do again. It's too soon, I'm still married. I'm just so torn. He makes me feel so alive, so why am I panicking?"

"Let's get something settled right now. You stopped being married to Edward the moment he hurt you the first time. Marriage is more than a piece of paper. It's the way you love and respect another soul. He stopped doing that a long time ago. The way I see it, your soul has been single for a very long time. Don't deny it happiness because of that douchebag."

How can someone I've only just met make everything sound so easy? Her words are making sense of my jumbled thoughts.

"He's a good man, Mia. One of the best. If you're having these feelings for him too, don't let your past ruin your future. I wouldn't let him anywhere near you if I was worried in the slightest, let alone let him lay you out on my couch and have you moaning."

Her words startling me, I look straight at her. "Oh god, you saw us, didn't you? I'm so embarrassed." My cheeks are burning, and I imagine them being bright red.

"Don't be. It was only for a split second. I woke feeling better and was coming down to check on you. I know you told me to stop, but anyway, last night may have cured me. As soon as I saw the two of you wrapped in such a passionate kiss, I quickly raced back to my room and woke Mason to tell him. Sorry not sorry. I was a little excited."

"Oh god, Paige, don't do this. I'm struggling trying to go slow as it is. Don't join the Lex camp. Can you just stay in the Mia camp for a little while? Be the big sister and pretend to scare him off or something until I get my head around it all."

We both look at each other and burst out laughing. Paige grabs me and we're hugging and laughing at the same time.

"Love you, Mia, it will all be fine. I just know it will. You will get your HEA."

I pull back and look at her. "That's what I call it, too! HEA!"

"Duh, we are sisters after all."

"I love you so much, Paige. Thank god we are finally together. Our own sister HEA."

"You got it, sis. Never apart again." She drags me off the bed. "Now let's go eat before there's none left."

"They better not have eaten it all, otherwise they'll find out what happens when sisters lose their shit at the same time."

"Oh, this is going to be fun!" Paige links her arm in mine, and we head out to join the rest of them for the morning.

I'm feeling a little lighter from my talk.

Amazing what it feels like to have someone to finally share my thoughts with.

Today life is good, and that's all I can ask.

"I can't believe you voted that Lex's pancakes were better than mine. You're supposed to be on my team, you know, being my girlfriend and all." Everyone is laughing at Mason as we finish cleaning up.

"Well, I can't lie, they did taste better. Perhaps you need more practice and need to raise your game." Paige winks at me from across the kitchen.

"I saw that, Tiger. Oh, I see how this is. You think if you tell me they were shit I'll cook them all the time until you say they're better than his. I'm onto you, woman. You better start running now before I catch you and spank that little bottom of yours." Paige is off before we know it, screaming the whole way as she's running up the stairs. Jack chases after them, wanting to play in the game too. Welcome to parenthood. There is no time to yourself. Maybe I've cured them of ever having children. I doubt it, though.

Watching them with Jack and Kayla, it's like they're born parents.

"It's good to see him so happy." Lex is beside me now. "Life hasn't always been easy for him since he came home from deployment. Carried a lot of baggage."

"Yeah, he told me some of it. He deserves happiness. He's a good person, and I couldn't wish for anyone better for my sister."

We both stand there for a moment. Again, the silence is eating away at me, but I need to tell him what I'm thinking. It's only fair that I push myself to bare some of my thoughts when he tells me so much of his.

"I know I'm going to keep freaking out, and as much as I try not to, I'll want to run when the panic sets in. I've been doing it for so long I don't know how to change it."

"Mia."

"No, let me finish, please. I'm going to want to run every time, but what I'm telling you is I want you to stop me. I like you, Lex, and I know deep down I want to be with you. I just have to keep working on myself before I can give me to you. I hope you understand."

"Every single word, Mia. Just so you know, I'm a fast runner, and I will catch you every single time you try. I'm not letting you go." Standing in front of me, he leans down so I can see his face fully. "Ever." Sneaking a quick kiss in, he then takes me in a tight embrace.

While my face is buried in his shoulder and he can't see my embarrassment, I say the other words that I'm hiding. "Last night was wonderful. And just so you know, one day I'd like you to do all that just like you said. When I'm ready." Feeling the shiver run through him, I know he wants that too.

"Oh Mia, me too. Until then, this is perfect, and more than enough." Feeling him kiss the top of my head, we both know this moment is short-lived. Jack will be back any moment, and I need to check on Kayla.

When we hear the voices coming down the stairs, our time is up, and we move apart, but this time we're both smiling. Sharing a secret bond that no other person feels.

Moving to the living room for us all to be together, Lex sits down next to me and has no problem with making sure he's close enough that we're touching. I try not to laugh. He is not subtle at all. He may as well hang a sign around my neck.

She's mine!

I'm not sure how he'll cope with slow, but at least he's trying.

"So, what's the plan for today?" Mason asks, and to be honest I have no idea.

"I want to know if you two will watch the kids. I'd like to take Mia out for coffee. If you would like that?" He looks so nervous for my answer. "We need to talk about Monday, and I think it will be easier without the kids around. Plus, I won't deny, I'd like to spend a little time with you. Alone without Mason and Paige playing big brother and sister."

Everyone starts laughing, and I laugh too, but on the inside I'm already nervous about leaving the kids.

"Of course, I'll watch all the children, Jack, Kayla, and Mason. All three are safe with me." Paige starts laughing at her own joke.

"Well, that headache yesterday didn't wipe away any of your sassy attitude, did it?" Mason pokes her in the side which has her laughing more.

"What do you say, Mia, do you think you can come with me?" I want to say no, I don't think I can, but Paige's little voice in the back of my head telling me not to let the past ruin my future pushes me to answer differently.

"Okay, but not too far away, and you can't complain when I call here ten times while we're at coffee. Is that a deal?"

"Anything you need, Mia. You know I don't mind. Now why don't you go and get ready and then we can leave. Plus, I have another idea for later if it's alright with you, Paige, since this is your house. I thought maybe we could have a framily dinner tonight. Order in some pizzas and just let Mia get to know everyone."

Oh god, what happened to slow, Lex?

"What a great idea. We'll get in touch with everyone while you're out. But you might want to explain to Mia what she's in for. No matter what Mason told me, that first night was so damn funny I ended up with sore sides from laughing so hard. Now get going before the cherubs get restless again."

Standing in my bedroom after changing into a pretty floral dress that Paige lent me, for the first time in a very long time, I care how I look. I know this isn't a date and we have some serious things to talk about, but it's nice to want to dress up a little bit.

As I slowly walk out into the living room, Lex's smile lights up his face. Paige tells me how lovely I look, and Mason just winks at me and then keeps playing cars with Jack.

Although I'm actually feeling a little excited, I also feel like I'm about to vomit. Leaving my kids here without me is a big deal. When we were in Lex's office, they were just down the hall from me. Now they'll be here, and I'll be there, wherever there is. Trying to count in my head like Mason taught me, the panic is staying at bay, but for how long once I leave the building remains to be seen.

Before I have time to think too much about it, I feel Lex take my hand and tell me to say goodbye to the kids.

"Bye, Mom, can you pick a chocolate donut for me? The one with the colored sprinkles." He looks at me with a smile and then goes straight back to the plane he's flying in the sky. Paige walks over with Kayla on her hip and leans her to me so I can kiss her and then walks away from me.

"Ready?" Lex whispers.

"No, but let's go anyway."

"Good girl. Keep pushing yourself. It will get easier." With that we are in the elevator before I know it and whizzing towards the underground parking. Paige had arranged a spot for Lex, especially since he's been here every evening since I arrived.

Walking me to his car, Lex opens the door and helps me in. Not saying a word and letting me settle in the space of just me and him and no kids.

Driving out of the parking lot, he looks across at me. "Is it okay if I just quickly go home to get changed and freshen up? I'm still in my work clothes from yesterday. I understand if you don't feel comfortable with that. Your call."

Oh, the poor guy, I had totally forgotten about him not having anything with him last night.

"Yes, of course it's fine. You poor thing, I'm sorry I didn't even think about that. Do you live far from here?" I'm sure he knows why I'm asking.

"Just ten minutes in the car, and then we will come back this direction and find a café, so we're still nice and close. Sorry, I just don't want you looking so beautiful and having to sit with sleep-wrinkled me."

"You look great, but I know what you mean."

We travel the rest of the trip in silence. I'm wondering what is in Lex's head as much as I'm trying to control what's in mine. We turn into a parking spot right out front of a building as tall as Paige's.

"I'll just leave the car here because we won't be long. I promise I don't take as long as a girl to get changed." Trying to make light of the moment, he always knows what I need. "Come on, you can see where I hide away from the world." Jumping out of the car, he comes around to open my door. Such a gentleman.

"Why do you need to hide away from the world?" I ask curiously as he takes my hand and we walk to the front doors.

I must admit it feels nice, holding his hand. I feel like I'm in high school again.

Walking past the front desk, Lex stops to talk to the doorman.

"Hi, Austin, this is Mia Kennedy. Please add her to my list of people who are allowed straight up, no questions. I will be giving her a security key, but if she doesn't have it, please let her in even if I'm not here." My mouth nearly drops open.

"Sure thing, Lex. Nice to meet you, Miss Kennedy. If there's anything you need just let me know. We are always here to help." With that, we are walking again to a separate elevator away from the others.

As I start to take in my surroundings, I'm now beginning to understand. Paige is rich, but I have a feeling Lex is in the same league as her. I knew I didn't fit into his world, but now I realize how far out of it I really am.

Entering the elevator, he pulls me to him.

"Stop freaking out, baby. No matter where I live or what I have, I'm still the same Lex, you know, and the frog you kissed last night to turn me into your Prince Charming."

I can't help but laugh. "What makes you think you've become

the prince yet? Don't they say you have to kiss a lot of frogs before you find the prince? Maybe you were just another frog."

That smug smile comes over his face. "So, you're telling me just a mere frog had you in his arms and begging me to take you over the edge?"

"Oh, well played, my prince, well played." The elevator comes to a stop and I look at the control panel which reads penthouse.

"Of course, you live in the penthouse." The doors slide open into his home.

"Well, where else do princes live?" Walking me into the room, my breath is again taken away. The view from Paige's home is spectacular, but Lex's is just as beautiful. Except he has a balcony that wraps around his living room.

"Welcome to my home, Mia. Please make yourself comfortable. I'll just be a minute while I run up and get changed. Take a walk out onto the balcony and check it all out." Leaning in and kissing my cheek, he is then gone and running up the stairs two at a time.

As I slowly walk around, this is just the sort of home I imagined for the Lex I first met, yet the more I've gotten to know him, this seems too stuffy. Everything is perfect. Not a piece of chaos anywhere. What a mess Jack could make of this apartment in seconds. The floors are a polished concrete and the furnishings all in dark brown, white, and black. I'm sure just the single sofa chair would be worth more than every item I own, including all the gifts from Lex. Careful not to touch anything, I open the sliding door to the balcony and step out. Luckily it turns out I'm not scared of heights. Before now I haven't been on a balcony this high off the ground. To the side of the door is a large daybed, big enough for two people, I'm sure. Next to it is what looks like a hot tub. My head starts to go to who has enjoyed that tub with him. I shake it off; I don't want to even let myself go there.

It really is astounding out here. Even though you are so high up, you can still hear the sound of the city. Yet it feels so safe. You aren't in the middle of all the people and all the hustle and bustle. Sitting on the daybed, I just take it all in. In my own little world, until Lex appears beside me and frightens the hell out of me. I let out a little scream.

"Mia, sorry I didn't mean to scare you."

"Lucky I wasn't near the edge, I might have jumped off with fright. I didn't hear you over the noise of the city below. Plus, I may have been daydreaming about being in the tower of my castle where no one could get to me."

"Then dream away, baby, because my castle is your castle, and you can spend time in my tower whenever you want. With or without me. I know what it's like to just lay here or spend time in the hot tub on your own. It's so peaceful at times to be away from it all."

"How many girls have you had in the tub?" Shit, I wish I wouldn't do that. Why can't I control my stupid inquisitive mind? "Shit, sorry, that was rude. That's none of my business. Ignore everything I just said." I'm now fumbling over my words.

"You look so cute when you get flustered over me. It's pretty hot, you know, this little jealousy thing you've got going on already." He takes my hands and pulls me up to be standing with him.

"I'm not jealous. That's ridiculous," I try to protest.

"Mhmm, you keep telling yourself that. And just so we're on the same path here, I've never had any women in my hot tub. The only body that has been in it is mine. I've never had any women in my personal bed in my room. But I'm a thirty-five-year-old single man. I've had sex and I've had girlfriends, just nothing serious.

"Have they been in this apartment? Yes.

"Have I fucked them here in my apartment? Yes.

"Yet I can promise you that I've never made love to any woman, let alone in my bed, or the tub for that matter." His hand takes my cheek and his thumb strokes it.

"Mia, when I finally take you to my bed, you will be the one and only that I have let inside my walls. Just like you, I have my bubble that I don't let people into. My reasons might be different to yours, but it's the same way of life. But I want you in my bubble, to hold onto me on those days and nights where we can just be us. You and me, and the world doesn't exist. Do you think you can see that in our future?"

"I hope so," is all I manage to say. He is so good with words, yet for me, three words and I struggle to even say them.

"Me too, baby. Me too."

Drawing my face to his, he kisses me like I'm the fuel to the fire burning inside him. I don't think I've taken enough time to talk to Lex and really get to know his deep dark secrets. He knows all of mine, yet I've just learned that I don't know his. His kiss wipes my mind of all rational thought, and that is pushed aside for another time. I've never been a big kisser, but damn I love when Lex kisses me.

"Come on, we better get going to the café. I promised I'd keep you close and not be gone to long, so I better do as I'm told on the first date. Otherwise I'll be in trouble from your family if I get you home after curfew. There'll be plenty of time to play hooky later when I've won your big sister over."

I giggle at him. "Like she doesn't already think you walk on water."

Taking my hand, we walk back inside, shutting the sliding door. "I like that. Let's keep that god image going when we're together with everyone tonight. About time I'm the king for once. Well, at least for one night anyway."

"There's that ego Paige was talking about this morning." I follow him into the elevator again.

"You better believe it. Mine's big, but wait until you meet Tate and Gray, they win the prize for the biggest egos, that's for sure."

As we're descending, another random thought hits me. "You had me there on my own. Why didn't you try to have sex with me?" I'm sure he's getting used to my casual outbursts.

"Because you're calling the shots, remember? You say what, you say when, and you say where. That will never change. As long as I can do this as much as you let me, then I'm a happy man."

He wraps me up in his arms, and this time it's not a firm kiss but a soft gentle one. One that he doesn't stop, instead just increasing the intensity the closer we get to the main floor. My hands slide up around the back of his neck and into his hair. I swallow his groan, and I crave more from him too.

The ding of the elevator letting us know we've hit the bottom doesn't make a difference. It's like I've developed an ever-increasing appetite for Lex's kisses. I vaguely remember hearing the doors open.

Then a voice sends chills through Lex, that even I feel as his whole body stiffens.

"Alexander Jefferson the third. Stop that sleazy public display right this minute!"

Chapter Nineteen

LEX

My body stiffens and the hairs on the back of my neck stand up.

This is not what I need right now, but then she has a habit lately of the worst timing to pick an argument with me.

"Is this why Austin wouldn't let me up to your apartment? What's going on with you? Is this little floozy the reason you broke off the engagement with Jacinta? I should have known there was more to it." She's almost stomping her foot to make her point as she stands in her rigid stance. Shoulders back, spine straight, and chin lifted, yet her eyes are glaring down at us.

Looking Mia directly in the eyes and making sure she understands me, I whisper to her, "I've got you. Don't let her behind your wall." Sliding her to the side of me and my arm around her waist, we step out of the elevator so the doors can close. There's no way I'm letting my mother into my apartment, and I don't even intend to stand here talking to her for long either.

"Mother. Stop that. You know we weren't engaged, and I'm not having this conversation with you. I don't even know why you are here, and I'm not sure I care. What I do expect you to do, though, is apologize for the disrespect you have just shown my girlfriend."

I feel Mia tense at my words, but I can't stop now to explain to her about this woman in front of me. But there is no fucking way I'm letting anyone make her feel small. Especially my mother. She has done it to me all my life, and like hell I'll let her push Mia back in her shell.

"Girlfriend." Her voice goes up an octave. "That won't be happening. You are becoming delusional. No son of mine will be with someone who is okay with being mauled like that in public."

Standing in front of me is the high-society woman with her uppity attitude. Although I always knew it deep down, I'm now understanding more, that she is so far from what I'm looking for in a woman. Her cream pants suit, perfectly pressed. Black sensible patent-leather dress shoes with a matching black handbag hanging over her arm. Her makeup plastered all over her face so that she looks like there isn't a single old-age wrinkle on her. Immaculate hairdo, like she's just stepped out of a hairdresser, which she probably has.

I want the messy bun on the top of a head. Wispy hair, hanging down the side of her face. Or her hair all hanging out and moving in the gentle breeze that's blowing in the sunshine. No makeup, or very little, like today. So I can kiss the hell out of her and not worry about me wearing her lipstick for the rest of the day. A free-flowing floral dress, that moves with her body as she walks across the room to me. Flat little sandals with straps that wrap up her delicate ankles. Showing me her cute toes that are peeking out the end of them. The same feet that I longed to massage to take away some of her strain.

"Mother, enough. Why are you here?" I just want to dismiss her and leave, but like I'm demanding respect for Mia, I can't show my mother the disrespect she deserves. It's not in my DNA.

"Because I haven't heard from you to apologize for the last outburst, so I decided I would need to come to you to hear it. Disgusting, really. But now I see why you haven't been home. You have made yourself busy." She rolls her eyes, and I just want to storm past her. "Now, are you going to open the elevator so we can attend your apartment? We don't need to be discussing these things here where everyone can hear." She places her hand on her hip. The signature move, when she wants you to bow to her commands.

I'm past obeying her.

"No, actually we are on our way out. So, it looks like that discussion will have to wait for another day. Before we leave, though, I would like you to meet my girlfriend, Mia Kennedy. You need to apologize to her for your harsh words because she is going to be in my life for a very long time to come. Mia, this is my mother, Elouise Jefferson, who is not showing her best manners today but I'm sure is happy to meet you. Aren't you, Mother?" I know throwing in the comment about her poor behavior, it will be killing her wondering what other people in the foyer are thinking.

One of my proudest moments comes from Mia happening just a split second later. Feeling her standing up that little bit taller, she holds her hand out to my mother as a peace offering.

"Lovely to meet you, Elouise." Although she is trying hard, her voice is very timid.

"Mrs. Jefferson to you." She thrusts her hand into Mia's with a lot of aggression behind it.

I am not prepared to put up with one more minute of this.

"Thank you for stopping by, I will call you next week. Have a nice day, Mother." She takes one look at me and knows I mean business. Not wanting to make any more of a scene than she already has, she drops Mia's hand.

"We will be speaking sooner than next week, Alexander. Good day." Turning on her heel, we listen to her stomps echoing across the foyer.

"Well, that's not quite how I was going to introduce you to my family, but too late now." I shrug my shoulders, not knowing what else really to do. "I'm so sorry, Mia, for the way she spoke to you. That little performance was more about me than you." I can see the unsure look on Mia's face.

"Have you upset her, Lex?"

"That's a very simple question which unfortunately has quite a complicated answer. Let's just say you aren't the only one with a fucked-up story to tell. But that's for another time. Right now, I'd like to take my girlfriend on our first coffee date before she tries to head for the hills, and this time not just to get away from me."

Taking her hand and walking towards the car outside, I know her head is spinning in circles again. My mother would do that to the strongest person upon meeting them, so poor Mia didn't even stand a chance of holding up a defense against the snarkiness of my mother.

"Why did you say that?" she asks as we're approaching her side of the car.

"Say what? There have been a lot of words since we finished that lip-smacking kiss in the elevator. Which, by the way, I would like to go back to?" I raise my eyebrows at her, trying to break the moment.

"Don't do that. It's not a joke, Lex." Her face becomes quite concerned.

"Sorry, baby. Say what?"

"That I'm your girlfriend? To your mother. Did you just say it to shock her?" Her face drops a little to look at her feet.

"No fucking way!" I lift her up into her seat in my SUV, standing in between her legs and sliding her tight against me.

"I said that because to me that's what you are. I'm proud to tell the world that. I don't give a shit what my mother thinks anymore. And just for the record, I have never been engaged to anyone, much to my mother and Jacinta's dismay after their manipulating behind my back."

She draws in a big breath. "Lucky you, Lex, unfortunately I have, and that ended up in a marriage. You can't be calling me your girlfriend when I'm still married."

Placing my hand on her neck, I feel her pulse point beating fast. "Do you feel married, Mia?" She shakes her head at me. "Then you aren't married in my eyes. After next week, we will have filed the divorce papers. It will be in the process and you will soon be free. But I want you to answer me this question."

"What?" Mia looks a little frightened at what I'm about to say.

"When your eyes are closed and I'm holding you, kissing you. Who are you dreaming that I am in your fantasy? Honest truth."

With a little hesitation she answers, "My future husband."

"Good answer. So, from today onwards, you are my girlfriend, and the rest I'll work on later. Just keep that dream alive." Kissing her cute little nose, I spin her around in the seat to buckle her in, and she suddenly starts to giggle, like a nervous laugh.

"What happened to slow as a snail?" I hear her say as I close the door. Running around to my door, I open it and jump in.

"Just picture me as a Jack snail. That'll work."

"There is no way that can even exist in this world, Jack doing anything slow. It's physically impossible." I love hearing her laugh, and to be honest, I wasn't sure how I was going to handle her reaction after that crazy encounter. Every day I see her getting that little bit stronger. For every time she stumbles, she comes back slightly more confident. If we can get through next week, I can't wait to watch that strength grow even quicker.

We sit down at the table in the quaint little café not far from Paige's apartment. There aren't many tables but more moon-shaped couches that circle around a little table that's covered in a few books and the daily papers. While we are waiting for our coffees and cake, I know I'm on limited time, so we need to have the talk that we've both been avoiding.

"Let's get the boring, annoying thing out of the way first. We need to talk about Monday and what's involved." Watching her body language change straight away, I keep pushing on. "Your court time is nine am on Monday morning. We need to be there about thirty minutes before. I will handle everything that is going to happen and all you need to do is answer any questions that the judge may have about why you believe your safety is at risk. We can run through some likely questions a little later, so you get comfortable with that. Does that sound okay?"

"No, but I have no choice if I want to end this." Her voice is a little short.

"Sadly, that's true. But I'll be with you every step of the way. Plus, we will have Ashton with us."

"I'd rather he stays with the kids, I don't need him, I'll be with you."

"That's what we need to talk about. Mia, we will need to go and stay in Bellevue on Sunday night to be there early enough for court. We can't afford to get stuck in traffic or have anything hold us up."

"I don't want to stay there." Listening to the panic coming, I know I just need to say it and let it boil over so I can help her through it. There is no way I can stop it from happening.

"I know, Mia, but we need to. Just take a deep breath and listen to my plan." Her walls are coming up, but I see her trying. "You, Ashton, and I will stay in a hotel together on Sunday night. Mason and Paige will look after the kids at home, and Ashton will have one of his team guarding the elevator entrance for her apartment as well. The kids will be completely safe the whole time. They won't leave home even once while we are away. I will also organize for the guys and girls to be around to help."

"Lex, no, I can't leave the kids. What if they need me? How will I know they're safe? What if they get scared and I'm not there? You're asking a lot." Her hands are fisted tightly on her lap and she's tapping her foot with nerves.

I know I can't take away the fear, but maybe Ashton can help with something. The thought has just crossed my mind.

"I'm going to ask Ashton to set up a nanny cam so you can watch the kids from your phone whenever you like. Plus, we can call Paige and Mason at any time and speak to Jack. You know he blurts out everything, so if there are any problems, we will hear about it. I mean, he seems happy to throw me under the bus all the time." I'm trying to lighten the moment but it's not working.

The waitress chooses that moment to arrive with our order. Mia tries to smile and be polite and it almost breaks her.

"Thank you," I tell the waitress, acknowledging her and waiting for her to leave.

I lean over and take both Mia's hands in mine. Slowly unfolding her fists until she is instead gripping my hands like a vice.

"You can do this, baby, for them you can do it. They need you to be strong and fight for all your freedom to live a life without fear. If you can't do it for you, then do it for the kids." Finally, I see her brain registering some of the things I'm saying.

She's processing the words.

"Even if I call them a hundred times?" she asks, looking at me for confirmation.

"I don't care if you call when we leave and don't hang up the phone until we get home again." Leaning in close to her and lifting her hands to my lips, I kiss them both gently. "I promise nothing will happen to them. They are already in here." I lift her hands and place them on my heart. "No matter what, I will always protect them."

"Thank you," is all she manages with her eyes welling up with tears.

Kissing her on the cheek then letting her go, I take her coffee from the table and put it in her hands.

"This will help you feel better, plus the chocolate brownie I ordered. Now teach me, is this an appropriate time to use chocolate?" I hold both my hands up beside me and shrug. A slight smile creeps up her face.

"Lesson one of chocolate and women. If you are delivering shitty news, then make sure there is some on hand ready. So yes, you passed lesson one."

"Thank god. I didn't want to crash and burn on the first attempt." Sipping my coffee, it is really hitting the spot.

"How do you do that? Always manage to change the conversation and have me feeling that I can do this."

"Ah, now that is my special trick and I can't tell you, otherwise you will find out how ridiculous I really am. You see, this super-hot and funny lawyer persona I've got going on is just a disguise. The guy underneath the costume is just some geeky man with a bad sense of humor." If only she knew how true that is. The man that's behind the career is not quite the guy they all think I am.

"Who said he's..." Mia sips her coffee, deliberately not finishing the sentence.

"If you say I'm not super-hot then we have a big problem." I point my finger at her to pretend she is on the hot seat.

"I was going to say funny, but the rest might be debatable too." She tries to move from me on the couch.

"Not a chance. You don't get to crush my ego and then leave me sitting here broken."

"Oh my god, can we add drama queen to that list too?" The more she's bantering at me, the more I know I'm pulling her back out of going inside her head.

"You wait until you spend time with Tate tonight. You will then learn I'm certainly not the drama queen of the group." I take a pause to see her body language when I mention tonight. She doesn't seem to act any different, which is good.

"I'm actually a little excited to meet everyone again. That first night is such a blur, and listening to you talk about them, they sound fun. I mean, that group text message, I couldn't stop laughing. You're lucky to have such great friends."

"That is so true. But be careful what you wish for tonight. You think my jokes are bad and ego is big. You ain't seen nothing yet." We both laugh and sit back trying to relax a little.

Mia's right, though. I'm so grateful for them, but I also know that tonight it's my turn to receive all the payback. That's what happens when you're happy to dish out on your friends in front of their new girlfriends. It comes full circle, and bingo, now it's my turn.

I try to keep the conversation light and away from anything that will make Mia sad. She seems to be hedging around wanting to say something but doesn't quite know how.

Noticing the time on the old-fashioned Roman-numeral clock on the wall, we've been here longer than I'm sure Mia realizes. I promised I wouldn't keep her away from the kids too long.

"As much as I could sit here and talk to you all day with no distraction, I should get you back home." It's like that was enough reason for her to blurt it out.

"What is it between you and your mother? That was intense. I've never seen you like that except with that other lawyer at your office. I just don't see you as that person, and you talk so much about how you love having a close family. Yet your mother is obviously not included in that."

Sitting back into the couch and running my hand over my chin, I try to decide how much to tell her right now. I don't want to hold anything back from her, but I need more than ten minutes to explain the world that is my mother and the constraints that come with high society.

"I'm not hiding anything from you, but to explain everything that I want to say is going to take more time than we have. But so you have an idea… My childhood was nothing like Jack and Kayla's in so many ways, but the biggest difference is that they are surrounded by a mother's love."

"Oh Lex." She puts her hand on my leg and squeezes it to let me know she's there.

"I was brought up by my nanny, more than my own mother. To her I am just a token to parade in her social circle. My father I've learned can't stand up to her either. Anyway, let's just say she isn't talking to me because I finally decided to take my own life back, and she isn't happy about it. Hence the little spat in the foyer. She doesn't know how to handle me not obeying her wishes."

"It's okay, Lex, you don't have to continue. I shouldn't have asked, I just couldn't get her horrible words out of my head."

"I just ignore them now, let them wash over me. If I keep my wall up, she can't hurt me."

"You are talking to the queen of walls here," she says, pointing to herself.

"Don't I know it," I mumble in a playful voice.

"I didn't ask for your smart-ass comment, thank you very much." Then shocking the hell out of me, Mia leans forward and kisses me on the cheek. "Just remember it works both ways with us. You need to share your soul with me too. When you're ready, I'm here to listen." Standing up, straightening her dress and picking up her bag, she looks down at me to make sure I'm following. I'm sure all she sees is my shock. This is the woman I know is hiding inside. The confident yet compassionate and loving soul that is the true Mia.

For once it's me that is at a loss for words, which rarely happens.

Today is the first day that I've ever wanted to tell anyone what I hide inside.

To be honest, I don't want to tell just anyone.

I only want to tell Mia.

"I can't believe you took poor Mia to a coffee shop for your first date." Grayson throws a scrunched-up napkin across the table at me.

"Well, we can't all be perfect and meet at a masked ball. I mean, when I think about it, that's probably the only reason you got the girl. She didn't really know what you looked like at first, then she didn't know how to tell you to get lost." Throwing the napkin back.

"Um, this little sparkly rock on her finger means she doesn't want to get rid of me. In fact, she's happy to have me hanging around for a lifetime," Grayson replies, looking proud as punch.

"You mean hanging around like a bad smell?" Mason smirks at him from across the table.

"Hilarious, Mason. Where did you pull that one from, is that one of Jack's jokes you stole?" Everyone is now laughing together.

"Hey, Mia, I can't believe you let the counselor here debate with you the reasons for letting him hang out with you. I mean, do you really understand what you're taking on? He's the most complex little man we know." Tate is laughing at himself, before he's even finished delivering the joke.

"Are you all finished here? I'm sure Mia doesn't need to hear every little, stupid story you want to bring up." I try to give the hint that it's time to let up on me.

"Maybe I do," she proudly announces.

"Please do not encourage them. They will just keep going and going. Honestly they have years of stories to call on to embarrass me." Looking at her and almost begging her playfully to help me out.

"Oh," Grayson blurts out, "do you remember that time he got

locked in the janitor's storeroom in high school?" The boys roar laughing.

"Shh you idiots, if you wake up the kids, I'll kill you. Plus, I wasn't the one who started that damn crazy idea. I just ended up the one to get caught in there." I can still picture that day.

"Spill the beans, I've got to hear this one." Tilly winks at me from across the table as I take Mia's hand and wrap mine around it.

"No, I don't think you do," I protest when Tate already starts, completely ignoring me.

"We were about fourteen if I remember correctly. And Lex had come to school with his first portable DVD player. He was always the first with everything because Mommy wanted to make sure we all knew they had money. Anyway, he had found this porn DVD of his father's and brought it for us all to look at. He thought we could watch it after school. But fuck that, I wasn't waiting until then. So, I suggested we sneak into the janitor's storeroom."

"Like we were ever going to all fit in there together," Mason complains, "but nothing like being up close and personal with your best friends when you're watching porn. What the hell were we thinking? That's just gross."

"What was gross was Tate thinking he was funny pinching our asses while we were watching, if I remember rightly." Gray slaps him on the arm.

"Oh my god, you did not do that," Bella snaps at Tate. "What is wrong with you? Is that where your fascination with sex started, locked in a storeroom with three other boys?"

Mason spits his beer out over the table and almost chokes from laughing so hard.

Looking at Mia, I don't think I've ever seen her smile so much and as freely.

"Yeah, baby, that's how it happened. Nothing to do with the hot little cheerleaders who wanted their turn with the football star." Tate looks proud as punch.

"Ugh, you are so full of shit," Grayson comments and then takes over the story. "Anyway, here we are getting to the part where the woman is moaning and he's going to town pounding into her, and the bell goes."

"Yeah, and Lex the goody-two-shoes panics," Tate says. "Trying to shut it down, but the DVD player gets stuck and it won't stop. So, we all start piling out of the storeroom because no one wants to get into trouble, and we assume Lex is following us. But when we turn back from our lockers, here is the janitor locking the door and walking away down the hallway. So poor Lex is stuck in there, DVD still going, and he's in there on his own."

Grayson has tears rolling down his cheek by this stage of the story.

Mason chips in, "If it was Tate locked in there, no one would bat an eyelid, but not poor Lex who was our worrier."

"That is not how the story goes at all," I say, pointing my finger at all of them. "You bastards took off and left me there with the evidence. I didn't hear anyone trying to help me stop the stupid movie. No, you all ran like little girls."

"So, what happened then?" Mia looks at me, laughing.

"This isn't funny, baby," I protest. "They are all bullshit friends. I'm always the one bailing them out of the shit, and when I needed them, they all ran for the hills."

"Not quite," Tate says. "We all waited in the bathroom until everyone was in class and then came back for you. Breaking into the door to rescue you from losing your virginity to a DVD player." He makes actions like he's jerking off.

"Fuck off, Tate."

"Oh, don't pick on Lex, you mean boys," Paige soothes before adding, "It sounds like you were all just jealous you didn't get to finish with him."

"Tiger, you did not just say that. I never want to have the vision of jerking off with my three best friends. That's just wrong on so many levels, no matter what age we were." Mason pretends to puke.

"No, god no. I meant finish the movie. You need to get your mind out of the gutter, Mason."

Bella laughs. "I don't think it's possible for any of them to keep their conversations clean. They have been like this for as long as I can remember, it's just gotten worse since you all came along. Now they're just bragging."

"Seriously, this story is done," I try for a subject change. "It went way off track, very quickly."

"No, no, no, you don't get to miss the ending, it's the best part," Tate declares.

"For who?" I'm looking at him like I'm about to kill him but that never makes a difference.

"For you, Lexy boy. It was a happy ending alright." All the boys are sniggering and trying to hold it together, but they're not doing a very good job.

"What do you mean?" Paige looks between me and Tate.

"I came in my pants. Are you all happy now? That's what fourteen-year-old boys do when they watch porn." Looking at Mia, she blushes a little and then can't hold it in anymore. She starts laughing hard like the rest of them.

"Oh Lex. You poor thing." Mia is trying to show compassion for me in between laughing.

"Don't feel sorry for him. He got to finish. The rest of us were walking around for the rest of the day trying to hide our hard cocks and also explain why the four of us were late to class."

You wouldn't think it's possible to embarrass a thirty-five-year-old man when it comes to sex, but I can tell you that you are wrong. On the inside I want to kill these boys for picking that story out of all the stories they could have chosen. Yet part of me is thanking them. Sitting here watching Mia laugh so much she's crying has been the highlight of the day. Her happiness is my weakness.

The night progressed with more of the same, but fortunately it involved stories of all of us and not just me. Until Tate gets a page from the hospital that he's needed for an emergency. It's late and it gets everyone up and moving with Gray and Tilly offering to drop Bella home as Tate makes the mad dash for the hospital. Even though he isn't on call, sometimes they just need his expertise and brilliant knowledge. He might be the biggest smartass I know, but he is also the most amazing neurosurgeon we have in Chicago.

After they've left and Mia and Paige are starting to clear the table with the last of the glasses and bottles, Mason taps me on the shoulder.

"You staying again tonight, man? The spare bed might be a little bit more comfortable," he says, giving me a little smirk.

"If Mia wants me to I will. But don't worry about the bed. The couch was just perfect last night, thanks."

"I bet it was, lover boy. Whatever you want I'm good with." Walking over to Paige, he kisses her on the top of the head and then takes the glasses out her hands. "Head up to bed, Tiger. Lex and I have got this. You and Mia have done enough playing host."

Both the girls start protesting, but we win in the end and Paige heads upstairs and Mia goes to check on the kids.

"I'm off to bed too," Mason says. "Be a good little boy tonight. See you in the morning." I want to tell him to fuck off, but it's not worth it. He'll just continue then.

"Goodnight." Letting him leave, I just take a seat on the couch waiting for Mia to come back out.

A few minutes passing, I wonder if she realizes I'm still here.

Eventually I hear her little feet padding down the hallway towards me.

Sitting down next to me, she kisses me on the cheek shyly.

"Thank you for tonight. It was just what I needed. I love your family."

"I do too, well, most of the time anyway. Tonight, was debatable."

"They love you, that's why they did it. I think it was also a little bit of just desserts for past performances. Am I right?" She turns sideways so she's on the couch now with her legs tucked up under her. Sitting on her feet.

"Oh, I totally deserved everything I got tonight. Now we're all square." I lean over and kiss her lightly on the lips.

"Mia, it's your call. Do you want me to go home or stay the night again? Just tell me what you want, and that's what I'll do." I lean my forehead on to hers.

"I want you to stay," she whispers.

"Then I'll sleep right here. The whole night."

"Can I sleep with you again here too?"

My heart skips a beat. "I'd love that. And one day I promise we'll make it to a bed. Lucky Paige has a comfy couch."

"You think this is comfortable, you should try sleeping in my bed."

"Don't tease me, Mia."

"Maybe it's not a tease," her little angelic voice replies, and I'm instantly hard.

Fuck, sleep is going to be a challenge tonight.

Chapter Twenty

MIA

Seeing the early morning sunrise, lying in Lex's arms is just so perfect. I love the silent peacefulness of this time of the day. I thought nothing could top that silence, but I was wrong. I know I should keep sleeping, but I can't. There is too much in my head.

How do I even try to separate the happy from the sad and anxious? It's impossible, so they're all mashing in together which just makes confusion.

Every time I think about Lex, which is easy lying here with him wrapped around me, my heart flutters.

Where did this man come from?

It's like everything I ever wished on a star for, the universe has delivered in one very hot and sexy package. But it's funny, that's just the side bonus.

I've never been treated like a princess by a man. But that's the only way to describe how Lex is with me. It's a strange sensation to be on the couch here and feel so safe with a man. A place I never thought I'd get to. Especially so quickly which still worries me, but I push that aside. I just hope that nothing will take this away from me. Surely the universe won't be that cruel again.

My happy place, however, keeps getting overrun by all the fear of the next forty-eight hours. I'm still not sure if I can leave my kids later today. I know Lex sees the pain it's causing me, but I'm not sure he can ever truly understand the worry that sits deep inside me. The practical part of my brain knows they will be safe here, and probably spoiled rotten. But the irrational part of it is thinking up all the things that could go wrong while I'm gone. It's not like I'm ten minutes away; three hours is a long drive if I need to get home in a hurry.

Then my biggest fear is seeing Edward.

I have no idea how this is going to go or if he'll even show up. I mean, what does he even have to gain from it, except putting me through more mental torture. Lex is probably right that without any money he won't be able to afford a lawyer so won't bother. I'm praying that's the case.

At least after tomorrow, there will be a barrier between him and us. I know it's cruel to take children away from a parent, but that's from a parent who deserves a relationship with their kids. It's comical that he even has that title, really. He's hardly ever changed a diaper or even fed them their bottles as babies, or played one second with Jack. It all stopped within weeks of them being born.

'That's the woman's job'

Asshole!

"You're thinking about tomorrow, aren't you." The soft deep sleepy voice comes from behind me. There is something so comfortable about spooning with Lex. It's like I fit perfectly against his body, and he is just the right size to wrap me in a cocoon. I could easily get used to this.

"Maybe." I blow out a breath I didn't realize I was holding when I was thinking about it.

"I'm not going to tell you to stop it, because we both know that's not possible. What I will say is let me share the load. Don't keep it all locked inside." He squeezes me a little tighter around the waist.

"I'll try." I'm pretending to sound a little confident, but I know I've failed.

Lex releases his arms and then rolls me over to face him.

Our bodies are tightly pressed together, and I know his body is reacting to how close we are. I can feel every inch of it slightly touching against me.

He kisses me on the forehead, then each cheek, landing on my lips and giving me the softest captivating kiss. Pulling back slightly, his words whisper over my lips.

"Morning, beautiful." Just the way his voice is first thing in the morning makes me tingle in places I shouldn't be thinking about with my kids so close by. Goddamn it feels nice, though.

"Good morning." Taking my chances, I lean in for another long passionate kiss before the kids are awake. I need to take it slow around them. Not that Lex got that memo.

"Mmm I like this kind of morning wake-up."

"Me too." I giggle a little. "I still can't believe you're here. With me."

"No self-doubt, Mia, that's not how you start a morning."

"Is that right? And how exactly do I start a morning, Mr. Perfect?"

His hands land on my ass cheeks and push me harder against his body. There is nothing I'm missing feeling on his body now. "Mr. Perfect, I'll take that. Now, how it goes is you lay here with me. Understanding exactly what you do to my body. Hopefully feeling a little hot and bothered by that. So it makes you start dreaming of what mornings will be like, one day. Because I can already tell you, lying next to you is pure pleasure and torture in one. So, once you are ready and give me the green light, there will be plenty of morning delights." His words roll off his lips without hesitation.

"I think I might like that." I'm blushing as I say it. He has a habit of making me say things I never thought would cross my lips.

"I'm sure we both will," Lex whispers in my ear before taking my earlobe in his mouth and sucking gently on it. Then I can feel his whiskers on my neck as he softly kisses it on his way down towards my shoulder.

Damn, the sensations running through my body are like pure sparks of electricity. Not like previously in my life. With Lex, I've never had to force myself to feel anything. His touch is like he's worshipping my body, and I'm all for it.

"Lex," I moan softly. He doesn't stop, and it only encourages my body to start responding. Previously, I've never been allowed to take time to explore a man's body at my own pace. But now I want to touch him and feel his body. I know I need baby steps, but he is making my brain forget that, and I want so much more. His hand is rubbing up and down my bare arm while he's feasting on my neck. My head is screaming for him to touch my breast as he skims up the side of it each time. It shouldn't be, because I always imagined that the fear would overtake me, yet it's nowhere to be seen.

My hips start pushing against his hard cock. Slowly riding him in the rhythm of his hand sliding down my arm.

This time it's me dragging the moan from his mouth.

"Fuck… Mia." His lips move to mine and then the kiss takes on a life of its own.

While I'm grinding against his cock, his hands are now roaming my back and ass. I want more but I'm too scared to ask. Instead I'm dry humping him like a teenager.

It feels amazing and is helping to soothe the burn that has been there since I climbed into his arms last night.

Letting my lips loose, he is gasping.

"Mia, you tell me to stop. You are in complete control." His eyes bore straight into my soul.

"Don't stop, but just like this, clothes on. Please don't stop."

"Baby, your wish is my command. I'll always listen." Our lips slam back against each other, tongues now exploring into new territory. I let my hands start to wander into places they haven't touched before. His ass is rock solid under my fingers. The vision of these tight buns of steel, naked, has me rising that bit higher with my sexual tension. I just want what he gave me yesterday. It's the orgasm I'm chasing again. I want the high that only he has been able to bring me.

Letting my hand slowly edge around to his hips I'm trying to debate if I can do it. Can I touch his cock? I don't want to make him so desperate to touch me that this will tip his patience over the edge and he'll push me past what I'm ready to do. So many times, he has asked me to trust him. But now it's not just him that I need to trust, it's myself.

My want is racing towards me taking that leap. Panting between our kisses, I'm barely holding on, and then he takes the first step for me. Letting his hand slowly slip over my breast has me gasping but reaching for his cock at the same time.

"Oh Mia, I want you so badly. Naked and like this. Desperate for me to make you come."

"What about you?" I'm now moaning as his hand gently squeezes my breast. He might be taking it slow, but I'm not.

My hand rubs up and down his cock. I had no idea it's even bigger than I'd been feeling against me.

"This isn't about me. Always about you, Mia, always." He groans as I grab him lower around his balls. "Can I touch other places? You can say no."

Both of us panting. I'm about to burst and I need more. "Yes... Lex, yes!" Feeling his hand disappearing from my breast, I ache with anticipation, while it's sliding down my body. So easily he could slip it into my sleep shorts, but I know he won't. Not one part of me is scared of him taking advantage.

My shorts are thin cotton, and I can feel every touch like it's magnified. The moment his fingers slide up my sex, I'm almost whimpering with need. And then he hits the spot that has me shooting to the stars. His hand keeps rubbing me through the orgasm while he swallows all my screams in the kiss that brings me back to earth.

"Lex, I'm sorry..."

"Hush. We will get there when you're ready. I don't care if it takes a lifetime." He looks at me with that beautiful smile, even though he must be almost dying.

"Where have you come from?" I ask, placing my hand on his cheek.

"A place I was buried in, a life that didn't let me truly live. I never knew happiness until I found you. It's somewhere I don't want to go back to. I only want to be here with you."

Taking my hand from his cheek, he kisses it, and we just cuddle in the ever-increasing light from the early-morning sunrise.

All of a sudden, the quiet giggles overtake me.

"What's so funny?" he asks.

"Do you need to use the janitor's closet?" I try to get out in between my giggles.

"Ugh, I'm never going to hear the end of that, am I?"

"It's pretty funny."

"For you. But I'll be honest, I do need the bathroom before the kids wake and Jack jumps on me. And, if you breathe one word to the boys of what I'm about to do, you will pay for it with all my man movies on repeat."

Lifting himself up and over the top of me to stand, he leaves me feeling so relaxed on the couch.

"Oh Lex, I'm …" I don't even get to finish.

"Don't you even say the word sorry. You have nothing to be sorry for. What we just shared was amazing, and it will just keep getting better. I promise. Now don't move, this won't take long, I can assure you. As soon as I close my eyes and replay what just happened, I'll be back here snuggling with you in the afterglow. Looking like you do right now." With that he is off towards the bathroom. I feel bad, but part of me is cheering that I got him so turned on that he needs to go and jerk off to relieve the ache, and that he is so kind that he never even contemplated asking me to do it.

Lex is more than a gentleman; he is an extraordinary man. One I hope I can keep.

"Mia, we really need to think about leaving," I hear Lex's gentle voice behind me.

Sitting on the bed holding Kayla asleep in my arms, I'm trying to hold it together before I face Jack. I can't let them see me crying. I need to give them the confidence to be here without me. I feel Lex's hand on my shoulder trying to give me the support I need.

I tell myself I can do this.

For them I can do this.

Standing up above her playpen, I kiss her on the cheek and place her down with her teddy that Lex gave her. Tucking her in snugly, she looks so peaceful. Turning into his arms, he hugs me, but I know I need to get out of here before I lose it. I can do that in the car.

Walking into the living room, I find Jack coloring with Paige on some pictures she found on the internet.

"Look, Mommy, Auntie Paige got me all these cars and trucks and planes and animals." He is so excited, and I don't want to change that. That's how I want to remember his face while I'm gone.

"I hope you said thank you. That's very special."

"I did. I promise. If I keep in the lines, she said we can get the delivery man to go to *McDonald's* and get a kids' meal. She said they come with a toy. Like on the television." His little voice is killing me. My love for him is like no other.

"That sounds awesome, bud. Now come here and give me a quick hug before I go." Jumping up, he is in my arms and hugging me tight. He has no idea how long it is until tomorrow, and hopefully I'll be back before he even has time to think it's been a long time.

"Now you be the best big boy for Auntie Paige and Uncle Mason. Help them with Kayla, won't you?"

"I will. I'm the besterest big brother ever," he proudly tells me.

"Yes, you are, my beautiful boy, you certainly are."

Standing quickly, I'm ready to leave swiftly as Lex leans down and also gives Jack a hug then a high five. Whispering something in his ears that has Jack giggling and running back to keep coloring. Then taking my hand in his, we head to the elevator with Paige following.

Turning to say goodbye to her, she grabs me and squishes me tightly.

"I'm so proud of you, Mia. I promise I will take good care of them. I'll protect them with my life."

"I know you will, otherwise I wouldn't be walking out of here right now," I say, trying to hold back my tears.

"You stay safe and do what you need to for this part to be over with. Be strong and let Lex take care of you." Now it's Paige that's teary too.

"Don't do that. You'll start me off and I won't stop," I mumble as we give each other the last big squeeze.

"Lex, we need to go." My voice is weak, and he takes control. Feeling his arm around my waist, he guides me into the elevator.

Watching those doors close is like knives stabbing into my chest. I fall against Lex as my legs feel weak. He does what he has been doing since the day I met him.

He catches me.

"I've got you, Mia, you can do this. Stay strong." His voice washes over me with a calmness like it always does.

Taking me to his car, we start on our journey. Not saying another word between us for around thirty minutes. He is so perceptive that he knows I just need space. To firstly settle my nerves and then to help clear my head of some of the fear.

After a while I start to come out of the fog a little, then it dawns on me.

"Where's Ashton?" I want to take it back as soon as I say it. That shouldn't have been the first words that came out my mouth.

"He has been following us in his car ever since we left." Lex just smiles at me and doesn't seem mad at how rude I've been.

My head swivels to look back and I see his big black SUV with the really dark tinted windows.

"I'm sorry I've been so quiet. I'm so rude," I say, looking back to the front.

"Don't be silly. You just need time to get over a pretty big thing you just did. We still have at least two hours in the car to torture each other with my dad jokes and you laughing hysterically at them." He looks sideways at me with that warming smile.

"Who said I'll be laughing?"

"And there she is, my sassy girl who hides from me at times. Welcome back."

"You say that like it's a good thing." I wonder what he thinks about my mood swings at the moment.

"It is. Because behind that sass is a pure heart. So, I know no matter how sassy you get with me, it's never in a nasty way, but in such a fun affectionate way."

"Not like her, the lawyer?" I question.

"Yeah, I suppose you're right there." It's like a bit of a lightbulb moment happened for him answering my question.

"Before we get to the dad jokes, which I honestly can't wait for, we have plenty of time. Do you want to tell me about Jacinta and your mom? I'm okay if you don't. I never want to pry. I, of all people, know what it's like to keep things deep inside." I reach out with my hand to touch him on the arm and give him a reassuring squeeze to know I'm here for support.

He goes quiet for a moment and then looks towards me again quickly and lets out a deep breath.

"Plus, you telling me your problems takes my mind off mine." Which is true, but I'm hoping it will help him to find the courage to tell me.

"Yeah, you know what? This is probably the perfect time. I'm not good at sharing feelings. Actually, to be honest, I've never really done it. Not even with the boys. So here, in the car, you have me trapped. I can't run from it when it gets hard. I don't want to hide anything from you, so some of this will be hard to say to you. Embarrassing. But I just want you to know, the guy I'm about to tell you about is not the guy I am when I'm with you. You have shown me the man I want to be. The man I didn't know was even possible in my world. Yet the person I'm becoming right now is someone I want to know more about and want you to get to know him too." As he turns to look at me, I see for the first time since I've met Lex, an emotion that actually makes me fall for him even more.

Vulnerability.

LEX

I'm not sure if I was ever going to find the right time do this, so Mia pushing me is taking that indecision away from me. The irony of it is that's what I've been doing to her since I met her. Asking her to trust me with her deepest darkest secrets and to let me behind her walls. She is far braver at this shit than I am.

"I already know that last man you're talking about. He's my Lex. The others don't matter to me if they don't matter to you anymore. I like to think of it like the spring. Where nature has shed its old skin and the new life is coming. I have to believe that there is a new life for all of us coming. Otherwise it's too hard to get up and move forward every day if we aren't moving towards something better. Let me help you shed that skin, Lex. You've pushed me to finally let go of some of mine."

What have I done in life to deserve such a caring soul to be sitting here beside me? No one has ever asked me what I'm hiding. Yet she sees the real me when I don't even know who he is?

"For someone who has been through so much, you are so strong and know all the right things to say. You have such resilience, which I admire." One of the things I want to help Mia work on is accepting that she is worthy of compliments. From what she's told me, she has been told most of her life how hopeless she is that she finds it hard to believe any of the good stuff. That needs to change.

"You know talking about me is avoiding the hard conversation, don't you?" Mia starts to giggle a little at me.

"See, you are way smarter than you give yourself credit for as well."

"Lex, start talking. We've been through this every time you try to talk emotional crap. Suck it up and get on with it."

"Wow, we can add bossy to that list too." Laughing at her, she just smiles and waves her hand in circles to indicate I need to get on with it.

"Okay, okay, little miss bossy pants. I get the hint."

"Good, now start talking. I'm all ears."

I drop my closest hand to hers because I want to hold on to it. To have it ground me. "I've told you some basic outlines of my life growing up, but not what it was really like. The relationship I have with my mother and father is not normal. Well, maybe in their world it is, but when I took my first steps out of the world of high society and old money, it became very clear how far from normal it was." I know compared to what Mia has lived this is trivial, and I don't want her to feel that I don't know that. How the hell do I tell her that, though?

"I know what I'm about to tell you won't sound bad, and your childhood was so much harder than mine..." I don't get to say anymore before she's cutting me off.

"Don't do that! Your emotions are no less important than mine. Don't put me up on some pedestal I don't deserve. Please, Lex, I need an equal in my life. I've lived too long with an unequal level of self-worth. I won't make that mistake again. It's equality in everything or not at all. Do you understand!" Her voice is more forceful than I've seen her. She is fighting for what she wants in her new life, and I'm so fucking happy to hear it.

"That's a fair comment. You know you would make an excellent lawyer with your counter arguments." I laugh at her screwing her nose up.

"And I can see why you are good at your job because you are the king of changing the direction of a line of questioning."

"Touché, baby, touché!" I'm actually laughing hard, at a time where I thought this would be difficult.

"We should have brought popcorn for this. By the time we're finished we will have analyzed and debated the whole fucked-up life of Alexander Jefferson the third." Trying to keep things light always helps.

"Not if you don't start talking, we won't. Man, when you were a child at school, did they have trouble getting you to focus?" Mia is laughing at me now.

"Yes, but that was more the friends who were sitting with me." I smile and try to look all innocent which she sees right through.

"Oh yeah, it's always the friends fault." She shifts herself in the seat until she is a little more side-on, so she has the perfect view to pin me with her glare.

Releasing her hand and taking a drink of water from my bottle sitting between us, I know I need to stop joking and get on with it, but maybe not with such a serious undertone.

"Alright, let's do this." Looking into those soft eyes, I know I can share anything with this woman and there is no judgment.

"My parents apparently had trouble getting pregnant, so by the time I came along, I should have been a treasured little baby. Instead I just became the perfect pawn in my mother's society ladder climbing. She needed to appear the perfect wife and mother, and our family a pillar of society. But behind the big wooden door of our home, that was so far from the truth." Pausing to take a moment to organize my head, I know I'm treating this like an argument in court. But I can't help it because that's all I know how to do. I don't know how to have a conversation about these sorts of hard emotions.

"Once we would arrive home from wherever we had been, Mother would walk inside, leaving my father or the hired help to get me out of the car and settled. We never ate a meal together without other people in the house, and then I wasn't allowed to speak unless directly asked a question. It was my Nanny Sue that I would run through the back door of the house to tell about my day at school, to show her the pictures I had drawn, or tell her about my marks on a test. All my mother cared about was the report she received from the school to tell her how I was performing and if my marks were still at the top of the class."

"I'm sad for that little boy, and I wish she understood what she was missing out on," Mia says with the utmost compassion for my younger self.

"Me too, but it was what I learned to expect. That and the other thing that I had drummed into my head from as young as my memory will go were the words: *'You will live the life I tell you, that's what good sons do. Your life will be as a lawyer and then move onto being the Chief Justice which will be the perfect point to move into politics.'* I look back now and realize she was brainwashing me. I grew up knowing no different. That's what my life was to be, so I just accepted it and aimed to fulfill it. It wasn't much different for most of my friends in middle school. I use the word friends loosely. They were the kids of the people my parents socialized with, who were also trying to keep their rank in the society ladder, by having their kids at the best school money could buy. So, we all had been pretty much told similar things of who we were expected to be when we grew up.

"I accepted it was just what happened, until high school where I met the boys. That's when my whole world opened up and it was the start of the friction between my mother and me." Laughing a little, I can still see the look on her face the first time she met them. Which was in the principal's office when we all got called in for being too disruptive in class. My mother was outraged, and I remember Gray's mom and dad trying not to laugh and pretend to act serious. That was the first day I wished my parents were different.

"Oh, dear I can imagine how that went down. Was Tate as cocky then as he is now?" Mia's laughing with me at the thought of it.

"He hasn't changed one bit since the day I met him, and I love that about him. Which of course really pissed my mother off every time she would see us together. Not that they came to my house very often. Mother made sure they knew they weren't welcome, and I was told bluntly how she hated my friends and that they weren't the right friends for my image. I mean, who the fuck tells that to a thirteen-year-old boy. Friendship isn't about your image, it's so much more than anything so superficial.

"Anyway, needless to say I ignored her, and we just always went to one of the other's houses after school. Gray's mom, Maxine, used to make such a big fuss at school in front of my mom about what a wonderful boy I was so that all the other mothers who loved Maxine – which was most of the school population to be honest—knew that we were friends and she approved. She was easy to love, especially compared to my mother. Then she sadly died unexpectedly, and the school community made a big fuss on how lovely it was that us boys were such a support for Gray. So Mother was stuck then and couldn't say a word in public and had to give up on banning me from seeing them. I then spent so much time at his house that I started to learn what a good father should be. Even in all his grief, not one day went past that Gray and Bella didn't know how much they were loved."

As much as I started trying to make this light with my humor, now I'm feeling the weight on my chest getting heavier.

"I'm sure your mother loved you then and still loves you now in her own way," Mia softly says.

"To this very day my mother has never told me she loves me, and I'm starting to believe that maybe she doesn't. Perhaps she is incapable of love, I don't know. But it's unexplainable to me now after seeing you with Jack and Kayla how a mother can't love her own child. Hell, I love your kids and they aren't even mine." Running my hand through my hair, I find myself at a complete loss, and the fact I just told her how much I've fallen for her kids too.

"So why wasn't I ever good enough for her to love, Mia? What is so wrong with me, that I'm not worthy of a mother's love?"

I sigh loudly. "I just wish I fucking knew, because I'm sure it would explain a lot of my life."

"That's where you're wrong, Lex. It's not that you feel unworthy of your mother's love. You are now at the point you believe you don't deserve anyone's love. Isn't that the real statement you tell yourself every day?"

I almost swerve the car off the side of the road. How the hell can she know that? I want to lie and deny it, but I vowed I'd never lie to her.

"Every. Single. Fucking. Day," I tell her the words from the bottom of my soul.

Chapter Twenty-One

LEX

"How do you know what's in my soul before I do?" It's like Mia's reading my mind.

"Because I live with that belief every day of my life too. And now I'll never be able to change that with my mother gone. You have time, Lex, and hopefully one day you'll get the answers you need too." Taking in what she's understanding, I finally see that though we've come from different backgrounds, we are the same. We both have craved our whole life for the love and acceptance of our mother.

"I don't know if that'll happen, but I've been proven wrong before." We drive for a few minutes without talking, Mia giving me the time to work out the next part of my conversation.

"Perhaps that's why I've lived my life the way I have. Not wanting to look for love because I don't think I'm worthy of it. I don't know, I'm just a guy. We're not supposed to know this crap."

"For someone who's not supposed to know this *'crap'* you are pretty damn good at sorting out my head when I need it." Mia giggles at me.

"Well, someone else's life is always so much easier than your own. Besides, can I just say that I've never done deep and meaningful discussions with anyone before you. So, I think it's more that I'm drawn to you which makes me in tune with you."

I shrug my shoulders as she tries to avoid my eye contact for a moment. "Anyway, this is the part of my life I'm not extremely proud of, and sharing it with you seems wrong in so many ways, but if I'm going to do this then I need to tell you all of it." Taking a deep breath, I look straight ahead because I don't want to see the disappointment on her face.

"I've used women for sex." I panic that came out the wrong way. "Shit, never in a harmful way, and every time it was completely consensual, but there was never any affection in it. We had sex, hot and hard. We both enjoyed it, but there was never anything more. To the point that I didn't even bother sometimes to ask for their number. I had no intention of seeing them again. I suppose it came from never seeing my parents act with any affection towards each other. In fact, I don't even know if they had sex. Besides when they had me, obviously. But I never heard them or even saw them touching each other. As a little boy, all I heard was them argue with each other or live the silent life that we all lived in that house. Of course, until we were out at a function and they were the perfect couple." I sigh at the sadness in my father's eyes. I think he's stuck in a life he doesn't want either, but he doesn't have the guts to do anything about it.

Mia's timid voice speaks up. "Lex, you said hard sex. You don't mean like the pain stuff, do you? I don't think I'll ever be able to do that."

"Fuck, sorry, baby. No, I'm not into BDSM. I could never do that to you. God, I am making a mess of this, I should have been clearer what I meant. Actually, I should have shut my mouth." Feeling flustered.

"It's okay Lex, as hard as it is, I think I have to hear it. I need to know everything, so I'm not left wondering or guessing what could be hiding under the surface. I won't make that mistake in my life again." Her face tells me it's hard, but she is standing strong. Sighing I continue to explain myself.

"Hard sex for me is where I'm the one in control and I'm letting go of my pent-up frustrations and emotions. It's purely physical. Shit, how do I explain this?" Trying to describe my sex life leaves me feeling tense.

"Mia, I've never made love to a woman. I've just fucked. Where we just get the gratification we both want. I've never wanted to worship a woman's body like I want to worship yours. Or to make sure the pleasure is all about you. To take things slow and savor every moment. That hasn't been something I've ever thought about." I look at her for the first time since I started talking about my sex life. "Until you, baby. Now it's all I think about."

Just nodding at me, she seems calm but isn't giving me too much of a clue on what she is really thinking.

"So how does Jacinta fit into all this with your mother?" Her voice now sounds a little stronger than her previous question.

"I knew her through my parents' social circles as we were growing up. She's a few years younger than me so when I went to high school which was an all-boys school, I didn't see her as often. Then as I finished law school, my mother started talking about her every time I saw her, and where she was up to in her studies. Me being a boy in my early twenties, I wasn't listening to anything from my mother. All I cared about was making a name for myself in the legal fraternity. There were plenty of women around for me to spend time with. I didn't even pick up on the clues, or should I say subtle hints, my mother was trying to give me. Then life moved on for a while, and I didn't hear about her for years. Later I found out it was because she had moved to England to finish her studies at Oxford University and stayed to work afterwards. She was in a serious relationship with someone she worked with. Unfortunately for her, after a few years it ended, and from reading between the lines I think he was cheating on her the whole time. The Jacinta that came home to Chicago was a woman who was married to the job. No emotions at all and ready to slay any man who stands in her way.

But what it did do, was make her a damn good lawyer. One of the best in Chicago. So of course, I started coming up against her in the courtroom."

"Let me guess, she pushed you to the limits and started beating you." Mia actually laughs a little at this story.

"Yeah, she challenged me, and while it pissed me off, it turned me on too. I like that she doesn't take shit from anyone, including me. So, one night we were at a charity function that my mother was hosting, and I was seated next to Jacinta. Which I thought was coincidental, but now I know was all orchestrated, by the master puppeteer, my mother. Anyway, we were drinking and discussing work, among other things. The drunker we got, the more I just wanted to have sex with her and see her for once without that hardass exterior. This is going to sound so disgraceful, but she was a challenge to me. Both in and out of the courtroom. So, we went home together that night. That was when I found out she was no better than I was. We just used each other for sex, and it was good for both of us. The next morning, she put forward a proposition like a business arrangement, which I see now is totally fucked up. That we would call each other whenever we needed sex. We meet, we get our satisfaction, and leave again, no strings attached, no emotions involved, and no talk about any work. Otherwise we would be in all sorts of professional trouble." Taking a quick sideways glance at her again, to see if there is a look of disgust on her face, but I'm pleasantly surprised.

"That sounds very clinical, but after meeting her, something I can totally imagine. You both chase the high of winning a case in real life, you started playing the game of chasing that high against each other in another way." Mia seems to understand this whole fucked-up situation better than I do.

"I suppose you're right. I never looked at it that way, but it makes sense."

"How long did this go on for?"

"Over six months. Mother started getting us tickets to events, and of course we always carried the persona of friendship. Then at the end of the night, we would fuck and then go home to our own beds. Sometimes I wouldn't see her for a week, but then other weeks we would meet for five nights in a row if one of us needed it. Stress is massive in our world, and sex is the only relief I knew besides hanging out with the guys. I didn't want to be one of those high-powered lawyers who is also an alcoholic, or worse, using drugs to get them through. So, this seemed like a harmless thing." Looking back now, I see how toxic a situation it really was, for both of us.

"Yet it wasn't harmless, was it?"

"No, and I hurt her which was never my intention. And not that she can see it, she hurt me too, just in a different way. We were supposed to say something if feelings ever started to develop for either of us. They never did for me. Instead I was drowning in my own life and just didn't realize it. I knew I needed to stop seeing her and try to work out what it was I wanted in my life. So just before I met you, I told her it was over, and I couldn't do it anymore. That it wasn't healthy for either of us. That we both deserved more than that. A real relationship."

Turning to Mia, I go on, "That was when I worked out the part I feel so terrible about. Jacinta had developed feelings for me, and I had no idea. When I asked to meet her, she thought it was to move us forward and I blindsided her. Let me tell you, as a lawyer, one thing you hate with a passion is to be hit from left field with new information. I know she seems like a bitch, and on the outside, she is, but I felt awful for hurting her. As time passed, I found out I shouldn't have wasted my time. She played me even though she may have felt something for me. She and my mother had been planning this all along. I was supposed to marry Jacinta, make the perfect power couple. She would support me to fulfill my mother's plans for me to end up in politics, and Jacinta would also get her boost in status."

"This all sounds so far out of reality for me. I didn't think this sort of thing happened anymore, you know, arranged marriages. That's crazy, Lex."

"It truly is. So, when I found out, you can imagine how gutted I felt. Yet I didn't share it with anyone. Not even the boys know about this. It just made me understand the restlessness I had been feeling in my life. I had known for a while I wanted more. Hell, I *needed* more. I've been seeing the guys all find a woman who lights up their world and I wanted it too. Then I took the leap and I stood up to my mother for the first time in my life and told her no more. My life, my decisions. As you can imagine that didn't go down well, and you saw yesterday the fallout from that. She is furious with me, yet I feel lighter than I have in years."

"So, when she saw me, that was like a red flag to a bull."

"You've got it, baby. A raging bull at that. She will calm down, but it'll take time. I need to stand firm, and she'll realize she either lets me live my own life and we have a relationship, or things will always be like this where she is cut from my life. Don't get me wrong, I'm hurt and I'm angry at her, but I still want my parents in my life. Does that make sense?" Man, this shit is hard!

"To others probably not, but to me it makes total sense. I carry so much anger at my mother, but what I wouldn't give to have her in my life in some way. And likewise, for my kids. I hurt for them knowing they will never have a father in their life. Some situations in our life just suck and we can't do anything about it." Picking up her own water, Mia takes a big gulp like she's trying to control her own emotions.

"Truer words have never been spoken. And I've finally learned that. The only one that can change this life is me." I reach out to grab her hand as she puts her water bottle down. "The amazing thing is, the moment I made that decision to change the way I looked at my world, you came running into it. Like the biggest sign that this is where I should be. Right here with you." For the first time, I know what Mia is describing when she says she feels a sense of calmness from me. She is now pushing it back to me. Unloading so much that I've been holding for so long is uplifting and brings a sense of peace.

Maybe we were meant to run into each other that night.

From a life where I have felt manipulated and nothing felt right.

The moment I started to question if there was more for me and asked for a sign.

The universe delivered Mia to me.

In all her beautiful craziness, falling into my perfectly ordered world.

She needed me, but what she didn't realize until now, was that I needed her too.

Just because life is a certain way, it doesn't mean it has to stay that way.

We have the power to change that.

It just means shifting the way we perceive it.

I've found my perception.

I've found my one.

My Mia.

We both sit for a while in the quiet of the car, listening to the hum of the engine and tires on the road. No music, just the silence of our thoughts.

If there is one thing we both appreciate it's the space we give each other. It's not asked for yet understood and appreciated when it happens. Something about our connection of souls just knows when it's needed.

About fifteen minutes has passed, and then Mia starts getting restless in her seat.

"What's wrong, are you getting uncomfortable? Do you need to stop and stretch your legs?"

"Sorry, I didn't want to say anything. But can we do a restroom stop, please? I should have gone before we left, like I would have made Jack do. I just wasn't thinking."

I can't help but laugh.

"Christ, Mia, you should have just told me. Although I must say, I'm sure you've lasted longer than Jack would have. So gold star for you, Miss Mia."

"You are such a smartass, seriously, Lex. Don't make me laugh, otherwise I'll be peeing my pants just like Jack does too. All over your nice leather seat."

"Shit, we need to find the nearest place to stop then before that happens. I mean, we can't finish this trip without some of my amazing jokes that'll have you laughing in hysterics. And by the sounds of it, that could cause you a *wee* little problem." I try not to laugh as I deliver the punchline.

"Oh my god, you did not just say that. Not helping, Lex." She rolls her eyes at me.

"I know, but it was funny, right?"

"Oh yeah, freaking hilarious. How old are you?"

"Old enough to know that if I don't stop right now you're going to kill me." I can't help it now, the laughter is coming out.

"Good answer."

I take her hand and lift it to my lips, giving it a light kiss. "Yes, because we don't want to be telling the kids the story when we get home of the Princess and the Pea – or is that *pee*?" Before I know it, the hand I was kissing is now smacking me in the arm.

"Stop it, I hate you." She's now crossing her legs.

I call Ashton on my phone while she's trying to distract herself.

"Lex, what's up, man?" His voice surrounds us in the car.

"We just need to make a little stop to stretch our legs and a bathroom break for me. Will be pulling off just up here."

"Perfect. Thanks, will see you shortly." Hanging up the call, Mia just smiles at me.

"You could have told him it was for me, but thank you for your chivalry."

"Who's to say I don't need to pee too?" I put on my signal to start pulling off the road. Looking for a parking spot.

"I love that you didn't say that until now, so I couldn't torture you and make you laugh. "You don't play fair, Lex." Her seat belt is coming off before the car is fully stopped.

"That comes from playing against the boys. There is no fairness in our games. It's every man for themselves. You'll need to remind me now I need to compensate for the lady." We're both out of the car and heading inside to the restrooms.

"Bullshit. Equal treatment in all things, remember? Game on, funny boy!"

Even by the time I've finished and washed my hands, I've still got the stupid grin on my face. I love when Mia's true personality comes out. I can't wait until her life is in a settled place and she feels safe to let her true self shine all the time in every situation.

Walking back out of the restroom, I find Ashton standing to the side just pretending to look through some magazines.

We give each other a chin lift as I get closer.

"How's she doing so far?" he asks.

"Better than I expected. Although we sort of got a little distracted."

"You're seriously hitting on her in the car." His deep chuckle starts.

"No, dickhead. Our conversation got distracted away from her, which wasn't a bad thing. But it also means she hasn't thought to call home once yet or watch the camera you set up. So, I'll take that as a win." I try to keep my voice low waiting for her to come out the door.

"It's still early, buddy. Don't expect her still to be talking to you by the time we get through this afternoon." Ashton signals with his eyes that she's approaching.

"That's a risk I'm prepared to take." I turn back to face her as she gets closer.

"Now I bet you wouldn't mind a snack for the road. Let's get something full of sugar while the kids aren't with us. That way we don't have to share or worry about getting Jack to sleep." I take Mia's hand and walk up the candy aisle.

"Who's to say we don't have a kid with us still." Mia laughs at her own joke while Ashton walks past her laughing too.

"Oh, she just burned you, man. I like this one. I think we might keep her. She doesn't let you get away with shit." Ashton slaps me on the shoulder.

"You're not keeping nothing, man. This sassy little lady is all mine now. Your job is to watch her, but you ever get any ideas about anything further, man, and you will be fighting me." I try to make it sound like I'm joking, but inside my heart is pumping. I know I'll fucking kill anyone that tries to go near Mia.

"Umm, excuse me. Right here, gentlemen," Mia says, pointing to herself. "If you want to try to go all macho on me, then you can both fuck off."

"She just owned you both," the lady behind the counter bursts out laughing.

"I totally did. Now they know who means business in this road trip." Mia places her candy and chocolate on the counter and winks at me as she steps back for me to set mine down.

"It was never in doubt, bossy pants."

Swiping my card, I bundle everything up including the little packet of stress relief suckers that I intend on giving Mia before we leave her, for the short period, once we get there.

The rest of the trip is uneventful until we get around fifteen minutes from Bellevue and the road signs start listing the town on them. I can see Mia's whole body language changing, and if I'm honest with myself, I'm feeling it too. It's a mixture of emotions of wanting to protect Mia, comfort her from how she's feeling, and the aggression that's building of wanting to beat the hell out of Edward for what he's done to her. I know I can't do that, but that doesn't mean I don't want to.

Looking across at her, I see that she's watching the nanny cams we set up for her. Just reassuring herself that they're fine. At times there's a little half-smile, which means Jack's probably doing something cute again.

To be honest, I'm like Mia and I just want to get this over with. The court hearing is actually the furthest thing from my mind because no matter what the judge awards, that bastard is never getting near Mia or the kids ever again.

I'll make sure of that!

MIA

"I might just call Mason's phone to talk to Jack for a bit before we get there if that's okay?" Watching them is keeping a lid on my nerves that are building, but hearing his voice will be even better.

"Not Mason," Lex jumps at me quite quickly. "Sorry, I mean not Mason's phone, in case Ashton needs to talk to him about anything. Call Paige instead." He's getting a little jumpy too, but I'm not surprised. This is not the kind of place that Lex would be used to.

"Okay, that's a good idea." I push her name on my phone and wait for her to answer. On the second ring, I hear her voice and my heart rate settles a little. I can only see Jack and Kayla on the screen so was feeling nervous, but I didn't want to tell Lex that.

"Hi, Mia, how's the trip been so far?" Her chirpy voice seems a little over the top, but maybe she's just trying to make sure I'm not worrying. I hate to tell her that's not possible, but I can't be snappy to her.

"Hi, Paige, yeah, okay so far. We're almost there. How are the kids? I can see them playing in the living room. Have they had their afternoon sleep yet?" I can't help it. I'm checking she's following my schedule.

"Yes, they just got up actually. They went down a little later than usual because Gray and Tilly have been here, along with Tate and Bella. So, they've been playing. The girls have just left to get some food, and we are going to make dinner here. Jack is going to make dessert with Bella. Don't panic, it's something easy, but I will let him tell you. Do you want to talk to him?" I'm not sure how I feel about Jack being near the kitchen without me, but in the back of my head I keep hearing Lex's voice, trust them like you trust me. They are your family.

"Please, if I can. I don't want to upset him, but I need to hear his voice." I'm honest with her, but I doubt I need to be worried.

"Mia, you can call a hundred times and I won't care or be offended. Remember, we understand and think you are being so brave. Now hang on and I'll take the phone to him." I watch her appear on the screen and his eyes light up as she tells him it's me.

"Mommy, guess what? We had *McDonald's*, and I got a toy and tomorrow if I go to sleep tonight, Uncle Mason says I can pick what we have for breakfast. Even ice cream if I want it." I can't help but laugh. Trust Mason to take the bribery to the next level.

"Oh, did he now? Well, you better have a big sleep then. What else have you been doing since I left?" I look at Lex who can hear everything on loudspeaker. He's laughing silently about the ice cream and mouthing the word *'asshole'* to me.

"I colored all my pictures. Played cars with Fruncle Grayson and Fruncle Tate, but I won."

"Oh, sweetie, it's Uncle not Fruncle," I say, correcting his mistake.

"No, Mommy, they told me to call them Fruncle." His voice sounds very sure of himself.

Lex cuts in before I can answer. "That's right, bud. They are your Fruncles, and you make sure you don't let them win any of the games you play. Tell them I said you are the champion every time." Lex is now mouthing at me he will explain later. I'm so confused but decide to run with it.

"I have to go, Mommy, Frauntie Bella and Frauntie Tilly are here and we're making cookies for our dessert with the chocolate chips like you make." Before I get time to say another word, I see him drop the phone in Paige's hand and run out of the camera screen.

"Mia?" Her voice comes back on the phone.

"Yeah, we're still here," I answer.

"Sorry, he got excited about the cookies," she tries to explain why he dumped me.

"It's okay, the attention span of a four-year-old is about zero-point-three seconds, which you are probably learning this afternoon."

"I'll sleep well tonight, put it that way. I can handle twenty board members in a meeting, and that's nothing like keeping up with Jack. I don't know how you do it every day."

"Because she's a super woman. That's how," Lex comments from beside me.

"Hey, Lex. Are you driving safely and looking after my sister?"

She's joking, and of course Lex starts smiling. I know this answer will be the same as the question.

"If you don't count the two cars I sideswiped, the truck I ran up the back of, and the flock of geese that shit so hard on the windscreen it shattered, then yeah, we're doing great."

"I swear, if I didn't have little ears around me, I would tell you that you are d-i-c-k-h-e-a-d among other things." Lex and I both burst out laughing. At the same time, the GPS in the car starts talking and I know we're getting close and Lex needs to concentrate. "That sound's my cue to leave you to it. Call anytime, otherwise we will call before bed so you can say good night. And don't worry about them, sis, they're doing great. Love you."

"Thanks, Paige. I couldn't do this without you. Love you too." The call ends and I see her pick up Kayla and disappear off the screen.

My heart feels sad again, but that won't change until I make it home again.

"You are doing great, baby. Just keep breathing and we will get through this." Lex is doing his best to comfort me, but to be honest, a cuddle would be better. Guess I have to wait until we get there for that.

"By the way, what the hell is a fruncle and frauntie?"

"Well, you think Jack has personality, wait until you meet Daisy. Since we are all framily then she decided we are fruncles and fraunties. It's kinda cute when you think about it. Something unique to our special little group."

"It's just perfect. Like all of you." Squeezing his hand is the closest I can get to touching him, so it will have to do for now.

"In five hundred feet you have reached your destination," the GPS system announces. Which makes me shiver all over.

This is the first time I've set foot back in my hometown since the night I ran.

I didn't live in this good part of town, but it's still close.

But looking up, this is far from the apartment block I lived in.

Instead, I see the beautiful *Peoria Marriott Pere Marquette*. It's a place I've only ever driven past on the public bus.

I won't fit in here. This is so far out of my league.

Feeling frozen in my seat, I don't know if I can do this.

I sense the door open next to me, and Lex's hand take mine.

His voice is soft in my ear. "I've got you, Mia. You can do this. Remember, you are doing this for the kids."

And just like that my legs move, and I step from the car to take the next step in facing my demons.

Chapter Twenty-Two

MIA

Walking towards the front desk, I'm in complete awe of everything. From the moment I stepped out of the car and there was a concierge there to take our bags and have the car parked. I knew then I was in another world to anything I have ever known.

Everything looks so expensive and lush. The front desk is a mixture of gold and brown with the lighting set perfectly to show the class of the place. Standing behind it are a woman and a man ready to greet us. Above their heads is a chandelier that runs the full length of the room. It's like there's a waterfall of glass raining down on them. The cost of that light is probably some crazy amount that I would faint over.

"Mia, just wait here with Ashton. I won't be long. Okay?"

Lex speaking has me snapping out of my fascination of where I'm standing. "Umm, okay." He continues on to the counter, and I feel Ashton's presence next to me.

"You alright, Mia?" he asks quietly.

"A little freaked out, I don't fit here," I whisper.

"Now that's where you're wrong. You belong anywhere you want to be. Only you get to decide that. No one else."

"I've never been somewhere like this." As usual with me, when I'm worried my words just keep coming.

"Then enjoy this. I've got an idea it won't be the last time you'll visit a hotel with Lex, or Paige, for that matter."

"They belong here, though. I don't."

"Bullshit. I won't accept that, and if Lex heard it, he wouldn't either." But before we can debate it any further, Lex is back from getting the room keys looking a little bit nervous.

"Yeah, let's go and get settled in. I'll show you where we're staying." Noticing my expression, it has him reaching his arm around me as we walk towards the elevator.

"You'll love it here. It's even got a big bath you can try out."

I know he's trying to help, but that's the last thing on my mind right now.

"What floor?" Ashton asks as the doors are closing in front of us.

"Top one, eleventh floor."

"Of course," Ashton replies with a chuckle.

"What?" Lex asks, looking like he has no clue why Ashton is laughing.

"Nothing, fancy boy." He rolls his eyes at Lex.

"If we have to stay the night, then I'm getting the best room I can for Mia. She deserves it." Lex pulls me closer to make sure he's still comforting me. "I can downgrade your room, though, if you like, smartass, to I don't know, perhaps the basement." There's something about Ashton that ruffles Lex's feathers.

"No can do, boss. Need to be near the pretty lady at all times. Looks like you're stuck with me close by, for the rest of the trip."

Lex is almost growling at Ashton. If I didn't feel so freaked out by my unfamiliar surroundings, I would be laughing at these two.

Arriving on our floor, we stop at the first door.

"This is your room, Ashton. Here's the key. We will be next door. I'll text you once we've settled in." Lex then places his hand on the small of my back, guiding me farther along the hallway. I can't stop looking around at the building. Everything is old world. Lush cream and brown, gold, and the soft furnishings just ooze class. Even the carpet in the hallway is thick and plush.

"This is us." We stop at the next door on the left of the corridor. Room 1102.

Holding the door open for me, Lex guides me inside.

Standing still, I just try to take it all in. This can't be my room. It's so pretty. I'm almost scared to touch anything in case I mark it or break it. I feel like a child again in a shop where you knew you weren't allowed to touch anything just in case.

In front of me is a round table with four chairs, all a plum velvet and a high-back chair to match. The couch is a cream velvet with the same plum-colored cushions. Lex isn't saying much, just letting me wander the room to check everything out. The farther I get into the room, I see a door that goes through to the bedroom. At the same time there is a knock at the suite door with the bellhop calling out to announce he has our bags.

"I'll just grab the bags," Lex says from behind me as I walk towards the open bedroom door.

Sheer panic runs through my body.

"Lex," my voice shakily calls him.

"Mia, what's wrong?" I hear him come rushing to me.

Standing at the end of the bed, I'm struggling. "There is only one bed. Do you have another room?" Maybe there has been a mistake, and Lex is staying with Ashton.

"It's okay, please don't panic. This is your bed. I'm sleeping on the sofa bed out there. They didn't have any two-bedroom suites so this was the best Greta could do for us. No matter what, I wasn't leaving you in a room on your own. And over my dead body were you staying in a room with Ashton."

"No, Lex, I'll sleep on the couch. I'm smaller, plus you're paying for the room, you should get the bed." I'm racing with my words but try to slow myself down. I don't care which bed I'm on, I just don't think I'm ready for that yet. No matter how much I dream about it at night.

"No way in hell are you sleeping on that sofa bed. I didn't ask Greta to book the best hotel she could find, for you to spend the night not sleeping in a big fluffy bed. Plus, you need your strength for tomorrow, so I won't hear another word about it." He walks in past me to put my bag on the luggage stand.

"What is it about you and sleeping on couches around me? How many nights have you slept in a bed since we met, Lex?"

There is no hesitation as he answers straight away. "Three, and that's three too many. God, Mia, I don't give a shit where I sleep as long as I'm near you. It's as simple as that." Standing in front of me, he puts his hands on my shoulders and gives them a gentle squeeze. "I need to know you're safe, baby. I'm sorry if that freaks you out, but I feel this pull towards you that I can't explain. So, I hope it's okay if I'm here in the same room so I can see you." The last part comes out as a whisper. This big, strong man is never afraid to show me his softer side, and I can't turn him away.

"Okay, but know that I'm not happy, and if I could, I'd do something about it. But this time I just have to suck it up and accept it, don't I?"

Trying not to laugh at me, he nods his head. Then leans forward and kisses me ever so sweetly on the lips. I need more. Taking the step to him, I circle my arms around his waist and hang on tight.

He now wraps me in his arms.

I bury my head into his chest and smell everything that is Lex.

My safe place.

LEX

I'm so fucking stupid.

I should have told her that before we got here. But she totally threw me in the car, when she got me talking. I forgot all the things that I wanted to say to her. Now I've just added to her stress.

"Why don't you lie down, relax, and test out the bed. Tell me how fluffy it is. I need to call Ashton to check everything is okay with his room. I'll be back." Sitting her gently down on the edge of the bed, I pull my phone out of my pocket as I walk back through to the little living room, closing the bedroom door behind me.

"Hey, man, everything as it should be?" Ashton knows I'm not

Lovable Lawyer

asking about his room at all. To be honest, as long as he has a bed and a bathroom then he's set. Guys need so much less than a woman. We travel light and keep things simple.

"Yeah, Mason and Ronan are about fifteen minutes away. I'll let you know when they're here, and you can break the news to Mia. Then let's get this shit done so we can relax for the rest of the night. There's a nice beer in my mini bar that has my name on it."

"You shouldn't be drinking on the job!" I snap at him. It's not really anything to do with Ashton, I'm just getting worked up about paying a visit to Edward.

"Yeah, and you shouldn't be fucking your client, so we're even."

"I'm not," is all I can say because he took me by surprise.

"Not yet, but it's coming. I'm telling you now, don't you hurt her, or you'll have me to answer to." Ashton is putting the big tough alpha hero voice on.

"Fuck off, Ashton. As if I would. Plus, you can stand in line behind Mason and Paige for that matter. Just remember what your role is here; to protect her, not hit on her."

"Man, you are such an idiot. Mia doesn't see another soul when you're in the room. Lex, she only ever sees you. So back off me. I don't want your girlfriend. Do I like her? Yeah, she's a great lady, a good friend. Do I want to fuck her? Not a chance, she's not even close to my type, and I wouldn't know how to care for her. Yet you two are perfect together, we all see it. So, don't fuck this up, Lex. Now, can you stop with the whole macho man at me every time I look at her. I'm doing my job, being her friend and yours, if you'll let me. She trusts me, man, I just need you to also. Then we can keep her safe." I didn't understand how rude I was being to him.

Letting out a breath, I roll my shoulders to try to release some tension.

"Sorry, Ashton. I don't know why I've been such a jerk. I've never had someone like her in my life, and I have this incredible need to keep her safe and not lose her. She's it for me, man, and like you said, I can't afford to fuck this up."

"Well, then don't. Let's do this together. You keep your girl, and I gain two friends. Deal?"

"Deal. Just don't be asking to be best man at the wedding, okay?"

"Buddy, they don't even make suits big enough to get across my shoulders. So, unless you're getting married on a beach in tank tops, I'm out. But heads up, let's get her divorced first, before we go planning that tropical beach ceremony."

"Thanks, man, for giving me the space to make a dick of myself and not holding judgement. I do appreciate it." I pace the room, quietly watching the clock. "We're lucky to have you."

"Damn right you are. But don't worry, I respect any man who is prepared to fight for his girl, treat her right, and take on any man who thinks otherwise of her. Even if they are twice his size and ten times stronger."

"Shut up, you idiot. I pack a mean punch when I need to."

"Oh yeah, and when's that, tough boy?" Ashton's now laughing at me.

"When I hit the punching bag at the gym. Let's hope I don't need to test it out today."

"Remember the plan, we're just talking, getting him to sign, and walking away. Otherwise I'll be practicing my punching skills on your nose. Got it?"

"Loud and clear. Message when we're ready to go." I hang up and think it over to myself. Ashton standing up to me and pushing me to get my head out of my ass was just what I needed. My head is now clearer, and I know what I need to do.

Opening the door to the bedroom slowly so not to startle her, I find Mia lying on the bed, curled up in a ball. Her eyes closed, and quietly singing to herself again. It seems to be her go-to when she needs to calm her brain.

Just standing listening to her angelic voice, I can't make out the song. It isn't one I've heard before

The search has always been for that place for me
Deep inside my soul, where only you can see
But even then, no one knows the real me
It's so hard for me to see, who I'm meant to be...

Her eyes opening a little, she startles as she sees me watching and listening to her. I walk to her and sit on the bed beside my beautiful, gentle soul.

"You have the most beautiful voice, Mia. I love to hear you sing," I say, sweeping her hair out of her face.

"Wait what, when have you heard me?" Sitting up in a hurry she nearly knocks me off the bed.

"The night you first arrived. I heard you singing in your room while you cried yourself to sleep. You have no idea how hard it was to stand at your door and not come in. I wanted to be there and comfort you, but you weren't ready then." Her shocked look subsides.

"I don't let people hear me sing, only the kids and Anna, my old boss at the diner. I'm too embarrassed." Her face looks down into her lap where she's fidgeting with her hands.

"You have nothing to be embarrassed about. Your voice is so angelic. Whose song is that, the one you were singing just now?" I crawl behind her on the bed, leaning against the headboard. Drawing her between my legs, I wrap my arms around her waist as she leans with her back against my chest. There's silence for a minute and then she finally answers me.

"Mine." The word is almost so quiet I didn't hear it.

"Mia, did you say mine?"

Her head just nods.

"Wow, is there more to it?" I ask, dying to know this secret side to her.

"Yes, plus others." She has no confidence, and I can tell she's struggling to even be admitting it to me.

"Will you sing it to me?" Her head starts shaking no in a panic.

"It's okay, I'm not upset. I understand. It's something obviously very private and important to you. Just know that anytime you're ready to share, I'd love to hear it. I don't think you understand what a talent you have hiding inside you."

"It's just something I do for me, it's nothing special."

"I think you're wrong, but I'm glad it brings you happiness." I kiss her on the top of the head and hold her that little bit tighter.

"Is that why Jack sings all the time while he's playing, and I've seen him sing to Kayla?"

"Yeah, I taught him from early on that when he was scared, he should sing because it always makes the bad things go away. He hasn't stopped since. Singing is his happy place. His singing voice is so beautiful. He used to sing to my boss Anna too. She was like a grandmother to the kids."

"Just like his mom too, by the sound of things. Well, I'm glad it makes you both happy and I hope you never stop."

Mia turns her head to the side to look up at me.

"Thank you for not pushing me."

"Never. You know you only ever have to share what you want to with me. The rest is yours, and that's okay." She's reaching up for a kiss when my phone chimes with a message.

Shit.

I already know what the message will be.

Mason: I'm in Ashton's room. On our way in.

Why did this seem like such a good idea at the time? Right this minute, I know it's probably the most stupid thing I can be doing. Mia is going to hate me, and if I get this wrong, my job is also on the line.

For the first time, I'm telling myself to keep breathing instead of saying it to Mia.

The knock at the door means it's go time.

"I'll grab the door, it's Ashton." Plus, another two, but I don't add that yet. I'm going to savor every little second left before she wants to rip my balls off.

"Hey, man." I shake Mason's hand and grab a quick man hug as he walks past, followed by Ashton and another guy, that must be Ronan. Before I even get a chance to speak to him, Mia is behind me in the living room.

"Mason, what are you doing here? Who's with my kids, what's going on?" Going right to her, I take her hands and lead her to the couch.

"The kids are perfectly fine. You just saw them and spoke to Jack. Paige is taking great care of them. Tate and Grayson are there with her. Plus, there's one of Ashton's guys in the foyer so no one can get to them. Just stay calm and let me explain." I know I'm talking quickly but I don't want her to go into a full-blown panic attack.

"Calm? Lex, what the hell is going on!" Her voice is raising now as she's getting more worried.

"Okay, just let me get all the way through this before you say anything. Mason is here to come with me to see Edward tonight. I need to make sure he understands that he is never to come near you or the kids again. To reinforce what the court is going to tell him tomorrow and have him sign your divorce papers to speed up the process. While Mason, Ashton, and I pay him a visit, Ronan who works for Ashton is going to stay here to keep you safe."

"No, Lex. You can't leave me. I can't be on my own. You said you wouldn't leave me on my own. You promised." The tears are running down her face and my heart aches at the pain I'm causing.

"You won't be alone, baby. Ronan will be here the whole time. We'll be back before you know it."

She's up and pacing the room now, glaring at me like she hates every word I'm saying. "Nope, that's not happening. What if he hurts you? He has friends in that building. They can help him. He's nasty. What if he's drunk? He won't care what he does to you."

I give her a few moments to try to take in what I've told her. The room isn't that big, but she seems to be able to find plenty of room to keep pacing.

"I know," she blurts out. "I'll come with you. I can make him stop if he tries to hurt you. He'll stop when he sees me." Her words are racing, and she isn't even looking at me when she speaks.

"No fucking way are you going anywhere near him," I almost yell at her.

"Over my dead body," Mason says at the same time.

"Okay, let's all calm down. Now I'm running this shitshow, so how about you all listen up. This is what's going to happen."

Ashton's voice is strong and forceful and has us all stop and pay attention.

"Unlike lover boy over here, I anticipated this problem. So, here is the plan, Ashton's version. We are all going to travel to Mia's old apartment. In my SUV that has the blacked-out windows. Mia will remain in the car the whole time with Ronan. She will not move one inch out of her seat. Us three will go in. Lex and Mason, you can say your piece to Edward, in words and no other form. Get him to sign the divorce papers and then we leave. End of story. I'm giving you fifteen minutes in the apartment and then we are out. Any longer than that and I will drag your asses out of there myself. Am I understood?" He is in full security mode and everyone just nods.

"Like you could even get near my ass," Mason mumbles under his breath.

"Not now, dickhead." Ashton scowls at him for being a smartass at the wrong time.

"I don't like this," I say, moving to Mia and taking her in my arms. She fights it a little and then finally gives in. Much to my relief.

"Well, that makes two of us," she sobs. "I don't want you near him, and to be honest, I don't want to see him either. But I can't sit here, without you. I'm already fighting the panic off." She buries her face into my chest.

"I know, baby, and I'm sorry. But I need to do this for you and for me. I can't sit back and let him get away with what he did to you and the kids. I also want to make sure he thinks twice before he ever does that to another woman. The only way to stop a bully is to stand up to them. I think we're both learning that." Her head nods up and down.

I'm thankful that the other guys are just staying quiet and letting Mia and I sort through this moment on our own. I wish there were an easier way, but unfortunately there isn't.

Ashton's voice pulls both of us out of our strong hug.

"Let's roll and get this over and done with. Then Lex is buying the beers tonight, he owes me big time, for more reasons than one. Mason, you ride up front with me. Ronan, you're in the back with

Mia, and Lex, like we talked about. That way she isn't seen at all, the whole time you wait for us."

"Got it, boss," Ronan replies.

Ashton starts towards the door, meaning it's time for us to follow.

Grabbing my briefcase, I take out the envelope I need and then we follow down the hallway. No one saying a word. I don't know how this is going to turn out, and to be honest, when the adrenaline passes, whether Mia will still be talking to me.

Sitting in the car I can feel the fear radiating from Mia's body next to me. Her breathing heavier than normal and her hand sweaty in mine. I can tell when we're getting close, by the way the buildings are changing. They're rundown and don't look like anyone gives the time of day to maintain them.

As we turn into the street, I don't even have to look. Mia gives it away.

"Fuck," she gasps as the home she ran from that night comes into view.

"It's okay, he doesn't know you're here. He can't get to you. I promise."

"I don't care about me. I can't lose you to him, not like I lost my own soul." Her whisper is loud enough that it hammers home why I'm here. To help claim back everything he took from her and the kids.

"You won't lose me, Mia, I'm yours for a lifetime." I kiss her hard on the lips so she knows how much I mean it. I don't give a fuck who is in the car with us. She needs to know how serious I am about it.

I need to move and do this quickly so I can get back to Mia.

"Don't move from this car, don't make a sound, and do as Ronan tells you," I lean in to whisper in her ear. "Sing if you have to. Even in your head, but sing those beautiful songs until I'm back."

Leaving the car and seeing the tears rolling down her face is hard, but I need to do this, and she needs me to do this for her too. If she didn't believe that, Mia would have stopped this.

Walking up the stairs, the smell of rotting garbage hits me, the noise of televisions from behind doors with paint peeling off. Carpet in the hallway that's stained so much it almost looks like it's meant to be part of the pattern. I can't even imagine my beautiful girl living in these conditions or sweet little Kayla crawling on the floor. They will never experience a life like this again, not when I can give them the world.

Standing in front of the apartment door, I take a deep breath and knock with force.

I hear footsteps stomping to the door. Well, that answers the question of if Edward is home.

Here goes, it's showtime.

The door opens to the sight of a pathetic man, who you can tell has been aged by his alcohol and drug addiction. Standing there in his black jeans, bare feet, and a white t-shirt that has some bar's name and slogan on it. I wouldn't call the shirt bright white because the stains on it offer a different picture.

"What ya want? I told the last guys. I got no money, the missus took it all, the bitch. Find her and make her pay." That's enough to get me seeing red, even if I wasn't already almost there before I even knocked on the door.

Feeling a hand on my shoulder, I know it's Ashton trying to calm me and keeping me from knocking him out cold.

"You Edward Walker?" My voice is coarse and grumpy.

"Who wants to know?" He's standing with a smug look on his face and arms crossed.

"My name is Alexander Jefferson the third. I'm a lawyer here on behalf of Mia Kennedy. We need to chat." Not giving him time to agree or ask any more questions, I shove the palm of my hand into his chest and put him off balance. He backpedals into the apartment as Mason, Ashton, and I follow him in. Hearing the door closing behind me, I know, we're on our own.

"That bitch owes me money and stole my kids. You can tell her from me I'm coming for her!" He tries to stand his ground and rolls his shoulders back to look tough.

That's when I do, what I promised everyone I wouldn't.

My fist collides with his face, and I hear him groan as he falls backwards and the blood starts running from his nose.

"For fuck's sake, I knew this would turn to shit. What happened to using words?" Ashton grumbles.

"That spoke a thousand words for me." My fist is throbbing, but I'm so mad I ignore it.

"Me too," Mason agrees.

"Get up, you coward. Not so tough now you don't have a woman to beat up?" I can't help it. I need to get out everything that's been building for days.

"What the fuck was that?" Edward is still trying to climb to his feet.

"That's the beginning of this conversation, and if you don't shut that big fucking mouth of yours it'll happen again. I'm here to give you a message loud and clear. So, I suggest you listen, and this will run a lot smoother."

"You can't walk into my house and hit me." Holding his face, his words are a little mumbled through his hand covering his nose and mouth.

"See, that's where you're wrong. I just did, asshole."

"Get to the point, man, do what you came to do." Mason's voice to my side is trying to bring back my self-control, before it goes up in flames completely.

"What, you think you're tough because you have your goons with you?" Edward makes the mistake of still talking.

Mason next to me, stands that little bit taller and his body moves back to that defensive stance.

"Shut your mouth and listen up. Before I finish what I started." I push him backwards into the seat next to the kitchen table.

"Tomorrow you're going to show up in court and tell the judge that you agree to the restraining order. Admit that you assaulted Mia. So she doesn't have to say a word in court."

"I didn't do nothing to that whore. She wasn't worth a piece a shit, just the money she brung home which was never enough." As my fist raises again, Ashton grabbing me is enough to hold me back.

"I swear you say one more word like that about Mia and I will end you."

"What, you fuckin' my wife, pretty boy? You seem mighty pissed for some guy who's just her fancy lawyer." How dare he disrespect Mia, talking about her like that. This guy has no brains, but before I can respond, Mason is in his face.

"If you want to live today, I suggest you get that smart mouth shut and let the man finish. Otherwise my friend here, who's trained in making people disappear, may have a job to complete for me." I'm obviously not the only one who's having trouble controlling his rage.

Ashton steps a little closer to reinforce Mason's words.

Finally, Edward is getting the message and just glares at us all, but I start to see a hint of fear in his eyes.

Trying to get myself under control, I start again.

"Like I said. Tomorrow you turn up, confess you are a fucked-up husband and that you will stay away from her and the kids. The judge will sign off on the restraining order. Then you will walk away and never see her again. And when you see her in the courtroom, you won't speak to her. Look down and do not make eye contact, and don't you even get close enough to think about touching her or I swear to god I don't care who's in the room, I will kill you!" Now his eyes are getting wider and his breathing quicker. While the blood continues to flow out his nose.

"Do you understand?" He nods his head once.

"Say it, asshole!" I'm nearly yelling by this stage.

"Yes, for fuck's sake," he grumbles.

"Don't think you can take off and not show up either, because we will be watching you, and if you try, I will find you. There is no hiding now. I fucking see you, you piece of scum, and I'm more than happy to make you pay for everything you've done. So, you either cooperate or I will make your life a living hell, more than it is now. I'm sure you'd look good as some guy's bitch in a jail cell with him. From what I hear, they don't like guys who bully women and kids. So, you'll fit right in." Now he's listening. I can smell the fear coming off him from where I'm standing above him.

"Alright, I get it," he mumbles.

"I'm glad we're finally on the same page. So, while you are being so agreeable, you will sign these divorce papers and grant full custody of the kids to Mia. I'm sure you're happy to do that, aren't you, Edward?" I pull the pen and papers from the envelope.

"Like I want those screaming brats anywhere near me, you can have them." Breathe, Lex, just breathe. Even though he just talked about Jack and Kayla like they're trash, just breathe. You need him to sign this.

Scribbling his name on all the places where I'm pointing, he then looks up and delivers the news I wasn't expecting but is the only thing that came out of his mouth worth anything.

"And as far as she goes, I didn't need to sign shit. We weren't even married properly. We made it up. My buddy wasn't even licensed. I just told her he was. I should have got rid of her years ago when she wouldn't put out when I wanted it. Good luck with my used goods."

There's no holding back now. I pick up my papers.

Put my hand on his throat and glare at him.

"Be there tomorrow or I will come for you, and don't doubt me. It's a promise. This is for Mia and every other woman you've hurt."

I stand and slam my foot into his balls and watch him scream in pain, falling forward. Turning, I walk out of the apartment as quick as I can, otherwise I know the next place I'll be will be in jail.

All I can think as I walk away, trying to breathe and calm myself, is that Mia is not married.

She's free.

And she's mine.

Chapter Twenty-Three

MIA

Twinkle, Twinkle, Little Star are the only damn words I can think to sing.

Where are they?

It's been forever.

I can feel my heart pounding in my chest. Breathing is getting harder. My nails are digging into my skin, and I can feel the pain but can't stop.

"Mia, I need you to breathe with me. Ashton told me about the panic attacks. Let's breathe." I can hear Ronan's voice, but it's in the distance. My gaze is focused on the door the guys entered, and I swear if they don't come out that door in the next minute, I'm going in.

"They're fine. I promise Ashton will keep them safe. Now breathe, Mia, please. The boss will kill me if I let anything happen to you." Then I hear the numbers. The ones Mason taught me to concentrate on. "Ten, nine, eight…breathe."

I take that first breath. The one that's always shaky and hurts the lungs to take.

"Good girl, seven, six, breathe…five, four…" I'm trying hard to do this. I need to hold it together.

Ronan's voice then disappears as I see Lex come bursting through the door by himself. Like there's a fire behind him. He storms towards the car. I can tell he's not just mad but furious.

Sliding across the seat, I can't wait, I open the door and run to him. I know I shouldn't be, but I need to get to him.

But before I even get to him, he shoves the envelope he's carrying in his pocket, and his arms are out.

The tears of relief are running down my face

"Are you okay?" I ask as I fall into his arms.

"Yes. Come on. In the car." His voice is not like usual. He sounds like he's trying to hold it together. A little short and there is definitely anger radiating from his body.

I don't get to hug him for long as he turns me and starts walking us forward. Reaching the car, the door still open, he's almost pushing me in and climbing in behind me. The door bangs shut, and before I can say a word, his lips are on mine.

There's an urgency in this kiss. Almost like he's trying to tell me something but doesn't know how to put it into words. The world around me disappears, and all I can see and feel is him.

Having him here safe is all I care about, and I'm giving him just as much pent-up emotion in return.

Eventually the kiss slows, and the intensity turns to a soft passion. Both of us pull back to breathe as Mason and Ashton arrive in the car. Both look back at us, not saying a word.

"What happened?" I ask tentatively.

"Let's talk when we get back to the suite. Everything is fine. You don't need to worry." Ashton starts the car and we drive off down the road. I want to know more, but I'm not about to ask. Poor Ronan is sitting awkwardly in the back seat with us and had to get the up close and personal picture of Lex and me, yet he doesn't seem one bit fazed by it.

Lex tucks me under his arm and holds me tight against him. Every so often he kisses me on the top of my head. The trip is done in silence, and it's making me feel uneasy. It's a little suffocating. I just want to scream at them all and say just talk. I'm not a child, I don't need them to hide things from me. But I respect Lex's wishes and keep my mouth closed until we arrive back to the hotel.

As we stand outside the car at the hotel, Mason walks to me and puts his hand on my arm.

"Are you okay, Mia? Your sister is blowing up my phone with messages for taking you there, so I need to promise her that you're alright. Otherwise, I'm apparently not welcome home tonight." He tries to lighten the moment a little without much success.

"Yeah, I will be when someone tells me what the hell happened in there." I glare at him and then Lex.

"Let's go upstairs and we can talk there." Lex calmly takes my hand.

"That sounds like my cue to leave with Ronan. We'll see you three back home tomorrow. Good luck with everything, but I'm sure it'll all run smoothly now."

"Thanks for coming here, man. I know you've always got my back." There's something about Lex's voice that sounds strained.

"Always, bro, and Mia's too. Try to get some sleep and behave." With that the boys hug each other, and Mason leans down and kisses me on the cheek, whispering in my ear, "He's a good man. Today he proved it, putting you before anything else in his life. Go easy on him." I have no idea what he's talking about, but I know he means what he says. Whatever went down in that apartment is serious, and I need to find out now. I'm done waiting.

This time it's me dragging Lex to the elevator and Ashton walking behind trying to stay close but not interfere.

I know I'm panicking and scared. But I'm sick of not being in control of my life.

Making decisions without me has to stop.

Approaching our rooms, Ashton says good night and slips into his room quietly as we continue along the hallway.

Lex swipes the card and I walk right past him into the room. I can't help pacing until I hear the door close.

Turning, I'm first to talk. "Tell me what the hell happened. I want to know, Lex. It must be bad if you wouldn't tell me in the car." I'm not calm and there's anger running through my body.

"Mia, let's sit down and I'll tell you everything."

"I don't want to sit." I'm too wound up, but as usual, he takes my hand and gives me the look that I can't resist.

"Fine." I'm acting like a child but that's probably because I feel like I'm being treated like one.

Sighing, Lex actually looks stressed, and I suddenly feel bad for the way I'm carrying on.

"Did something bad happen, is that why you won't tell me?"

"No, baby. Well, yes, but not what you're thinking. Edward is still alive and breathing. Not that I didn't get tempted to kill him a couple of times."

I gasp with my hands over my mouth. "Shit."

"Okay, so here's how it went. We arrived at the apartment, convinced him to let us in to talk. I then explained who I was and that I'm representing you. He said something disgusting, and I punched him in the nose and made it bleed."

Fuck.

"Lex, it was supposed to be talking. God, what did he say?"

"It doesn't matter. Just know I won't let anyone talk shit about you, no matter who they are. Anyway, I then explained how tomorrow will work, what he has to do, and what the repercussions are if he doesn't show. Got him to sign what I needed." He doesn't look happy, though.

"So, if he signed them, that means he can't take the kids, right? That I'm free from him, isn't that what you said? If we got him to sign them that it would all be over after tomorrow? So why don't you look like it's a good thing?" My anger has left, and the anxiety is building in my body again.

"Yeah, and that's true, but there are a couple of things we need to talk about. The first involves me. I need you to know that if he reports me, I will lose my job and won't be able to practice law anymore. Because funnily enough, as a lawyer you can't go around hitting the people you're against in a case." He looks shattered and it's all my fault.

Before I can even say anything, he grabs my hands.

"Don't you dare take on any blame for this. I would make the same choice every single time."

"Lex, you can't do that. I'm not worth it. See, I'm trouble wherever I go. I knew I should have left that first night."

"No, Mia. Stop. This is not your fault. I'm a big boy who makes my own decisions. I knew going there today, I was putting my job on the line. I don't give a fuck if I lose it. You and the kids are the most important thing in my life. Full stop, end of story. You need to understand that. Nothing, and I mean nothing, comes before you."

I can't help the tears that are running down my face. Now everything Mason said to me makes sense. As he takes me in his arms, I try to hold it together but it's hard. Now I've ruined someone else's life too.

"Shh, please don't cry. It's only a problem if he complains, and to be honest, I think I scared him enough that he won't want to say a word, and it's his word against three of us. So, he knows it won't be worth it."

But that's not even the point, I think to myself. *I have made you do something that goes against everything you stand up in court to defend.*

I feel terrible.

We've been sitting for a few minutes when Lex then sits me up facing him again.

"There is one other thing I need to tell you, and I know it'll make you feel both happy and sad, and I totally understand that."

"Damn, what else could go wrong now." I don't even have the energy to guess.

"What I'm going to tell you will be a shock and not something you could've expected. So take your time to let it sink in, and remember you had no control over this either."

"Just tell me, Lex," I demand.

"Edward told me you two are not legally married. His friend wasn't licensed. So, they forged it all. You're single and completely free of him."

I can hear the words he's saying but it makes no sense. "He's lying, I have the certificate he got from when he registered it. It's in my papers at Paige's place. I can show you. It says married." I feel like I want to vomit.

"I know, that's what he wanted you to believe. I'll have it all checked out by Greta in the morning, but I don't think he would have lied to me today. He was scared as hell by the time we were finished with him. I know it's hard to hear, but you need to think of the positive side to this. You're single and don't have to wait for a divorce to move on with your life. He signed over full custody of the kids to you, and tomorrow we get the restraining order in place and you get to live your life. Any way you want to, Mia."

I feel numb. I don't know what to say. Should I feel sad I was never married and made to look like a fool? Or should I be happy for all the reasons that Lex said? Edward has no hold over me, and I should be ecstatic. Yet all I feel is hollow. My whole life, I never knew who I was or where I belonged, but for that short time, I was someone. A wife who was part of a family.

Instead I'm back to being nobody.

The person no one wants.

He didn't even love me enough to marry me properly.

"I'm sorry, Lex, I need a shower. I just…I just need a bit of time."

Standing on auto pilot, I leave him and walk into the bathroom, closing the door.

Stripping bare and turning on the water, I step into the warmth and slide down the wall to the floor. Bringing my knees up to my chest. Hugging them as tightly as I can to make myself as small as I can.

The crying starts and I don't want it to stop. I need to let this out. To ever be free of Edward, I need to let the hurt go. Every time I've started to cry before, I've needed to shut it down to look after the kids. But I know they're safe, and although he's not in the room, with Lex close by I know I'm safe too. Mason is right, he is a good man. I feel bad I walked away from him, but I need this time for me, and Lex being the beautiful man he is, is letting me have it.

All I can hear is the water mixed with my sobbing, I'm that broken I can't even sing. I'm not trying to be quiet or hide anything.

I'm done hiding my pain. I'm just plain done hiding. They all want to help me to move forward.

But the truth is, the only person who can fix me, is me.

Slowly standing up, I finally stop the tears that have just about run out anyway.

I lean my head back into the streaming water, close my eyes and let it run over me. I'm washing my past off me.

Nothing Edward can do now will hurt me as much as he already has. I'm not giving him that power anymore.

It's time to talk to Lex. The poor man will be out there worried sick. If the roles were reversed, I would have burst through the door by now.

I have no idea how long I've been in here. Turning off the water and stepping from the shower, it dawns on me as I grab the towel. I didn't grab my bag and I have nothing I need. I dry myself and then wrap the towel around myself while I decide what to do with my dilemma.

The choice is to put dirty clothes back on or go out in a towel to find my bag. Knowing I don't want to put any of the clothes on that feel tainted from earlier, I turn to walk out the door. It's then I spot the note that is on the floor. Lex must have slipped it under the door.

> *Your bag is outside the door*
> *Take your time*
> *I'm here when you're ready*
> *I'm sorry*
> *Lex xx*

And there is the contrast I needed to see.

Maybe this is the universe's way of giving me direction.

Making sure I know where I should be heading.

I'm hearing you loud and clear.

Softly opening the door and sliding my bag inside the bathroom, I can't help but smile. On top of the bag is a heart chocolate, which is from the bag we bought on our pitstop while traveling. Like a peace offering, but also, he knew it would make me laugh. Nice point scoring, Lex. Yes, this is another time chocolate is always a must for a woman who has just had an emotional breakdown. And you thought you were crap at this. I beg to differ.

Once again, you are the star in my dark world.

Taking a deep breath, I leave the bathroom, walk out of my bedroom to the living area.

Lex, sitting on the couch with his head resting in his hands, startles as I walk in.

Jumping up, he stands but isn't sure what to do. He's nervous and unsure if he should touch me.

"Mia, are you okay? I wanted to come to you but …"

Putting the poor guy out of his misery, I walk right into his arms.

I feel some of the tension leave his body the moment we connect. Our embrace is so tight he nearly squashes the air out of my lungs.

"I'm sorry I hurt you," he whispers into my ear. Oh god, I've broken this man too.

"You didn't hurt me, Lex, you just delivered the news. I actually need to thank you."

"Me, what for?" He pulls back to look me in the eyes.

"No one has ever stood up for me like you did today. Let alone put both their own safety and career on the line. I'm truly grateful to have found you." I'm not sure what is coming over me but it's a sense of peace I'm not sure I've ever felt before.

"You're worth it, and I've never been more grateful for anyone in my life than I am for you." Lex looks very emotional, and I think we need to move past this.

"Well, technically I found you when I ran into you. So, I'm taking the points for the first date." Lex just looks at me and starts laughing. What starts as a small laugh, builds until we're both laughing like crazy kids.

"I can't believe you just said that. No way do you get points for that." Lex takes my hand and we sit together on the couch.

"Why?" I ask, snuggling into his side.

"Because a date is supposed to be fun and you need to have a good time, and that *run-in* was neither fun nor a good time. Plus, I already claimed the first official date was coffee, so you can't take that back."

Feeling a little more confident now, I answer with another sassy comment. "So that's the kind of guy you are, hey, get a girl coming with your dirty words and then take her out for coffee. That's very classy, sir." With that I jump up before he can grab me and tickle me or something to make me suffer for my comment.

"Right, that's it. You wait, you'll pay for those words. The next time you're begging me to touch you, I'll politely decline, because apparently we need to do coffee first." He looks very pleased with himself.

"You always have an answer for everything, don't you, Counselor?" Laughing, I hold my hand out for him to take it. "Let's go and get something to eat. I've somehow found my appetite. I think you owe me a date, something more than coffee." I'm being brave, but there are limits. "But can we just stay in the hotel, please?" I feel a little silly, but his smile lets me know that he doesn't care one bit.

"Sounds perfect. Can you just give me five minutes to shower? That's if you left me any hot water." Walking past me, Lex slaps me on the ass, picks up his bag, and keeps walking. "They always say women hog the showers, but you must have taken the record being in there for fifty minutes. I'm not sure how you thought you could improve on perfection."

Then the door closes, and he leaves me smiling. What a swing of emotions today. No wonder I feel so exhausted.

Taking a quick moment, I message Paige to check on the kids and let her know I'm okay. Actually, that I'm better than okay.

The word great is what my fingers are typing to her.

Time for change, and it starts with me.

"I'm in a food coma. You made me eat too much." I'm lying with my head in Lex's lap on the couch. I didn't think I was hungry until he ordered me this amazing fettuccini carbonaro. The sauce was so creamy and the freshly made pasta was to die for. Nothing like the sort of meals we made at the diner. This restaurant was something else. I didn't know what to even pick and I was so glad when Lex just took the reins. All I said was pick me something simple. He rolled his eyes and then laughed at me. I'm sure his plan is to make me put on weight with the amount of food he always serves me.

"Hey, I just ordered the meal. I didn't force-feed you. The first time or the second time you went back for more after telling me you were full and couldn't possibly eat another thing." Him laughing makes my head bounce up and down on his lap.

I could stay here all night, but I know that's not what either of us need.

"We should probably try to get some sleep. It's been a long day, and I can't imagine tomorrow will be much fun either," I say, looking up at him.

"Yeah, I agree about today, but don't you worry about tomorrow. I'll make sure it will all be fine. Trust me, I've got this."

Leaning down, he kisses me lightly on both cheeks and then my forehead.

"Why don't you go and get ready for bed and I'll make up the sofa bed."

Scowling at him, he just laughs.

"We've had this argument, now just ignore it and go do what you need to before bed." He slowly lifts me up to sit before I stand and stretch.

"Hmmm, well I'm still not happy about it," I say as I start walking towards the bedroom.

"Old news, baby." His laugh always makes me smile.

After using the bathroom and changing, I'm folding down the bed when Lex knocks on the door even though it's open.

"Can I just use the bathroom before you jump into bed?"

"Of course. I'm all done." He walks past me, and I notice for the hundredth time tonight his hot ass in those jeans. Whatever he does at the gym, he needs to keep that shit up.

"Are you perving on my ass?" he calls me out, looking at me from the bathroom door.

"What if I am?" I giggle, blushing a bit.

"Then I say keep going. It's all yours to check out as often as you like." With a big grin on his face the door closes, and I can't help but keep giggling. This guy can go from so serious to being the teenage boy with the big ego in the flip of a dime.

It's one of the things that attracts me to him. Although you think he's this intense lawyer, that is so far from the truth. There's so much hiding behind that mask that no one has ever seen. I'm not sure he's ever let himself really be who he's meant to be in life, until now. I feel a little thrilled that it's me that's drawing that out of him, and he feels comfortable enough to share the real Lex with me.

I'm sitting on the side of the bed when Lex comes out of the bathroom still smiling.

"You look happy with yourself," I say to him.

"Why wouldn't I be? I have the hottest girl in town checking out my ass."

"Oh my god, get over yourself Lex and go to bed."

Now standing in front of me, he takes my hands and pulls me to my feet.

"I need to say goodnight first." His face gets closer.

"Goodnight," I manage in no more than a whisper.

"No, not in words," is the last thing I hear as his delicious lips gently start touching mine. Lightly kissing me, his hands hold my face exactly where he needs me to be. I'm lost in the moment of our mouths dancing with each other. I can feel the need to escalate the kiss but both of us are holding back.

I take in a breath as he pulls back, my head spinning.

"What was that?" I murmur.

"My goodnight." His thumb strokes my chin as he slowly pulls his hands from my face.

"Jesus, if that was goodnight, I can't wait for good morning." I look at him in my fuzzy haze.

"We've already talked about what your mornings will be like, baby. All in good time. Now try to get some sleep. I'll see you in the morning." He hesitates and then starts walking out of the room, about to close the door.

"Lex?"

He looks over his shoulder at me. "Yeah, baby?"

I feel a little unsure all of a sudden. "Umm, can you leave the door open, please? So I can see you." I feel embarrassed to even ask.

"Sure thing, as long as you don't snore." I can always count on Lex for some humor when I need it.

"Well, you're about to find out, aren't you."

Climbing into bed, I'm mesmerized, watching him slowly lift his arms up over his head and pull his shirt up his back. I'm feeling all sorts of things through my body the more skin he's exposing. I know I've seen him with his shirt off before, but I wasn't ready to really look. Tonight, though, I don't care, and I'm pretty sure he wants me watching too.

His back to me, he undoes the button on his jeans and my heart is skipping beats because it knows what's coming next.

His hands slide under the jeans over his ass and push them down his body.

Fuck me.

I thought his ass in jeans was hot. That is nothing compared to seeing him standing in front of me in his white briefs. Fuck, who said white underwear on a guy is like an old man? I can assure you there is nothing old man about Lex. My eyes follow his legs down as he pushes the jeans to the floor. His body is pure muscle, from his shoulders all the way to his feet. I can feel my palms getting sweaty and I'm suddenly overheating.

He turns to look at me as he starts to slide into his bed.

Bastard is grinning. He knows exactly what he's doing to me.

Well, I hope your sleep is going to be as hard as mine. Or that something else is hard which won't let you sleep, more like it.

The room is now dark except for the little lamp that's left on in the living room. It puts a soft glow around the room. Enough to see just a little but not enough to keep you awake. Well, in theory, anyway. After the strip show I just received, I'm not going to sleep anytime soon. If he had taken the briefs off, I'm pretty sure I would have self-combusted. If I was in a room on my own and him not so close, I would be taking things into my own hands right now. Although, I know nothing I do to myself will be even close to the feelings Lex gives me. What I wouldn't give to have him touching me right now.

I'm moving restlessly in the bed because I can't get comfortable. Even though the bed is like a big fluffy pillow.

"Mia, are you okay?" I hear Lex calling to me in the dim room.

I want to say yes just so he doesn't know, but I'm no good at lying.

If I'm being honest with myself, that's not the answer.

"No... because I'm scared."

"You're safe, baby, I promise," his voice gently echoes in the quiet.

"No, I'm scared if I don't say this now, I'm not sure when I'll get the courage."

"Say what?" I can hear his sheets moving.

"That I want you in my bed, touching me like you do. I need you, Lex." I can feel the tears I'm holding back with the emotions that I feel.

Seeing him standing at the side of the bed in the lamplight is like all my fantasies coming to life.

"Are you sure, Mia? Like, really sure? I don't want you to do this because you're running from your fears." I can hear the strain in his voice.

"Can't you see? This is me running *to* my fears. The fear of taking my life back, and that starts with you. I don't know where you came from or why, but all I know is you are meant for me, Lex. I can't stay away any longer. I want you." I'm breathless with anticipation of what he's thinking.

"Fuck, Mia. I have wanted you from that first night. I keep holding back because I don't want to hurt you, after the nightmare you've been through." He's torn, but I need him to understand I don't want him to treat me like glass.

Sliding across in the bed, I hold up the covers.

"Please, Lex, this is what I want, don't make me beg."

He's in beside me before I even blink. Taking me in his arms and our bodies pressing hard against each other. I know what I want, I have to tell him, though.

"Undress me, Lex, I want you to touch me, naked. I need to know I'm more than the nightmare. I want to feel again."

"So much I want to do with you, I just don't know where to start." Oh god, how much I love that sexy voice. The one he saves just for me.

"Kiss me...all over." My voice is all breathy. Lordy, where is this coming from? I never asked for anything, or even known what I want. Yet with Lex I know I can, and I feel in the safest place I've ever been in my life, right here between the sheets. It goes against all logic, but I don't care, I'm taking what I want.

"When I'm finished with you, baby, you won't remember anything from before this night. Tonight, you're mine, and I intend to worship every single part of your body. But if you need to stop, say the word and everything stops, and I won't care one bit. This is all at your pace. You make the rules. If it doesn't feel good, then you need to tell me. Promise me." Rolling me onto my back, he's above me, and I know he's testing how I react. I should be freaking out, but I'm not, and I know it's because it's him. My world is different with him in it.

"Thank you. For letting me take control of my body, but fuck, Lex, if you don't touch me soon, I'm going to explode in anticipation. Please don't treat me like a victim. I want to be the strong woman you make me feel I can be."

Hearing him groan and feeling it vibrating through his chest, I know he's as sexually frustrated as I am.

"You are the most beautiful and the strongest woman I've ever met. I have never seen you any other way." His mouth touches my lips and the world around me disappears. Tonight, I'm not a mom, or a sister, not even a wife or the poor little orphan girl. Finally, I'm just Mia.

Our lips unleash the heat that has been simmering just under the surface in both of us for days.

His hand is now sliding up under my tank top, lifting it finally so we're skin to skin. He breaks our kiss quickly to take it over my head. My nerves escalate at him seeing me naked.

"So sexy, you have no idea how fucking sexy you are." Before I can even argue, his mouth is kissing down my breast until he reaches my nipple. His tongue taking the first swipe has me lifting off the bed. But he doesn't wait for me to settle. He takes me in his mouth and sucks while I feel his hand on my other breast.

Oh, I can't breathe.

In the best fucking way possible.

I'm surrendering to him and his touch.

And I feel my heart breaking wide open.

"Oh…Lex…oh…"

Chapter Twenty-Four

LEX

Her moaning my name is the most incredible feeling. I'm just getting started and don't plan on stopping until there is no breath left and my name is a mere whisper.

Her skin tastes like the forbidden fruit, the one I've been able to see and almost touch. But never really taste. Just hints of her on her lips but nothing like this.

The more I feast on her breast, the more her body moves under me. I know she wants more from me, and fuck, do I want to give it to her. But she deserves more than a quick fuck.

This is the woman I plan on making love to for the rest of my life, so she deserves that from the beginning. I need to show her the stars.

Moving to take the other breast in my mouth, my right hand now slides down her body. Making sure she feels every single tingle as I move from the side of her waist to swiping my fingers across her stomach and around her navel. Finally running a finger slowly across the top of her shorts' waistband.

Over and over again.

Teasing her as I suck her harder and taking her nipple between my teeth and gently tugging on it.

"Lex, please take them off...I can't...I don't...fuck, I can't take it much longer." Her pleading is the sweetest way of her trying to tell me she's ready to orgasm any moment.

Releasing her breast, I sit up straddled over her body. Trying to stop myself for coming just at the sight of her half naked and baring more than her body for me.

"This is just the beginning, Mia. We have all night, and I'm going to make sure you can take it over and over again until you can't scream my name anymore." Her mouth drops open as I slide her shorts and panties down her legs.

My cock is throbbing so hard, and I can feel the pre-cum leaking, I just need to hold on, but the sight of her pussy right there for me to touch is making it near impossible. I know her breasts were like the forbidden fruit, but this is going to be like tasting the whole goddamn tree.

Moving my legs to between hers, she bends her knees and lets her legs fall to the side. Like an invitation. But I don't care what her body is telling me, I need her head to be telling me the same thing.

"Are you okay, Mia? I need you to say it."

There's a disgruntled moan which almost makes me laugh.

"If you stop now, I will kill you, Lex. Fuck, do something!" She's demanding now and I fucking love it.

"Oh, you want me to touch you, do you?" Playing with her a little, slowly dragging my finger up her inside leg but not quite reaching where she wants.

"Yes!" Her body rises off the bed where my finger goes.

"Lex, higher." Seeing the pure fire in her eyes for the first time has me wanting to fuck her. She is so primed and ready to let her body come to life.

I'm aching to be inside her.

Playing with her is the perfect way to take her out of her head. She can't think of anything except the frustration I'm giving her, but that will only last so long.

"Higher, like this?" My finger lightly swiping through her sex for the first time.

"Oh fuck…" She moans at the same time those same words leave my lips too.

"Oh fuck, baby, you are so wet for me."

She's biting her bottom lip trying to hold on as I slowly do it again, but this time stopping on her hard clit that is desperately waiting to be touched.

"This is what you need, isn't it, beautiful."

Her body is now matching the rhythm of my fingers as I leave my thumb on her clit and the others are rubbing her up and down just like she wants.

Suddenly her hand comes from her side and grabs my cock. I almost come instantly just having her touch me through my briefs.

"Off, take them off. I want to touch you. I'm choosing to touch you." This dominant Mia is such a fucking turn-on. Having her take control of her own body is more than I hoped for.

"No, you get to take them off. It's yours to unwrap."

I stand next to the bed for her, as she moves as fast as she can in her totally heightened state.

"Are you my reward?" she says with tears in her eyes.

"I'm your star, baby," I whisper as she drags my underwear down, and I kick them off for her. I don't move, to give her time to take what she wants from me. Her eyes look up at me and never leave me. Her hands exploring my cock, I feel like I'm in heaven. Her hands are so small and delicate, her touch so soft. Nothing like I'm used to but my new favorite thing. She's had tears running down her cheeks slowly ever since I said I'm her star, and I know they're happy tears, so I leave her be. She's reaching the pinnacle of claiming her life back and this is a massive thing for her.

Ownership and control of her body.

Lowering herself to the floor on her knees, she takes me in her mouth and I'm hanging by a thread.

"Fuck, Mia, that feels so good…that's it, baby, just like that." I can't help but start rocking gently in and out of her mouth. I don't grab her head because I won't trap her in any way.

But I need to stop this, the moment she grabs my balls that are so sensitive and sore from being blue for days.

"Mia, stop, I need you to stop. I'm going to come, and I can't go first, it needs to be you. I need to be inside you right now. Oh god, I'm desperate to feel you." Reaching down with my hands under her arms, I pull her up to me.

"You are my world. I need to show you just how much you mean to me." I kiss her as I pick her up and lay her down on the bed and crawl on top of her.

Both of us completely naked, pressed together for the first time.

As soon as I'm on top of her, the grinding of our bodies starts.

"Please tell me you're on the pill? I don't have a condom. I wasn't expecting this."

Her head nods as she's struggling to say yes.

"I'm clean, I promise. I've never gone without." It's me who's begging now.

"I trust you."

The three words that kill me.

Her eyes tell me everything I need to know. She's not only saying the three words, she feels it deep in her soul.

Taking my cock and running it up and down her pussy a few times to prepare her, I stop at the entrance. I need her to look at me. To really look at me and tell me she wants this. Not because she's fighting demons or proving anything to herself.

But because she wants me.

"I will never take this for granted. It will always be like this."

As I slide inside her, my world finally shifts to where it belongs.

Inside her.

Deep inside her.

"You own me, Mia. I'm yours forever."

Her mouth open and head back, we dance our own form of sex.

The perfect kind.

The one that comes from a place of two souls joining, never to be parted again.

Both of us come together, and the high of the orgasm is such a rush that neither of us can say a word because there's no air left between us.

Making love with a soul mate.

I can never go back from this.

MIA

Lying in his arms, the words *'I'm your star'* keep playing over and over again in my head.

It's all I ever wanted in my life. Someone who just wants me. Believes in me but gives me the space to be who I'm meant to be. They are the person I look to for guidance when times are tough. Just like I looked to the stars every night and wished for a better place.

Right here in his arms. This is my better place.

No doubt in my mind.

His hand rubbing up and down my arm feels so reassuring. My head on his chest and hearing his heart beating. I've never felt such peace.

"Are you okay, Mia?" The words vibrate through his chest as he's speaking.

"Perfect." One word sums it up.

"Then I can't improve on that." His hand lifts my chin up to look at him.

"But are you really okay? I know that was a massive step for you, and I understand if you need to talk about it." This man is incredible.

"Lex, you're amazing. Constantly checking in on me." I reach up to kiss him.

"That's what boyfriends do. We take care of our girlfriends."

"Well, it's new territory for me." Thinking a bit about what he said, I need to ask. "I know this is going to sound weird, but is that what it's always like for you? Sex, I mean. Is that what it's supposed to feel like?" How ridiculous at the age of thirty-eight and I'm asking about sex.

"Mia, firstly, you need to know you can ask me anything. Never worry about that. And secondly. Damn, I hope so. I'm going to be honest. What I just felt between us is nothing like my previous times. With you, it is as you said, perfect. So perfect I think I need to check to make sure I wasn't dreaming. I mean, if we try again and it's the same, then we know for sure. What do you think?" That rogue smile gets me every time.

"Nah, I think that's enough. You only get one crack at perfection, so we don't need to do it again." Trying to keep a straight face isn't working.

"You had me for about two seconds until your body shivered at the thought of me touching you again. Like this." His hand moves from my arm and grabs my breast. "See that electricity that's running through your body? You can't turn that off. And I hope we never lose it."

His lips take mine again, and I'm totally lost in the world we're creating together. The one where I feel safe, treasured, and never have to share with the outside world.

All our intentions for sleep are gone, and I don't care one bit.

I'm ready to take on tomorrow no matter what happens.

I'm stronger than I think.

Just like Anna told me.

Remembering back to last night and the hours I spent with Lex, being worshipped, I'm trying to keep myself distracted from where we're driving to.

We talked, touched each other, made love, played a little too much, but one of the parts I loved was the easy conversations in between. About what I had tried, what I liked and didn't like. How Lex's sex life had previously been. I've never had a person to talk such intimate subjects with. We talked about my sex life and the hard parts I couldn't tell him before. Edward had only forced me a few times, and I know once is more than enough, but I had it much easier than others have in their life. Lex was compassionate and tried to hide his anger. But also kept saying how he knows I'm hurting but he loves that I'm not married. The strange thing is, that after I got over the initial shock, I'm happy about it too. After we get through this morning and the custody of the kids is approved by the courts, then Edward has no hold over me.

"How you holding up?" Lex's voice pulls me out of my thoughts.

"Better than I expected. I mean, that will probably change when I see him. But right now, I'm coping. How do you feel, are you worried?"

"Not one little bit. Nothing he can do will hurt me. Even if he submits a complaint, I don't care. I've got the one thing he can't have in life, and that's you. Nothing else matters."

"I'm not a pawn in a game, you know." I feel a little put out by his comment.

"Shit, Mia. I didn't mean it that way. I would never treat you like that." The worried look on his face reminds me that he wouldn't.

"Sorry, Lex, that wasn't fair. Maybe deep down I'm not as calm as I'm trying to convince myself." He reaches over from the driver's seat, taking my hand and squeezing it tight.

"Lean on me, baby. I've got you. Nothing that happens today can change the fact that you and the kids are safe and have an amazing new life. No matter what, you will always have me."

Taking my hand up to his lips, he kisses it, and I feel the same little tingle I always get. The one that keeps me coming back for more.

"Remember that offer when I'm the crazy woman standing in the courtroom shortly, who can't breathe and is freaking out like an idiot." Saying I'm fine really wasn't quite true. Deep down, the fear of a man I lived with for five years is simmering and ready to boil up and over.

"I'll be the man next to you, holding you, counting with you, and making you laugh when you need it. Because it's been proven I have the best dad jokes around. Do you want me to show you again, or better still I can call Tate and we can have a joke-off contest, and you can judge it?"

"Oh my god, did you just say you and Tate can have a jerk-off contest? Lex, what the hell?" I start giggling and can't stop.

He shakes his head at me. "Far from it. I can tell you now, the only person who will be jerking me off will be you, Mia. Plus, that's just weird to be jerking off with Tate. He might be a jerk at times, but that's as far as it goes."

I'm laughing so hard now I'm almost peeing my pants. "You're ridiculous, you know that?" I'm trying to get out in between my fits of laughter.

"I might be ridiculous, but you love it, and I've just proven my point that I have great jokes." He looks very proud of himself.

"Lex, you weren't even trying to say a joke, it was just the words you used, so that doesn't even count. No points for that one." It's then I hear the GPS say the words that make my laughter stop and my heart start to race a little faster: *'You have reached your destination.'* Looking out the window, I see the courthouse that I've seen before on the television news broadcasts, and now I'm about to enter it to help secure my safety.

"I can do this," I say out loud, trying to convince myself.

"Yes, you can, Mia. But I also want you to remember that if you can't, that's okay too." Our voices have changed from fun-loving to quiet and solemn.

"Okay, let's get this over and done with." I don't want to sit here and just stare at the building. I need to stand strong and march in there with my head held high.

"That's my girl." Lex exits the car and comes around to my door. Opens it and waits for me. Not rushing me, not saying a word. He lets me do this in my timeframe. Taking a big deep breath, I undo my seat belt, turn to him, and give him my hand to help me out.

"One more step to happiness for my kids." We start walking towards the courtroom, hand in hand.

"And your happiness, Mia, which is just as important."

"Mhmm," is all I say as he opens the door for me.

Watching Lex in work mode always shows him in a totally different light. From the moment we step through the door, he drops my hand and takes control. The voice he uses to speak to the court attendants is a firm one with direction. He is running the show now, and I just need to sit back and let him. It feels so good to have someone in my corner.

"Just take a seat here with Ashton, I'll be back in a minute." Lex talks to one of the desk clerks, hands him over an envelope, and then signs off on something. They're talking intently as the clerk goes through whatever was in the envelope.

I'm concentrating on Lex when I hear the noise of high heels marching down the marble floor of the courthouse corridor. I'm not paying too much attention to the noise, but it's something that stops Lex in his tracks, and he turns to give whoever it is his full attention. The look on his face is strained and it worries me, trying to work out what's going on.

Then the footsteps stop right next to me.

Turning, I see the stone-cold bitch-face of Jacinta.

"Mia Kennedy, I'm Jacinta Nordick, your legal counsel for today." She throws her hand out at me as Lex arrives by my side.

"Mia, this is Jacinta. I thought with the events of yesterday between me and Edward, it's best I don't represent you as your lawyer but just stand beside you as your boyfriend. I contacted Jacinta last night and asked her to attend on my behalf, and she graciously agreed. I don't trust anyone in the courtroom more than I trust Jacinta." He doesn't need to be a mind reader to know I'm pissed off. Why didn't he tell me? He had plenty of time last night or this morning. I know he thinks he's doing the right thing, but I hate these surprises all the time. Fuck. And why her? This woman hates me. I took the man she thought she was about to marry from her. She's not going to care about me or my case. For all I know, she'll happily throw me under a bus when we get in there.

I need to just get through this. Remember you are stronger than you think.

Standing and taking her hand, I put on my armor that I had started packing away, and get on with it.

"Thank you for your help, Ms. Nordick. I didn't know Lex had asked you, but I appreciate you coming at such short notice." Lex flinches at my words; he knows he's done the wrong thing.

"He's lucky that I didn't have court today, but the early start wasn't much fun." Taking her hand back.

"I'm sure. Thank you again."

"Mia, can I talk to you for a minute?" Lex asks from beside me.

"No, we don't have time. I'm sure Ms. Nordick needs to talk to me or you about what's going on today." I need to maintain this anger to get through the next hour in the courtroom.

"She's right, have you secured a meeting room?" Jacinta is very direct in her tone. Her coming here for this would have been a big ask, and I'm not prepared to upset her.

"Yes, but we only have ten minutes before we'll be called," Lex says, rubbing his chin. That's when I know he's worried about me. It's his nervous tell sign.

"Then let's move," she says, already walking away. He reaches over to take my hand, but I don't think now is the time. With Jacinta here, and Edward could walk in at any moment.

Getting the message, he points in the direction of the room we're in and we follow him, with Ashton quietly in the background, but always close by. I feel totally safe, but between my anger at Lex and the anxiety of Edward, I feel like I could just walk back out the front door and keep going.

I'm tired.

You can only live on your adrenaline stores for so long. I have a feeling mine are getting close to running out.

I'm sick of a life full of drama.

I just want this over.

Watching Lex and Jacinta work and her asking me a few questions, I understand why he called her. She's good at her job. In fact, to me she looks like she thrives on it.

There's a knock at the door, and I shiver as they tell us it's time.

"Lex, you shut your mouth in there. Do not engage with Edward one bit, not a word, not a look. Nothing, do you hear me?" Jacinta is treating him like a child, but I wonder if this is his punishment for leaving her, or her disappointment in him as a lawyer, that he stepped over the boundary with Edward. And me, for that matter. I'll never know, but I can tell she's using this time to make him feel as small as possible, and I could never have seen him being happy with her. She would never have met the real Lex like I have. He wouldn't have been given the space to grow or just be himself.

I might be angry at him, but I'm still so grateful I have him in my life. If it weren't for him, I wouldn't be doing this today, and I never would have found out about the fake marriage. Jacinta may see him as a weak man, but she has him all wrong.

So totally and utterly wrong.

He has so much strength that he openly shares with me every day.

Jacinta marches down the corridor like she owns the place and opens the courtroom door like she's been in here a million times before. Following her in with Lex to my side, I stop in my tracks two steps into the room. My hand grabs Lex's and squeezes it so hard like I'm about to break his bones. My breathing speeds up and things are getting blurry. The only thing I can see is Edward sitting on one side of the room with his head down and looking a mess.

"Breathe, baby, I've got you. Ten, nine, eight, breathe…" I hear whispering in my ear. "That's it, nice and slow, let it out. Seven, six, five, and breathe." The room is coming back to me. "Lean on me. Four, three, breathe." I can feel my body slowing slightly. "You're doing great. You are strong. Two, one, big deep breath… Now let it out slowly." I didn't notice that he was rubbing his thumb back and forth over my hand making sure I knew he was there, but as I come back to him, I can feel his never-ending calmness.

Looking up into his eyes, my anger is gone, seeing only his pure heart shining through as he protects me from myself before anything else.

"Thank you," I whisper.

"One foot in front of the other," he whispers back but waits for me to take that step. He never pushes me and always makes me take the leap.

As I start to walk again, I know I should let go of his hand, but I can't. He is my strength and I need him.

I don't look sideways at Edward, just sit straight down on the seat next to Lex. My body is shaking slightly, and I know that won't go until I leave this room.

"Do I need to start with the dad jokes?" I hear his whisper next to me.

Oh, Lex, I adore you. No one else would say something like that to me and know that it's the perfect thing to pull me out of my head.

"I promise it won't be one about jerking, though." I can't help it, even though it's not the time. I let a little grin creep on to my face and look up at him from where I was staring into his lap.

"All rise," the bailiff calls as the judge walks in. Any smile I had is gone. The tight chest is back, and in my head, I'm chanting the words.

'Do it for the kids, be strong for the kids.'

Standing and moving to the desk with Jacinta feels like I walked a mile, but in fact it was three steps. I didn't realize how much I would miss the touch of Lex beside me, though.

But it makes me understand as much as I need him, I actually need to do this on my own. To prove to myself I can be the woman I want to be, I must stand strong and fight for the life I want.

It's fucking hard, but I'm doing it, and no one including Edward can stop me now.

"Counsel, please approach the bench." The judge's voice startles me.

Shit, what does that mean?

Is there a problem?

Fuck, has he made a complaint?

I didn't even know he had a lawyer here.

Don't panic, don't panic. It will be okay. Lex promised me it would be okay.

Turning and looking at him, he just mouths the words to me that I love to hear.

"I've got you. It's okay." Yet his eyes aren't as confident as I would like them to be right now.

My foot is bouncing under the table, and I can't help myself. For the first time, I look across at Edward.

He looks up, maybe sensing my gaze.

His nose is swollen and his eyes are sunken. A shell of the man I thought I fell in love with all those years ago. He has aged so much, and the alcohol and his lifestyle are slowly killing him. All the bravery in him has left, and he looks like a scared little boy sitting there. It makes me wonder why I ever felt so frightened, but I already know the answer to that. He had me trapped in a situation I had no way of getting out of, and above all, I would never do anything to put my kids in danger. His pull over me was more a psychological one than the physical one.

Jacinta's shoes walking back towards me have me quickly turning to her.

As she sits down next to me with her straight face and tense body language, I can't read her because to me she always looks the same.

"Mia, Edward's lawyer has put forward that her client has agreed to comply with the restraining order and the claims you have made. He has advised that he has signed the documents for you to have sole custody of the children that Alexander has filed with the courts this morning. His only request is that you and Alexander also stay away from him. He wishes to have nothing to do with you either. Do you agree to these conditions?"

Agree, what the hell would I disagree with? But I'm not letting him get off that easy.

"Yes, I agree, of course, but I have one more condition and I'm not sure you can say this in front of the judge or just his lawyer. But he has to agree to never say anything about the meeting he and Lex had with each other. I don't want him to hurt Lex in any way. If he agrees to that, I'll happily walk out of his life for eternity. If he doesn't, then I will report him for fraud on the illegal marriage stunt he pulled." Once the last word is out of my mouth, I see Jacinta looking at me slightly differently. I don't know what I've said or done, but whatever it was, I think she liked it.

"Give me a moment and I'll have this finished and ready to sign off on." Leaving me sitting here alone, she talks to Edward and his lawyer. He nods in agreement, then both the lawyers approach the judge at the bench again to discuss something, and then she returns to sit with me.

The few moments of silence are almost killing me and then the judge finally starts speaking.

"I have awarded the restraining order against Edward Walker to not be within fifty miles of Mia Kennedy, Jack Walker, and Kayla Walker. All custody of the children, Jack Walker and Kayla Walker, is temporarily awarded to Mia Kennedy until the full orders for custody are heard by the court. This matter is now closed. Thank you, counsel. Ms. Kennedy and Mr. Walker, you are free to go." She bangs her gavel on the desk and my heart starts racing in excitement this time.

"Next case," the judge calls, and Jacinta looks at me.

"Time to move, we'll talk outside." Whatever that look was before is gone and she's back talking to me like a child.

To be honest, I don't give a shit.

Standing and following her, I just want to jump into Lex's arms, but I know I can't. He's smiling at me like I've won the lottery, but I can see he's physically restraining himself too. We don't need to talk or touch. We're both saying it all with our eyes.

I'm free to be me, and I made sure he is too.

For the first time in my life, I got to make my own choice.

I took control.

As I'm about to step away from the courtroom doors to follow Jacinta down the corridor, I stop to take one last look at Edward.

We both share a moment.

For me it's one of letting go of my past.

For him I hope it's one of realizing what he lost and the changes he needs to make.

I can't help but give him a small smile of thanks, which will seem strange to the outside world. But I have two amazing, beautiful children that are a gift he gave me. He may not have wanted them, but I did, and will cherish them until the day I die.

Even in the darkest times, there are bright twinkling stars.

Chapter Twenty-Five

LEX

I hate being here in the public seats and not knowing what's being said. It's taking every part of my patience to stay seated and not interfere. But I made that choice yesterday when I punched Edward and placed my hand around his throat. I'm not proud of myself, but I will stand up for Mia again in a heartbeat if she needs me to.

While Mia sobbed in the shower last night, I knew I had no choice but to call Jacinta. I was surprised she even answered my call. But I couldn't risk not having someone here to represent Mia if Edward filed any complaint against me. We needed this restraining order in place and the temporary custody orders while we wait for the permanent ones to be completed. I couldn't have my actions risk her safety.

Jacinta gave me a tongue lashing about how stupid I was and how I've put my law career and any future political career in jeopardy. I took it all. I could have argued she's talking about a political career I never wanted or intended to pursue. But I needed her here, so I shut my mouth and agreed. Seeing my father in me, for the first time in my life. The way he just says nothing and lets my mother go with her rants, I get it now, I really do. I may have been a little harsh on him in some parts of my feelings, but I still won't forgive him for not caring enough to stand up for me. No matter what, he should have stood up and protected me from her. Or at least shown me that he loved me.

Those damn shoes on the floor get my attention every time. It's her power move in the courtroom and it makes me snap out of my thoughts.

Wait, why is Jacinta talking to Edward's lawyer? Shit, this is killing me.

Is it about me? Has he done what I assumed he wouldn't, by saying something that he knew would hurt Mia?

She finishes talking and they both approach the bench, and I'm holding my breath. I don't care about me, and I should never have shown violence towards Edward, but please don't let my actions hurt her.

Jacinta heads back to her seat and talks quietly to Mia, giving me no signs. The bitch is making me pay for this. No questions asked, she is making sure I suffer for hurting her by not letting me know what's happening. She knows how much it will be killing me, and she is loving having that power over me, especially here.

A courtroom is my domain. The place I have control and feel a sense of power in my life.

Somewhere that has always felt like home.

Today is different.

It feels ugly and sad. A place where people's worst sides are shown. There is never any joy in that. Even though I always show compassion, I thought there was a thrill in the fight. I selfishly took joy in the wins and got pissed at the losses like it was about me in a way. I now see it in a completely different light.

Today, it repulses me.

Something I never imagined was possible.

The judge starts talking and the words are like pure gold coming from her mouth. Mia is free to go and live her life.

Mia is safe!

It's all I can think. I can't speak, but watching her turn and look at me, her eyes tell me everything I need to know. Her cage is lifted, and my beautiful girl is free to fly.

I've known for days, but last night sealed it for me. I'm in love with Mia. A love like I've never known.

I can't tell her, it's too soon and she's not ready to hear it, but I'm trying to tell her in my unspoken way, hoping she can see it when I look into her eyes.

I see love in her gaze, but she can't trust herself with it yet.

That's okay, I can wait. When it's time she won't be able to hold it back anymore.

Following her down the aisle and out of the courtroom, she stops and looks back at Edward. I can't look at him, because part of me still wants to kill him. But I see in the small smile she gives him, she finally feels the fear leaving her.

She has control, and I couldn't be happier for her.

After going through the motions in the courthouse, I still haven't spoken to her or touched her. Because I know when I do, there won't be any stopping for a few minutes. Here in front of Ashton, Jacinta, and in a way Edward, it's not the place.

It's all very clinical with Jacinta, and I know I can't leave it like this.

Walking to the cars, Mia stops to talk to Jacinta. "Thank you for everything today. I'm sure I'm the last person you wanted to help, but I'm very grateful." Mia holds her hand out to her, and Jacinta takes it a little less aggressively than the first time they talked this morning.

"You're right, I didn't, but nobody deserves to live in fear. I'm glad it ended up being settled quickly and simply for you, and that the idiot here didn't wreck it." Oh man, she points at me. Nothing like getting her point across.

"Mia, can you and Ashton head to the car? I just need a minute with Jacinta to say goodbye." Mia's smile tells me she understands. This is not just a goodbye for today. This is my final goodbye to someone who needs help to move on with her own life.

Mia gives her a little wave. "Thanks again, Jacinta." And I want to fist pump the sky when Mia reaches up on her toes and kisses my cheek before she leaves. In her own way, she is claiming me in front of Jacinta. She's fighting for her man, and I'm fucking ecstatic. Funny thing is there's no need because she has me, hook, line, and sinker. But it feels amazing to know she wants to make sure.

As she disappears towards the car with Ashton, my eyes still following her, I hear Jacinta behind me. "I underestimated her. She showed me today that she is far more than she seems." Her voice is softer than I've heard before.

"Behind those walls is one hell of a woman who has more to give this world than she knows, and an inner strength that she underestimates."

Jacinta's whole face softens. "You love her, don't you."

"I haven't said those words yet, and she needs to be the first to hear them, but yeah, she's my one. There will never be another woman who makes me feel what she does."

"I thought I loved you, Lex, but watching you right now, I now know I was wrong and I'm sorry. What I felt was nice, convenient, and easy. But love isn't that easy, is it?" Why haven't I seen this side of Jacinta before now?

"No, it's not. It's messy, hard, and like nothing else you'll ever experience, but at the same time, it's the most amazing, powerful feeling that you'll never be able to describe. I won't lie, and I've told Mia this. What you and I had was great, and it served us both well at the time. You were my safe place and I hope I was yours." Giving me a little nod, she confirms I was too. "I just want you to know, that no matter what our parents or society tell you on how you should live your life, they are wrong. That whole life is fucked up. I want this for you, Jacinta, I really do."

I look towards where Mia is sitting in the car and then back to Jacinta. "You can still be the best kickass lawyer I know but live a life with a man you love, no matter who he is. He can be a man who cleans toilets or the President of the United States. It doesn't matter as long as you love him, and he loves you back, and you're both happy with your lives. Don't let them tell you any different. Where you are in your career, you got there on you own ability, not on any connections or push from your parents. I wouldn't have trusted anyone else I know with Mia's case. And as hard as it was for you to come here today, I can't tell you how grateful I am. I knew you would keep her safe, and I needed a friend on my side. We might be in opposite camps in the courtroom, but I will always count you as a friend. I hope you'll get to a point you can too."

I hope everything I've just said lets her know that I do care about her. Although I didn't understand it at the time, part of me always cared for her. We both just had a fucked-up way of showing it.

I didn't think it was possible, but a few stray little tears roll down her cheeks.

"I want to believe you, Lex, I'm just not sure I'm strong enough to fight those expectations."

"Maybe not now, but when the right man comes along, you will be. Just don't settle until you find him. You deserve the best."

Stepping forward, I take her in my arms and hug her. Dropping her briefcase, she wraps her arms around me too. She knows this is goodbye and the tightness of her hug tells me she's holding on to that final touch. We have never connected like this in all the times we were together. It doesn't last long, and she puts her walls back up and pulls away from me. On the inside I'm laughing at her, knowing that she will be hating how vulnerable she's been with me.

"Don't worry, Jacinta, I won't tell a soul that under that bitch face you are a good soul," I say, laughing a little at her to help break the moment.

"You better not or I will deny it all. Now I need to go, because I have a long drive back after making a trip to save some friend's ass, after he lost his mind for a moment."

"Like I said, love is a powerful thing. Try it sometime."

"I'm glad you're happy, Lex, and I truly mean that. But fuck, your mother is going to die." This time it's Jacinta laughing at me.

Groaning at her comment, we both turn and walk towards our cars.

Her last words to me as we part put our relationship where it should be. "See you in the courtroom the next time I whip your ass."

"We'll see." I smile and turn away from her towards my new life in more ways than one.

Mia is sitting in the car and on the phone, I'm assuming to Paige, when I get there. Ashton is standing guard outside waiting for me. I feel bad for the way I treated him to begin with and didn't understand how jealousy can taint your vision. He's someone I know will be part of both our lives for a lifetime now.

"That woman could stop an army on attack, dead in its tracks, with just her stare. Even I'm scared of her and that's saying something. Imagine fucking that sass right out of her." He's still checking her ass out as she walks away.

"I did." I smile, waiting for the penny to drop.

"Holy shit. Of course, you did. Mia know that?" Ashton starts laughing.

"Yeah, man, she knows it all. Every sordid detail of my fucked-up life and even the bits I didn't know existed until she started asking questions. Not sure she shouldn't have been the lawyer in this relationship. She has a way of pushing me to spill my secrets like no one before her."

"She's a special lady. Even I can see that. You are one lucky man. Like I told you, don't fuck it up, bro." Ashton slaps me on the shoulder as we get ready to part. "Any planned pit stops on the way home? You know, so you can celebrate in style." He laughs to himself as he walks towards his car behind mine.

"I wish, and thanks for putting the thought in my head to torture me now." Asshole. I can already feel the pain in my balls.

"You're welcome," he calls as he climbs into his car.

Opening the door and climbing into the driver's seat, I take the phone from Mia's hand that's holding it to her ear.

"Sorry, Paige, we'll call you back in a minute." I hang up the call.

"Lex," is all Mia gets out before I take her face in my hands and our lips collide. Kissing her like I haven't been able to breathe from the moment we left here an hour ago. I need her to know how I feel. That my heart is hers and to please be gentle with me.

Her hands are in my hair and our bodies are now pressed hard together from the chest up. The acknowledgment that the worst is over pouring out of both of us. This woman does things to me just in the way she touches my body.

Finally coming up for air, we look at each other and then she starts giggling. "You hated that, didn't you, not being in control."

"Every fucking minute of it. Topped with the fact I couldn't touch you just about killed me." I place my hand on her cheek. "I am so proud of you. You were amazing, and I hope you understand how strong you are now."

Her smile lights up her whole face.

"I'm stronger with you in my life," she says with tears in her eyes.

"Maybe so, but you did that in there all on your own. Never forget that. You claimed back your life today, and that had nothing to do with me. Now let's go home and celebrate."

"Umm, I have kids, remember?" I fucking love her giggle.

"Yeah, but they have to sleep sometime, right?" I sit back properly in my seat and pull the seatbelt on while starting the car.

"Lex, you are not fucking me on Paige's couch."

"Nope, you're right, but we'll work that out. And that's something we need to start thinking about for your future. You need your own space. But today let's just celebrate my kickass girlfriend who just started her new life." Before Mia gets to say another word, my phone rings, and answering it on Bluetooth seeing it's Paige, I know what's coming.

"Lex, unless you were just kissing the hell out of my sister, then you better explain why you cut me off. You might have some sort of spell over her, but I still come first. I'm the sister." I know she's joking, but part of her is still telling me that I better be prepared to share Mia with her. She only just found her sister and isn't ready to hand her over to me yet. Poor deranged woman has no idea it's already happening whether she likes it or not.

"Well, I'm guilty as charged so you can calm down, big sis. So, for the record, that was the boyfriend celebrating with the girlfriend, so you definitely come second." I didn't realize we were on speaker on her end until I hear Mason laughing.

"Can you two wait a second while I make some popcorn? This is going to get good, I can just tell," Mason's voice booms through the speaker.

"Mason, don't be a dick," Paige scolds. We can hear the slap on his arm from here.

"Are you two finished fighting over me now? Not that I'm complaining, I've never had this before and I kinda like it." Mia is smiling next to me as we start driving out of town.

"Then bring it on, Paige. If my girl likes it, I'm happy to debate with you for the rest of the drive home. You know I'm pretty good at it." I laugh at Mia rolling her eyes at me.

"You wish," Paige says. "With your job as a lawyer, you debate against one person in a courtroom. I boss around twenty businessmen in a boardroom, and not one of them is brave enough to speak by the time I'm finished." Sounding proud of herself, I can't help bursting out with laughter.

"Mason, good luck is all I can say."

"You think I put up with that shit at home, Lex? Not a chance."

"Okay, very funny, you two. Now can we get back to Mia, please? Remember the lady in the car who just slayed her dragon today," Paige says with such pride in her voice, and I can see the blush on Mia's cheeks from the compliment.

"You should have seen her. I'm so proud of her."

"We are too," Mason chimes in.

Then in the background we hear the kids laughing.

"What's Jack doing?" Mia asks.

"Um can I just say now it's Mason's fault, but Jack is blowing, or attempting to blow raspberries on Kaylas's tummy. Turn on the camera, it's the cutest thing, you need to see it. I'm sure he's covering her in spit, but she just giggles every time he does it." I can picture it now, but Mia is opening up the app on her phone and has the biggest grin on her face.

"Oh my god, Mason, can you video that so I can show Lex later and keep it for when they get older? I love those two little munchkins so much." Happy tears shimmer in her eyes.

"We all do, Mia," Paige says. "You did good, sis, they are the most adorable kids."

Mia is emotional now and just nods her head, unable to speak.

"Okay, we need to get off the phone now, I need to call Ashton for a minute about the direction we're driving home. So, we'll see you soon."

Everyone quickly saying their goodbyes, I end the call and just enjoy the quiet for a moment.

"Aren't you going to call Ashton?" Mia softly asks without taking her eyes off the kids on the video app on her phone.

"No, I'm good."

Her face looks up at me now and then smiles at me with a stupid grin.

"You didn't need to call him, did you?"

"Nope, but you needed a break from your sister." I take a quick look at her reaction and then back at the road.

"What would I do without you, Lex?" Her hand reaches for mine and gives it a squeeze.

"Let's never find out." I take her hand and kiss it which is one of my favorite things to do. She just smiles and nods at me, then goes back to watching the kids but still hanging on tight to me. Just the way I like it.

We drive for a while in silence. Just lost in our own thoughts of the morning and what it means to us both. I know what I want moving forward, but I need to give Mia time to find her feet, and this is going to test my patience more than it's ever been tested before. My mind racing about the changes coming in my life are halted when she starts talking.

"Lex?" Her voice is calm but a little quiet.

"Yeah, baby."

"You pissed me off today, and I need to tell you that." I want to laugh but I can't. The way she is so sweet, but obviously has been stewing on it since Jacinta walked into the courthouse.

"I know, and I'm sorry about that, and I promise I won't do that again. But I knew if I told you it would make you worry more than you already were. There is only so much stress one person can handle." I hope she understands my intentions were good.

"That's true, but you need to let me decide what I can handle or not. I've spent all my life without having much choice. I won't put up with that anymore. So just so we're clear, no matter how much you think something will hurt me or piss me off, please tell me anyway. Then be there to help me deal with it." If I wasn't driving right now, I would hug her so tightly. She's taking control of her life with so much gusto, and I just want to cheer her on.

"That sounds like a perfect plan. I promise from now on, I won't make any decisions for you. As long as you promise to lean on me and never run from the hard choices."

Closing her eyes, I can tell this is hard for her to say, but finally she opens them and replies, "I promise never to run again when life gets hard." As she looks out the window, I know there will be a silent tear running down her face, and that's okay. That is a huge promise for her to agree to, and I treasure that she made it to me.

Giving her a few moments, I just keep driving towards home.

"Lex?" I'm starting to worry every time she starts a sentence with just my name and nothing more. It's usually something deep or I'm in trouble. It's her way of sorting out her thought process in her head and what she needs to say.

"What's wrong?"

"Nothing, I just need to ask your opinion on something."

"Sure, fire away."

"Paige has offered me a job as her PA." I did not see that coming when she started speaking.

"That's awesome, Mia, but how do you feel about it?" I know the fact she's talking to me and hasn't accepted it means that she hasn't worked that out yet.

"I was shocked when she said it. It was after that day she was sick, and I helped her out and she seemed to think I did a good job. I just don't know if I'm capable of being the person she needs. I mean, do you think she just offered to be nice, you know, to make me feel important? A pity job?" I can see the inner turmoil in her eyes. But I know my answer without a doubt.

"I can honestly say I don't think Paige would offer you such an important role in her company if she didn't think you could handle it. Sure, she might have offered you a job if she felt sorry for you, but it would have been just in the office or helping someone far lower down the food chain than the CEO of a multi-billion-dollar company. As harsh as this sounds, Paige is a businesswoman first and your sister second. She needs someone to help her run her company and her life. If she didn't think you had talent hidden, then she wouldn't have asked you. Do you know what I mean?" I hope I haven't been too blunt but explained it plain enough for her to see the truth.

"I do, and that's what scares me. It excites me, it really does, but scares the shit out of me at the same time. What if I make a mistake that costs her money or her reputation?" I can see the internal anxiety she's dealing with.

"Then you apologize and help fix it. We all make mistakes in life, but it's how you deal with it afterwards that's the important thing. No one is perfect. I mean, look at Paige, she chose Mason, which she will regret for the rest of her life." I laugh at myself.

"Lex, you are awful, I'm being serious."

"I was too."

"Very funny. But honestly, do you think I can do it? The job, I mean."

"Baby, I think you can do anything you want to. If you truly want this, then go for it. You will never know if you don't try. You have learned the hard way that you need to dream big and fight for it. You have never given up trying to make life better for you and the kids. This is another step in you gaining the independence you crave." I let that sink in before I say the last part. "But know that no matter what you choose, I will support your decision."

"Am I bad mother for leaving the kids while I work?"

"No way in the world. You thought they couldn't survive a night without you, and how did that work out for you? They've spent time learning new tricks that make them both laugh hysterically, and you were so wrapped up in me that you didn't even have time to worry about them. I'm all for more Mia time." I wink at her.

"You are terrible, Lex. I don't know how you survive in a courtroom. You can't seem to hold a serious conversation for long."

"You'd be surprised. I'm as boring as they come in my work, but then again, I never had a client as sexy as you," I say, shrugging at her.

"I hope you don't give all your clients the special treatment you give me."

"Let's clear this up right now. You are not my client and you never were. That may have been what you thought, but to me, it was always more than that. And besides, as of this morning I'm no longer your lawyer. Jacinta is, and I can guarantee you will not get the kind service you got from me, with her."

"See? Remember, serious conversation, can you hold it together for longer than five seconds?"

"With you, not a chance."

I can see she's thinking hard, and then out of nowhere she blurts out, "I'm going to do it. I'm going to take the job."

"Good for you. Paige will be so excited, and it gives us another reason to celebrate."

Then her smile turns a little sexy. "Lex?"

Shit, what now? "Yes."

"Does Ashton have to follow us all the way home?"

"Just until we hit Chicago, why?"

Biting on her bottom lip, she looks at me. "Any chance we can christen that bed of yours to celebrate before we go home to the kids?"

My cock is instantly reacting, and these business pants aren't made for the extra room I now need.

"Fuck, how fast am I allowed to drive? Because I'm all for your excellent suggestion, I'm just not sure I'll make it upstairs to the bed the first time. You know how partial I am to couches." While she's blushing and giggling, I call Ashton. As soon as the call connects, I don't even give him a chance to talk.

"As soon as we reach the outskirts of Chicago, you're on your own. Thanks for your help."

His laughter roars through my speakers. "Okay, lover boy, you lasted longer than I thought. You got it, man. Have fun, you two, and I'll talk to you tomorrow."

Mia just laughs as I reply, "Oh, we will, there is no doubt about it."

"Ashton," she says between giggles. "Seriously, though, thank you for everything. I couldn't have gotten through all this without you by my side."

"Anytime, Mia."

I cut him off before he says anything smart about me again. "Yep, thanks, Ashton, now you're off duty and I will be taking care of my girl."

"Lex!" she yells at me, and Ashton just chuckles, saying goodbye as I disconnect the call.

Shaking her head at me, I see her texting a message which I'm guessing is to Paige to let her know we'll be a little later than expected. My thoughts are confirmed when she giggles and looks at me.

"Paige said you better make sure it's worth it. Mason is ready with every smart comment for when we get home. Apparently, he's messaging the boys now."

"Asshole, but I don't give a shit. I'll take anything he's got to get some time with you right now. I hope you know this is not a ten-minute stop, baby."

"If you ever think I'll be happy after ten minutes, you underestimate the heaven I was in last night. I want more, a whole lot more of that, and I am not ashamed to say it."

"Fuck, yeah."

Chapter Twenty-Six

MIA

Two weeks later

"How long is your lunch break?" Lex mumbles as he throws his jacket onto the chair in the corner of the hotel room, his pants already undone and the shirt coming off.

"Less talk, more skin. We have forty-five minutes before I need to be back." My skirt falls to the floor and my hands try to get the shirt buttons undone as quickly as I can.

"Don't you dare take off that garter, stockings, and heels, you look so fucking hot," he moans, coming towards me while I giggle and edge backwards to the bed.

"Aren't you supposed to be in a meeting?" I try to distract him as the backs of my legs hit the bed.

"I am. A very important meeting with my girlfriend who needed some help." His hands settle on my waist. He drops his head and the first kiss on my neck already has my whole body on fire. "Helping her to remember what this feels like." His hand grabs my breast and starts squeezing it. "And this." His mouth is now licking up my neck and the goosebumps follow. "But most of all… this." His finger slides under my black lace panties, and the moment he touches me my legs almost collapse out from under me.

"Oh, Lex…" I'm quivering as he rubs up and down.

"See, you need reminding because between your kids and your sister, I can't get time to make you feel like this." My hands drag down his chest and I can feel every rock-hard ab, and honestly I want to lick them too. His fingers are now moving faster, and I want more.

"Fuck, Lex, I want you. I need to feel you." I move my hand to take his cock that's standing tall, pushing against my stomach. I love the groan that comes out of his mouth. The power he gives me when we're together is such a turn-on for me.

"Oh, you're going to feel me alright." He takes his hands off me, which almost has me screaming at him to keep going, but instead he quickly lowers me to the bed. My anticipation of what is about to happen has me panting and my heart is racing.

"I hope you brought a spare pair." His sexy voice has me almost coming before he touches me again. Before I even have time to answer no, he's ripped the lace and his mouth is on my pussy. I can't even breathe as his tongue keeps sweeping slowly up, and the hair on his face stimulates everything around it.

"More…fuck…Lex… I need…" I can't even say what I need. But it doesn't matter because as he pushes his fingers inside me and bites down on my clit that's throbbing hard. I scream.

"Leeeexxxx!" The room spins and my whole body shakes as the orgasm screams through me. His hands continue to stroke me to keep me going, and he leans over the top of me.

"That's my girl. Now, I need you." Kissing me hard, he pushes his cock inside me. While I'm sliding down from the first high, my body instantly reacts to him as he pounds into me.

"You are so tight, fuck, you make me want to stay here all day." Wrapping my legs around him, my heels that he wanted left on are now digging into his ass.

"Fuck, you need to come again because I can't hold it much

longer." I'm so close that I'm almost scared of the sensation that's taking me over the edge. He knows that, because he reads my body so well. Just as I'm teetering on the edge, he grabs my tit and pinches my nipple, hard, and doesn't stop while I scream through my second orgasm, and he roars my name as he lets go.

I'm sure I almost black out as he slowly pushes inside me a few more times, enjoying every last moment of his orgasm. He starts kissing softly on my shoulder and up my neck, nibbling on my earlobe, which he knows I love.

"I missed you last night, in my bed." He sounds like a little child sulking.

"I know, but I have to be with the kids." I'm giggling now as he starts on my neck again. I never knew how ticklish I am there.

"Well, your sister is mean because she has banned me from her couch. Damn Mason told her he found a white stain on it."

Nearly dying with embarrassment, I try pushing him off.

"No way baby, I'm not done with you yet."

"Lex, oh my god, was there really a stain? Shit, we never have full sex on it, but maybe I dribbled out of my mouth last time." I'm freaking out and all he can do is laugh at me.

"Mia, ignore him. There is no stain, but it's his way of trying to tell your sister that I'm cramping his style as much as he's cramping mine." He lets out a big sigh and lays beside me on the bed. "I've lost you in the moment now, haven't I. You're too busy freaking out about a non-existent stain. Now fucking Mason is cockblocking me too, just like Paige and the kids."

I roll on my side and lean my chin on his chest, looking at him.

"It's okay, sexy Lexy, we still have time before you go."

"What did you just call me?" Oh shit, I've never said that to his face before, but it just slipped out.

"Umm sexy Lexy." I pause to see his reaction. "I mean, it's true, so I just call it how I see it." I try to keep a straight face and not laugh.

"You think I'm sexy, huh?" He moves his hands under my arms and drags me on top of him.

"No, I think you're so ugly, I just close my eyes while we have sex." I can't help it any longer and the laughter bubbles out.

"So sassy today, aren't we. I don't think you should work with Paige anymore, she's rubbing off on you." The sparkle in his eyes tells me how happy he is.

The last few weeks have been amazing, and although a massive learning curve, my new job makes me feel like I belong in this family, and I'm creating a future for my own little family. I even got to have my first girls' night out. Not that I could tell Lex much of what happened that night.

I mean, how do you tell your boyfriend that you spat your drink across the table when Fleur called the guys the Fuckalicious Four and no one bats an eyelid? My Lex, I can vouch that he is definitely fuckalicious.

The girls are hilarious, as is my sister when she's drunk. It's one of the other things I've learned in the last few weeks, that people can drink and enjoy themselves and it doesn't make them nasty or escalate the evening to something more than drunken fun and really bad karaoke songs. Not that I was drinking, and I certainly wouldn't get up and sing for them. I keep that close to my chest and still won't even sing for Lex.

My life is finally coming together, and I'm starting to see a future in this world of theirs.

"Where did you just go?" Lex's voice brings me back.

"Just thinking about how happy I am. You might think I'm changing, but I hope it's for the better."

"Mia, I don't seriously think you're changing. I believe this is who you've been all along, I just think you needed to feel safe enough to let the real you shine."

He always knows what to say to me when that element of doubt slips in.

"I love… how you make me feel." I nearly let it slip, but I can't, I'm just not ready yet. I know the moment I say it, something bad will happen. I just need to keep it inside. For a bit longer anyway.

Before he has time to say anything, I start kissing him, knowing we're running out of time and he'll want more before he leaves.

"You have ten more minutes, and you know I want the whole ten." It's enough for him to be distracted about my slip with the L word, and within seconds I've forgotten too, because he already has me moaning with his touch.

Sexy Lexy is in the house again.

"You better hurry up or you'll be late for court. I can be late back from lunch, but you can't. Jacinta will just use it to score points."

Watching him dress in his suit will never get old. It doesn't matter what he dresses in, I love every style, but a black business suit, holy hot balls. This man is to die for. I never thought I would even look at man in a suit, let alone love him. I know I love him, deep in my bones. In a way that is as amazing as the way I love my kids but on a whole different level. It's the feeling that you can't describe in words. You can't force it and you can't even stop it when it happens. It's that powerful and overwhelming. I can't wait for the day I can tell him. I know it's coming because it's getting harder to hold it in.

"Oh, she can try, but I've got her right where I want her in this case. My guy is innocent, and today I intend to prove it. Because it's about time for me to end this once and for all." He bends down and ties up his laces on his shoes.

As he is standing up, I kneel up on the bed, still naked except for the stockings and garters, holding his tie in my hand.

"Here, let me do this."

"Fuck, woman, how am I supposed to leave you looking like that? You're a naughty dream but I'm able to touch you in real life." I can see the tension in his face and the problem in his pants.

"Well, you need something to look forward to later. You just told me tonight you'll need to celebrate." I try to knot his tie while he's feasting on my neck again.

"Lex, you need to stop, or you'll be explaining more than just being late to the judge. That hard-on in your pants may give away

Lovable Lawyer

where you've been." His hand gives me a tap on my bare ass. He stands up straight again, and I fix the tie so it's perfect.

"Tonight, you're mine. Tell Mason his punishment for being a dick is he's got the kids and you're sleeping at my place. I'm done sharing you. And then tomorrow we start looking for an apartment for you. Better still, move in with me, Mia. You and the kids, come and live with me."

No, no, no. Don't do this, Lex. It's too much pressure yet. I love you, but I still need slow.

"I can't Lex, it's too…"

"Soon, I know, I shouldn't have said it. But you know I would love it. I'll wait. There's no rush. Please don't freak out on me. Let's talk apartment hunting tonight, okay? Your own space and the next step."

My heart is racing on the inside, but I try to show him I'm fine when I'm freaking out just like he said.

"You better go, and I'm fine. Yes, tonight let's talk. We can't have any more stains on couch incidents." I shoo him with my hands as he's looking at me to make sure I'm telling the truth.

"Can't wait." He leans in and kisses me one last time. "Get dressed and good luck spending all afternoon with no panties. If I have to suffer being in court with a hard-on, then you can be thinking about me all afternoon too." His smile is the last thing I see as he blows me a kiss, closing the door behind him.

Flopping back on the bed, my mind is racing. I know he loves the kids, but are they starting to become a problem for him? Is it too much to expect him to take on an instant family? I can't just stop being a mother to become a girlfriend to Lex. I need to work out how to be both, and I'm not sure that he's ready for the type of commitment he just asked for.

Lex's apartment is neat and tidy. Everything in its place and not a mark on a wall, a fingerprint on the windows, or food smudged into the floor rug. I know he sees it at Paige's place, but he still gets to go home to his ordered life and the peace and quiet of his sanctuary. With Jack and Kayla, there will never be peace and quiet for at least twenty years. Oh god, how the hell do I even work this out?

Every time I take a step over a hurdle, another pops up in front of me. I need to push this out of my head and get dressed for work. Although I told him I could be late, I never would be. Paige might be my sister, but that doesn't mean I want to be treated any different. I'm her PA, and I need to be the same as every other employee in that company, abiding by the rules of the job.

It'll be okay, I just need to talk to him tonight about giving me time. He'll understand. He always does.

Getting up to head to the bathroom to freshen up, there's a knock at the door. Grabbing the hotel robe on the chair, I know it'll be Lex because no one else knows I'm here. Well, except for Ashton, who will be nearby somewhere. We've worked out our arrangement where he's in the background but still there when I'm on my own. Until the case with Bent is complete, Lex and Mason don't want to drop the security on Paige or me. I've gotten used to it now, and he has become a great friend, to both me and Lex. He keeps our secrets and I know I can trust him with anything.

"Miss me already?" I say, giggling as I open the door, only to stop breathing when I face the person who hates me most in this world.

Lex's mother.

"Umm Eloise, sorry, I thought you were Lex." Sweat starts pouring out of me under her gaze. The way her eyes are looking me up and down. I'm standing in heels, stockings, and a hotel robe.

I must look just like she expects, a hooker.

"Mrs. Jefferson to you. We need to talk." Not even giving me a chance to say anything, she storms into the room that smells like sex, and the bed proves the point with my clothes strewn all around it.

Standing stunned at the door, I see Ashton out of the corner of my eye. I know I could call him over and he would deal with her, but I can't. This is Lex's mom.

"It's okay," I mouth to him, when it's really not.

"Sure?" he whispers.

Nodding my head, I slowly close the door and turn to face the firing squad.

"Umm Elou…I mean, Mrs. Jefferson, why are you here?" I pull

the robe tighter around my body and curse Lex the whole time in my head, because I don't even have panties on.

"For goodness sake, get dressed so I don't have to look at you like that." She glares down her nose at me.

I want to tell her to fuck off, but at this stage I agree. I need clothes on. This is so uncomfortable. Scooping up my clothes and rushing into the bathroom, I quickly dress while trying to keep myself from falling into a panic attack. I haven't had one since that day in court, and I'll be damned if today will be the day to fall back into that place.

Standing in front of the mirror, I look as pale as a ghost. This is not how this meeting should have been. She has totally caught me off guard. Running my hand down my skirt and buttoning up my jacket, I take a deep breath and imagine Lex's voice in my head. Telling me he's got me and to breathe.

Okay, let's get this over and done with.

"At least you have learned how to dress more appropriately since the last time I saw you." She's standing in the middle of the room like she doesn't want to touch anything. It's not like we're in some cheap-ass hotel. This place is five star and not somewhere that hires rooms by the hour. Although it just dawns on me, that's exactly what we've done.

"Thank you for the compliment, I think." I'm biting my tongue and it's already getting old.

"So, what did you have to discuss with me that couldn't have been done with Lex around? Because that's why you are here, isn't it? To talk without him here."

"You watch your tone, young lady, and his name is Alexander." She shifts her weigh from one foot to the other, and I can see she's winding up, ready to take aim at me.

"I don't know who you are or where you come from, Mia, but I do know you aren't the right person for my son. There are certain expectations on him, and you fall far short of those. I mean, look at where we are. He brings you to a hotel for sex in the middle of the day. No gentleman of his status would even contemplate that. It's disgusting."

I'm stunned, but I can't argue with what she's saying. It's what we did, and if I'm honest with myself, deep down I know I'm not in the same league as Lex.

"The truth is hard to hear, isn't it, Mia." Her stare is like a knife piercing my soul. "You need to know some facts about my son. He was born into a social circle you can never fit into. One that is centuries old and something that you being an orphan will never understand, a family heritage."

Oh god, breathe, Mia, breathe, count… What are the numbers? Shit.

"I know your life and I know how you're pretending to try to fit into your sister's world, but you don't. You haven't been brought up in this world and will never be accepted. I can't have your background being dragged out of the shadows for Alexander when his political career takes off. And he will become a politician. I haven't worked all my life to make that happen and then a little tramp comes in and derails that. Jacinta was the perfect woman to partner him through it all, but you wrecked that and now she wants nothing to do with me either."

Ten…that's it, ten. What comes after ten? My chest is screaming for air. I can't think. All I can do is hear her words. They won't stop.

"So, it was fun while it lasted, and he has got his little fling out of his system, but it's time for him to stop and get on with his life. I'll be damn sure I won't let you keep up this little game you're playing trying to take all his money. So, I'll just set you straight now. I control his money. That's right, you can't get your hands on it and neither can he until he's married to someone I approve of, and then I sign his trust fund over. So, if he's stupid enough to think he can stay with you, then you both will live in poverty together. But then again, you'd be used to that, wouldn't you, Mia. Because that's where you belong, not trying to play happy families with your little bastard children."

Nine, it's nine, breathe. Just breathe. Block out her words. Make it stop. Her voice, it won't stop.

"I'm not surprised you have nothing to say. You have no argument because you know everything I'm saying is true."

No, it's not true. I can't breathe to talk.

Eight, seven…breathe. I just want to run. I need to run.

"I think I have explained the situation clearly enough, but there is one last thing you need to remember. I know my son lost his head and assaulted a man because of you. He may have been lucky so far trying to cover that up, but if I choose to make it known, Alexander will never work as a lawyer again and that will be all your fault. But if you disappear from his life, then it will never be heard of again."

I promised I wouldn't run, but I can't breathe. Six, five…it's not working.

"The choice is yours, Mia. Keep fucking my son and dragging him down to your level, or walk away and let him live the life he is destined for. I'll be watching for your decision. Good day."

I know she's moving, I just can't see properly as the room is spinning. Four…air, that's it, keep dragging in that breath. The air helps the pain stop. Hearing the door click, I fall on to the bed, my legs giving way as the tears are falling.

Three…breathe. I don't know if I even want to breathe anymore.

The kids…breathe for the kids. I need to think about the kids. Sing, you need to sing. Make the bad lady's voice go away in my head.

Two…breathe. Oh, Lex, I'm so sorry. I just can't do this. I don't know how to breathe without you.

The sound of the door opening has my vision slowly coming back, but the tears won't stop as I look up to see Ashton standing there, with a face that says he wants to kill someone.

"One… that's all I'll ever be is just a lonely one."

"Mia, I'll call Lex," Ashton says with his phone in his hand.

"No! Please no. No one can know. Please, Ashton no." My chest is getting tight again and my breathing starts to race.

"Okay, okay. You need to breathe with me, Mia. You can do this. We know you can. Let's count. Ten, nine, deep breath…" He doesn't understand. I don't want to breathe without Lex, and I know now I can't have him. I love him too much to do that to him.

Ashton places his arm around my shoulder and keeps talking

and counting for me. On the outside, it might look like I'm coming out of it, but the only place I'm going is to my dark corner. The one in the back of the room where no one can see me. The place I'm used to, and where I know how to function. I don't have to keep being happy, I just stay numb. It doesn't hurt as much there.

I don't know how long I've been sitting here with Ashton on the bed when I finally stop crying. He doesn't talk, he just sits and holds me. Like I said, he knows my secrets and I trust him with my life. He and Mason have become the brothers I never had.

"I'm sorry, Ashton, you shouldn't have had to see that."

"Bullshit. I stopped being your bodyguard the moment I met you. I'm your friend first, and I chose to keep you safe second. I'd do it even if Lex wasn't paying me."

"Wait, what? I thought Paige was paying you." I sit up taller and look at him as he pulls back a bit.

"No, Mia, Lex took over weeks ago, and don't you dare complain. If you were my girlfriend, I would do the same. He wants to protect you any way he can, so he knows if he can't be with you then at least I am. I respect that." Ashton stands up and gives me a bit of space.

"Oh god, this just keeps getting worse," I mumble.

"What does? Mia, talk to me. This stays between us. What did that woman say to you? Because no normal mother leaves a person in a full panic attack like you just had."

"You wouldn't understand even if I told you. Just know that if I ever turn out like her to my children, you have permission to shoot me or lock me up, either will work."

"Right now, I'm pretty sure I want to shoot her, and I don't even know what happened. But I know you would never be like her, it's just not in you, Mia. And knowing Lex, it's not in him either, thank god."

I just sit for a few minutes and my phone starts vibrating in my bag.

"Shit, Paige, she'll be wondering where I am." I fumble with my bag trying to find my phone.

"It's okay, I messaged her to say you weren't feeling well and I was going to take you home. She's probably just calling to check on you. Because there is no way you want to go back to the office looking like you do, no offence."

"None taken, I can't even look in the mirror. Thank you. I'll call her from the car if that's okay. I just need to get out of here."

"Sure, let's go. I'll have one of my guys meet us at the apartment, and after you're settled, I'll go back to the office and get the kids from daycare. Even though Jack will hate me for picking him up early. He loves that place and all his new friends. I think he has them eating out of his hands with his natural charm." He smiles at me and holds out his hand to pull me up from the bed.

"Ugh, don't remind me. Imagine that boy as a teenager with testosterone kicking in. He'll be a nightmare, I'm sure."

"Probably, but he's your nightmare so I can just sit back, watch, and laugh." We both laugh a little as he opens the door for me.

"Wow, great friend you are. Thanks for the support." I feel like I'm doing the walk of shame to the elevator after what Elouise said. She made me feel so cheap and dirty. I thought I was past feeling that, but in a moment, she put me right back there.

Today I learned one thing.

Money doesn't make you a nice person if you were born a nasty one. That woman is nasty to the core and nothing will ever change that.

I can't stop her from hurting me, but I can stop her from hurting Lex.

Which in turn just makes me hurt more, and that's what she wants too. To punish me for Jacinta.

Once again, I'm responsible for wrecking another life.

I should have listened to my head when it was saying to stay away from Lex, but I stupidly followed my heart thinking this time it would finally be different.

I didn't even have to tell him I loved him.

Just thinking it and feeling it so strongly in my heart was enough to ruin it anyway.

Edward always told me I was no good and no one would want me in their life.

I should have believed him.

Sitting in the back of Ashton's car, I just stare out the window trying to get my head together on what I need to do. I'm not sure Paige believed me that I was sick when I talked to her, but she went with it and for that I'm thankful. I just need this afternoon to make a plan and then I can move forward.

"Ashton?"

"Yeah?" he replies, looking at me in the rearview mirror.

"You don't happen to know any apartments for rent, do you? I think I need to start my new life, on my own. It's the only way I'll ever be able to prove to myself that I am who I am by my own merit." I look back out the window in my daze as the world is a blur passing by.

"You really sure that's what you want? Because there's going to be couple of fights over that decision."

"I know, but yeah, I'm sure. I need to become the true Mia Kennedy before I can be anyone else to others."

"I totally understand, and I will stand behind you one hundred percent. As for the apartment, funny you should ask. The lady next door to me moved out yesterday, and it's still vacant. It's not as fancy as what you're used to, but it's nice and it's safe. And has the best neighbor, or so I hear."

"Thanks, Ashton, it sounds perfect. Will you help me? I have no idea how to even apply for it." I try to give him a smile.

"As soon as we get home, I'll make the call. And don't worry, the universe has a habit of making things happen the way they're supposed to. Out of the darkest times there is always a door that will let in some light."

"Thanks, Ashton, for everything. I couldn't do this without you. And like I said, please don't tell anyone what happened. Not a word."

"And like I told you, I think that's a mistake and you should tell Lex the truth, but I respect your choice and my lips are sealed. I'm going to hell anyway, so what's one more lie."

"No one as caring as you goes to hell, Ashton. It doesn't work that way."

"I'm not sure I believe that," he replies.

Well, I need to believe that, otherwise what I'm about to do is going to send me to hell for the rest of my days, even while I'm still living.

Sing, I need to sing. I just wish I could.

But for the first time there's no star to be seen.

And nothing to wish on.

My light is dimming and I'm heading back to the dark.

Chapter Twenty-Seven

LEX

Leaving Mia in that room, looking sexy as fuck, was not an easy task.

It was hard, very, very hard.

Listening to the judge hand down the verdict doesn't even make my heartbeat change today. I'm happy for my client who didn't deserve the charges brought against him. I could see plain as day that he was innocent.

It's now that I really know there's only one reason my heart beats, and that is for her.

My Mia.

"Congratulations, Counselor," Jacinta says as we walk side by side out of the courthouse to our cars.

"Thanks. You knew he was innocent all along, better luck next time." We both laugh a little. Since the day we talked with the most honesty we'd ever had with each other, our friendship has developed to a good place.

"You know I'll never admit to that, don't you?" she says, trying to keep a straight face.

"I'd be shocked if you did."

"By the way, can you talk to your mother? Seriously, that woman is ridiculous. I've been avoiding her and all her millions of phone calls and text messages for two weeks, but I'm just about to take out a restraining order on her ass. She just never gives up!"

"Ah, and now she gets it." We laugh as we reach our cars that happen to be next to each other. "I'll do it over the weekend. Sorry she's such a pain. I've just been enjoying my time in my little mother-free bubble. But I can tell you this now. It's Friday, I've booked babysitting, and it's date night with my girl. So, nothing short of a big explosion is going to stop me from spending the night with Mia."

"Lex."

"You know I like hearing you call me that. Alexander is only reserved for the wicked witch." I roll my eyes at her.

"Oh my god, you can't call her that. You're right, but still. Anyway, I just wanted to tell you something." She hesitates a little. "I've been thinking about what you said, and I just wanted to say thank you. Things are looking a little different now and you made me think in new ways. I never felt like I had a choice. So, thank you." She is a beautiful woman when she smiles an actual happy smile.

"Hey, I just laid out the arguments. You connected your own dots, but I'm glad. So, does this mean no more bitch-face Jacinta who thinks she has bigger balls than me in the courtroom?"

"Fuck no! I didn't say I grew a heart or anything. That Jacinta will never leave, but she might just take time out every so often, if she can find the right man to do that with."

"And there she is. Welcome back, Counselor."

"You can be just as big an asshole at times too. Now go home. There's some crazy woman who for some reason is waiting to see you. Some people just can't be helped." She places her hand on my arm and gives me a little squeeze as she opens her door and places her briefcase inside.

I walk to the other side of the car, and I'm about to hop in when I call her. "And Jacinta? I can't wait to meet him."

"Who?" She looks confused.

"The man who removes those balls for good."

"Ugh, goodbye, Lex." She's just shaking her head at me as she gets in her car, and I open my door already planning my night with Mia.

I call and she picks up after a few rings. "Hey, baby, are you ready for tonight? I'm just leaving work." There's a little silence on the other end, which is unusual not to hear the kids, but maybe she isn't home yet.

"Hi, Lex." Her voice is flat with absolutely no emotion.

"Mia, are you okay?" I'm already putting that accelerator pedal down a bit harder than I should be.

"Yeah, I'm fine. Just not feeling great. Is it alright if I come over for a while but don't stay tonight?" Now I'm getting concerned. She almost sounds like she's crying, but I can't tell.

"Of course, but don't worry, stay home and I'll come and stay with you." I don't want her to have to leave if she doesn't feel like it. Date night can wait. Hell, we'll be having date nights for the next fifty years.

"No! I mean, no, it's okay, the quiet at your place is what I need."

What the hell is going on?

"Okay then...I'll come by now and pick you up."

"No, it's okay, Ashton is heading that way now. Mason just got home so I'll meet you at your place in about twenty minutes. Is that alright?"

No, but I can't say that because I know that she needs control in her life, and something has definitely derailed her since I last saw her, so I have to let her run this show.

"If that's what you want, Mia, I'll see you soon. I'll be waiting to make whatever it is that's not right, better."

"Thanks, see you soon." And then she's gone, and the line is dead.

The wheels squeal a little as I turn into my parking spot. My senses tell me something is not right, and until I see her, I can't work out what it is.

Banging the elevator button several times wanting it to open quicker I'm sure I'm about to break it.

My mind is racing, which is unlike me. Maybe she's just unwell. She could have eaten something bad, that's probably it. Was she rushing after lunch and got something from one of those sketchy vending machines? Shit, I should have fed her. We use up a lot of energy when we're together. What kind of boyfriend am I?

I need to talk to Paige. She needs to make sure there's lunch delivered every day. Something healthy and full of energy. Plus, water. Yes, lots of water to keep her hydrated. Ashton, I'll give him that job. Make sure she always has a full water bottle.

Walking into my apartment where it's so quiet, I stop for a moment and realize I'm thinking like an idiot. Mia is a grown woman who can look after herself. I have to wait until she gets here and then I'm sure she'll tell me the little thing that's worrying her. We can sort it out and then Sexy Lexy can make it all better.

Oh shit, I know what it is. I freaked her out about asking her to move in with me. I'm such an idiot. That's what it is. Feeling my body relaxing a little, I take off my suit jacket and kick off my shoes and socks in the bedroom. I know I can solve this one easily. I don't care where she lives, as long as there's a place for me there.

I turn on the music and open the balcony doors to let the fresh air in. The city is starting to light up for the night and the Friday night noise is wafting up from the street. Behind me I hear the elevator sound that she has arrived, and I pad across the floor in my bare feet, while rolling up my shirt sleeves and getting more comfortable. Hopefully these clothes won't be on for much longer anyway.

The doors open and Mia steps out with her shoulders slumped. Her face is pale and a little puffy around the eyes.

"Hi, baby, are you okay?" Walking to her and not waiting, I take her into my arms. She slumps into my body and her arms wrap so tightly around me. Her head buries in my chest and it reminds me of that first morning in my office where she seemed so lost.

"Mia, talk to me. You look terrible." Slowly her face lifts up and I know she's been crying, and by the look of her eyes, a lot.

"Can we sit down?" Her voice is quiet and with no strength to it.

"Sure." I leave my arm around her and lead her to the couch.

She sits down and I sit next to her and lift her into my lap. Her head drops onto my neck and she snuggles against me. I want to scream at her to say something, but I know I can't. This is her way.

After a few minutes, I can't take it anymore.

"Mia, please, you're killing me here. Whatever it is, just talk to me. I can't fix it for you if I don't know what it is."

Feeling her take a big breath, she sits up and looks me in the eye. "That's just it, Lex, you can't fix it. No one can. I need to start fixing things on my own."

"You know what I meant."

"Yes, I do, and I appreciate it, I really do. But if I don't start doing things for myself, I'll never know if I can. I don't want to look back and wonder, could I have done this on my own?"

"But you are, baby, look at you. Your life is turning out perfectly. You have a great job, the kids are happy, we're happy."

"Lex, please. I have things I need to say. Can you just not say anything until I'm finished? Otherwise I'll never get through it." The tears are there, and she's barely holding on.

"Okay," is all I can say.

She starts to move off my lap, and now I know this is about to turn to shit.

"From the moment I ran from Edward, I haven't been on my own. First Bent put us in that apartment, and although it was for all the wrong reasons, he still fed us and we had somewhere to live that was clean and safe. Then that all went crazy and I ran from the danger straight into your arms and that of my sister. You all took me in straight away and cared for me and the kids. You on that first night running out and buying us a lifetime of supplies was so overwhelming." I go to say something, but she gives me a look to tell me not to open my mouth. "Then you helped me with all the legal things I needed to make sure the kids and I were safe and able to move on with our lives. You gave me friendship when I needed it the most. Paige and Mason have given me a home and a family that I have longed for all my life, and now this job is where I know I belong." Her hands are clenching open and closed, just like my heart is.

"But as much as I tried not to, I let you into my life as more than a friend. Lord knows I fought you off in my head, but my heart kept giving in to you. You can be very persuasive when you try. I guess that's what makes you so good at your job as a lawyer. And then as much as we tried to go slow, it never happened. Then today a few things made me stop and think. I don't know who I am."

Fuck!

"I can't be the woman you need, until I know the woman I even am without you. Otherwise we won't work, and that's not fair to you. I know that doesn't make sense to you, but it does to me. I need to find out who Mia Kennedy is. The single mom who is raising her children in her own apartment, using her own money from working her job. Just like all the other single parents in the world do. I need to be an *'I'* before I can be an *'us.'*" The tears are running down her face, and I can't move my body to wipe them away because my own tears are now running too.

My heart is breaking open, actually shattering into pieces right here in front of her. I'm supposed to be the one supporting her, but this time I can't. I don't know how to cope myself.

"You're running, aren't you?" I whisper.

"No, this time, I'm finally learning to walk slowly, so I don't have to run anymore." She lifts her hand and starts to wipe my tears from my face.

"Why?" I can't say more than that.

"Because it's the only way. I'll never be accepted in this world until I prove I belong here." For once she is stronger than me.

"You don't need to prove a thing. You belong with me. You can't deny that, Mia. Fuck, I'm in love with you, don't do this." I never wanted to tell her like that, but if I don't say it now, I may never get a chance again.

"I know. One day I can hopefully say that too. Just not today." I can't sit here any longer, so I stand and pace back and forth.

"Space, is that what you need? Was the moving in together too much? It was a stupid thing to say. Ignore it. Just don't push me away. Just tell me what you need, and I'll do it." I'm almost begging her.

"That's just it, Lex, you can't keep doing this life for me. I need to go learn it myself, and hopefully one day I'll feel I'm an equal."

This can't be happening.

Fuck, fuck, fuck.

As I stand looking out the windows, I feel her behind me. Will I always feel her even when she isn't with me? What's that shit saying?

If you love someone let them go, and something about if they don't come back, they weren't yours.

Yeah, fuck that right off.

"Lex, tomorrow I'm moving into my own apartment with the kids."

"What!" I spin to see her right behind me. She flinches at my yelling. Stop, you idiot, you're scaring her. This is the last thing she needs and will be expecting from you.

"Sorry, Mia, I just… I'm really struggling here. You keep knocking the air out from me."

"I know, and your hurt is killing me too. I don't want you to freak out, but I'm moving into an apartment next door to Ashton."

I'll fucking kill him. If he even touches one hair on her body, I will kill him. I try so hard to pull it in and not show her my anger and frustration.

Breathe, fucker, before you start losing your shit.

"That way he can keep me safe but not be in my face. And thank you for paying him, but I will be taking over from today. I have borrowed money from Paige as a loan and will start to pay her back gradually. Just like I would like to pay you back for all the things you bought for me and the kids."

"Not happening." I'm almost growling. "I bought those for you."

"Yes, with your money which I appreciate, but…"

"But nothing. That's right, with my money that I can choose to spend how I like. I choose to spend it on you. That's what you do for people you love." I know I'm losing it and that was a cruel thing to say.

"Okay, let's forget that then."

"Mia, what happened today? I'm so confused, I left the love of my life, glowing from some amazing sex, and five hours later we're here. Help me out, please."

"I know it's hard to understand, but it's the best thing for both of us. I just need you to believe me and…" Taking a deep breath, she says the two words that smash my heart, what is left of it. "Trust me."

I grab her into my arms as we're both sobbing. I have never cried like this, but I don't care. Nothing has ever hurt as much as I'm hurting now.

"Lex?" Shit, I know what's coming.

"Nope, I'm not answering."

"Then I won't tell you, but I need to go."

"Nope, not letting you go. Mia, I don't know if I can." I take her face in my hands, I know for the last time. I just need one more taste.

"Mia, I love you and that will never change." I kiss her on the lips, the ones that I have made my own but now I'm sadly saying goodbye to. As we pull apart, she just nods with her tears pouring down her face. I know she's done and not able to say another word.

Slowly she takes a step back until our joined hands slide apart and the last touch is broken.

She walks backwards to the elevator like she too is taking every last second to memorize what we have. Pushing the button, the doors open, and as she steps in, I call to her, "Mia. When you're done running, you know where to find me. I'll be waiting."

My last vision of her as the doors closing is her nodding and hugging herself in a desperation to stop the pain.

And behind she is leaving a shattered man.

My words from this afternoon have never felt truer.

The only thing that would keep us apart tonight would be a huge explosion.

Fucking boom!

MIA

"Mia." No, please Lex, no more.

"When you're done running, you know where to find me. I'll be waiting."

The elevator doors close, and I collapse to the floor.

My heart's gone.

I left it with him, and I'll never get it back.

He claimed it, and I know he will always treasure it. Even when his is bleeding from the pain. He will still protect mine. That's just how my Lex is.

The doors of the elevator open, and I look through the tears to see Ashton and Paige standing there waiting for me.

He leans down and picks me up and carries me away from the one person who feels like home.

I don't think I have any more tears to cry.

I'm curled up on the floor under the window, trying to find a star. Just one is all I need tonight. But all I see are dark clouds, and every so often a glimmer of the moon from behind the clouds.

I know I'm doing the best for Lex, and in some ways for me, just the pain is more than anything I can describe. Why, if it's the right thing, does it feel so wrong?

When Mason got home from going to check on Lex, he came to try and comfort me.

Telling me that Lex will be okay, and that he understood why I did what I did.

It was total bullshit, because if Lex loves me like I love him, then he's not okay, and he won't be okay tomorrow or the next day either. Tonight, he probably hates me more than he loves me.

In one of our after-sex deep and meaningful talks, we both confessed we never really gave our heart to anyone because we were so afraid of the hurt. Because we knew what it felt like to long for love and not have it.

Then today I did exactly what he always feared.

I broke his heart.

Tonight, I need to let the hurt and pain pour out, because tomorrow I have to pick myself up and learn to move on.

To show the world that I am worth something.

That I deserve to be loved.

Because you can never truly feel love until you're ready to believe you are worthy of it.

LEX

I don't want to move from this daybed on the balcony.

I've been lying here since Mason left, trying to find a star, just one.

I need to know she can see one. If I can't be her star, she needs the ones that get her through a day. That make her feel safe.

But just like I feel, the sky is dark and has no light tonight.

Mason promised he would watch over her. But he's not me.

When I asked him what the hell happened, he either didn't know or couldn't tell me, but my gut feeling is nobody really knows. Mia knows how to put up a wall that no one can climb over.

She asked me to trust her which I have no choice but to do.

My phone starts buzzing next to me, and I jump to grab it in case it's her.

The name on the screen makes my blood run cold.

"You fucking touch her, and I will kill you with my bare hands," I scream at Ashton down the phone.

"For fuck's sake, of course that's what you think. I thought we got past this shit, dickhead."

"Yeah, until you organized to move her in next door to you, asshole."

"Lex, I know you're pissed, so I'll let you off this once for talking to me like that. Now shut your mouth and listen. I shouldn't be calling you, but I know how much you love her, and you need to know this."

I sit up so quick my head is spinning a little. "What do you know, what did she tell you? Start talking now, Ashton, or so help me god I will hurt you." I'm sure half of Chicago can hear me I'm yelling down the phone that loud.

"If you shut up for five seconds then I will. Damn, you are such a lawyer."

"Ashton!"

"Contrary to your belief, I moved Mia into the apartment next to me—that I own, by the way—so she can afford something nice even though I'm charging her about the quarter of what it's worth."

"I'll pay you."

"Shut up, dickhead. I did it because I can keep her safe for you and we both know that she is going to need a friend. I'm that friend, you idiot, to both of you. She trusts me and she doesn't want to ruin your friendship with Mason and Paige and put them in the middle, so I'm it. Now you might not like that, but it's the way it is. So, when your anger simmers down a bit, you'll see a little clearer that I have done this for you as much as I did for Mia."

"Keep going," I mumble.

"Oh, now he wants to listen."

"Not the time for humor." I'm still hanging on by a thread.

"She needs to see if she can do this on her own, and I know you're going to say that she doesn't have to, but she thinks she does and that's all that matters. So, if you want my advice, you let her try. You back away and let her find her feet. Let her realize what we already know, that she can do anything. She's got such an inner strength that she doesn't give herself enough credit for. Man, what she did today to walk away from you took more courage than some of the bravest soldiers I know. And before you ask why she did it, that's her story to tell you, Lex. Just hang in there, and when she's ready, you'll know. Because there is no way in this world that woman will be able to stay away from you forever. Even a dumbass like me can see that."

I totally owe this man my life, because once again I have shown him the worst side of me.

"I don't know what to say to you, Ashton. Except you're right, I'm an idiot. No matter what I tell myself, I just don't see clearly sometimes when it comes to Mia. She leads me around by my balls and that blurs my vision at times. I'm sorry for what I said and... thank you for being there when she won't allow me to be."

"I bet that hurt coming out your mouth." Bastard's laughing at me.

"Nothing could hurt more than my heart does right now. Take some advice from me. Do not, under any circumstances, let a woman past the wall on your heart, man. You think the bullet burned going through your chest? Well this is one hundred times worse." I lie back down on the daybed and take a deep breath.

"Noted. I'm going to leave you to try to sleep, but can I just say one more thing?"

"Sure," I say, looking up to the sky.

"From the outside looking in, I don't know your story, but maybe this is your time to work out what you really want from life too. Maybe Mia isn't the only one who has some soul searching to do. Just think about it. I'll stay in touch, and if you value my help, you keep your mouth shut and these phone calls just between us. Understand?"

"Totally, and I'm grateful. Hopefully one day I can repay you."

"I've already recorded the IOU in my memory, buddy. Talk soon."

"You better believe it."

The phone call ends, and I think one of the bricks I had been stacking back around my heart fell off the wall. Just leaving that little hole. Just in case, one day someone might want to peek back through the wall.

Staring at the sky, the clouds part just for a split second, and there it is.

The lone star.

Just one, hovering in the darkness.

Mia's star watching over her from above.

The last two days have been the longest of my life.

Not leaving my apartment almost killed me, especially when I knew everyone else was helping Mia move and settling into her new place. The guys have been calling and messaging, wanting to come over, but I didn't want visitors. I had a lot to sort through in my head, and to do that I needed to be alone.

Walking into work right now feels like the numerous visits to the principal's office in high school. You know the outcome is going to make your parents mad, what you do and say will disappoint others, but by the time you walk out, you know that life is going to get better after the visit.

Speaking to Greta late last night made me feel better, and she's already here and ready for me. That woman has never let me down, since the day I met her, and today I hope I can repay her.

"Hey, boss." I look up and there is her happy face, with my coffee like usual. When she hands it over, I look to see what stupid name she gave me today. But instead it just says one word.

'Proud'

"Likewise. Couldn't have done it without you. Now let's do this before I look like a girl here, hugging you because you made me emotional."

"Heaven help us, you show you're normal. The world could end."

"Do you ever get up in the morning and think, I'm going to be nice to Lex this morning?" We start walking down the corridor together.

"Nope, never, not a chance, and you know that won't change, right?" We both laugh.

"Poor Blaine. Can't say I'm sad he's the number one man in your life. He is welcome to that spot."

She just rolls her eyes at me. "Like you were ever in the running for it."

"I know, but it's been fun driving him crazy with it since the day you met him."

"Asshole."

"Every day."

We stop outside the office door that will change my journey, and until this moment, I didn't know if I could do it.

But this feels like the first step towards my HEA, wherever that may be.

Knocking and then entering the boardroom to see the six partners of the law firm, I can feel the weight already lifting.

"Good morning, everyone, sorry for the early morning meeting, but it's important."

Turning to look at Greta, she smiles at me and mouths the word *'proud'* which is all I need.

"I know this will come as a shock to you all, but I'm resigning this morning, effective immediately from close of business today." You could have heard a pin drop in the room, but inside me all I can hear is the biggest sigh of relief. "I have asked Greta here with me today because I want to strongly recommend her to be promoted to take my position. She knows every one of my cases probably better than I do and is so dedicated to this company that I personally believe you would be fools to let her go. And before you ask, I'm not joining another firm, I'm no longer going to be a practicing criminal lawyer."

This time the room is not silent but filled with gasps of shock instead. "I've known for a long time this job wasn't for me anymore, but it took a woman far smarter and stronger than me, to make me see that light. So, I thank you for every opportunity and all your friendships over the years. I'm grateful, and I hope you show the same mentoring to my successor Greta. I'm going to head to my office now to empty out my desk, but I'll leave you with Greta for a moment so you can discuss her new position and when you can get the contract drawn up for her." With my last closing argument presented, I lean across the desk and shake each of their hands. Laughing to myself that I should also be picking up their jaws off the table for them.

Turning to walk out of the boardroom, I tell her the same, mouthing *'proud'* and then leaving her to it as I hear her voice starting her opening argument.

Taking my first step to freedom, part of me feels sad, because the one person I want to share it with, I can't.

I send a message through the universe and hope she still feels me like every part of my body still senses her.

'Tell her thank you, I couldn't have done it without her push.'

A wise lady, who at the time I thought was crazy, told Bella about my life. Storms were coming and the woman with the negative energy had to go before I could see my light.

Well, I've found my light, so now it's time to remove that negative energy. At the time I thought it was poor Jacinta; how wrong could I have been.

Time to visit Mother!

Chapter Twenty-Eight

LEX

"Master Alexander, I didn't know you were arriving today for a visit. Your mother didn't mention it." Standing up out of the car, I shake Charles's hand and give him a man hug.

"That's because I didn't tell her. But I'm sure the gossip train has already reached her. She'll be expecting me. And fair warning… run for the hills, my good man. This is not going to end well." I chuckle to myself as we walk to the front door, possibly for the last time.

"Lord help us, what have you done now, Lex?" He stops with me on the top step before opening the door for me.

"Something I should have done a long time ago. Started to live my life. The one I choose to live."

He pats me on the shoulder.

"Good for you, my boy. About time."

"Well, some of us take time to grow up, or better still, to stand up."

"You are here now, so get in there, and do what you need to. I'll warn the rest of the staff to bunker down as this one's going to be a rough cruise. Stormy seas ahead for a while, but like everything, they too will eventually pass."

"Oh, I wouldn't bet on it with this one. You might want to name this Hurricane Lex. It's no ordinary storm." With that, he opens the door, waves me through, and quietly disappears into the back of the house.

I don't need to ask where she is. I can hear my mother tearing strips off my father on the phone.

"You get to that office right now! I don't care if you are due in court. You tell them he is unwell and made a mistake and to please ignore his rash actions. Tell them he was delirious on medication or something…"

"But I wasn't." She stops mid-sentence and glares at me. I've been on the end of plenty of my mother's death stares, but I would say this one has to take the cake. The best part of it is, though, it has zero effect on me. There is no power there anymore.

"Dustin, forget it. He's here…yes, I expect you home right now." She's listening to him, but her eyes never leave me. "What do you mean you don't care? I can't believe you. Ugh, I will deal with you later." Slamming down the house phone, I know she's winding up and just doesn't even know where to start.

Storming past me and into my father's office, she stands at the door expecting me to follow. Because she thinks behind this door that the hired help won't hear what we say. Her voice can be heard in every corner of this house when she yells, but sure, let's hide in the office.

She doesn't even know how to close the door without banging it.

"What the hell have you done, you stupid boy!" It's almost comical watching her stomping around the room.

"Always a pleasure to visit you, Mother." I can't help baiting her.

"Pleasure, what pleasure is it! Tell me there's a mistake. Tell me you did not just resign and tell them you are no longer going to be a lawyer. Because that is not happening. I've worked too hard to get you where you are and lay the platform for your rightful place in politics."

Letting her pace, I take a seat in my father's office chair.

"See, that's funny, because I could have sworn it was me who attended college, worked my ass off for good grades, then spent countless hours working up the corporate ladder in my job and have an amazing record in a courtroom of proving my clients' cases and winning. Just remind me again… what part of that life of mine did you participate in, Mother?" Her mouth drops open but not for long.

"What is wrong with you, Alexander? We need to get you to the doctor's because you aren't thinking clearly." She starts looking for the phone on the desk.

"Actually, to be honest, today I'm thinking clearer than I ever have in my life, and it feels amazing." I lean back in the chair and put one foot up on the other knee.

"That's it. That little whore, the one after your money. It's her, isn't it." Don't let her bait you. That's what she wants. Don't yell, just set her straight.

"If you are referring to my girlfriend, Mia, then I suggest you stop right there. I will not let you talk about her like that, because every word you just said couldn't be any further from the truth. Mia has never taken one cent of money from me, nor has she even asked. Not that it's any of your business, but she works hard to support her family, and I'm very proud of her for that. And if I *ever* hear you call her a whore again, I promise it will be the last time you see me or any future grandchildren I may have." Deep down inside, though, I know today is the last time I'll probably see my mother, and it's for the best.

"I told her to stay away from you! I told her she would never get your money until I release it, so she had better be gone before you know it, and if she wasn't, that I would ruin your career and tell everyone you physically abused her husband."

"You fucking bitch, it was you! How could you do that to your own son?" I stand so quickly the chair goes flying to the floor. "How could you hurt the woman I love with such venom and stand here proudly boasting that's what you've done? I thought you were evil but that there had to be a good person in there somewhere. I was wrong. You have no heart. You've never loved me, and you couldn't take it that finally someone else actually does. Well, fuck you, Mother. You thought you could blackmail Mia with my career? You like to think I'm the pawn in your game of life? Well, fucking checkmate! I screwed you first. Nothing you can say or do now will ever make me forgive you for what you have done. Goodbye, Mother. I can't even say it was nice knowing you, because I never did."

Ripping the door open, I'm storming down the hallway as I hear her heels following me.

"I did it all for you, Alexander!" she's yelling behind me.

"Bullshit, you did it for you." Stopping at the front door, I turn back to face her. "My name is Lex. Alexander is gone, thanks to you."

I knew it!

I fucking knew something had happened that day, and Ashton knew too because he had to have seen my mother with her.

Screaming out the driveway in my car, I'm heading home. My plans just got moved up, and as much as I want to see Mia and tell her I know everything, I know what Ashton said is right. I need to let her do this her way. It's going to kill me, but maybe I need the space too. Mia doesn't need to see me like this. No one does.

Mason was right the night he told me that Mia brings out the best part of me I didn't know existed. But my mother brings out the worst. I need to get rid of that side of me for good, and then when my girl is ready, I will be the man she needs me to be. Not just the man she thinks she sees.

Pushing his number, I wait for him to answer.

"Hey, man, plans just changed. I'm heading home to pack now and leaving. I need to get out of here to clear my head."

"You okay? I'm a little worried."

"To be honest, no. But I will be. Thanks for your help with this and everything else. Never thought I'd say this to another guy again and least of all you. But I love you, bro, and I couldn't do this without you."

"Stay safe, and I've got your back."

"Deep down, I never doubted it."

Hanging up the call, I try to work out what else I need to do before I leave. I don't know how long I'll be gone so I need to make sure any loose ends are tied up.

The next call is far easier than it would have been a month ago.

"Lex, I just heard. Are you okay? What happened?" Hearing Jacinta's voice is surprisingly calming.

"Hi there. Yeah, quite a morning, hey? I bet the rumor mill is running wild." I can't help but laugh now.

"Um, you could say that. Plus, you mother is blowing up my phone, as is my mother. I don't care one bit about them, but I want to know, are you okay?" The concern in her voice is one of a real friend. Who would have thought we would ever be at this point?

"To be honest, I'm probably the best I've been in years. It just wasn't me anymore. The truth is, it was never really me. It was what was expected of me, but not where my heart lies."

"And where is that, Lex?"

"With Mia, but unfortunately my mother got to her too."

"Oh Lex, no!"

"It's okay, I've got this. I'm not worried, and I'll never admit it but in a weird way my mother may have done us a favor. Sometimes the universe works in weird ways." I pause to take a deep breath.

"But I need a big favor, I need you to take on Mia as a client. She has a few things that need finishing, and I won't be here, not that I could represent her even if I was. Bit of a conflict of interest when you're sleeping with your client."

"Like it stopped you when you stepped over the line the first time. Of course, I'll look after her, as long as she's okay with having me. Anyway, just have Greta send over the files. And then we can chat."

"Um, that's the thing, I'm going off the radar for a while. I'm not sure how long, so I need you to just look after her. It's the permanent custody of the kids and the case against Bent which I told you about. I don't think that will actually make it to court, because with all the evidence they have against him, the last I heard he's going to take an early plea for a reduced sentence. So, fingers crossed she won't have to even get involved. All the notes are in the file and Paige and Mason know everything. I'll send them all an email to explain."

"Lex, you aren't going to do something stupid, are you?"

"Me? I'm the most sensible person you know." I laugh at my own joke. "But thanks for checking on me, though. No, I'm all good, I just need some time to think and I can't do that here. You think your phone is blowing up? Imagine what mine will be doing. I've just used the word fuck to my mother so many times, and then ripped her whole life out from under her. So yeah, I'm out of here for a while."

"I don't blame you one bit. Look, I have to run, I'm due in court shortly. But promise me if you need anything you'll call me."

I smile to myself at how far she's come in such a short time with opening up.

"As long as you promise to look after Mia, and if you're worried about anything, you message me and I'll be here in a flash."

"Deal. Talk soon, Lex, and safe travels."

"Thanks for everything, it means a lot."

"Stop with the mushy shit, you'll ruin my reputation."

"Okay. Bye, bitch. Better?"

"Better, asshole. Bye."

Now one last stop to make and then home to pack.

Standing in my apartment with my last bag, I look around for the last time for a while. I pick up my phone and type out the message to tell him the letters are on the table and Austin will let him up to get them when he gets here.

By the time I walk back into this apartment, I'm not sure if I'll still fit this place when I get back, but I do know I will always remember it being my safe place, my home until I learned that home is not a building.

Home is where your heart is.

Mia is my home.

MIA

Two months later

"Mommy, when is Lex coming back from his holiday? I miss him," Jack asks while we sit and read a bedtime story on his red racecar bed.

"I miss him too, bud, every single day."

"Why can't we go and visit him?" he innocently asks.

"Because Mommy and Lex agreed we should stay here until the time is right?" I look out the window at the night sky.

"What does that mean?" I try not to giggle too loud and wake Kayla up in her bedroom next door. She's turning one next week and is up and walking although still just a small amount. It won't be long, and I won't be able to stop her. Just like her talking. With Jack trying so hard every day to teach her new words, I think Kayla will be running this house before long.

I try to distract Jack, ignoring his question.

"Okay, I think we've finished reading for the night. Time to say goodnight, dream big, and make your wish on your star." It's the same thing we do every night. I wanted both the kids to know that dreaming is important and not to be afraid to wish for those dreams to come true.

I never would have gotten to this point if I hadn't done that every night.

He closes his eyes tight and then opens them and looks out his window.

"Done. Now your turn, Mommy."

I close my eyes, then open them and look up to the stars and make my wish.

"What did you wish for?" he asks as he wriggles down under the covers.

"The same thing I do every night. For you to go to sleep." Leaning down and kissing him on the forehead, I put Ted in under the covers with him.

"That's a silly wish," he mumbles a little as his eyelids start closing.

I walk out of the room thinking to myself. Let me assure you, buddy, after the week I've had and the phone call just before I left work, if you go to sleep and let me just crawl into bed right now, then it will be the best wish ever.

Going through my nightly routine, I clean up after the kids, stack the dishwasher, and triple-check the apartment is locked up tight, before getting ready for bed. Then the last thing is to text Ashton to tell him I'm getting into bed. He has become a great friend to me. Someone I can vent to when working with Paige gets too much, or that friend who can watch the kids when you need ten minutes to have a shower. I never thought I would be so close to a male again, but he is a great guy. There is so much more to him, I think, than he lets anyone see, but I suppose that can be said for all of us in life. Including me.

After sending the message, I climb into my bed that seems way too big now just for me. It took some getting used to having the kids in their own rooms, but it was the best thing for them, and me in the long run too.

I've become such a routine person, basically because it's the only way to get through a day.

Nighttime is no different.

Lying down on my pillow, I take my phone and open up the last message I got from Lex.

Lex: When you find yourself then come find me. I'll be here waiting no matter how long it takes. Don't ever forget that when you need me, look to the sky and find your star. Make your wish and know that I'm seeing your star too. I love you, Mia.

Then I do as he told me. I look to the star and make the same wish I make every night.

'Goodnight, Lex, I love you too.'

Letting sleep claim me is never a problem these days because my dreams are always a happy place. The place I know I want to be, where Lex is waiting for me.

Saturday mornings have become a lazy time. We sleep in—well, I try but that doesn't always happen. We make pancakes, using the recipe that Lex taught Jack, and Ashton joins us for breakfast.

"What's my score today?" I ask the boys. I was never much of a cook, but living on my own, I'm trying new things and getting better.

"Oh, I think a solid eight out of ten today. What do you think, Jack?" I poke my tongue out at Ashton as he tries to be funny.

"Ten!" he yells. "But still not as good as Lex's." I get the same answer every week. Damn kid. "Maybe Lex will make them for me when he comes back from his holiday?" He looks at me with hope.

"If he ever comes back," I mumble under my breath.

"He won't," Ashton replies.

"What do you mean? He's coming back, right? Eventually?"

He looks up from his pancakes with a stupid smile. "Yeah, after you go find him."

"Ashton, what the hell are you talking about? What do you know? Oh my god, you know where he is, don't you?" I drop my knife and fork and jump from my seat. Pacing the room.

"Mia, sit down and finish your breakfast. You're going to need your strength. Then if you think you're ready, I may have an idea where he is."

If the kids weren't here right now, I would choke him.

I do as he says, my mind racing. Is that what I want? Am I ready?

I can't eat, and Ashton just starts laughing as I jump up from the table and grab my phone.

Mason's voice is rough with sleep. "Mia, what's wrong? You do know it's only seven am, right?"

"Mason, tell Paige I'm bringing the kids over for a sleepover." The words are tumbling out so fast I doubt he even understood.

"Wait, what?" I hear her sleepy voice come through the phone. He must have me on speaker.

"The kids, they're coming for the weekend."

"Mia, what's going on?" Mason demands.

"I'm going to find my man." I giggle excitedly down the phone.

"About time, woman! What took you so long?" Mason cheers through the phone. "The gang's getting back together."

"Mason, stop it. She hasn't seen him yet." I can hear Paige slapping him.

I grab a bag. "And I'm telling you right now I've got a lot of time to make up for, so the gang will have to wait for a little while. Not sure I'll be ready to share for some time."

"Deal," Mason cheers. "Now get your ass in that car and start driving." By this stage, I'm throwing things into the bag.

"Drive, I don't even know where to." I can't stop giggling.

"Ashton does."

"Wait, Mason White, have you known where he is and not told me?!" Paige is yelling at him now.

"No way, Tiger, Lex isn't that stupid. I just knew that Ashton knew. Lex knows what you're like, Paige, you would've gotten it out of me if you thought I knew. Especially in those early days when Mia was a mess."

"Umm still here, guys, so can we not discuss how much of an emotional basket case I was? Nobody needs to relive that. Now instead of me bringing them over, you two get your asses out of bed and over here. I'll pack their bags, but the faster you get here, the quicker I can leave." I hear all the rustling of them moving.

"But, Tiger, I had plans," Mason complains.

"Well, if you ever want to have plans with me anytime soon, I suggest you move. Otherwise, this body is off your calendar indefinitely. She's going to get her man. Don't you dare stand in the way of love. Your magic wand can wait."

"Oh god, again, still here, people, but I'm hanging up now. My ears are bleeding."

Hanging up, I think about texting Lex but decide I want to see him in person. The poor man has waited this long, he deserves his first hello to be followed by the words that I feel are about to burst out of me. Hold on, words, not much longer now.

Paige and Mason must have made record time to my apartment and were so busy pushing me out the door I don't even really know what I packed.

"Are we close?" I ask Ashton probably for the hundredth time since we left.

"Do I have to answer that?" He laughs at me.

"Yes. I'm anxious, and it helps me to know."

"Which I would never have guessed. And because I'm smart and anticipated that. I've been stretching the truth on the time since we left. So, we are about one minute away."

"Oh... I um, oh, a minute. Shit, Ashton what if he doesn't want to see me?" I can feel my heart pounding at the thought of being so close to him now.

"I don't think you need to worry your pretty little face about that. When I spoke to him yesterday, he told me to tell you he loves you. Which he has done every day since he left."

"Ashton!" I can't help but scream at him.

"What, you weren't ready to hear it. What would be the point of him staying away if he was sending you messages every day? Man, you two are hopeless. I'm glad this is finally getting wrapped up and I can get on with my life."

"Oh Ashton, I'm so sorry. I didn't even think about you in all this mess."

"Don't be silly, I needed to find my feet in civilian life again, so you did me a favor too."

Then he turns the car off the road and on to a gravel drive and stops just inside the gate.

"Mia, this is where your trip finishes with me. You have to go this last part alone. But that was the point of this whole thing, wasn't it? For you to understand you can do it alone."

Feeling emotional, I just nod at him.

"Then you have reached your destination, and I'm so proud of you. Now can you get out and go find him? That poor man has been dying out here on his own."

Leaning across the car, I kiss him on the cheek.

"Thank you, for everything. For keeping us both safe when we needed to find ourselves."

"I'll always be here for you and Lex. That's what friends do." Squeezing his hand, I look out the window to a gravel road that goes down with trees on either side of it.

"Just follow the road in. You won't miss the ugly guy who'll be there waiting for you. Good luck and see you in a few days. Don't rush home. It may be the only alone time you get for quite a while."

"Oh, I know that. See you soon." Taking my bag from the backseat, I step away, and Ashton reverses out the driveway.

"Deep breath. Today is the day."

Stepping that first foot forward is always the hardest, and then the other just tends to follow.

LEX

It's a little early for Ashton's message today.

I know it'll be him because he's the only one who knows where I am, and the only one that I've answered since I left.

The letters I left for everyone explained that I needed this time and that I was okay, so they respected my wishes. Well, after about day five when they just simply gave up when I didn't reply.

Ashton: Special delivery!

What is he talking about? I'm just about to call him when I hear her voice, singing to me and calling me like a siren.

My Mia.

I can't get up out the chair on the porch fast enough. Running to the side of the cabin, I see her come from the edge of the trees.

We both freeze and all I can do is stare at her. I almost pinch myself to make sure I'm not dreaming. Then she takes one foot to move forward, and in what feels like slow motion, we end up standing in front of each other. Not moving.

"Lex, I love you, I'm finished running." I can't wait. I take the last step and take her in my arms, kissing her like she is my lifeline.

We break apart just for a second. "I love you too."

"I know." She giggles and my body reacts to the sound it has missed so much.

Kissing her a little softer this time but with just as much hunger, we both come up for air.

"Home."

"What?" she whispers

"Home is where the heart is." I take her hand, placing it over my heart. "You have always been my home."

"Oh, Lex, I've missed you, show me what it's like to be home."

"By the time I'm finished, you'll forget you ever left. I hope you ate breakfast, because you are going to need the extra energy." I laugh as I pull her tight against my body, so she fully understands.

"Maybe I had a different sort of breakfast in mind. I seem to remember you promised me some morning delight." She gives a little giggle trying to hide her blush.

"Then a promise is a promise."

I grab her bag and hand it to her. "Hold this."

Then I scoop her into my arms and start towards the house.

Opening the front door and carrying her in, the last words she hears before I lay her on the bed and make hot passionate love to her is, "Sexy Lexy is in the house! Welcome home, baby."

Epilogue

LEX

"You told me not to run, but you ran too, Lex. Why?" Her sweet voice lingers in the silence.

Lying on our sides, naked in bed with her back to my front, we're both enjoying the view from Ashton's lake house.

When I told him I needed to get out of town, that it was all too much, he told me about the place that he inherited from his grandparents years ago. That it was a little run down, but I was welcome to it if I spent some time working to fix some things. It seems he has a habit of providing a safe house for us all, both mentally and physically.

"I was hurting like I had never hurt before, and then Ashton gave me a bit of a kick up the ass to make me realize that you weren't the only one that needed time to look deep inside and make some changes. I knew it was time to show you the true man I am," I say kissing her shoulder.

"I already knew."

"How could you, I didn't know him properly then either. But the funny thing is my mother doing what she did pushed us both to find our true selves."

Mia rolls over so quick I almost get hit by her elbow on my face.

"What did you say about your mother?" Her face looks a little worried.

"It's okay, I know what she did. The bitch had the nerve to throw it in my face the day I resigned from my job."

"You know everything?" She's hesitant but I can tell she wants to know.

"Yeah, baby, every revolting detail, including the blackmail. I am so sorry she put you through that, and I told her I will never forgive her for it, and I won't be seeing her again."

Then she goes silent and her head drops a little. "Why didn't you tell me? I might not have run."

"Because if I did that, you never would have stopped running. I couldn't do that to you. You took that last huge step, and I needed to back off and let you." Taking her face in my hands, I lightly touch her lips with mine. Her breath hitches and I feel a little shiver run through her body.

"But by choosing me, you've given up your trust fund. You don't deserve that."

"Mia, I don't care what my mother thinks about my trust fund, or how she thinks it gave her power. She has no idea that I have never spent one dollar of that money since I started working. It just sits in an account and she can take it all back if she wants to. I have my own money and it's built up quite a little nest egg. Money means nothing to me, but you Mia mean everything to me. I'll choose you every time." I'm devastated at how my mother's words that day made her feel.

"I'm so sorry, Lex, I hurt you."

"Yes, but I hurt you too, by smothering you. I never gave you a chance. I'm sorry for the hurt, but I'm not sorry it happened. Looking back, I don't regret one moment. Well, maybe the fifty-eight days of blue balls, but other than that," I say which earns me a slap on the shoulder.

"Are you happy?" she asks

"I truly am, especially now I have you back in my arms."

"Me too."

I'm trying really hard not to show her again how happy I am, but I know she needs a rest. The last few hours have been fucking intense, literally.

"Lex?"

I gasp a little and try telling myself not to panic. "Yes?"

"What have you been doing the last two months?" Relief fills me at the question, and it's something I've been desperately waiting to share.

"Promise you won't laugh."

"I would never laugh." Rolling onto my back, Mia replies now leaning up on my chest.

"I wrote a book." I wait for her reaction and feel like I can't breathe

"Oh Lex, that's amazing. What sort of book?"

"Our love stories. A book full of love letters. I know you're thinking it sounds strange, me being a guy and all, but you inspired me."

"Me? Why me?" She's giggling looking confused.

"You taught me to dream. That in your eyes, all stories have an HEA, regardless of the darkness and pain that come before it. But most of all, you taught me how to love."

Tears are rolling down her cheeks.

"Can I read them?"

"Not yet, but one day maybe, the story is still being written."

"Oh, wow this tastes amazing, I've missed your cooking." Her eyes closed, she drags the spoon slowly out of her mouth with the moan of pure bliss following it

"And I've missed watching you eat it like you're making love to your meal."

Giggling, she just rolls her eyes. "Lex, you can't say things like that. You have to get in the habit for when we get home to the kids."

"Well, you stop looking so sexy when you eat."

My nerves are already going crazy and she's just making me worse.

"It's so beautiful out here at night under the stars."

"Do you like it here?"

"I love the peacefulness and that it's just us and our bright stars."

I take her hand and pull her from her seat. "Come down to the dock on the lake, the view is spectacular."

She follows behind me in her bare feet with little pink-painted toenails, which are a new addition that I'm quite fond of. She has the same flowy sun dress on from our first date and her hair is down blowing gently with the breeze.

As we clear the tree line and step onto the dock we stop to take it all in.

"Lex, oh wow, look at all the stars. It's incredible."

"It's ours," I whisper

"What's ours."

"All this." I sweep my arm around in a three-sixty circle. "I bought it from Ashton, for us. I knew eventually you'd come back to me, and I wanted to make sure we never forget tonight or any of the days that follow. So, this is our special place. Just you and me and our stars."

Dropping to one knee in front of her, I pull the ring from my pocket.

"Mia, will you be my star for the rest of our days? The one I share my dreams with, make my wishes with, and most of all fall asleep with every night. I love you unconditionally and will always be your equal. I promise to be the best father I can be to your children and hope we can be blessed with a few more. I knew when you walked away from me that I couldn't let you go. I quit my job, packed my bags, and bought this ring. So, when this day came, I would be ready. I know you want slow, but the last two months have been a lifetime for us.

"Marry me and let me love and treasure you forever."

As always with Mia when emotions are hard, she loses her words, so instead she's nodding and crying.

"I need to hear it."

This is the last time I'll push her.

"Yes, oh Lex, yes." I jump to my feet and twirl her around as she keeps screaming yes for all the stars in the sky to hear.

Putting her down and taking her hand, I slide the white gold star-shaped diamond solitaire onto her finger.

"We will always be joined by our love and the stars."

We seal our words with a kiss in our new home.

The place where our hearts will always be.

"I love you, Mia."

"I love you too, Lex," she whispers.

"Don't forget the *sexy* in that sentence."

"Like you will ever let me forget!"

MIA

Twelve months later

"Mia, come on through now." Walking into Dr. Bridge's office for the first time is on the list of the hardest steps I've taken in the last few months. Each week gets a little easier, but it's still hard.

"How are you today?" she asks as I take a seat.

"Tired and a little overwhelmed, but nothing too serious."

"Okay, you know we just let these therapy sessions go wherever you take us at the moment, so let's start there, with the overwhelming, shall we?"

I love that about her, in that she doesn't force me to places I can't go yet, but slowly she is bringing out everything I had packed in my box and slammed down the lid to try to survive.

Lex and I are both seeing therapists separately and have had a couple of joint sessions which have been helpful. I should have listened to Mason a lot earlier, but I just wasn't ready. Now I want all my pain of the past to be dealt with before more new life comes along.

The letters that my mother wrote for me and Paige, I couldn't even open or read until I started with Dr Bridge. However, she made me see that to have the future I want I need to deal with the past. The letter was short and just explained what we suspected, that she gave me up out of fear. The last line gave me the closure I longed for with her words: *'I will always love you no matter where you are.'* She longed for a better life for me and it may have taken time, but now I couldn't be happier.

So much for Lex and his slowness. We married six months after that night at the lake house and spent our honeymoon creating a new life. If I thought his alpha protectiveness was bad before, it just hit overload. Hence the therapy, so we never get to a point where we stop communicating our fears.

Lex is already an amazing dad, but part of him is worried his upbringing will come out in him as the kids grow older. He has been having a few therapy sessions with his dad to try to work on their relationship, since his dad left his mother. His dad wants to be a grandfather to the kids, and I know deep down Lex wants that too but it's a work in progress. What I do know without a doubt, is that there is no chance of Lex being a bad dad, his heart is too big, and Jack and Kayla already have him wrapped around their fingers. So, the twins Remi and Gabe being born will make no difference. It's just another little boy and girl to add to the list in this house to drive him crazy but suck him in at the same time.

Anna has been to visit us a few times now and the kids have started to call her Franna. It's their version of Nanna for the framily. She loves Lex and he adores her. I overheard him one night telling her how grateful he was for her keeping us all safe before he found me. They shed a few tears together and I quietly did too. I'm so glad she is still part of our lives.

Slowly running my hand over my pregnant stomach, I'm smiling. The bigger the family the better.

Secretly I can't wait.

Our little family and our big framily I wouldn't trade for the world.

Them or my life under the stars.

Fifteen years later

"Do you think he needs me? I mean, what if he panics? He's never panicked before and he won't know the counting. Remember the counting, Lex? I should have taught him…" Before I can finish the sentence, Lex kisses the air back into my lungs.

"Mia, stop. Otherwise I will make you count." He hugs me tight and kisses me on the forehead. "Baby, Jack is fine. You've heard him. The crowd will love him." The lights dim, and the crowd is starting to cheer.

"Hey Chicago!" My Jack's voice booms into the concert hall. "Thank you all for coming tonight for the first concert of our national tour." The crowd is now starting to go wild. I can feel the electricity in the air as Lex pulls me back against his chest and wraps his arms around me.

"Look at our boy, Lex," I say as he leans down to kiss my cheek.

"Yeah, baby, we did good."

"My name is Jack Jefferson or JJ as my dad calls me. Before we start tonight, I want to just give a shout out to my huge framily who are a here tonight to support me, my two sisters Kayla and Remi, my little brother Gabe, and my dad, Lex. But there is one special lady who I need to tell something, and if I can get through this then I can get through anything in life."

My heart drops and I'm crying already.

"My mom lived a hard life when I was little. She did everything she could to survive and protect my sister and me. The memories are blurred, but there is one thing I will never forget, and that's how she used to tell me to sing away the fear. So, from the age I could talk she taught me that my happy place was when I was singing, which I have never lost. Mom and Dad, tonight is for you, and I have a special surprise for you. I found this book a few years ago in a box of family memories, that you had packed away. You may recognize the words of this brand-new song, Mom. For everyone out there, these are the words my mother wrote on a piece of paper in my auntie's bedroom over fifteen years ago, while she watched over me sleeping. I hope you love it, as much as I will always love you both."

I can't stop crying and my heart is so full seeing Jack truly happy on the stage where he was always meant to be. He takes a breath, and in my mind, I say the only words that make sense. *'I've got you, just breathe.'*

"Tonight, for you, Mom, I'm dreaming big and wishing on my star that same wish I remember from way back then. I wished for you to find someone to be your star just like you have always been mine."

I blow him a kiss, and I feel Lex's tears on my cheeks too as he whispers in my ear, "Home is where the heart is."

Looking at my big extended family around me.

I know this will always be my home.

THE END

Read on for the first chapter of Gorgeous Gyno & Love's Wall

COULD THIS BE MY TIME

Mia's Song

The search has always been for that place for me,
Deep inside my soul, where only you can see.

But even then, no one knows the real me.
It's so hard for me to see, who I'm meant to be.

Today was the same as yesterday and
Tomorrow I can't see any change.
A day of me trying to be who I think they want to see,
But instead you came along and showed me a place for us to feel free.

A lifetime of trying, fighting for happiness.
How hard does it have to be?
I'm being pushed and shoved in your chosen direction,
But what you failed to see, was it was never right for me.

I had to look deep inside, to see where I wanted to be,
To see who I really had growing within me.

Then today was the day, change is upon me.
You've seen past the fuss.
It's you being you, and I'm learning to be me,
Today we can be us, and tomorrow hoping for the same.

If this change can stay, then the pretending goes away.
People come and go as just part of the show,
But tonight, I know you and I are more than before.

I look back now at the grief I was made to feel,
Those silent punches into my soul they didn't see.
I had to believe and hope that in time
The circle will keep moving to set me free.

Bonus

Now that I'm finally in a place to be me
You want me to keep believing in who I can be.
My eyes are open wide and all I can see
Is my heart now beating outside and it's not just for me.

A safe place for us is where we are now standing.
Put your strength in me and we can finally be
Who we always should have been.

To the critics stay on your road
And that life, you don't know how to alter.
But I'm no longer on your train
To the place you said I should be.

The time has come to tell you all
That this place was never for me.
Because finally he was the first to see
What's been buried deep inside me.
This is my time, his time,
Our time, the time to live the dream.

LEX'S LOVE LETTERS

BONUS LETTERS
If you would like to receive some of the beautiful letters
Lex wrote for Mia in his time at the Lake House.
Subscribe to my newsletter for more of Lex and Mia's love story.
www.karendeen.com.au

LIST OF TITLES

The Complete TIME FOR LOVE Series is now available:

LOVE'S WALL #1
LOVE'S DANCE #2
LOVE'S HIDING #3
LOVE'S FUN #4
LOVE'S HOT #5

Standalones:
GORGEOUS GYNO
PRIVATE PILOT
NAUGHTY NEURO
LOVABLE LAWYER

Gorgeous Gyno

Matilda

Today has disaster written all over it.

Five fifty-seven am and already I have three emails that have the potential to derail tonight's function. Why do people insist on being so disorganized? Truly, it's not that hard.

Have a diary, use your phone, write it down, order the stock – whatever it takes. Either way, don't fuck my order up! I shouldn't have to use my grown-up words before six am on a weekday. Seriously!

I'm standing in the shower with hot water streaming down my body. I feel like I'm about to draw blood with how hard I'm scrubbing my scalp, while I'm thinking about solutions for my problems. It's what I'm good at. Not the hair-pulling but the problem-solving in a crisis. A professional event planner has many sneaky tricks up her sleeve. I just happen to have them up my sleeve, in my pockets, and hiding in my shoes. As a last resort, I pull them out of my ass.

I need to get into the office to find a new supplier that can have nine hundred mint-green cloth serviettes delivered to the hotel by lunchtime today. You would think this is trivial in the world.

However, if tonight's event is not perfect, it could be the difference between my dream penthouse apartment or the shoebox I'm living in now. I'll be damned if mint napkins are the deciding factor. Why can't Lucia just settle for white? Oh, that's right, because she is about as easy to please as a child waiting for food. No matter what you say, they complain until they get what they want. Lucia is a nice lady, I'm sure, when she's not being my client from hell.

Standing in the bathroom, foot on the side of the bath, stretching my stockings on, I sneak a glance in the mirror. I hate looking at myself. Who wants to look at their fat rolls and butt dimples. Not me! I should get rid of the mirror and then I wouldn't have to cringe every time I see it. Maybe in that penthouse I'm seeing in my future, there will be a personal trainer and chef included.

Yes! Let's put that in the picture. Need to add that to my vision board. I already have the personal driver posted up on my board—of course, he's sizzling hot. The trains and taxis got old about seven years ago. Well, maybe six years and eleven months. The first month I moved to Chicago I loved it. The hustle and bustle, such a change from the country town I grew up in. Trains running on raised platforms instead of the ground, the amount of taxis that seemed to be in the thousands compared to three that were run by the McKinnon family. Now all the extra time you lose in traffic every day is so frustrating, it's hard to make up in a busy schedule.

I slip my pencil skirt up over my hips, zip up and turn side to side. Happy with my outfit, I slide my suit jacket on, and then I do the last thing, putting on lipstick. Time to take on the world for another day. As stressful as it is and how often I will complain about things going wrong, I love my life. With a passion. Working with my best friend in our own business is the best leap of faith we took together. Leaving our childhood hometown of Williamsport, we were seeking adventure. The new beginning we both needed. It didn't quite start how I thought. Those first few months were tough. I really struggled, but I just didn't feel like I could go home anymore because the feeling of being happy there had changed thanks to my ex-boyfriend. Lucky I had Fleur to get me through that time.

Gorgeous Gyno

Fleur and I met in preschool. She was busy setting up her toy kitchen in the classroom when I walked in. I say hers, because one of the boys tried to tell her how to arrange it and her look stopped him in his tracks. I remember thinking, he has no idea. I would set it up just how she did. It made perfect sense. I knew we were right. Well, that was what we agreed on and bonded over our PB&J sandwich. That and our OCD behavior, of being painfully pedantic. Sometimes it meant we butted heads being so similar, but not often. We have been inseparable ever since that first day.

We used to lay in the hammock in my parents' backyard while growing up. Dreaming of the adventures we were going to have together. We may as well have been sisters. Our moms always said we were joined at the hip. Which was fine until boys came into the picture. They didn't understand us wanting to spend so much time together. Of course, that changed when our hormones kicked in. Boys became important in our lives, but we never lost our closeness. We have each other's backs no matter what. Still today, she is that one person I will trust with my life is my partner in crime, my bestie.

Leaning my head on the back wall of the elevator as it descends, my mind is already running through my checklist of things I need to tackle the moment I walk into the office. That pre-event anxiety is starting to surface. It's not bad anxiety. It's the kick of adrenaline I use to get me moving. It focuses me and blocks out the rest of the world. The only thing that exists is the job I'm working on. From the moment we started up our business of planning high-end events, we have been working so hard, day and night. It feels like we haven't had time to breathe yet. The point we have been aiming for is so close we can feel it. Being shortlisted for a major contract is such a huge achievement and acknowledgement of our business. Tapping my head, I say to myself, "touch wood". So far, we've never had any disaster functions that we haven't been able to turn around to a success on the day. I put it down to the way Fleur and I work together. We have this mental connection. Not even having to talk, we know what the other is thinking and do it before the other person asks. It's just a perfect combination.

Let's hope that connection is working today.

Gorgeous Gyno

Walking through the foyer, phone in hand, it chimes. I was in the middle of checking how close my Uber is, but the words in front of my eyes stop me dead in my tracks.

Fleur: *Tonight's guest speaker woke up vomiting – CANCELLED!!!*

"Fuck!" There is no other word needed.

I hear from behind me, "Pardon me, young lady." Shit, it's Mrs. Johnson. My old-fashioned conscience. I have no idea how she seems to pop up at the most random times. I don't even need to turn around and look at her. What confuses me is why she is in the foyer at six forty-five in the morning. When I'm eighty-two years of age, there is no way I'll be up this early.

"Sorry, Mrs. Johnson. I will drop in my dollar for the swear jar tomorrow," I mumble as I'm madly typing back to Fleur.

"See that you do, missy. Otherwise I will chase you down, and you know I'm not joking." I hear her laughing as she shuffles on her way towards the front doors. I'm sure everyone in this building is paying for her nursing home when they finally get her to move there. I don't swear that often—well, I tell myself that in my head, anyway. It just seems Mrs. Johnson manages to be around, every time I curse.

"Got to run, Mrs. Johnson. I will pop in tomorrow," I call out, heading out the front doors. Part of me feels for her. I think the swear jar is more about getting people to call in to visit her apartment. Her husband passed away six months after I moved in. He was a beautiful old man. She misses him terribly and gets quite lonely. She's been adopted by everyone in the building as our stand-in Nana whether we like it or not. Although she is still stuck in the previous century, she has a big heart and just wants to feel like she has a reason to get up every day and live her life.

My ride into work allows me to get a few emails sorted, at the same time I'm thinking on how I'm going to solve the guest speaker problem. Fleur is on the food organization for this one, and I am on everything else. It's the way we work it. Whoever is on food is rostered on for the actual event. If I can get through today, then tonight I get to relax. As much as you can relax when you are a control freak and you aren't there. We need to split the work this way, otherwise we'd never get a day or night off.

The event is for the 'End of the Cycle' program. It's a great organization that helps stop the cycle of poverty and poor education in families. Trying to help the parents learn to budget and get the kids in school and learning. A joint effort to give the next generation a fighting chance of living the life they dream about.

Maybe if I call the CEO, they'll have someone who has been through the program or somehow associated with the mentoring that can give a firsthand account of what it means to the families. Next email on my list. Another skill I have learned: Delegation makes things happen. I can't do it all, and even with Fleur, we need to coordinate with others to make things proceed quickly.

As usual, Thursday morning traffic is slow even at this time of the day. We are crawling at a snail's pace. I could get out and walk faster than this. I contemplate it, but with the summer heat, I know even at this time of the morning, I'd end up a sweaty mess. That is not the look I need when I'm trying to present like the woman in charge. Even if you have no idea what you're doing, you need people to believe you do. Smoke and mirrors, the illusion is part of the performance.

My phone is pinging constantly as I approach the front of the office building. We chose the location in the beginning because it was central to all the big function spaces in the city. Being new to the city, we didn't factor in how busy it is here. Yet the convenience of being so close far outweighs the traffic hassles.

Hustling down the hall, I push open the door of our office.

'FLEURTILLY'.

It still gives me goosebumps seeing our dream name on the door. The one we thought of all those years ago in that hammock. Even more exciting is that it's all ours. No answering to anyone else. We have worked hard, and this is our reward.

The noise in the office tells me Fleur already has everything turned on and is yelling down the phone at someone. Surely, we can't have another disaster even before my first morning coffee.

"What the hell, Scott. I warned you not to go out and party too hard yesterday. Have you even been to bed yet? What the hell are you thinking, or have the drugs just stopped that peanut brain from even working?! You were already on your last warning. Find someone who will put up with your crap. Your job here is terminated, effective immediately." Fleur's office phone bangs down on her desk loud enough I can hear her from across the hall.

"Well, you told him, didn't you? Now who the hell is going to run the waiters tonight?" I ask, walking in to find her sitting at her desk, leaning back in her chair, eyes closed and hands behind her head.

"I know, I know. I should have made him get his sorry ass in and work tonight and then fired him. My bad. I'll fix it, don't worry. Maybe it's time to promote TJ. He's been doing a great job, and I'm sure he's been pretty much doing Scott's job for him anyway."

To be honest, I think she's right. We've suspected for a while that Scott, one of our managers, has been partying harder than just a few drinks with friends. He's become unreliable which is unlike him. Even when he's at work, he's not himself. I tried to talk to him about it and was shut down. Unfortunately, our reputation is too important to risk him screwing up a job because he's high. He's had enough warnings. His loss.

"You fix that, and I'll find a new speaker. Oh, and 900 stupid mint-green napkins. Seriously. Let's hope the morning improves." I turn to walk out of her office and call over my shoulder, "By the way, good morning. Let today be awesome." I smile, waiting for her response.

"As awesome as we are. I see your Good Morning and I raise you a peaceful day and a drama-free evening. Your turn for coffee, woman." And so, our average workday swings into action.

By eleven-thirty, our day is still sliding towards the shit end of the scale. We have had two staff call in sick with the stupid vomiting bug. Lucia has called me a total of thirty-seven times with stupid questions. While I talk through my teeth trying to be polite, I wonder why she's hired event planners when she wants to micromanage everything.

My phone pressed to my ear, Fleur comes in and puts her hand up to high-five me. Thank god, that means she has solved her issues and we are staffed ready to go tonight. It's just my speaker problem, and then we will have jumped the shit pile and be back on our way to the flowers and sunshine.

"Fleurtilly, you are speaking with Matilda." I pause momentarily. "Hello, Mr. Drummond, how are you this morning?" I have my sweet business voice on, looking at Fleur holding her breath for my answer.

"That's great, yes, I'm having a good day too." I roll my eyes at my partner standing in front of me making stupid faces. "Thank you for calling me back. I was just wondering how you went with finding another speaker for this evening's event." I pause while he responds. I try not to show any reaction to keep Fleur guessing what he's saying. "Okay, thank you for looking into it for me. I hope you enjoy tonight. Goodbye." Slowly I put the phone down.

"Tilly, for god's sake, tell me!" She is yelling at me as I slowly stand up and then start the happy dance and high-five her back.

"We have ourselves a pilot who mentors the boys and girls in the program. He was happy to step in last-minute. Mr. Drummond is going to confirm with him now that he has let us know." We both reach out for a hug, still carrying on when Deven interrupts with his normal gusto.

"Is he single, how old, height, and which team is he batting for?" He stands leaning against the doorway, waiting for us to settle down and pay him any attention.

"I already called dibs, Dev. If he is hot, single, and in his thirties then back off, pretty boy. Even if he bats for your team, I bet I can persuade him to change sides." Fleur walks towards him and wraps him in a hug. "Morning, sunshine. How was last night?"

"Let's just say there won't be a second date. He turned up late, kept looking at his phone the whole time, and doesn't drink. Like, not at all. No alcohol. Who even does that? That's a no from me!" We're all laughing now while I start shutting down my computer and pack my briefcase, ready to head over to the function at McCormick Place.

"While I'd love to stay and chat with you girls," I say, making

Deven roll his eyes at me, "I have to get moving. Things to do, a function to get finished, so I can go home and put my feet up." I pick up my phone and bag, giving them both a peck on the cheek. "See you both over there later. On my phone if needed." I start hurrying down the corridor to the elevator. I debated calling a car but figured a taxi will be quicker at this time of the day. Just before the lunchtime rush, the doorman should be able to flag one down for me.

Rushing out of the elevator, I see a taxi pulled up to the curb letting someone off. I want to grab it before it takes off again. Cecil the doorman sees me in full high-heeled jog and opens the door knowing what I'm trying to do. He's calling out to the taxi to wait as I come past him, focused on the open door the previous passenger is closing.

"Wait, please…" I call as I run straight into a solid wall of chest. Arms grab me as I'm stumbling sideways. Shit. Please don't let this hurt.

Just as my world is tilting sideways, I'm coming back upright to a white tank top, tight and wet with sweat. So close to my face I can smell the male pheromones and feel the heat on my cheeks radiating from his body.

"Christ, I'm so sorry. Are you okay, gorgeous?" That voice, low, breathy, and a little startled. I'm not game to look up and see the face of this wall of solid abs. "You just came out that door like there's someone chasing you. I couldn't stop in time." His hands start to push me backwards a little so he can see more of me.

"Talk to me, please. Are you okay? I'm so sorry I frightened you. Luckily I stopped you from hitting the deck."

Taking a big breath to pull myself back in control, I slowly follow up his sweaty chest to look at the man the voice is coming from. The sun is behind him so I can't make his face out from the glare. I want to step back to take a better look when I hear the taxi driver yelling at me.

"Are you getting in, lady, or not?" he barks out of the driver's seat.

Damn, I need to get moving.

"Thank you. I'm sorry I ran in front of you. Sorry, I have to go." I start to turn to move to the taxi, yet he hasn't let me go.

"I'm the one who's sorry. Just glad you're okay. Have a good day, gorgeous." He guides me to the back seat of the taxi and closes the door for me after I slide in, then taps the roof to let the driver know he's good to go. As we pull away from the curb, I see his smile of beautiful white teeth as he turns and keeps jogging down the sidewalk. My heart is still pounding, my head is still trying to process what the hell just happened. Can today get any crazier?

Grayson

'I'm just a hunk, a hunk of burning love
Just a hunk, a hunk of burning love'
Crap!
What the hell!

I reach out to grab her before I bowl her over and smash her to the ground. Stopping my feet dead in the middle of running takes all the strength I have in my legs. We sway slightly, but I manage to pull her back towards me to stand her back up. Where did this woman come from? Looking down at the top of her head, I can't tell if she's okay or not.

She's not moving or saying anything. It's like she's frozen still. I think I've scared her so much she's in shock.

She's not answering me, so I try to pull her out a little more so I can see her face.

Well, hello my little gorgeous one.

The sun is shining brightly on her face that lights her up with a glow. She's squinting, having trouble seeing me. She opens her mouth to finally talk. I'm ready for her to rip into me for running into her. Yet all I get is sorry and she's trying to escape my grasp. The taxi driver gives her the hurry along. I'd love to make sure she's really okay, but I seem to be holding her up. I help her to the taxi and within seconds she's pulling away from me, turning and watching me from the back window of the cab.

Well, that gave today a new interesting twist.

Gorgeous Gyno

One gorgeous woman almost falling at my feet. Before I could even settle my breathing from running, I blink, and she's gone. Almost like a little figment of my imagination.

One part I certainly didn't imagine is how freaking beautiful she looked.

I take off running towards Dunbar Park and the basketball court where the guys are waiting for me. Elvis is pumping out more rock in my earbuds and my feet pound the pavement in time with his hip thrusts. I'm a huge Elvis fan, my music tastes stuck in the sixties. There is nothing like the smooth melodic tones of the King. My mom listened to him on her old vinyl records, and we would dance around the kitchen while Dad was at work. I think she was brainwashing me. It totally worked. Although I love all sorts of music, Elvis will always be at the top of my playlist.

"Oh, here's Doctor Dreamy. What, some damsel in distress you couldn't walk away from?" The basketball lands with a thud in the center of my chest from Tate.

"Like you can talk, oh godly one. The surgeon that every nurse in the hospital is either dreaming about fucking, or how she can stab needles in you after she's been fucked over by you." Smacking him on the back as I join the boys on the court, Lex and Mason burst out laughing.

"Welcome to the game, doctors. Sucks you're on the same team today, doesn't it? Less bitching and more bouncing. Let's get this game started. I'm due in court at three and the judge already hates me, so being late won't go well," Lex yelled as he started backing down the court ready to mark and stop us scoring a basket.

"Let me guess, she hates you because you slept with her," I yell back.

"Nope, but I may have spent a night with her daughter, who I had no idea lives with her mother the judge."

"Holy shit, that's the funniest thing I've heard today." Mason throws his head back, laughing out loud. "That story is status-worthy."

"You put one word of that on social media and I won't be the one in court trying to get you out on bail, I'll be there defending why I beat you to a pulp, gossip boy. Now get over here and help me whip the asses off these glamour boys." Lex glares at Mason.

"Like they even have a chance. Bring it, boys." He waves at me to come at him.

Game on, gentlemen.

My watch starts buzzing to tell us time's up in the game. We're all on such tight work schedules that we squeeze in this basketball game together once a week. These guys are my family, well, the kind of family you love one minute and want to kill the next. We've been friends since meeting at Brother Rice High School for Boys, where we all ended up in the same class on the first day. Not sure what the teachers were thinking after the first week when we had bonded and were already making pains of ourselves. Not sure how many times our parents were requested for a 'talk' with the headmaster, but it was more often than is normal, I'm sure. It didn't matter we all went to separate universities or worked in different professions. We had already formed that lifelong friendship that won't ever break.

Sweat dripping off all of us, I'm gulping down water from the water fountain. Not too much, otherwise I'll end up with a muscle cramp by the time I run back to the hospital.

"Right, who's free tonight?" Mason is reading his phone with a blank look on his face.

"I'm up for a drink, I'm off-shift tonight," Tate pipes up as I grin and second him that I'm off too. It doesn't happen often that we all have a night off together. The joys of being a doctor in a hospital.

"I can't, I'm attending a charity dinner. It's for that charity you mentor for, Mason," Lex replies.

"Well, that's perfect. Gray, you are my plus one, and Tate, your date is Lex. I'm now the guest speaker for the night. So, you can all come and listen to the best talk you have witnessed all year. Prepare to be amazed." He brushes each of his shoulders with his hands, trying to show us how impressive he is.

We all moan simultaneously at him.

"Thanks for the support, cock suckers. My memory is long." He huffs a little as he types away a reply on his phone.

Mason is a pilot who spent four years in the military, before he was discharged, struggling with the things he saw. He started to work in the commercial sector but then was picked up by a private charter company. He's perfect for that sort of role. He has the smoothness, wit, and intelligence to mingle with anyone, no matter who they are. He's had great stories of different passengers over the years and places he's flown.

"Why in god's name would anyone think you were interesting enough to talk for more than five minutes. You can't even make that time limit for sex," I say, waiting for the reaction.

"Oh, you are all so fucking funny, aren't you. I'm talking about my role in mentoring kids to reach for their dream jobs no matter how big that dream is." The look on his face tells me he takes this seriously.

"Jokes aside, man, that's a great thing you do. If you can dream it, you can reach it. If you make a difference in one kid's life, then it's worth it." We all stop with the ribbing and start to work out tonight's details. We agree to meet at a bar first for a drink and head to the dinner together. My second alarm on my watch starts up. We all know what that means.

Parting ways, Mason yells over his shoulder to us all, "By the way, it's black tie."

I inwardly groan as I pick up my pace into a steady jog again. I hate wearing a tie. It reminds me of high school wearing one every day. If I can avoid it now, I do. Unfortunately, most of these charity dinners you need to dress to impress. You also need to have your wallet full to hand over a donation. I'm lucky, I've never lived without the luxury of money, so I'm happy to help others where I can.

Running down Michigan Avenue, I can see Mercy Hospital in the distance standing tall and proud. It's my home away from home. This is the place I spend the majority of my waking hours, working, along with some of my sleeping hours too. My heart beats happily in this place. Looking after people and saving lives is the highest rush you can experience in life. With that comes rough days, but you just hope the good outweighs the bad most of the time.

That's why I run and try not to miss the workouts with the boys.

You need to clear the head to stay focused. The patients need the best of us every single time. Tate works with me at Mercy which makes for fun days and nights when we're on shift together. He didn't run with me today as he's in his consult rooms and not on shift at the hospital.

I love summer in Chicago, except, just not this heat in the middle of the day when I'm running and sweating my ass off. It also means the hospital struggles with all the extra caseload we get. Heat stroke in the elderly is an issue, especially if they can't afford the cool air at home. The hospital is the best thing they have for relief. My smart watch tells me it's eighty-six degrees Fahrenheit, but it feels hotter with the humidity.

I don't get the extra caseload, since I don't work in emergency. That's Tate's problem. He's a neurosurgeon who takes on the emergency cases as they arrive in the ER. Super intense, high-pressure work. Not my idea of fun. I had my years of that role, and I'm happy where I am now.

Coming through the front doors of the hospital, I feel the cool air hit me, while the eyes of the nursing staff at the check-in desk follow me to the elevator. The single ones are ready to pounce as soon as you give them any indication you might be interested. Tate takes full advantage of that. Me, not so much. When you're an intern, it seems like a candy shop of all these women who want to claim the fresh meat. The men are just as bad with the new female nurses.

We work in a high-pressure environment, working long hours and not seeing much daylight at times. You need to find a release. That's how I justified it, when I was the intern. I remember walking into a storeroom in my first year as an intern, finding my boss at the time, Leanne, and she was naked from the waist down being fucked against the wall by one of the male nurses. Now I am a qualified doctor who should hold an upstanding position in society, so I rarely get involved in the hospital dating scene anymore.

Fuck, who am I kidding? That's not the reason. It's the fact I got burnt a few years ago by a clinger who tried to get me fired when I tried to move on. Not going down that path again. Don't mix work

Gorgeous Gyno

and play, they say—well, I say. Tate hasn't quite learned that lesson yet. Especially the new batch of interns he gets on rotation every six months. He is a regular man-whore.

Am I a little jealous? Maybe just a tad. Both me and my little friend, who's firming up just thinking about getting ready for some action. It's been a bit of a dry spell. I think it's time to fix that.

Pity my date for tonight, Mason, is not even close to what I'm thinking about.

My cock totally loses interest now in the conversation again.

Can't say I blame him.

Just then the enchanting woman from today comes to mind and my cock is back in the game. I wish I knew who she was.

Now this afternoon's rounds could be interesting if my scrubs are tenting with a hard-on.

The joys of being a large man, if you get my drift.

There's no place to hide him.

Love's Wall

Zach

Heading across the bedroom, steam still swirling around from the shower, I paused. The view of the mountains brought a smile to my face as I stood naked at the window, enjoying the morning in all its glory. The breeze carried the bird's morning song and the sounds of the cattle in the paddocks through the open window. Nature was busy getting ready for the day. I pulled my clothes on for the office. Part of me wished that I could just jump back into my farm jeans, shirt and boots and head out to the barn to saddle up for a ride. I could use one more day to relax in this tranquil place like I had been for the last two days.

Thinking back on the weekend I could see that, although I loved my life, it was missing something. Or perhaps someone. My life was full. I had an amazing family and a business that made me happy to get up and go to work every morning. My home was my safe-haven, it gave me a place to just be myself with no expectations. It also gave me a place to hide. With all of the things that were right in my life, there was still a part of me that was empty. After letting my mind drift, I knew I needed to get my head around the start of a new week. Jumping in the car, I placed the same call that I made every Monday morning as I drove out of the gate.

"Good morning, Zoe, how was your weekend?" I smiled, waiting for the usual answer.

"Morning, Zach. Let's just say that several words can describe it. My weekend was fun, crazy, drinking, partying - all of which have led to my head paying the consequences this morning!" Zoe then launched into stories of the weekend and we spent time laughing about her nights out.

As I turned down the entrance to the highway and felt my foot press down on the pedal, my body pushed back into the leather seat that wrapped around my body so well. The buzz of driving a nice car at speed brought a smile that inched up my face.

"So, the big question is, Zoe - did you spot your Mr. Right out there somewhere?" I let out a little chuckle, hearing Zoe sigh and then laugh. She got ready to joke it off, but I knew deep down under the party girl exterior it was no joke. She was a young lady who would give anything to have a man to love and protect her, to plant her feet on the ground. My gut feeling was that man would be my brother, Luke, but the two of them just hadn't worked it out yet. The sexual tension between them could light up Times Square, yet they both fought so hard to keep that 'friend wall' up. One day something was going to flick that switch and the explosion would be more impressive than the Fourth of July fireworks. I'd just sit back, watch, wait and then say, 'I told you so' because I knew all along.

"Now Zach, you know as good as I do that there is no good man out there who will pin me down. Living the dream, Zach, living the dream". I burst out laughing at Zoe's comment, knowing she was trying to convince herself of that. "Tell your head that this morning, Zoe. Anyway, as much as I hate to hurt that little brain of yours, what's on the agenda for today? Also, did you get that email I sent you re the plans for Branch Street that need to be at council by 10.00am?"

"Yes, yes," she sighed. "Already done, you know I am always one step ahead of you!"

Love's Wall

Zoe joined our building development company five years ago straight out of secretarial college and had been my assistant from day one. It was a match that could have spelled disaster. She walked in on a day that had me dragging myself up off the couch in my office. I was trying to make the bathroom to throw up the bottle of bourbon I had consumed the night before. Tragically, I stumbled and managed to throw up on her shoes and then lay moaning at her feet.

Our relationship could have gone either way. She could have turned around and walked straight back out, cursing me as she left, never to return. Instead, Zoe just looked down at me and burst out laughing. She proceeded to tell me to take my hungover ass and grovel back to the couch while she changed and cleaned up my mess. She walked over and threw her shoes in the bin, mumbling that she expected two new pairs of shoes to replace the ones which were now laying sadly in the bottom of the bin. It hurt my head to laugh, but I couldn't help but let out a quiet chuckle. We would get on just fine.

Zoe spent our first day of working together in her gym clothes. Luckily, they were in her car and clean. Me? I was in the singlet and jeans I had on from the night before, minus the shirt. It had a new home in the bin with her shoes!

Zoe had cleaned me up, poured coffee that was as thick as tar down my throat, along with bottle after bottle of water and plenty of pain relief. We managed to get to the end of the day and she never asked what happened. And I never told her. From that day forward, we had been great friends, as well as work colleagues. She knew I would be there to stand up and protect her, no matter what. Zoe would jump in front of anyone trying to take advantage of my soft caring heart. If I was the builder of the wall in front of my heart, Zoe was the guard at the gate. We just clicked that way. Although I already had two sisters, Alesha and Lilly, Zoe had become like my third and I was just as protective of her.

"Ok, so if you are one step ahead of me, what am I doing today, Miss Smarty Pants?" I heard the tapping of her long-painted nails on the keyboard as she called up my calendar.

Love's Wall

"You will be in the office in approximately thirty minutes. Oh wait - what are you in today, the SUV or the BMW?"

Waiting for the smart answer that would come back, I replied, "The BMW, so you better adjust the time frame." I pushed the speedo up and got into the fast lane. One of my weaknesses was the love of a fast fancy car. Although I had not indulged myself in the last few years, I still loved my BMW. It may not be the highest priced or the fastest model, but it appealed to me with its style and lines. That was me, I was always looking at how something spoke to me before I acquired it. I had to feel it was meant to be part of my world before I proceeded.

"Ok, you will be in the office in twenty minutes, so we can have a coffee and run through this week's planning. Then you have the family meeting at 12pm for lunch. You will need all your files for that. I've put the updates and proposal for the Branch Street property on your desk. Bob Walter is meeting you at 4pm with the legal papers for the eviction notices for Branch Street. Then you have dinner booked at 6pm with your Grandmother at Waters Edge. Your older control-freak brother, Grant, is picking her up at 5.40pm from home. I have the birthday present wrapped and on your desk as you asked. How am I doing so far?"

"Wow! What would I do without you, Wonder Woman?" I grinned as I looked out the window, trying to hold my laughter inside.

"Screwed, I'd say. Now, can I get off the phone, so I can get a coffee, otherwise that morning smile you are wishing for will be non-existent."

As much as I loved Zoe like a sister, you never crossed her before the first coffee in the morning. "Just quickly before you start having a meltdown, I am going past Branch Street before I come to the office. I want to take a few more photos, so don't worry about my coffee. I will grab one on my travels"

"Ha, like I was getting you one anyway. Bye." I hung up with a smile, knowing she would have had one on my desk when I walked in the same as she did every other morning. I was such a creature of habit. I also knew I never got to say goodbye because she always liked to have the last say. Typical woman.

Zoe always believed she was one step ahead of me. I loved to humor her, but the truth was, I knew everything she told me this morning because I was a fine-details person. She was my back up and was damn good at it. Her job was very important to her. It kept her out of the mess of a life she'd worked so hard to rise above.

I put my head back on the headrest and searched through music playlists to get my Monday morning going. I loved all sorts of music, but when you are cruising down the freeway with the sun shining, there was nothing better than good ol' solid eighties rock to sing along to.

The Monday morning drive into the office of our family owned-property development and building company always gave me time to prepare mentally for the week ahead. I loved the challenge of my role - sourcing properties in need of development to increase their value. Or finding those sitting on the market needing to be demolished. My true passion, though, was to restore homes and buildings to their former glory whilst modernizing them with the comforts of the twenty-first century. These properties were hard to find, and I was very selective of the ones I purchased, due to the cost of restoration in relation to what they would sell for.

Sometimes, though, there was that special property that came along that spoke to me. The costings became less important and the project became about me. That was the case for my home, which I purchased two years ago. It was situated on fifty acres of land, thirty minutes outside of the city. The day I saw the listing pop up in my real estate watchlist, I knew I had to have it.

The first photo I saw was of a two-storey farm house with wide verandas all the way around the house. The front of the house had a beautiful set of stairs that opened out like welcoming arms, just like that first warm embrace of a loved one. The stairs led straight up to solid double doors at the entrance. When opened, they gave the first glimpse of a home full of love and laughter. The problem was that the love and laughter had been sucked out of this home.

Love's Wall

The previous family had spent ten years battling over the proceeds of the deceased estate of an elderly couple.

I had later found out the previous owners were Tom and Nellie Smithton. They had built this home after marrying seventy-five years ago. The two souls had spent a lifetime devoted to each other and their home. Tom and Nellie were never able to have children, but it never changed the amount of love they'd had to share. Many friends from church had taken their children to spend time on the farm. Nellie enjoyed baking for the children and fussing over them. They became known as Poppy Tom and Nanna Nellie to generations of children who'd loved them dearly.

They passed away within a week of each other, Nellie from a stroke in her sleep and Tom from a broken heart six days later. The farm was left to the church in their will. But, as it happens so often these days, the will was challenged by two great-nieces and a nephew. The nephew challenged to try and stop his greedy twin daughters. They were spoilt little rich girls and never felt that generous wealth was enough. The nephew had always said he would gift back to the church if he was successful. He had disowned his daughters for their terrible behavior. Needless to say, it dragged on to become a lengthy court battle where the only winners were the lawyers. In the end, the decision was that each would receive part of the estate. The property needed to be sold. That became my lucky day. In my heart, I hoped to bring their property back to being a place that was a treasured home.

When I saw the home listed, I rang the agent straight away. I offered the asking price without any haggling, on the condition that it be pulled from the market immediately and a quick settlement negotiated. I wanted this house more than I had wanted anything in my life. Well, except for the one thing that I would never allow myself to have again. My heart could not take that.

I didn't tell my family I had even put in an offer on the property until I had already settled the purchase. Grant was pissed, to say the least, because he had not been consulted whether he thought it was a good investment. Ever since my parents had retired, Grant had become the self-appointed head of the family, whether we wanted it or not.

Luke had complained, but only because he had to put up with Grant's grunting. The silent treatment always happened in the office when Grant believed one of us had stuffed up. Of course, the girls both questioned why I had bought a house so far out of the city - it would be like going to the end of the earth to have to travel that distance every day to civilization. Apparently, life ceases to exist past the Central Business District of Cashmore! Nobody sold coffee or shoes that were up to the standard of my fashion conscious, latte-sipping sisters. Zoe just raised her eyebrows and gave three reasons why it was a dumb idea - no night clubs, no girls and no life!

I remember the feeling of the grey cloud my family had painted getting heavier over my heart. For once, I felt like I had finally found a place to just be me and make my mark on the world, but they were raining on my parade. It hurt, but I would never let them know that. I did what I had always done for many years - painted a smile on my face. I loved my family with every part of my being and would never hurt them. I had kept a part of me hidden from them, as well as from the rest of the world. I would never again be vulnerable to having my world shattered. Love is amazing and the most comforting emotion, but it could also rip you to shreds. After being on both sides of the wall, I had chosen my side. The side which was comfortable and safe. I had built my wall just that little bit higher, thicker and stronger so it kept me safe and stopped any future intruders from crossing over it.

It hurt to think of my life before then. I had never completely shared with anyone what truly happened, nor would I ever. No matter how much you moved on, pushed it down, stepped on top of it and tried to climb above it, there'd always be a part of it that would pull you down.

Regardless of what my siblings and Zoe had thought, the house was right for me and I would make it my home by bringing back its dignity. Maybe that was what I'd needed to do to help me see value in my own life. To feel like I had dignity again. That was a thought I kept to myself.

Love's Wall

When my Mom and Dad came home for a few weeks, in between travelling the country in their motorhome, it was their opinions that mattered the most. My father was the typical all-American, hardworking, self-made, protective alpha male who valued his wife and children above money and power.

My grandfather had died from a heart attack when Dad was ten years old. Dad took on the responsibility of becoming the man of the house and looking after my grandmother. He took it very seriously and, as an only child, Grandmother had no one else to lean on. Dad grew up faster than most kids his age. He was a great man and worked hard to be the best father he could, providing us with all that we needed. He always loved us. We knew we were loved unconditionally. While the love for his children was big, the love in his heart for our Mom was huge. They had that connection of love that made their souls melt into one, their lives intertwined around each other's hearts to keep them safe.

My mother was the opposite to Dad. Dad was the foundation of our family tree. He was strong and solid and lifted us all up to the sun. My Mom was the softness of the leaves, the beauty of the flowers and the memorable moments of their scent. She was the branches that twisted, curled, intertwined and reached out to protect her family tree. They were the perfect couple that you always heard about. The ones women swooned over in those trashy romance novels, like the ones Zoe read when she thought I wasn't watching.

I grew up with the perfect family around me. I'd forever be grateful for the love we had and the feeling of always being safe. Many aren't so lucky to have grown up in such a home. My parent's life, although it was perfect for them, was one that I had decided was not going to happen for me. While thinking my siblings would all at some stage find that special person to love, cherish and share a life with, it was no longer in my life map. I was resigned to be the uncle who was always there to be fun, protect, guide and love any nieces or nephews that came along. I hoped there'd be plenty, but being a father was no longer an option for me. I always imagined I would make a good dad. I'd visualize it and see a little boy with brown hair and brown eyes like me. Or perhaps a little girl with ringlet curls like my sisters, with big eyes that would suck her Dad in every time.

My family would never know why, but the uncle life was the path for me. They would be the ones to benefit from the love I had to give, without the pain that could come in return when giving out that love. Family was your safe place. Well, it was for me.

When Mom and Dad arrived at the property for the first time, I held my breath. Although I knew I had made the right decision for me, their opinions were so important.

As their truck came slowly down the gravel drive from the front gate, I wondered what they thought of the house at first sight. Did they see it the same way I did? Was I the only one whose heart had skipped a beat on their first trip down the same strip of gravel that they now travelled?

The drive to my home was lined with maple trees that were bare at the time the property became mine. They stood tall, solid and strong, yet sparse as I'd crawled slowly towards the house that memorable day. They looked like they were reaching out to find someone to love the property and, in turn, them.

The truck crawled to a stop in front of the staircase where I stood at the top, looking down. Mom jumped out and raced around the front of Dad's truck, which was his pride and joy. He always told us, 'every man needs a truck so they can work hard and provide for their family'. Mom always giggled at that statement, but all of the boys in our family owned trucks, even if we had other vehicles. It was in our blood that every man needed a truck to be as big a man as our Dad. He was our hero.

Mom took the steps at a jog and jumped into my arms with a big tight hug. I wrapped my arms around her and buried my head into the crook of her neck. I took a deep breath and with it, the scent that was my Mom. My safe place. It was the scent that took you back in time to when you scraped your knee and she kissed it better. Or the time you were sick in bed and she sat all night holding your hand while you battled the fever. Mom was always home, no matter what.

I lifted my head up and looked down at her face which, now aged a little with many laugh lines (as she called them), had the loving smile she saved just for her kids. Although she was having a ball travelling with Dad, she missed her kids terribly. And although Dad would never admit it, I think he did too. Mom always said they were travelling now so that by the time grandkids were arriving, they would have that bug out of their system. There was no way in hell she was missing one moment of being a grandparent. God help her grandkids, they were going to be smothered with love! Then again, what more could any child want but to feel the love of a whole family?

Mom was not a short woman, standing at 5'7". To my 6'2" height, her head sat perfectly under my chin and leant against my heart, taking it all in. When she looked up at me finally, her eyes were damp. There was warmth shining out of them and her smile lit up her whole face. It told me her heart had skipped that beat on the trip down the gravel driveway too.

"So, what do you think, Mom? Does it give a good first impression?" I asked, thinking I already knew the answer.

"Oh Zach, it is wonderful! What a precious looking home. It looks just perfect. I can't wait to see what you do with it. I would love to hear all your ideas for it. Take us on the grand tour and share what your dreams are!" Mom bounced with excitement and talked quickly as she dragged me towards the front door.

"Hang on a minute, woman! Can I get a word in, or at least a hug from my son?" boomed Dad's deep voice as he climbed from his truck.

"Hey Dad, thanks for coming to check the place out and give me your thoughts".

"Zach, my boy, good to see you," he said, giving me the typical Dad man-hug with the compulsory man-slaps on the back. Always three slaps. When we were little, I asked Dad why he always did three slaps on our backs. He laughed and hugged me, his arm around me with his hand on my shoulder blade. He slowly slapped me and said, "This first slap is to let you know I am glad to see you. The second is to let you know that I am always there for you. The last is the most important. It is to remind you that, no matter what happens in your life and no matter where you are, I will always love you."

I have carried that memory with me every day since. For a man who always appeared to the outside world as the strong alpha male, he also had a soft spot that he only showed to his family. Even now, as grown adults that were out living their lives in the world, we immediately got the hug and three slaps from Dad. Only after Mom had hugged the air out of us first, though!

Dad pulled back from the hug and looked up, casting his eyes over the house. He went quiet and started to wander off around the outside of the veranda, lifting his eyes up and down and taking in the structural elements.

As I stood and watched him with anticipation, Mom tapped me on the arm and grabbed my attention. "Come on, Zach. Let him go. You take me inside and show me around this gorgeous new home of yours."

I looked down at the excitement in her eyes and took her by the hand. We turned towards the front door and I lead her into my new world. The one I was creating to live in.

"I have so many ideas, Mom. I feel like my head is going to explode with the amount of activity that is going on in there. It's hard to concentrate on work when my mind keeps coming back to here. I want to bring life back to it and show the house as it once was. There is so much beauty in the original architecture and building materials, but it has been left to rot. It's been neglected for the last ten years, some of the house is past just a paint job. Some of the timber will need to be repaired or replaced to return it to its original state."

Mom started to run her hand along the walls as we stood in the entry and fell silent while she assessed the sight that played out in front of her. What was she doing rubbing the walls, I wondered? It's not like she was testing for wood rot or structural soundness, because Mom would never make a builder. After she stood for a minute, she turned to me with a serious look on her face. As she contemplated whatever she was thinking about, the wrinkles on her forehead relaxed and the corners of her mouth began to curve up towards her eyes, bringing out the warm smile.

"Um, Mom - what are you thinking?" She let out a nervous giggle, sighed and looked me straight in the eye.

"This house has a great vibe to it. It will make a perfect home for you, Zach, you can feel the love in its walls. It was built to be filled with the love of a family. It will be a special place for you to bring home a bride one day. The two of you will fill it with love and a family of your own. It will be magical for this house to be the home it was built to be by the old couple. There is magic here, Zach, I can feel it."

My heart stopped beating and my brain froze. How do I break my mother's heart and tell her that would never happen? There would be laughter and smiles here, but the love of a family would only be here when they came to visit. I stared at her while she continued to talk ten-to-the-dozen, but I didn't hear a word. Doubts began to creep into my mind. Did I do the right thing buying this property? Was it meant to be a home for some lucky family who would have kids running around screaming, laughing and climbing the trees? A dog chasing at their heels as they rode their push bikes from the house to the front gate and back?

"Zach…..Zach………ZACH!" Mom started waving her arms madly in front of my face. "Where did you zone out to, Zach, this isn't like you? Are you okay, honey? Did I scare you with all the talk of a bride and kids?" She sniggered to herself. "Don't worry, plenty of time for that. Let's get the house fixed up first and then you can go looking for your bride to make it a home."

Just paint on that smile again, Zach, and it will be okay. Take a breath and just relax. Breathe in, then out, in, then out. Every breath in is helping put another layer of bricks between the safe side of the love wall and the other side that I can't go to.

"Zach, are you okay? You look pale and have lost that excited look you had when we first walked in."

"Sorry Mom, just got lost in a daydream about the renovations" More like a nightmare, I thought to myself. "How about I show you through the downstairs living areas, then we can take a look upstairs at the bedrooms and bathrooms. What do you say?"

I held my arm out for her to take, and the moment she linked her arm in mine, the calmness of a mother's love warmed my body. I relaxed into her side as we stepped together down the hallway through to the formal lounge room. This was the room where I had visions of me after a long day at work, sitting back in my leather recliner in front of the open fire. I'd watch the flames dance over the wood as it burned. The warmth would spread through the room, enveloping me and seeping into my body, relaxing my muscles. My body would sag back into the cosiness of the chair and I could lose my thoughts gazing out the large bay window facing the front of the property. I would look towards the surrounding open space of the farm, with the beautiful trees that line the drive and the mountains in the distance. A great way to unwind with a glass of red wine and just contemplate the world.

As we studied the room, I explained my visions in broad terms to Mom. I wanted to keep part of my dream as mine for a while until such time as it was completed or I was ready to share it. Mom loved the room and all that I was going to do to bring it to life. The rest of the tour went much the same as I lead her from room to room until we ventured upstairs.

"Wow, look at the size of this master bedroom, it's huge! Especially for the era the house was built in. And the views from this window to the river and mountains are spectacular! I can imagine what it would look like at night lying in bed looking out to the stars over the mountains. Zach, you could not have found a more perfect home!"

"Thanks Mom, it means a lot to hear you say that. You know, Grant didn't talk to me for a week when I told him and Luke that I had bought it."

I jumped a little as Dad's voice came from behind us unexpectedly. "Your mother is right, Zach. This is a great buy with plenty of potential to bring it back to its prime. Don't worry about your brother. He is just sulking because he had to realize you don't need

Love's Wall

him to hold your hand. I swear he thinks he is the father of this family, frickin' control freak!"

Mom nearly choked as she burst out laughing at my Dad. "Gee, Mitch, I wonder where he gets that character trait from?"

"Bite that cute little tongue of yours, Sophia," he said as he strode across the room and wrapped her up in those big manly arms of his. He leant down and placed a very tender kiss on her lips and whispered, "Or will I have to shut that cheeky little mouth for you?" He winked, making her blush.

As much as I love my parents, there were times when I thought, I do not need the vision of you both doing anything else other than kissing and cuddling.

Mom stretched up on her toes to whisper in Dad's ear as I turned to stare out the window. I didn't need to share in that private moment.

"Like I said, Zach, the house is structurally sound, and I look forward to seeing what you do with it". As we stood staring out to the farm sprawling before us, Dad asked me what I planned to do with the worker's cottage.

"I am going to fix it up first to a neat livable standard, then move in there to live while I work on the house. That way, I can take my time on the house and continue on it at night after work. I won't have a thirty-minute drive home each night after I finish."

"Sounds like you have it all thought out, son. I am proud of you and know you'll do a good job."

"He had a good teacher, Mitch." My Mom's pride showed in her eyes as she looked up into my Dad's.

"She's right, Dad, you taught us all so well. Not only about building, but how to be a man. I hope I have lived up to that for you." In my heart, I didn't think I had. But it didn't stop me from desperately wanting to hear it from my father.

"As I said, Zach, I am proud of you and who you are. Just as I am of your brothers and sisters. You have all grown into great people. Your mother and I are excited everyday watching you all embrace life."

Love's Wall

"Thanks Dad, it means a lot," I whispered as I stood trying to process the emotions created by what he'd said.

"Now enough of this mushy crap. What's a man got to do around here to get a feed and a cold beer?" Laughter echoed off the bare walls and the moment was gone. Another rare glimpse of Dad's soft side to store in my memory bank.

The day ended with us in the local steakhouse. We chatted over the house plans and heard about their last trip. Dad wanted to get up to speed on where work projects were up to. He might be retired, but always liked to keep his finger in the pie. The day ended with Mom probing me for gossip on my siblings.

We'd made a pact years ago. Mom got the everyday gossip, but anything serious we kept to ourselves, so the person involved could share it when they were ready. It worked most of the time until Mom hunted for confirmation that one of us was in need of her help. The thing was, she was usually spot on the money. I guess it was part of a mother's sixth sense, like when you were younger, and she already knew what you'd done wrong.

I would always look back on that day with a smile and the memory of my parent's love, feeling so at home and safe. As I floated back into the present, I saw the edge of the city and heard the sound of horns above the tail end of Bon Jovi's "Living on a Prayer".

Acknowledgments

ACKNOWLEDGEMENTS

Writing a book is such an amazing feeling. Taking the characters that are in your heart and your head and putting them out there to share with the rest of the world. Hoping that the readers will love your words and see your vision.

For every one of you that have read my books, thank you for giving me a place to share my stories. Your love and support keep the words flowing and the stories brewing. Let's see where it may take us next.

Lex's book took me by surprise and stole my heart. I had no idea how big the story would end up being, but this love story could not be rushed. They deserved the time to both find themselves as well as each other. Their story is about finding your life and not the one that you feel you should live, but the one you want to live. About taking the direction you choose. I hope you all can take something from their story.

I need to thank my beta readers who I left dangling for days at a time, with no answers in sight. You girls are amazing, and I love you all dearly. To Nicole, Linda, Shelbie, Vicki, Di, and Nicole, from the bottom of my heart, thank you for all you do for me. Next book I'll try not to rip your hearts out… maybe.

Linda and the Foreword PR team. Every book you keep making my life easier, and I'm blessed to have you in my corner. You hold my hand, you push me when I need it, and most of all, you believe in me when I doubt myself. So grateful for everything you do and for your friendship. Some nights I just need to laugh, and you always manage to deliver. Just one of your many skills that I adore you for.

Contagious Edits – thank you for your amazing editing skills. I love that we live on opposite sides of the world and we make it work in our different time zones. Also, that you are way better than me at placing commas and you catch all my mistakes which is no mean feat. I can't imagine another editor putting up with the last-minute chapters being handed over not long before it should be out to the readers. Yet you never complain which I'm eternally grateful for. Thank you.

Sarah Paige at Opium Creatives, thank you for making my Lex into a Sexy Lexy Lovable Lawyer. You make my covers look stunning and I appreciate it so much.

To the beautiful Kellie who has taken my words, and formatted them into a book to make them look perfect for you all. Thank you for all your help and encouragement.

Friends and family, you have supported me from day one. Your support has been so encouraging, and I love that each one of you has given me something to add to my journey. You are my circle.

My beautiful mentor. I know you won't see this, but I tell you at every opportunity how much I appreciate your guidance and love you for it. So, in that next hug, I'll add a little extra from my Lex.

My supportive husband and children, you are my reason. It's that simple. I will always love you and be grateful to you for letting me live my dream.

To my readers, supporters, bloggers, fellow authors. Thank you so much and until next time, I'll meet you in between the pages.

Last but not least.

To the stars that guide me home. Thank you

Karen xxx

Printed in Great Britain
by Amazon